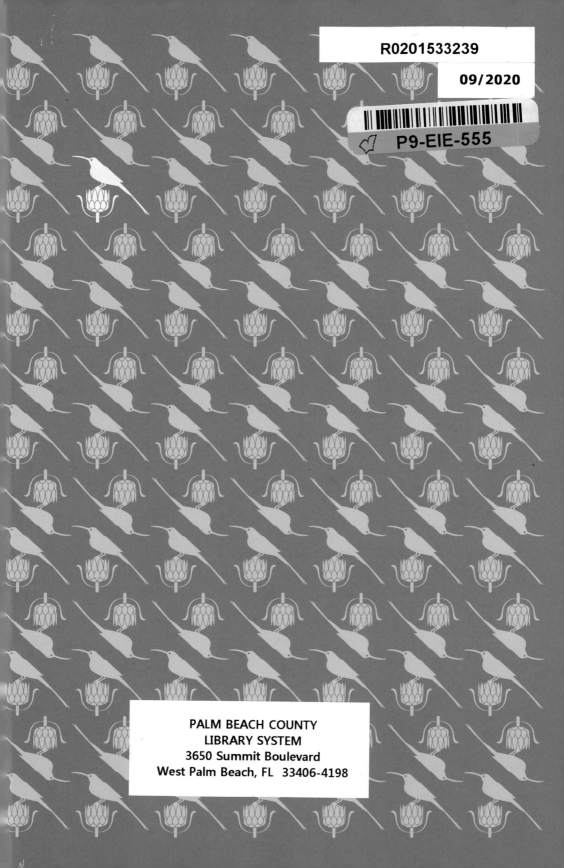

Praise for the novels of

WILBUR
SMITH

"Read on, adventure fans."
THE NEW YORK TIMES

"A rich, compelling look back in time [to]
when history and myth intermingled."
SAN FRANCISCO CHRONICLE

"Only a handful of 20th century writers tantalize
our senses as well as Smith. A rare author who
wields a razor-sharp sword of craftsmanship."
TULSA WORLD

"He paces his tale as swiftly as he can with
swordplay aplenty and killing strokes that come
like lightning out of a sunny blue sky."
KIRKUS REVIEWS

"Best Historical Novelist—I say Wilbur Smith,
with his swashbuckling novels of Africa. The
bodices rip and the blood flows. You can get lost
in Wilbur Smith and misplace all of August."
STEPHEN KING

"Action is the name of Wilbur Smith's game
and he is the master."
THE WASHINGTON POST

"Smith manages to serve up adventure, history and melodrama in one thrilling package that will be eagerly devoured by series fans."
PUBLISHERS WEEKLY

"This well-crafted novel is full of adventure, tension, and intrigue."
LIBRARY JOURNAL

"Life-threatening dangers loom around every turn, leaving the reader breathless . . . An incredibly exciting and satisfying read."
CHATTANOOGA FREE PRESS

"When it comes to writing the adventure novel, Wilbur Smith is the master; a 21st century H. Rider Haggard."
VANITY FAIR

ALSO BY WILBUR SMITH

Non-Fiction
On Leopard Rock: A Life of Adventures

The Courtney Series

When the Lion Feeds	*Blue Horizon*
The Sound of Thunder	*The Triumph of the Sun*
A Sparrow Falls	*Assegai*
The Burning Shore	*Golden Lion*
Power of the Sword	*War Cry*
Rage	*The Tiger's Prey*
A Time to Die	*Courtney's War*
Golden Fox	*King of Kings*
Birds of Prey	*Ghost Fire*
Monsoon	

The Ballantyne Series

A Falcon Flies	*The Leopard Hunts in*
Men of Men	*Darkness*
The Angels Weep	*The Triumph of the Sun*
	King of Kings

The Egyptian Series

River God	*The Quest*
The Seventh Scroll	*Desert God*
Warlock	*Pharaoh*

Hector Cross

Those in Peril	*Predator*
Vicious Circle	

Standalones

The Dark of the Sun	*The Diamond Hunters*
Shout at the Devil	*The Sunbird*
Gold Mine	*Eagle in the Sky*

ABOUT THE AUTHORS

Wilbur Smith is a global phenomenon: a distinguished author with a large and established readership built up over fifty-five years of writing, with sales of over 130 million novels worldwide.

Born in Central Africa in 1933, Wilbur became a full-time writer in 1964 following the success of *When the Lion Feeds*, and has since published over forty global bestsellers, including the Courtney Series, the Ballantyne Series, the Egyptian Series, the Hector Cross Series and many successful standalone novels, all meticulously researched on his numerous expeditions worldwide. His books have now been translated into twenty-six languages.

The establishment of the Wilbur & Niso Smith Foundation in 2015 cemented Wilbur's passion for empowering writers, promoting literacy and advancing adventure writing as a genre. The foundation's flagship program is the Wilbur Smith Adventure Writing Prize.

For all the latest information on Wilbur, visit: www.wilbursmithbooks .com or facebook.com/WilburSmith.

Corban Addison is the internationally bestselling author of four novels and was the winner of the inaugural Wilbur Smith Adventure Writing Prize. An attorney, activist and world traveler, he is a supporter of numerous humanitarian causes. He lives with his wife and children in Virginia.

WILBUR SMITH

WITH
CORBAN ADDISON

CALL OF THE RAVEN

ZAFFRE

First published in the United States of America in 2020 by Zaffre,
an imprint of Bonnier Books UK

Typeset by Scribe Inc., Philadelphia, PA.
Printed in the USA

10 9 8 7 6 5 4 3 2 1

Hardcover ISBN: 978-1-4998-6229-4
Canadian paperback ISBN: 978-1-4998-6230-0
Paperback ISBN: 978-1-4998-6238-6
Digital ISBN: 978-1-4998-6231-7

For information, contact
251 Park Avenue South, Floor 12, New York, New York 10010

www.bonnierbooks.co.uk

This book is for my wife, Nisojon, because my admiration for her and the unequivocal love she spreads keeps my heart and mind constantly beating.

Dear Reader,

It's been forty years since the publication of *A Falcon Flies*, the first novel in the bestselling Ballantyne Series featuring a character that my fans both love and love to hate: Mungo St. John.

Some might say that Mungo St. John is the incarnate of evil itself: a slave trader who steals native Africans and sells them to plantation owners in the United States. But Mungo, charming, intelligent and irresistible to all around him—both men and women—shows compassion for his slaves and even demonstrates a hint of doubt about his place in this dark chapter of the history of mankind. His complex personality makes the beautiful and determined Robyn Ballantyne question her feelings for him and allow herself to see him as something other than a slaver. Like all good characters, Mungo is full of contradictions: he is both evil and heroic, a complex character who reflects the historical times he lived in.

Since launching my Facebook page I have been asked by many of my readers, "When will the story of Mungo St. John be continued?" I went back and revisited *A Falcon Flies* and found myself drawn to this man again, who was both Dr. Jeckyll and Mr. Hyde. Where did he come from? What motivated him? Why was he the way he is in *A Falcon Flies*?

Call of the Raven is my answer to those questions. It is, without a doubt, the most interesting historical novel I've worked on in some time as it made me question the history of slave trading and its impact on racism in our world. How does evil become acceptable in society? How is it appropriate for someone to hold another human being as their property?

I was fortunate to work with a co-author who was perfectly suited for the task of helping me explore 1840s New Orleans and Virginia. Corban Addison, a very accomplished novelist and a resident of Virginia himself, helped bring Mungo's world to life.

We hope you will find *Call of the Raven* a fascinating exploration of the dying days of the slave trade. It feels like an important contribution to our understanding of a period in history which continues to throw long shadows into the darkest aspects of the human soul.

As ever,

Wilbur Smith

No man can put a chain around the ankle of his fellow man without at last finding the other end fastened around his own neck.

Frederick Douglass

I

THE *BLACKHAWK*

The chamber was packed. Young men in evening dress squeezed ten-to-a-row on the benches; more stood around the edges of the room, bodies pressed together. The lamplit air hung heavy with sweat and alcohol and excitement, like a prize fight at a county fair.

But no blood would be spilled tonight. This was the Cambridge Union Society: the oldest debating club in the country and the proving ground for the nation's future rulers. The only sparring would be verbal, the only wounds to pride. At least, those were the rules.

The front of the room was set up like a miniature parliament. The two sides faced each other from opposing benches, divided by the length of two swords. A young man named Fairchild, with sandy hair and fine features, was addressing the audience from the dispatch box.

"The motion before you tonight is: 'This house believes that slavery should be abolished from the face of the Earth.' And, indeed, the case is so self-evident I feel I hardly need to argue it."

Nods of agreement; he was preaching to the converted. Abolitionist sentiment ran high among the Cambridge undergraduates.

"I know in this house we are used to debating the fine points of law and politics. But this is not academic. The question of slavery speaks to a higher law. To keep innocent men and women in chains, to tear them from their homes and work them to death: this is a crime against God and all the laws of justice."

On the facing bench, most of the opposition speakers listened to his oration glumly. They knew they were onto a losing cause. One leaned forward and twisted his handkerchief through his hands. One stared at the speaker with such melancholy he looked as if he might burst into tears. Only the third seemed untroubled. He lounged back nonchalantly, his mouth set in a lazy smile, as if he alone was privy to some enormous joke.

"If you have one ounce of humanity in you, I urge you to support the motion."

Fairchild sat down to sustained applause. The president waited for the noise to die away.

"To close for the opposition, the chair calls on Mr. Mungo St. John."

The man who had been lounging on the front bench rose. No one applauded, but a new force seemed to charge the room. Up in the gallery, where a few well-bred young ladies were allowed to observe proceedings as long as they stayed silent, crinolines rustled and stays creaked as they leaned forward to see better.

You could not ignore him. He was twenty, but he loomed half a head taller than any other man in the chamber. His dark hair flowed over his collar in a long, thick mane; his tanned skin shone with a luster that no wan English sun could have produced. His suit was cut to accentuate his figure: a slim waist that rose to broad, well-muscled shoulders more like a boxer's than a Cambridge undergraduate's.

If he felt the hostility aimed at him, it did not shake the easy grin from his face. Indeed, he seemed to feed off the crowd's energy.

"You have heard a great deal this evening about the supposed evils of slavery. But has anyone here ever been to the great tobacco plantations of Virginia, or the cotton fields of the Mississippi?"

His smoky yellow eyes surveyed the room.

"That is my native soil. I was born and raised in Virginia. Slavery to me is not sensational reports in the newspapers, or hell-raising sermons. I have seen the reality of it."

He lowered his voice. "Is the work hard? Yes. Do rich men profit from the labor of others? Again, yes. But do not be gulled by these fantasies of brutality and violence you are peddled. At Windemere—my home, on the banks of the James River—my father keeps four hundred workers, and he cares for each one.

When they work well, he praises them. When they are sick, he tends them. If they die, he grieves."

"That is because each one is worth a thousand dollars to him," said Fairchild.

The audience laughed.

"My friend is quite right," said Mungo. "But think of something you own that is worth that much. A fine horse, say, or a necklace. Do you beat it and disdain it and leave it in the mud? Or do you take superlative care of it, polish it and watch out for it, because it is so valuable to you?"

He leaned on the dispatch box, as comfortable as if he were leaning on the mantelpiece of his drawing room enjoying a cigar.

"I am a guest in your country. But sometimes, it takes a stranger's eye to observe what the natives do not see. Go to Manchester, or Birmingham, or any of your other great manufacturing cities. Visit the factories. You will see men and women laboring there twelve, fourteen, even eighteen hours a day, in conditions that would make my father sick to his stomach."

"At least they are free—and paid," said Fairchild.

"And what use is freedom, if it is only the freedom to live in a slum until you are worked to death? What use is a wage if it does not buy you enough to eat? The only thing that money buys is ease for the consciences of the mill owners. Whereas at Windemere, every one of our people enjoys three square meals a day, a roof over his head and clean clothes to wear. He never has to worry if he will eat, or who will take care of his family. I promise you, if any English loom worker or coal miner glimpsed life on the plantation, he would swap his life for that in a second."

On the opposite bench, Fairchild had risen. "A point of order?"

Mungo gave a languid wave to allow it.

"Even if we accept this preposterous picture of African slaves holidaying in some benevolent paradise, the gentleman is rather coy about how those persons came to his country. Will he admit that the slave trade is nothing but a trade in suffering? Or will he try to convince us that millions of Africans willingly took a pleasant cruise to America to enjoy the benefits of the climate?"

That drew a laugh. Mungo smiled broadly, enjoying the joke with everyone else.

"The slave trade has been illegal in Britain and America for over thirty years," he said. "Whatever our fathers and grandfathers may have done, it is finished now."

Fairchild's face flushed. He tried to calm his emotions—gentlemanly behavior in these debates was prized just as much as sound arguments—but he could not hold them in check.

"You know perfectly well that despite our government's strenuous efforts, traders continue to flout the law by smuggling blacks out of Africa under the very noses of the Royal Navy."

"Then I suggest you take up your complaint with the Royal Navy."

"I shall," said Fairchild. "Indeed, I may inform the house that as soon as I have completed my degree, I shall accept a commission in the Preventative Squadron of Her Majesty's Navy, intercepting slavers off the coast of Africa. I will report back from there as to the accuracy of Mr. St. John's picture of the *delights* of slavery."

There were cheers and approving applause. Up on the ladies' balcony, more than one corset strained with admiration of Fairchild's manly virtue.

"If you are going to Africa, you can report back how these negroes live in their own country," Mungo shot back. "Hungry, filthy, ignorant—a war of all against all. And then you can go to America, and say if they are not better off there after all."

He turned to the room. "My virtuous opponents would have you think that slavery is a unique evil, a moral abomination unparalleled in the annals of civilization. I urge you to see otherwise. It is merely a name for what men practice wherever they are, whether in Virginia or Guinea or Manchester. The power of the strong and wealthy over the weak and poor."

Fairchild had started to object again. Mungo ignored him.

"That may be an awkward truth. But I say to you, I would rather live my life as a slave on a plantation like Windemere, than as a so-called free man in a Lancashire cotton mill. They are the true slaves."

He looked around the tight-packed chamber. Only the briefest glance, yet every person in the room felt that his gaze had settled directly on them. On the ladies' balcony, the fans fluttered faster than ever.

"Perhaps what I say offends your moral sensibilities. I will not apologize for that. Instead, I beg you to look beyond your distaste and examine the proposition with clear-eyed honesty. If you sweeten your tea with sugar from the West Indies, or smoke Virginia tobacco, then you support slavery. If your father owns a mill where they spin Alabama cotton, or a bank that underwrites the voyages of Liverpool ship owners, then I say again you support slavery."

He shrugged. "I do not judge you. I do not lay claim to any superior moral virtue. But the one sin of which I am wholly innocent is this—I will not play the hypocrite and weep false tears for the choices I have made. If you agree with me, I urge you to oppose the motion."

He sat down. For a moment, silence gripped the room. Then, slowly, a wave of applause began from the back and swelled until it echoed around the chamber. The undergraduates might not agree with his politics, but they could appreciate a bravura performance.

Though not all of them. As the applause rose, so too did an answering barrage of boos and catcalls. Yells of "murderer" and "blood on your hands" were heard.

Mungo sat back, reveling in the discord.

"Order!" shouted the president. "The house will divide."

The audience filed through two doors, one for "aye" on the right, and one for "no" on the left. The queue for the "ayes" was noticeably longer, but a surprising number turned the other way. Mungo watched the count from his seat, the grin on his face never wavering.

The president announced the result. "Ayes to the right, two hundred and seven. Noes to the left, one hundred and eighteen."

Mungo nodded, accepting the result with perfect equanimity. He shook hands with his teammates, then took two glasses of wine and crossed the room to where Fairchild was talking with his friends. He pressed a drink into Fairchild's hand.

"Congratulations," said Mungo. "You spoke with great conviction."

Fairchild took the glass reluctantly. By convention, the society's debates were about rhetorical skill and argument; winning or losing was less important than behaving like gentlemen afterward. But Fairchild could not hide his disdain for Mungo.

"You take your loss in good part," he conceded.

"That is because I did not lose," Mungo answered, in the soft drawl of his native Virginia.

"You heard the result. I carried the motion by almost two to one. You lost."

"Not at all," said Mungo. "I wagered ten guineas that I could get at least a hundred votes against the motion. Nobody else thought I would get more than fifty. And though the glory of victory is very fine, I would rather have the extra gold in my purse."

Fairchild stared. All he could think to say was, "I should have thought you had already made enough money out of slavery."

"Not at all. My father has vowed that when he dies, he will free all his slaves. The will is already written. I will have to find some other way of making my fortune." Mungo clapped Fairchild on the shoulder. "So, you see, I will never make a penny out of that institution you revile so much. Whereas you—" he grinned—"will depend entirely on the slave trade to make your living."

Fairchild almost choked on his wine. "How dare you—?"

"You are joining the Preventative Squadron, are you not? You will be paid to capture slave ships."

"Yes."

"And that is a very fine and noble profession," Mungo agreed. "But if you ever actually succeeded in exterminating the slave trade, you would be out of a job. So it is in your interest to see that slavery endures."

Fairchild stared at him in horror. "Arguing with you is like arguing with the Devil himself," he complained. "White is black, and black is white."

"I should have thought you of all men would agree that black and white are created equal. They—"

Mungo broke off. The room was still full with undergraduates milling about, talking and drinking and carrying on the argument. But a young man was barging his way through the crowd, upsetting drinks and knocking people out of his way.

As he reached the front, Mungo recognized him. It was Sidney Manners, a stocky young man who had only got his place at Cambridge because his father owned half of Lincolnshire. With his thick neck, squat shoulders and heavy breathing, he looked like nothing more than a prize bull.

"I have been looking for you," he said to Mungo.

"I hope it did not tax your energies. I was not hard to find."

"You have offered the most grievous insult to my sister."

"Insult?" Mungo smiled. "You are misinformed. I offered her nothing but compliments."

"You seduced her!"

Mungo made a dismissive gesture. "Where I come from, gentlemen do not discuss such matters."

"Then why have I heard of it from five different people?" Manners took a step closer. "They say you had her in the organ loft of Trinity Chapel, while the choir were rehearsing."

"That is not true. It was during Evensong."

Manners's eyes bulged. "You do not deny it?"

"I deny that I made her do anything against her will. Indeed, I could hardly have resisted her advances if I had tried."

Mungo carefully put down his drink, then gave a conspiratorial wink. "I may say, your sister is a perfectly devout young woman. Always on her knees in chapel."

Manners's face had gone a deep shade of puce. His collar seemed to have shrunk around his neck. He struggled to breathe; his mouth flapped open, but no words emerged.

Eventually, his anger burst out the only way it could. He drew back his arm and swung a fist wildly at Mungo's jaw.

His size gave him power, but he had no training. Mungo boxed every week, taking lessons with a former champion of England who had retired to Cambridge. He dodged Manners's blow easily, grabbed his arm, then swept his feet from under him and dumped him on his backside.

Manners jerked on the ground. Mungo looked down at him and, for a second, his eyes flashed with an anger so fierce, anyone who saw it would have feared for Manners's life. In that moment, you could not doubt that Mungo was capable of anything.

Then the anger faded, as sudden as a summer squall. Mungo's smile returned. He nodded to the circle of spectators around him. They edged back, though they could not look away: captivated by the spectacle, yet frightened of Mungo's power.

"If you will excuse me, gentlemen."

The crowded room emptied in front of him as he made his way to the door. He heard Manners staggering to his feet behind him, but he did not look back. Outside, he put on his hat and strode back toward his college. The summer night was warm, but not as warm as it would be at home in Virginia. Windemere would be turning green now, as the young tobacco plants were transplanted from their winter seedbeds out into the fields.

He had enjoyed his time in Cambridge. He had learned everything he could, made some influential friends who might serve him well later in life, and met more than a few young ladies like Clarissa Manners who were eager to share their charms with him. But he would be glad to be home.

The moon was rising behind the tower of Great St. Mary's Church as he turned into Trinity Street. It was past curfew. The gates of his college would be locked, but that did not trouble him. He had an understanding with Chapman, the porter.

"St. John!"

An angry voice hailed him from the end of the street. Mungo kept walking.

"St. John! Stop, if you are not a coward."

Mungo paused. Slowly, he turned back. "No one has ever accused me of cowardice."

Manners stood there, silhouetted against the street lamp. He was not alone. Two of his friends flanked him, sturdy young men with ham fists and broad shoulders. One of them carried a poker, and the other a wine bottle, which he gripped by the neck.

"If you were a gentleman, I would challenge you to a duel," sneered Manners.

"If you were a gentleman, I would gladly accept. But as that is clearly not the case, I will bid you goodnight."

Mungo tipped his hat and turned away—as if completely oblivious to the armed men behind him. Manners stared after him for a moment, stupefied by his opponent's insouciance. Then anger took over. Snarling like a dog, he charged.

Mungo heard the footsteps on the cobbles behind him. As Manners closed on him, Mungo pivoted on the balls of his feet and delivered a perfectly aimed uppercut to Manners's chin. Manners stopped dead, howling in pain. Mungo followed up with three quick jabs to the ribs that sent Manners reeling away, clutching his abdomen.

As Manners retreated, his friends moved in. They circled around Mungo, with the shambling gait of men who have been drinking. Mungo watched them carefully, calculating the effect the alcohol would have. It might make them slower—but also more unpredictable.

They waited, calling encouragement to each other. None of them wanted to suffer the same fate as Manners, but they did not want to look weak. At last the one with the poker stepped forward.

"I will give you a lesson, you American bastard!"

He swung the poker at Mungo. Mungo took the blow on his shoulder, moving away so that he barely felt it. As he did, he grabbed the poker with both hands and tugged it forward, pulling his opponent off balance. Mungo thrust the poker back so that it hit him in the stomach, then twisted it out of his hands and cracked him over the shoulders. The man stumbled back.

Now Mungo was armed, he liked his odds better. He swung around, brandishing the poker. Manners's friends edged backward. They were not so devoted to Manners that they wanted their heads cracked for him.

"Are you afraid of this Yankee upstart?"

Manners had stood up. He snatched the bottle that his friend carried and broke it on the cobbles so that he was left with a jagged and glittering stump. He advanced again, more cautiously this time. Two encounters with Mungo had taught him that much, at least.

"I would not do that," Mungo said.

If Manners had been sober, he might have heard the lethal warning in Mungo's voice. But he was drunk, and angry, and he had been humiliated. He jabbed the bottle at Mungo, swiping the broken glass toward his face.

Mungo avoided it easily. As Manners brought the bottle back, Mungo whipped the poker through the air and cracked it against Manners's wrist. The bone snapped; the bottle flew out of his hand and smashed against a wall.

Manners howled and dropped to his knees. His two friends

took one look at Mungo, the poker raised like the sword of an avenging angel, and fled. Manners was left alone with Mungo.

Mungo could have walked away. He had done so once already that evening. But Manners had tried to kill him, however incompetently, and that had unlocked a rage he had rarely felt before. He stood over Manners like an executioner, the poker raised. Strength coursed through his arms. He was not minded to be merciful. At that moment, all that existed was his rage. He would break open Manners's head like an egg.

But as he moved to strike, a firm hand gripped the poker and stayed the blow. Mungo spun around to see Fairchild's earnest face, teeth gritted with the effort of holding back Mungo's arm.

"What are you doing?" Mungo hissed. "Do you think you can save this loathsome rat?"

Fairchild's grip did not loosen. "I am not saving him. I am saving *you*. From yourself."

"I do not need saving."

"If you kill him, you will be hanged for murder." Fairchild prodded Manners with the toe of his shoe. "Is he worth that?"

The two young men stared at each other, both holding the poker. Mungo knew that what Fairchild said was true, but he could not bring himself to let go. He tried to twist the weapon from Fairchild's grasp, heaving with all his might. Fairchild's fingers flexed; he was not as strong as Mungo. His grip threatened to break. But he had an iron will and would not yield.

They might have stayed locked in that position all night, but at that moment footsteps sounded on the street. A sturdy man in a long dark coat emerged from the porter's lodge and came straight toward them.

"Mr. St. John, sir?"

It was Chapman, the college porter. If he was surprised to see Mungo with a poker raised like a weapon, Fairchild wrestling him for it and Manners kneeling helpless at his feet, he made no comment. Chapman had known Mungo since he arrived three years ago, and nothing the undergraduate did could surprise him.

"A letter arrived for you, sir. It was marked 'urgent.'"

Mungo blinked. The poker dropped to the ground. Manners took advantage of his reprieve to scuttle away, whimpering and clutching his wrist. Mungo wiped his hands with his handkerchief, then adjusted his cuffs and his cravat. Only then did he take the letter. It was franked from Norfolk, Virginia, dated six weeks earlier. The address was written in a clear, large script, careful letters formed by a hand that was not used to writing.

Mungo showed no emotion as he slit it open and read the contents.

"What is it?" Fairchild asked.

Mungo ignored him. "Have the servants pack my trunk," he said to the porter. "I must return to Virginia at once."

A storm threatened to break. Dense clouds covered the sun and turned the dawn sky gray. In their shadow, the water of the Patapsco River had the look of rain-washed slate. The channel to the inner harbor of Baltimore, normally busy with shipping and pleasure craft, was nearly empty on this morning in August, 1841. The double-masted brig *Aurora*, fifty-eight days out from Southampton, was the only ship presently underway.

On an empty patch of foredeck, a small crowd of first-class passengers had gathered, wrapped in coats against the unseasonable chill. Mungo stood among them, peering through a spyglass. He could make out the battlements of Fort McHenry, where only thirty years earlier the fledgling American republic had come close to surrendering its flag to the British, and the tall masts of the docked merchant ships emerging from the fog behind it.

His thoughts darkened. He was a practical man, who never wasted energy on problems he could not solve. There was nothing to be done at sea, and so he had been able to put the news he had received that night in Cambridge two months earlier out of his mind. Now, with landfall, he could no longer ignore it.

He took the letter out of his pocket and read it again, though he could recite it like the Bible.

Your father is dead. Windemere is bankrupt and they say it is to be sold. There is nothing to harvest for nothing was planted. Come home at once or we will all be lost.

With love and deepest affection,
Camilla

He touched the paper to his lips. There was still a trace of scent on it, though almost worn away now. The smell of dogwood blossoms: ripe, sticky and vaguely obscene. Had Camilla been picking them when she wrote the letter, or had she rubbed the petals on the paper deliberately to remind him of home? He imagined her poring over the paper, tongue sticking out as she concentrated on forming the unfamiliar letters. It must have taken a huge effort. What desperation drove her?

Despite her childish handwriting, Camilla was a full-grown woman, two years Mungo's junior. But she had never sat in a schoolroom. She had been born a slave, and from the age of eleven had served Mungo's mother, Abigail, as her maid. When Abigail died, Mungo had persuaded his father not to sell Camilla.

"I will soon bring home my own wife," he had argued, "and she will expect me to provide a good lady's maid."

That was not the whole truth of it.

Mungo strolled back along the rail toward the quarterdeck. The bosun's mate greeted him with a tip of his cap, as did the officer of the watch when he climbed the ladder. In the nearly nine-week voyage, Mungo had been a regular on deck. He had befriended the officers, swapped stories with the sailors, fine-tuned his knowledge of the winds and currents of the North Atlantic, and even learned to read the sextant. He loved the sea. In another life, he would have liked to be a mariner and then a master of his own vessel.

That was not the life he had come back to.

The *Aurora* docked at the quay, a stone's throw from the Waterfront Hotel. Stevedores shouted and hauled in the lines, and seamen manning the masts furled the sails and stripped them down to bare poles. Mungo collected his sea bag from his cabin and descended the gangplank. Unsteady after weeks at sea, he made his way through the crowd of dock workers to the livery yard at the Admiral Fell Inn. He had planned to hire a hack to ride to Windemere, but when he introduced himself, the groom led him at once to the stables. Two familiar faces greeted him.

"Jack," Mungo cried in delight. "Bristol."

In reply, he received happy whinnies of recognition. Two

Arabian horses trotted forward and nuzzled him. They were the finest horses in the yard, one patterned with high white markings, the other midnight black. They were not large, but they had the strength and stamina to outdistance any other breed.

"How do they come to be here?" Mungo asked.

"A negro boy brought them from Windemere," answered the groom. "He said you would call. Paid two months' board in advance and left this for you."

He gave Mungo a leather bag hung from a nail. Inside was a riding cape and hat, a purse and a slim wooden case, surprisingly heavy. Mungo knew without opening it what it contained. He wondered why she had felt the need to send him a pistol.

There was also a note, again in Camilla's familiar hand. *Come quick. Be careful.*

Mungo pocketed the paper. He tossed the groom a coin and mounted up.

"Don't you want breakfast, sir?" the groom asked. "You must be hungry."

"I have no time to waste." Mungo put on the broad-brimmed riding hat that Camilla had sent along with the horses. He snapped open the wooden case, loaded the pistol and stuck it in his belt. "I have a long ride ahead."

He navigated the streets of Baltimore at a trot, then spurred Bristol into a canter when he reached the King's Highway, with Jack loping behind. He set a pace he knew the athletic Arabians could keep until sundown. The road stretched out before him, a trail of hard-packed dirt and occasional gravel that wound through field and forest, hamlet and metropolis.

He passed by Washington, as the sun climbed the sky and descended again, the humid summer air soaking the cotton of Mungo's shirt with sweat. Twice, he stopped at a creek to allow the Arabians to drink, but he gave the horses no time to graze. His lunch was a wedge of hard cheese and a handful of carrots, the latter shared with Bristol and Jack. At dusk, as the moon rose above the leafy trees, he reached the outskirts of Fredericksburg. There, he halted for the night at an inn.

Next morning, he crossed the Rappahannock and turned west on James River Road. The timberlands of the Piedmont, thick with maples and oaks, poplars and sweet gum, gave way to the plains and marshes of the low country. Mungo knew the contours of this land like his own face, every homestead and plantation, every creek and hill and bend in the road. His father, Oliver, had made sure of it, leading Mungo on countless excursions to hunt deer and rabbit and the elusive gray fox.

"This is your heritage," Oliver had said. "A man should never forget where he came from."

Could his father really now be dead?

It was the afternoon of the second day, and the oppressive heat was at its peak, when Mungo arrived at the gate that stood at the entrance to his home. Unlike the wooden fences that surrounded it, the gate had been wrought out of black iron and gleaming brass, the pattern of interlinked whorls and fleur-de-lis framing the St. John family crest. Mungo's great-grandfather had carried it with him from Scotland in the 1750s. The unlatched gate stood half-open. A sign was planted in the earth beside it.

By order of the Fidelity Trust Bank of Charles City.

And in block letters beneath that, a single word:

FORECLOSURE

Mungo peered closely at the sign. He had never heard of the Fidelity Trust Bank of Charles City, though it was the nearest town and all the estate's business was done there. A host of questions swarmed in his mind, but they were beaten back by the force of his anger. In a single motion, he drew the pistol from his belt and pulled the trigger. At point-blank range, the lead ball blasted the wooden stake into splinters and left the announcement lying face down in the dirt.

He spurred Bristol into a gallop toward the house. By the first week of August, the fields on either side of the gravel path should have been green with tobacco plants ready for the harvest. But they were barren. There were no slaves tending them, or children playing—only crows picking through the weeds.

At the end of the drive stood the house, overlooking a lawn and the blue sweep of the river. It was constructed of red brick and laid out in the Georgian style favored by the American colonists. It had two wings: on one side the slave quarters and the kitchen, and on the other a colonnaded addition that housed the drawing rooms and the library.

Mungo left the weary horses tethered to a post beside the garden gate and ran to the porch. There was no one to open the door, but it was not locked. He threw it open himself, so hard that the heavy oak slammed into the pillar behind.

He waited a moment to see if the noise would bring anyone, but no one came. He crossed the threshold. Even though it was his property—his home—it felt different. Like stealing into someone else's house as a thief.

His footfalls echoed on the marble hallway. Everything was in its place and as he remembered it, except for a film of dust on the furniture. His eyes swept the adjoining rooms: the formal parlor where his parents and grandparents had entertained so many distinguished guests, including three of America's first five presidents; the youth parlor where his grandfather had taught him to play chess and poker and where, at his mother's insistence, he had dabbled with Beethoven on her Chickering piano; the dining room with its walnut table large enough to accommodate a party of twenty; and the long staircase to the bedrooms on the second floor.

But Mungo sensed a vast emptiness. Three years ago, when he left for Cambridge, fifteen servants—slaves—had lived and worked in the house. Whatever the season, the house had always hummed with life. Now it was as quiet as a burial chamber.

"Camilla!" Mungo called out, striding through the empty rooms. He left the dining room by way of the butler's pantry and walked down the hallway toward the servant quarters. He tried other names: Esther, the family's talkative cook; Old Joe, the chief carpenter; Charles, his father's personal attendant; Nora, the maid who maintained the ground floor, and her sister, Amelia, who looked after the upper chambers. He listened closely, sure that someone would respond, but no one did. He entered their rooms and found beds made and clothing still in closets. It was as if the entire staff had simply vanished.

If his father was dead, then they should all have been set free. But where could they have gone?

He went back downstairs and crossed the colonnade to the library in the east wing. This was the only room in the house that was not covered in dust; someone had used it recently. The ink in the inkwell was fresh, and papers were stacked on the desk. He took a handful and scanned them quickly, searching for any clue as to what had happened. Many of them bore the same letterhead he had seen on the foreclosure sign: the Fidelity Trust Bank of Charles City. There were also a great many bills of sale that recorded the dismantling of the estate, all signed with the same name.

From the hallway, Mungo heard a door click. Then footsteps. He listened. Ten minutes ago, all he had wanted was to hear another human sound in the empty house. Now, he was suddenly cautious. His pistol was empty from being fired at the sign and he had no time to reload it, but a penknife lay on the desk. He palmed it, just as the study door swung open.

The man in the doorway stood a head shorter than Mungo, with thinning hair and hunched shoulders that even his well-cut coat could not improve. His face was unremarkable: if you passed him on the street, you would barely notice him. And yet, if you caught his eyes you would not forget him. They burned with a bright purpose, unsettling in its intensity, as if he was fixed on a future that others could not see.

But now those eyes were staring in shock.

"Mungo."

"Chester," said Mungo evenly.

He had mastered his surprise quicker than Chester, perhaps because Chester's name was the one scrawled on all the bills of sale he had been reading. Chester Marion was the family attorney, a man with a unique talent for turning the St. Johns' plans into contracts, mortgages and conveyances that advanced the interests of the estate.

In truth, Mungo had never liked him. There was something cold and ferret-like in his bearing. He rarely looked you in the eye, and if he did it was always with an air of calculation.

But now he was the man who might be able to give Mungo answers.

"What happened? The estate—the crop, our people. Where are they all?"

Where is Camilla? he wanted to ask, but he doubted Chester would know one slave from another.

"Your father died."

"How?"

Chester sucked his teeth. "It is a long story. Perhaps it is best I tell it from the beginning. That way, I can answer all your questions in the right order."

Mungo nodded.

"Your father did not have a mind for business," said Chester. "I tried to advise him as best I could, but he would not listen. He was headstrong, like all the St. Johns, but without the good sense your grandfather had."

Mungo's grandfather, Benjamin St. John, had been a towering figure. His uncompromising ambition had built Windemere from a smallholding into a great estate, while his ruthless methods had kept the slaves in such a state of terror that they made it the most productive plantation on the James River. Even Mungo had feared the old man.

"My father wanted to be a better man," Mungo said quietly.

Oliver had inherited none of Benjamin's brutal enthusiasm for slavery. Where Benjamin refused to waste money on slave quarters and consigned the hands to wooden hovels, Oliver built solid brick cottages to house them. Where Benjamin had dictated whom the slaves would marry—"the better for breeding good stock," he had said—Oliver let them choose their partners and live with the families they created. Benjamin would sell a slave the moment he became unproductive; Oliver preferred to keep the old slaves doing light chores, so as not to split up their families.

Did that make him a good man, when every minute of his life was provided for by slavery? Did it matter to the slaves that Oliver kept them in bondage only reluctantly? Perhaps Oliver believed it.

"No doubt his methods flattered his conscience," said Chester tartly, "but they did nothing for his profits."

"It was enough for him to live comfortably."

"No!" Chester banged his hand on the table. "Did you learn nothing from your grandfather? He built this estate by borrowing aggressively. But the only way he could pay his debts was by continuing to expand. As soon as your father decided to rest on his laurels, the debts became unsustainable."

He leaned forward. The look in his eyes reminded Mungo of a schoolmaster he'd had at Eton, a man whose passionate purpose was to make his pupils understand the Latin subjunctive, or flog them raw if they failed.

"On any plantation, even in a good year, the profit from the crop is spent before the first seed is planted," Chester explained. "The income from the harvest goes to repay the debts. The structure that your grandfather and I had put in place meant that the estate had to expand constantly to survive, either by acquiring more land or by making the existing fields more productive. But your father would not take the measures necessary to force the slaves to work hard enough. Instead of rising, production fell. He had to borrow more, simply to pay the interest on what he already owed. Eventually, the bank lost faith in his ability to repay and foreclosed."

He sighed. "Credit is as vital to a man as the air that he breathes. Cut it off, and he dies."

There seemed to be more regret in his voice for the financial loss than for the death of Oliver St. John.

Mungo had grown impatient. "This is all very well, but I doubt my father starved to death. How did he die?"

"The old-fashioned way." Chester pointed out of the window, where a great oak tree spread its branches over the lawn. Mungo's grandfather had reckoned it over three hundred years old. "The slaves found Oliver there at dawn one morning, with a pistol in his hand and a bullet in his skull. Facing financial ruin, it seemed he did the only honorable thing."

Mungo closed his eyes, imagining the scene. "He would not have done it merely because of the money," he said. "My father never cared about that."

"Not nearly enough," Chester agreed.

"If he was bankrupt, he would have had to sell the slaves to pay his debts. That would have broken his heart."

"He was always too soft on them. He never understood that they were assets that should be made to turn a profit."

"He saw them as human." Mungo looked out the window, to the empty fields that had once been so full of people. "Where are they now? Have they been set free, as he wanted in his will?"

Chester leaned back against the door frame. A smirk curled on his lips, and Mungo realized how very rarely he had seen the lawyer smile. Chester took a cigar from his pocket and struck a match to light it. The end glowed red.

"The *will*." The word hissed out with a cloud of smoke. "Such an extraordinary document. I hardly had the stomach to write it down when he told me what he wanted to do. The notion of freeing his slaves to salve his conscience—ridiculous."

"Your job was to execute his wishes, not judge them."

"Of course, of course." Chester leaned forward. The light in his eyes burned brighter than ever. "Why should I dare to have an opinion? Chester the pen-pusher. Chester the numbers man. Chester the loyal dog, waiting in the corner in case someone throws him a bone. Chester who works night and day to make the St. Johns richer than he will ever be, only to see them piss it away. What right do I have to judge?"

He met Mungo's gaze, clear and full. For the first time in his life, Mungo saw through those shifting, deceitful eyes and into the bitter soul behind.

"What have you done?"

"I sold the slaves." He saw the protest rising on Mungo's lips and waved a hand to hush him. "They fetched a good price. It will be a shock for them to finally learn the meaning of a hard day's work."

Mungo stared. He had never been lost for words before, but now he could hardly speak.

"You betrayed my father's wishes."

"When he died, the will could not be found."

Mungo gripped the desk tight enough to crack the hardwood. "You were his attorney. Surely you knew where the will was kept."

Chester shrugged. His attitude only stoked Mungo's anger.

"I will find the will and prove you had no right to sell them. I will make you track down every last one of our people and buy their freedom."

"You do not have to look for the will." Chester reached inside his coat and pulled out a densely written piece of paper. Mungo could not read it at that distance, but he recognized his father's bold signature scrawled across the bottom, stamped with the notary's seal. "I have it here."

"Then why . . . ?"

Mungo did not understand what was happening—all he knew was that he had been betrayed. He flung himself at Chester. He wanted to sink his fists into that soft flesh and break every bone in his body. He wanted to wring his neck and rip his head off his shoulders. He wanted—

He did not make it more than halfway. From a holster under his coat, Chester had produced a small pearl-handled pistol. He held it straight out, aimed at Mungo's heart, and even in his rage Mungo had the sense and the self-control to stop moving. Until ten minutes ago, he would never have believed Chester had the courage to pull the trigger. Now, he did not know what the man was capable of.

Chester sucked on the cigar until the end burned bright red. Without taking his eyes off Mungo, he lifted the will and touched the corner to the glowing ember. A dark stain spread across the paper, then burst into flame. Mungo gave a stifled cry, but the pistol in Chester's hand did not waver. Chester twisted the paper this way and that, until the fire took hold, then dropped it on the floor. Mungo could only watch as the paper shriveled into wisps of ash. His father's last wishes—gone.

Chester ground out the embers with the heel of his boot.

"That is not the end of it," Mungo warned him. "Even if the courts believe my father died intestate, I am still the only heir. Windemere is mine."

"You are too late. The property was foreclosed this morning. I signed the deed myself, on behalf of the Fidelity Trust Bank of Charles City." Chester spread his free arm with a proprietorial grin, dripping cigar ash on the hardwood floor. "Windemere has a new owner now."

"You?" The fury boiled up inside Mungo, but reason kept an iron grip on him. "How?"

"Because I own the bank. I used it to acquire the debts your father owed—cheaply, I might add. The other banks were keen to be rid of them. Then I called in the loans. Your father could not pay, so he forfeited the entire estate to me."

Again, Mungo cursed himself for being so blind to the evil within Chester.

"My father did not bring all this on himself. You led him down the path to bankruptcy."

Chester did not deny it. "It was not hard. He had no head for business, and he trusted me completely. He did everything I told him, even as it brought him to his own ruin."

"Whatever my father may have done, you killed him as surely as if you had pulled the trigger yourself."

If he had meant to wound Chester, he failed. The smile that spread across Chester's face was terrible to see.

"You are more right than you know. I *did* pull the trigger myself."

"You?"

Chester nodded, as if accepting a compliment. "I had hoped that bankruptcy would drive him to despair. But even in his ruin, he did not have the wit to see what he should do. So I took it in hand myself." He sighed. "Even at the end, I had to do everything for him."

"I will kill you," Mungo hissed.

"I think not." Chester reached out a fist and rapped twice on the wood paneling. "Only a fool would kill the wolf and let the cub grow up to avenge him."

Behind the desk there was another door that led to the billiards parlor. Now it snapped open. Mungo turned to see half a dozen men spilling out of it into the room.

"I saw you coming the moment you crossed the county line," said Chester, drawing on his cigar. "We were ready for you."

Two of the men grabbed Mungo's arms. A third pulled Mungo's pistol from its holster and tossed it aside. These were not soft

Cambridge undergraduates; they were rough men with strong hands. Stubble darkened their cheeks, they had knives and pistols strapped to their belts, and by the smell of them they'd spent time in Oliver St. John's whiskey cellar. Their leader wore a maroon hat pulled low over his face, and an open-necked shirt that revealed a livid scar circling his throat.

"Granville," Chester said to him. "Take this boy outside and deal with him."

The men hustled Mungo outside. He had no false hopes. None of the neighbors had seen him arrive at Windemere; apart from a stable boy in Baltimore, no one even knew he had come back to America. His family were dead. Chester's men would kill him, and no one would be any the wiser. Wherever Camilla was, she would never know he had received her letter and acted on it.

Bristol, still tethered to the hitching post, whinnied at the sight of Mungo as the men dragged him past. They were taking him to the oak tree on the lawn, the same place where his father had died. Glancing back, Mungo saw Chester watching from the library window. Savoring his final victory.

Mungo had not resisted his captors. He hung his head and slacked his muscles, like a man resigned to his fate. That put his captors off their guard. Then, suddenly, he stopped dead. The men who held him stumbled forward; their grip loosened. Not much, but enough for Mungo to move his arm.

Couched in his hand, he still had the penknife that he had taken from the desk. He let the blade slip out between his fingers, and stabbed it to his right. The man let go with a cry. As he sagged to the ground, Mungo grabbed a long hunting knife from the man's belt and deftly reversed it into the man on his left, who stumbled backward clutching his belly.

Before Mungo could move, two more of Granville's men leaped for him. They grabbed his shoulders and tried to wrestle him to the ground. Mungo was too strong. He took three steps backward and slammed them into the trunk of the oak tree, so hard they let go and reeled away.

Mungo had been in his share of brawls. Yet he had never experienced this kind of violence before—half a dozen armed men trying to kill him. It did not terrify him; instead it unleashed the same focused fury he had felt with Manners in Cambridge. Everything seemed to move more slowly. The men who had attacked him had pistols in their belts. Before they could get up, Mungo snatched them both, spun, and discharged them both at point-blank range at the rest of Granville's men.

One of the men collapsed, clutching his shoulder where a bullet had shattered his collarbone. But the other ball had gone wide. Through the cloud of smoke that the pistols had disgorged, Mungo saw Granville and one of the others coming at him. Meanwhile, the men he had slammed against the tree were getting to their feet.

Granville swung at Mungo with a knife. Metal rang on metal as Mungo blocked it with a pistol barrel, jarring so hard that Granville dropped the blade. For a moment he was defenseless: Mungo had an opening to attack.

But if he went for Granville, there were three others ready to grab him. He could not beat them all. His only chance was to flee. He ran across the lawn to where Bristol was tethered. He slipped the bridle off the hitching post and swung himself into the saddle. Bristol had smelled the danger and began to move even before Mungo landed on her back. He kicked her flanks hard, leaning low over her neck as she shot away. Her mane blew back in his face; her hooves thundered over the hard ground.

Over the din, he heard the crack of a gunshot. A bullet flew by and buried itself in one of the oaks to his left. He glanced back. Chester had run out of the house and was standing on the porch, holding his pistol. By the tree, Granville and two of his henchmen stumbled after him. But they only had pistols, and against a moving target at that range they stood no chance.

Mungo passed the slave quarters, the drying sheds and the cooperage, and left the house behind. He rode across the soft earth of the empty fields, giving Bristol her head. Where now? After Chester's betrayal, he did not know if he could trust any of Windemere's neighbors. Richmond was a better bet, but it was miles away. Bristol had already done almost two hundred miles hard riding in the last two days. Already, Mungo could feel her beginning to slow. Behind him, he heard the barking of dogs and the neighing of horses. Chester's men must have mounted up to follow him.

Half a mile from the main house, he entered a knot of trees where a creek led in from the river. He guided Bristol down the bank and splashed into the creek. Halfway across, he slid out of the saddle and dropped into the water. The horse looked at him curiously.

"Go on."

Mungo took his sea bag from the saddle where it was still tied on, then slapped the horse on her rump. She trotted away and up the far bank, leaving a deep trail of hoofprints in the mud. At the top of the embankment, she paused again and looked back.

"Go," Mungo said again.

With a whinny, she tossed her head and vanished into the trees. With luck, Chester's men would see her tracks and be led a merry dance before they realized their mistake.

Mungo did not follow her. He turned downstream, holding his bag above his head and breasting through the water. Toward the mouth of the creek, where it met the river, an island had formed in the stream. There had been a bridge once, but it was gone now. A row of rotten pilings poking through the surface were all that remained.

Mungo hauled himself out and climbed onto the island. The thickly wooded ground rose up the slopes of a long hill, a pocket of the pre-colonial wilderness that had survived the St. Johns' improvements to the land. There was only one path, almost invisible and seldom used. Mungo prayed that Chester did not know it.

The air in the forest was quiet and dank. Briars and branches overhung the path, but it was not completely overgrown. The thicker branches still wept sap from their splintered ends where an ax had pruned them roughly back. In hollows where the earth stayed damp, Mungo saw footprints that must have been made since the last rain.

He took out the pistol case from his sea bag and reloaded the gun he had taken from his captors. He continued cautiously up the path. The forest deadened sound, but in the distance he could still hear the barking of dogs. He hoped the creek had washed clean his scent.

At the top of the hill, the trees thinned out into a clearing. A red brick building stood in its center—an octagonal shape with a domed roof. Mungo's grandfather had built it as an observatory and Mungo had spent many nights there with the old man, studying the stars through the heavy telescope that Benjamin had imported from Italy. After his death, Mungo's father sold the telescope and left the observatory abandoned. The forest had drawn in, and a canopy of leaves now blocked any view of the heavens.

But it had other uses. Someone seemed to be there now; the door stood open, and a pair of skinned rabbits were strung up from the bracket where a lamp had once hung. They were freshly killed; their blood pattered down on the carpet of leaves.

Mungo advanced into the clearing, gun ready. He had been playing in these woods since he could walk, and knew how to move silently. Barely a leaf stirred as he approached the door.

He waited outside. He could hear snuffling inside, a sort of snoring. Someone was in there. But if they were asleep, perhaps Mungo should pass by and not disturb them.

Then some sixth sense prickled down his spine. He turned,

pressing his back to the wall, to see a figure emerging from the forest. Her white dress shone bright among the gray wood.

His heart lifted. For the first time since he had landed in Baltimore, he felt a spark of hope.

"Camilla!" he called.

A stack of firewood tumbled from her arms and she gave a yelp of fear, turning to joy as she recognized him. She ran across the clearing and threw herself at Mungo. He caught her in his strong arms, wrapped them around her and hugged her close to him as he kissed her on the lips. Even in the chaos and ruin of that afternoon, for that moment at least the world seemed to hang still in perfect peace.

She buried her head in his chest. "Thank God you are here. I prayed every night that you would come."

He held her back so he could study her face. Her skin was the color of mahogany, a beautiful reddish brown that seemed to glow with the fire of an inner warmth. She wore her hair in two braids tied back behind her neck, framing an oval face with full lips and wide round eyes. She must have been in the forest some time; her features were drawn, and she had lost weight. But the spark inside her, the one that Mungo remembered so well, remained undimmed.

"I wish I had come sooner," Mungo said. A thousand questions crowded his mind, but he had no time to ask them. "Chester knows I am here and has put the hunt up. We must escape."

"It is not so easy."

She pulled free and led him into the observatory. Inside was a single dim room, empty apart from a makeshift bed of ferns and dry leaves in the corner. A white-haired man lay there, next to a balled-up blanket he must have thrown off.

"Methuselah," said Mungo softly.

The old man had worked the plantation as long as anyone could remember. Among the slaves he had served as headman, judge, shaman and spokesman. He was also Camilla's grandfather.

"What happened?" Livid welts criss-crossed Methuselah's back, gleaming with the ointment Camilla had rubbed on them. "Who beat him?"

"Chester said all the slaves were to be sold," said Camilla. "Methuselah said we belonged to the St. Johns, and once Mr. Oliver was dead we should be free. Chester had his man, Granville Slaughter, thrash him nearly dead."

She raised her eyes to look at Mungo. "Do you know Granville?"

Mungo rubbed his arms, still bruised from the hands that had gripped him. "I've met him."

Camilla shuddered. "Of all the men I ever met, black or white, I never saw one who scared me like him."

"Did he touch you?"

"No. That night, before we were to go away, me and my Granddaddy managed to get out. He couldn't go far, but I remembered this place. How you and me used to come here."

She dropped her gaze shyly, remembering the first night they had gone there together. Mungo had been eighteen, and she sixteen, on the cusp of womanhood.

"If Chester had touched one hair on your head, I would tear him apart like a dog." Mungo's voice was cold and resolute. "As it is, a bullet may suffice."

He rose. "But I do not like the odds at present. We must go."

"We can't." She took Mungo's hand and pressed it against Methuselah's forehead. "Feel him. He took sick from his wounds—he's burning up with a fever."

Mungo looked into her eyes, hating the pain he saw there.

"If I had been here, I could have put a stop to all of this."

Camilla looked as if she might be about to cry, but she caught herself. "It's not your fault."

Mungo's touch had woken the old man. Methuselah stirred, and seemed to mumble something. Camilla leaned over and placed her ear beside his mouth. He murmured again and turned onto his side, pulling his knees toward his chest like a baby.

"Not making any sense," she said, straining to listen. "Something about a . . . black heart. And . . . thirst."

A withered hand reached out toward Mungo, clawing the air to beckon him. Camilla moved aside to let Mungo move closer.

Methuselah let out a cough that shook his battered body. His eyelids opened, revealing the yellow-white of his eyeballs. They rolled back in his skull—sightless orbs that fixed on Mungo like two moons.

"Beware the black heart," the old man croaked, "and the thirst that never quenches."

A cold shiver went down Mungo's spine. The words meant nothing, yet they seemed freighted with menace. He knew the slaves venerated Methuselah as much more than an elder or a foreman. Unlike most of them, he had been born in the soil of Africa; he alone had been inducted into the old mysteries of their people. He was their shaman, a seer who could commune with their ancestors' spirits across the divides of time and oceans and death.

"What do you mean?" Mungo whispered. "What did you see?"

For a moment, Methuselah went rigid: as stiff as a dead man. Then his body relaxed. His eyes closed, his breathing eased and he sank back into the mattress.

From outside the observatory, Mungo heard the barking of dogs again. It was louder now; they must have crossed the creek and picked up his trail. He shook off Methuselah's grip, angry for letting himself be gulled by the old man's mumbo jumbo. He should know better.

"We must go," he said abruptly.

"Leave me here," Camilla said. "There is nothing they can

take from me. But you know what they would do to you if they caught you helping a runaway."

"Two years in jail and a thousand-dollar fine," said Mungo. "I can afford both."

He said it lightly, though he knew that was the least of it. For a white man to help a fugitive slave, especially the scion of a famous family like the St. Johns, was to betray every principle the South was built on. Mungo would be ostracized. His friends would melt away; his associates would disown him. Strangers would cross the street to avoid him, or stay so they could spit at him. In his fight with Chester, he would be left without a single ally.

"You are not a runaway," he told Camilla. "You should be free."

She stiffened. "The law says I belong to Chester."

"I intend to prove otherwise."

"Which will be easier if you are not in jail yourself."

"But I do not care to let him have you."

Mungo smiled. It was a look she knew well, the same charming smile he had worn when they met in the observatory that first night. The look of a man whose will was as unyielding as granite.

In a part of her mind, she wondered what truly drove him now. Was it love for her, or simply the determination to have what was his? When he had her in his arms, he was so tender she felt that their souls were joined and there was nothing between them. Yet even then, his heart remained impenetrable to her. And whatever she felt for him—a terrifying, breathless knot of feelings—she had never been able to escape one immutable fact. Just as much as the fields and the buildings, down to the last stick of furniture in the great house, she was his family's property.

The dogs were getting closer. Now she could hear shouts and the snap of branches as men fought their way through the undergrowth.

"Granddaddy cannot travel," she said.

Mungo ignored her. He lifted the old man off the bed and carried him outside in his arms, like a child.

"Where are we going?"

"Mud Island. You know it?"

Camilla nodded. It was a low-lying islet in the middle of the James River.

"The dogs will not find us there. Old Jonah the boatman used to keep a raft in the creek opposite. We should be able to get across."

At that moment, a dark shadow sprang out from the trees and raced into the clearing. It was a bloodhound, daubed with mud and snarling through its ferocious jaws. Mungo had the pistol in his belt, but his arms were full carrying Methuselah.

The hound bore down on them. Mungo did not have time to reach his pistol. Then something small and bloody sailed through the air and landed just in front of the hound. Camilla had snatched one of the skinned rabbits hanging by the obser-vatory door and thrown it at the hound. The scent of fresh meat drove out every other thought from the dog's mind. It stopped its charge and began tearing the rabbit carcass apart.

It would not be distracted for long. Mungo laid Methuselah on the ground, drew the pistol and shot the dog through the chest. The animal collapsed without a sound. Two more dogs had followed it into the clearing; now they halted, sniffing at their fallen companion and whimpering.

Mungo grabbed the pistol case from his bag and began to reload. But he was out of time. Even as he rammed home the ball, the dogs' owners burst into the clearing. There were six of them, all on horseback and all armed: Chester, Granville and one of his men, and three men in the blue coats of the Charles City County Militia.

They spread out in a loose circle, rifles raised. Mungo stepped forward, putting himself in front of Camilla and Methuselah.

"Have you called in the army now to do your work for you?" he asked Chester, nodding at the militia men.

"We were riding by the gate from our muster when we heard shots. We came to investigate." The leader of the militia was a stern-looking man of about fifty, with a lieutenant's insignia on his shoulder. His name was Jeremiah Cartwright and Mungo knew him well; he owned the neighboring plantation to Windemere. "What in God's name have you done, Mungo?"

"He trespassed on my property, attacked my men and then tried to escape," said Chester, before Mungo could speak.

"I cannot trespass on what is rightfully mine," Mungo retorted.

"I am the owner. These two negroes—" Chester pointed to Camilla and Methuselah—"belong to me. And this man has been helping them escape."

"Don't listen to him. He is a thief and a murderer," Mungo replied.

Cartwright looked uncertainly between the two men. Chester Marion was nothing more than a county lawyer, a man of no background or family; the St. Johns had been the masters of Windemere since before the War of Independence. Yet there was no denying the evidence of his eyes. Why else should Mungo be out here in the forest—bloody, filthy and unshaven—with two fugitive slaves?

"Please, Jeremiah," Mungo said humbly. "Would you do this to my family?"

It was lucky the militia had arrived so soon, Mungo thought. If Chester and Granville had found him themselves, they could have killed him quickly; his body would never have been found. Now there were witnesses, men Mungo had known all his life. The balance had shifted.

"Chester killed my father and he has swindled me out of my inheritance," he told Cartwright. "For the close bonds that have always tied our families together, give me the chance to prove it."

The low sun shone through the trees over Cartwright's shoulder, so Mungo could not see his face under the shadow of his hat. He waited, wondering what Cartwright was thinking.

"Oliver St. John was a good man, and I was proud to call him my neighbor," Cartwright said.

In fact, Oliver St. John had been a sanctimonious pain in the ass—treating his slaves too soft, giving them notions above their station. Ideas like that had consequences; slaves gossiped with each other. Cartwright had lost count of the beatings he'd had to give his own field hands because they'd been infected by Oliver's hands' way of thinking.

All that passed through Cartwright's mind as he looked at Mungo. That, and a great many other things. He gave Chester a sideways glance and nodded.

"These are serious charges. Best take him to the jail."

"He doesn't need a trial," Chester complained. "The evidence of his crime is all around you. I say we lynch him here."

Cartwright looked horrified. "That wouldn't be lawful."

"Are you always so nice about points of law?"

"Mr. St. John may be a criminal, but he is a gentleman. We're not stringing him up like some common negro."

Mungo saw Chester's finger twitching against the trigger of his gun. But he could not murder Mungo in cold blood in front of witnesses. He swung down from the saddle and walked across the clearing. He did not look at Mungo, but went straight past him to where Camilla kneeled beside Methuselah.

"I am obliged to you for restoring what is rightfully mine," he said to Cartwright.

He drew his pistol, aimed it at Methuselah's chest, and fired.

The bang echoed around the clearing, startling a flock of black birds from their roosts. The old man's body jerked once and went still. Camilla screamed and threw herself over her grandfather. Mungo lunged for Chester, but Granville read his intentions. He spurred his horse forward and struck Mungo's shoulders hard with the butt of his rifle as he cantered past. Mungo was knocked flat onto the ground.

Granville dismounted. He grabbed Camilla by her arms and wrestled her off her grandfather, her dress now stained with blood and earth. Chester walked over to Mungo. He planted his boot on the back of Mungo's head and squeezed down, pressing Mungo's face into the mud.

"The old man was worthless," he said, "and I have no time for assets that do not turn a profit." He bent down, lowering his voice to whisper in Mungo's ear. "As for your little black whore, I did intend to sell her with the others. But now she's gotten a taste for freedom, no one will pay good money for her. There's nothing you can do with a bitch who's gone wild—except shoot her down."

Mungo rose out of the mud so suddenly Chester was thrown onto his back. Careless of the armed men around him, Mungo lunged for his enemy. If he could get his hands on him, he would snap his neck and witnesses be damned. He would not let Chester kill Camilla.

But Mungo could not touch him. The militiamen leaped off their horses and piled into Mungo. He fought them off with all his strength, but they were fresh and strong. Even then, they could not overcome him until Cartwright managed to get a loop of rope over his head. He fastened the other end to the pommel of his saddle and spurred his horse forward. The rope closed around Mungo's throat. He had to stagger after the horse or he would be throttled.

He twisted his head back, staring at Camilla on her knees beside Methuselah, mouthing words that only she could see. He would never forget the way she looked back at him. Her eyes were wide with the shocking knowledge she was about to die, the frantic disbelief of a small bird cornered by a cat. Mungo clawed at the rope around his neck, but Cartwright was moving so fast he could not loosen it.

Back in the clearing, Chester raised his pistol and aimed it at Camilla's forehead. The sight tore at his heart, but Mungo forced himself to keep looking. Even if the world did not recognize it as a crime, he would witness it—and bring Chester to justice.

Chester half turned, almost as if he wanted to make sure that Mungo had gone. He caught Mungo's gaze; his mouth opened in a terrible sneer of triumph. Mungo wanted to shout at him, to warn him of the vengeance he would inflict if he hurt Camilla. But the rope was so tight, it only came out as an impotent gurgling sound.

The trees blocked his view as Cartwright dragged him on down the path. Camilla vanished from his sight.

From the clearing, a solitary pistol shot rang through the forest, then slowly died away.

Once they reached the road, Cartwright put him on a horse, and Mungo did not resist. They took him to the courthouse jail in Richmond. In the cell, he asked for pen and paper, and found a dollar in his pocket to pay a boy to take the message he wrote.

When he was alone, he sat on the bench in the cell. He took out a silver locket that he wore around his neck and stared at it, thumbing it open and snapping it closed. The clack of the metal rang off the hard cell walls like the echo of the pistol shot from the clearing. Mungo gazed at the picture inside, his face unreadable.

He had not been waiting fifteen minutes when the boy returned with the jailer.

"Your bail's been paid," the man grunted. "As long as you don't pass the city limits."

"I do not intend to go that far," said Mungo.

The sun had long since set, and the moon was high as Mungo made his way through Capitol Square to the large house on the hill above. Mungo was conscious of his appearance. He hadn't shaved since the *Aurora* landed in Baltimore, and the stubble poked through the mud that still caked his face. His clothes were ragged and filthy. He could hardly have looked more out of place as he climbed the steps of the elegant, Greek-revival mansion. If any of the neighbors had seen him, they would certainly have summoned the constables.

Yet the door opened at once to his knock, and the butler—a black man with white whiskers, named Carter—did not raise an eyebrow at Mungo's appearance. He ushered Mungo into the drawing room, where a plate of cold ham and a glass of wine were waiting for him. A maid discreetly swept up the mud that Mungo had tramped through the hallway, but Mungo did not notice her. He was staring at the portrait that hung over the fireplace.

It was his mother. She stood on the lawn of Windemere with the house and the river behind her, dressed in a saffron-colored dress that the artist had made to sparkle with the sunlight. Mungo knew every brushstroke on the canvas, but it never ceased to captivate him. Though Abigail's expression was prim and proper, her honey-colored eyes conveyed the humor with which she regarded all the pomp and self-importance in the world of men. She never took anything, including herself, too seriously. It was a trait that had exasperated her parents even as it endeared her to every man who had made her acquaintance.

A voice behind Mungo startled him out of his reverie.

"She was a rose among the thorns. I have never forgiven fate for taking her so young."

Amos Rutherford, Mungo's maternal grandfather, stood in the entrance to the drawing room. He was dressed in a fashionably tailored frock coat and waistcoat, his cravat as white as the hair of his beard. In his hand was an ornate pipe encrusted with decorative gold. He placed the stem between his lips and puffed on it as white smoke encircled his head.

"I confess, I never expected to see the day I would have to bail a St. John out of jail for stealing a slave," he said.

"She was mine," said Mungo. "And free by the terms of my father's will."

It hardly mattered now. *Camilla is dead.* He said it to himself again—the thousandth time, and each repetition was another twist of the knife inside him. He wanted the pain; he savored it. Let it be the fuel to forge his revenge.

None of it mattered to Rutherford.

"What happened with Chester Marion?"

Quickly, Mungo related everything that had happened that day. Rutherford listened in silence, puffing on his pipe and frowning.

"Chester Marion is a monster," Mungo concluded. "I am

going to kill him, just as he killed my father." There was no emotion in his voice, merely an icy statement of fact.

"But therein lies your difficulty." Rutherford fiddled with the bowl of his pipe. "Chester may be an upstart lawyer with no breeding, but he is now one of the biggest landowners in Virginia, and that carries its own weight. You do not go up against a man like that with only a half-dime in your pocket."

"All I need is a gun and a bullet."

Rutherford shook his head. "I thought you had a cooler head on your shoulders. Putting a bullet in Marion's heart might give you a moment's satisfaction, but you would not live to enjoy it. You would be branded a murderer."

"Not if I challenge him to a duel."

"Duels are illegal."

"When was the last time the authorities enforced that law against a prominent man?"

Rutherford laid a hand on Mungo's arm. "Chester would never accept your challenge. If what you say is true, he has spent the best part of three years at least getting his hands on Windemere. He will not risk his victory now."

"Then how do you suggest I proceed?"

Rutherford's caution had only stoked Mungo's temper. The old man's next words were more incendiary still.

"I suggest you do *not* proceed."

"I will not let Chester live!" Mungo hurled the plate into the fireplace; it smashed into fragments. "I will destroy him, and every man who has helped him. I will not stop until Windemere is mine again, along with everything that pertains to it."

Rutherford had lived the best part of seven decades, and in the course of his life he had encountered more than his share of dangerous men. Some he had done business with; others he had removed from his path. But he had never seen such lethal purpose in another man's eyes as he saw in Mungo's now. Experienced as he was, it made him shiver.

He gestured for Mungo to sit in a leather-upholstered chair, and rang a bell for the butler.

"You look like a man who needs a drink. What'll it be?"

"Whatever you're drinking," said Mungo.

"Alas . . . the doctor doesn't allow it. After my last seizure, he said if I drank again it'd kill me." Rutherford gave a resigned sigh. "But I have a very fine French cognac that I've been waiting for someone to finish."

The butler poured the cognac from its decanter into a glass and withdrew. Rutherford took a seat opposite Mungo.

"I know the blood runs hot in a young man's veins," he said. "But take some advice from a man who has lived long enough to learn wisdom. At the moment, Chester holds all the cards. You, on the other hand, are a penniless outcast who will shortly go on trial for slave stealing. People know your daddy's reputation as soft on negroes—they will make you out to be some crazy abolitionist. A white man who betrays his race? Chester wouldn't even have to bribe the jury to make an example of you."

Mungo sipped his liquor and did not argue the point.

"I feel the anger you must have in you." Rutherford glanced at the painting of Mungo's mother on the wall. "Abigail loved Windemere more than any place on earth, and she wanted you to have it when she and your father were gone. So let me help you get it back."

Mungo sat stiff in his chair, his yellow eyes watching Rutherford carefully.

"What do you propose?"

"You will leave the country."

"I am already accused of slave stealing. Would you have me add bail jumping to the charge sheet?" Mungo asked drily.

Rutherford tapped his pipe against the arm of his chair. "You will need money to go against Chester Marion, and your family is bankrupt."

"Not all my family." Mungo nodded at the sumptuous

furniture in the room, the fine paintings by Turner and Constable that had been brought from England.

Rutherford stiffened. "This is not my fight. I gave Abigail the finest dowry a daughter ever had, and your father squandered it lavishing perquisites on his negroes. I have not forgotten that."

His voice was harsh, a tone Mungo had never heard before. Until then, he had only ever seen Rutherford through a grandchild's eyes—kind and doting. Now, he saw the face Rutherford showed to the world. He had not accumulated his fortune by kindness and happy chance. He was a businessman, an opponent you would not want opposite you at the negotiating table. An enemy you could not afford to make.

If Mungo had glanced at a looking glass, he might have seen that the hard light in Rutherford's eyes mirrored itself on Mungo's face. He might have recognized it for what it was. Utter ruthlessness.

"There is a ship I have an interest in, the *Blackhawk*," said Rutherford. "She sails out of Baltimore in three days and when she does, you will be aboard as crew. Her master, Captain Sterling, is a friend of mine and entirely trustworthy. She stands to realize two hundred thousand dollars profit from the voyage and—in Abigail's memory—I will grant you a one percent share. If I receive a good report of your conduct from Sterling, I will raise that to five percent on the next voyage. If that is profitable, I will make you a full partner in the venture."

"Where is the ship bound?" Mungo asked.

"Africa."

"We will be gone for months." Mungo tried to keep his temper, but all he could see in his head was Chester, the smirk on his face as he aimed his pistol at Camilla. "It will be months—years, even—before I am in a position to challenge Chester."

Rutherford shrugged. "That is how it must be. My offer is not negotiable."

Mungo went silent, his mind calculating possibilities like a chess player. Rutherford must have read his thoughts on his face.

"If you are not on that ship when she sails—if you pursue your vendetta against Chester, or go back for your slave girl, or anything else—I will post the bounty for your capture myself," he warned. "You will go back to prison. If Chester Marion is half as ruthless as you have said, he will find you there and make sure you are dead before you even see the inside of the courthouse. Do I make myself clear?"

Again, Mungo glimpsed the steel inside his grandfather. Whatever ideas he might have had about defying Rutherford, he let them go at that moment. Camilla was dead; there was nothing to gain by haste. He would take his vengeance at his leisure.

Mungo drained the last of his cognac and stood. "I will sail aboard the *Blackhawk*."

The air in Windemere's storeroom was heavy with the musty sweetness of dried tobacco. In normal times, the room should be full of casks of packed tobacco ready to be shipped to England and beyond. Now it was empty—except for Camilla. She lay on the floor amid the sweepings, curled in a ball. She was surprised to be alive, though she did not yet know if she should be glad of it.

Her mind went back to the clearing, her last sight of Mungo as he was dragged away by Cartwright's horse. On her knees in the mud next to her grandfather's body, with Chester standing over her. He had raised his pistol and she had been certain she would die.

Then she had felt a movement beside her. Methuselah's eyes flickered open and saw Chester. With his dying breath, he tried to rise up to shield Camilla. It was a feeble hope: he did not even have the strength to lift himself off the ground. But the motion distracted Chester. He turned the pistol on Methuselah and shot him point-blank through his skull. Camilla started to scream, but was abruptly choked off as Granville pressed his palm over her mouth. He put the blade of his knife against her throat.

"Shall I do it?" he asked Chester.

She had seen in Chester's eyes that he was considering it. Then something changed.

"Mungo was sweet on her," said Chester. "I remember three summers ago, he could barely keep his hands off of her. Maybe I should keep her around a little longer, a trophy of my victory."

He nodded, the decision made. Granville's hands relaxed the pressure on her skull.

"Take her down."

They left Methuselah unburied, lying in the clearing for animals and birds to devour. Chester's men made bruises all over Camilla's body as they dragged her from the observatory—not gently. Granville had been particularly rough, letting his hands roam all over her. She still remembered the look he gave her as he threw her into the room, his hungry eyes and his teeth stained yellow with tobacco.

Still, she forced herself not to weep. At least she was alive.

Through the small, high window she could see night had fallen. She hugged her arms around herself, and wondered where Mungo was. She did not believe the militia could keep him captive for long. He was rich and important; his family were the greatest in the county. And she had never seen him in a situation he could not maneuver his way out of.

She wished she had explained more in her note. He would have come better prepared, but she had been so fearful of the letter being intercepted she had not dared say more. And she did not fully understand what had happened herself. How had Chester Marion gained such power so quickly? How could Mungo not be the master of Windemere, after his father had died? Why was she not free?

Footsteps sounded outside. Under the door-sill, she saw the glow of a lamp approaching. Could it be Mungo come to rescue her? She knew in her head it was unlikely, but her heart still sprang with hope. She could not believe he would abandon her.

The door swung on its hinges, and the light grew into a wedge. The lamp appeared, but the face beside it was not Mungo. It was the man who had stolen everything from her—Chester Marion, with his wispy hair and pale skin and those unsettling eyes. They were looking at her now, shining with a fervor that made her shiver.

"Where is Mungo?" she asked.

She knew she shouldn't have asked it, but the question was so hot in her mind she couldn't help herself. The moment she said Mungo's name, Chester's face lit up with fury. He kneeled down and slapped her face with a stunning blow.

"Never say his name," he hissed. "Mungo has no right to

Windemere. He will never set foot here, and you will never see him again."

He reached up and hung the lamp on a hook in the ceiling. Then he kneeled beside her again. Camilla cowered back, but there was nowhere to go in the tiny storeroom. All she had on was the dress she had been wearing that morning, torn and filthy from her rough passage back to the estate.

Chester reached for the hem of the fabric, his breathing ragged, and slid his hands under her dress. She felt his fingers crawling over her skin: up her thighs, over her waist and her young belly, lifting the dress higher and higher until she was completely exposed. He grabbed her breasts, wrenching and squeezing them.

She did not think about what she did next. Instinctively her hands curled into claws. She raked her fingernails across his back, sank her teeth into the curve of his neck. He roared in pain, the lust in his eyes turning to rage. He took hold of her hair and yanked her head back so hard he almost snapped her neck. He tore off her dress and tossed it aside.

"I will have you," he growled, "and I will make you pay."

He tugged down his trousers. Camilla fought him like a wildcat, poking his eyes with her fingers, scoring his flesh with her nails, kicking his groin with her feet, and resisting all his attempts to pin her arms and legs. Small and supple though she was, she fought with desperate strength. Her arms were strong from working; Chester rarely wielded anything heavier than a pen. Even though he was bigger, he could not get the advantage.

But he was not alone. Granville had been waiting outside, and he rushed in when he heard his master's distress. He grabbed Camilla's arms, pulled her off Chester and threw her to the floor. She tried to get up, but he was too strong. He rolled her over onto her stomach and put his knee on the back of her neck to pin her, while his hands gripped her wrists like manacles.

Chester wiped blood from the bite she had left in his neck. He forced her thighs apart and lifted her toward him.

"I will teach you obedience."

She didn't know how long Chester raped her, but eventually—with a grunt of satisfaction—it was done. He lifted himself off her, wiping himself with her dress. Granville Slaughter, who had held her down the entire time, let go. Camilla had almost lost consciousness, but through the haze she heard Chester say to the overseer, "I have softened her up for you. Your turn, now."

She'd thought she was immune to pain. But the thought of it happening again was more than she could bear; she would not survive it. Her body convulsed. Chester saw it, and laughed.

"This will teach Mungo St. John to mess with my property."

She did not have the strength to resist. Granville dropped his trousers and squatted over her. She bit her lip, and prayed it would be over quickly.

The door banged open. Camilla could not lift her head to look, but she felt Granville pause.

"I told you we were not to be disturbed," said Chester peevishly.

"Yes, sir." A new voice—one of his men. "But word just came from Richmond. Mungo St. John walked out of jail three hours ago and ain't been seen since."

Chester swore. He lashed out with his boot, kicking Camilla so hard she felt one of her ribs crack.

"Granville—get your men. I want them guarding the house day and night. That man is a wild dog and there's no telling what he may try to do."

"What about the girl?" complained Granville. "I ain't had my turn yet."

"Leave her," said Chester. "There'll be time later."

Angrily, Granville let Camilla go. The men went out. When Camilla heard the lock click shut, she curled into a ball on the floor, her eyes half-open but seeing nothing. Her chest heaved with sobs, but no tears came. All she had to cling to was hatred. She imagined Chester's end, his blood running red upon the ground, his flesh mutilated, rotting from within until only the bones remained. She imagined Mungo standing over his corpse. The news that he had escaped gave her new hope.

Surely he would come back for her now.

The taverns and public houses of Fells Point were lit up with revelers when Mungo handed Rutherford's horse to the stable boy at the Admiral Fell Inn. He retrieved the luggage he had left in store after his voyage from England, and took out the clothes he would need for his new life. There were not many. To these he added a few prized possessions: a long-stemmed pipe he had acquired from James J. Fox in London, along with a supply of the finest smoking tobacco; a compass and spyglass his father had given him before his first voyage to England; a spear-point Bowie knife with a gilded handle and intricate scrollwork on the edges of the blade; and a silver locket.

He packed it all into a new sea bag—everything except the Bowie knife. Then he tucked the knife in his waistband where the coat hid it, and went to get drunk.

The Waterfront Hotel was jammed with sailors downing pints of ale and shots of whiskey and shouting to be heard over the tunes of an Irish banjo band. Mungo sank three drinks in quick succession, letting the liquor numb him. He had been in Baltimore only a week ago, but it felt like a different life. Then, he had stepped off the boat as the new master of Windemere. Now, thanks to Chester Marion, he had nothing.

He raised his fourth glass of whiskey and drank a silent toast to Nemesis, the goddess of revenge. He tried to picture her as he had seen her in an engraving in the museum at Cambridge—a fearsome woman, wings outstretched to speed her revenge, a whip raised in her right hand. But when he imagined her face, all he saw was Camilla.

In the booth at the back of the tavern, a group of sailors were deep into a poker game. They must have been paid recently, for they were playing for high stakes. Coins jingled and flashed on the tabletop.

Rutherford's advice echoed back to Mungo: *you do not go up against a man like Chester Marion with only a half-dime in your pocket.*

Mungo did not know yet how he would bring Chester down—the pain was too raw to think—but he understood the truth of what his grandfather had said. He needed money.

The glittering coins on the poker table seemed to wink at Mungo. He felt a sudden, overwhelming pull toward them, almost as great as his thirst for liquor. He pushed his way through the crowd to the poker table.

Six men sat squeezed into the booth, cards in hand. Mungo's eyes took them in at a glance and settled on the man opposite. It was clear from the mound of chips in front of him that he was an accomplished card player, which was lucky, for he would never trade on his looks. His beard was so full it looked like an extension of his close-cropped hair. His eyes were green but bunched too close together, and his nose was elongated and hooked at the tip. Mungo disliked him on sight.

The man looked up from his cards and saw Mungo staring at him.

"Something I can help you with?" he asked. There was a dangerous note in his voice.

"Is there room for one more?"

"No."

"Not so fast, Lanahan," one of his friends protested. "Let's see the color of his money."

The man called Lanahan scowled. It made him look even uglier.

"There's a twenty-dollar buy-in with a one-dollar minimum bet. No paper, only silver. Are you game, or is that too rich for your blood?"

"I can afford it."

Mungo had not expected to find seamen playing for such high stakes. Rutherford had advanced him forty dollars to get him to

Baltimore, and he had thirty-two dollars and forty cents remaining. It was all the money in the world he had to his name.

He had no intention of losing any of it. Poker was his game, and had been since his first days at Eton, when the boys had called them "lying games" and placed bets with pennies and shillings, and dealt with cheating with their fists. Mungo had learned then that he had a quick mind for calculating odds and probability, but an even more unusual knack for reading the faces of men. More than any other game of chance, poker was about the man, not the cards.

Mungo pulled up a stool and squeezed in to the group. He placed the coin purse on the table, watching as the other men finished their hand. The man on his right, with a permanently dour mouth and a crooked nose that told of many fights, was the least skillful of the players. Although Mungo couldn't see his cards, he knew by the way the man's eyes wandered back to them that he had a weak hand. Sure enough, the man folded, his expression turning into a proper sourling frown.

The man beside him was younger and better-looking, with an embroidered shirt and clever eyes, but he, too, had a nervous tic. Before he raised the bet, he touched his right eyebrow, which suggested to Mungo that he was bluffing. The man after that was the fattest among them, his torso nearly as wide as it was tall. He was the most expressive, his face constantly in motion, which made his tell less obvious. Mungo had an idea what it might be, but he needed another hand to test out his theory.

As for Lanahan, his skill showed in his carriage. He kept stone-faced, his eyes on his opponents, not his cards. Besting him would not be easy.

By the time the bet reached Lanahan again, it had increased to seven dollars. The pot in the center of the table was piled with coins, mostly half dollars, but a few Liberty dollars. Lanahan called the fat man's raise and all the remaining players showed their cards. As Mungo suspected, the sourling had only a pair of jacks. He wrinkled his nose when he saw the younger man's trio of tens and shook his head in frustration at the straight displayed by the fat man. Then Lanahan laid down his cards. He had a full house.

"What do you know?" said Lanahan, raking in the pot. "I've always had a fancy for Lady Luck, and it seems she fancies me in return. Another hand?"

The rest of the players agreed, and after everyone had put in their dollars, the dealer dealt the cards. Mungo waited to take his until the others had collected theirs, scanning the faces of his opponents. By the way the young man touched his eyebrow and the sourling puckered his lips, Mungo knew they had nothing. The fat man was motionless, mesmerized by his cards, which confirmed Mungo's intuition about his tell. Whatever he had was stronger than three tens.

When Mungo shifted his gaze to Lanahan, he realized his opponent wasn't looking at his cards. He was staring at Mungo. He held Mungo's gaze without blinking, his eyes hard and hostile. Mungo stared back at him.

Only when he had studied all his opponents did Mungo look at his own cards. Nothing but a pair of red eights. He watched the others draw their cards. The sourling was even sourer, and the fat man was still lusting after his cards. But the young man was no longer touching his eyebrow. He was sitting back smugly in his chair.

Mungo traded in the unmatched cards and placed the fresh cards in his hand without looking at them. He caught Lanahan studying him again, and held his gaze until the sourling grunted, "What'll it be, mister mate?"

Lanahan blinked. "Three dollars." He looked away from Mungo and tossed a pair of silver dollars and a pair of half dollars into the pot.

Mungo looked down at the cards he had drawn. His flat expression gave the other players no hint of what he had.

"I'll match your bet and raise."

Before he had time to place six dollars in the pot, the sourling folded. Mungo turned to the young man and saw his confidence waver. He had only eight dollars left on the table.

"I'll call," the young man said, and his hand trembled as he parted with his money.

"Six dollars to me," said the fat man, eyeing his cards. He looked up at Mungo. "Since we seem to be fond of doubling, I'll raise it to twelve."

The young man gasped, and the sourling arched his eyebrows. Lanahan took the bet in his stride.

"Mr. Jeffers," he said, "I'm delighted to see you've finally been dealt a hand as generous as your girth. Unfortunately, I like mine just as well." Lanahan tossed nine dollars into the pot and another eight. "Make it an even twenty."

All eyes turned toward Mungo. Twenty dollars was the buy-in, the total of the coins he had laid on the table.

"I'll call," Mungo said.

In the face of such a bet, the young man returned to fondling his eyebrow. He pushed his last coins into the center of the table.

"I'm all in."

The fat man blinked as beads of sweat formed on his upper lip. Mungo watched for the moment he decided to fold. When it happened, the man seemed to deflate. He threw down his cards and muttered a curse.

Now it was Lanahan's turn. When he glanced at his stack of coins, Mungo knew what he was going to do. He said the words with a flourish, even as he turned his hands into a wedge and laid down the gauntlet.

"Like Reese here, I'm all in."

The dilemma before Mungo was as plain as it was painful.

Either he had to walk away from twenty dollars in silver to preserve the other fourteen and change in his purse, or he had to risk the lot.

If he lost, he lost everything. He could not go back to Amos Rutherford for more funds.

He picked up his purse and poured the remaining contents onto the table.

"Thirty-two dollars and change are all I brought with me, gentlemen," he said. His golden eyes surveyed the table, showing no fear. "Let's see what you have."

Reese, the young man, placed his cards on the table. He had a flush: all hearts, king high. The fat man coughed and mumbled. Lanahan gestured toward Mungo with cold triumph in his eyes, but Mungo shook his head.

"I placed the last bet. I believe the turn is yours."

"Very well." Lanahan laid down his cards. A full house, aces full of queens. "Now I thank you for your business and ask you to get the hell away from my gaming table."

Mungo gave a resigned sigh, and laid his cards beside Lanahan's. The mate had already started to reach out to scoop up his winnings. Mungo watched the man's face as he turned up his cards one after another. Eight of diamonds. Eight of hearts. Eight of clubs.

Lanahan's left eye began to twitch. The tavern seemed to fall silent, as if every man in the room was waiting on Mungo's last card.

"Get on with it," Lanahan grunted.

Mungo flipped the last card. The alcohol was warm in his veins; he felt a cruel delight in the way Lanahan's mouth dropped open as he registered the long row of eights—diamonds, hearts, clubs and now spades—and realized that his full house had fallen to a superior hand.

"I thank you for the game."

Mungo swept his winnings off the table into the coin purse.

The bag was as heavy as a weapon in his hand, and that too gave him a savage sense of joy.

But Lanahan did not accept his loss gracefully. As Mungo turned to go, he heard the scrape of the table as Lanahan burst out from the booth. He curled his fingers into fists and came at Mungo with a haymaker.

Mungo had no interest in tavern brawls. But Lanahan gave him no choice. He ducked the punch and landed an uppercut squarely on his attacker's jaw. The man's knees went weak. Before he could recover, Mungo grabbed him by the collar, took hold of his belt and heaved him back onto the table. Empty glasses flew aside and shattered on the floor.

The entire tavern looked on in silence, holding its breath. Mungo stared down at the other poker players. His yellow eyes burned bright; he felt himself willing them to come at him. Punching Lanahan had released something that had been building inside him for a week. It made him feel whole. All he wanted was to do it again.

The men at the table stared back. All were hard men, proud, and not averse to using their fists. But none of them moved. The fury radiating from Mungo's face pinned them to their seats.

Mungo turned slowly around the room, defying anyone to challenge him. More than that: he *wanted* them to challenge him, to give him an excuse to hit them like he had hit Lanahan. No one did. They had seen what he was capable of.

He gave a final scowl of disappointment and contempt.

"I'll bid you goodnight."

At nine o'clock the next morning, Mungo presented himself at the wharf. The fine suits and expensive shoes he had brought from Cambridge were packed away at the inn. He was dressed now as a sailor, in a light cotton shirt and trousers rolled up over bare feet, with his long hair tied back in a queue. He was no longer Mungo St. John.

"That name is too notorious," Rutherford had warned him. "You will have to travel under an alias."

So Mungo had chosen a new name, Thomas Sinclair, that had seemed right to him. The St. John name, like the clothes, had been put away.

I will retrieve my own name, he promised himself. *And a great many other things that have been taken from me.*

He touched his hand to the locket around his neck. He thought of Camilla, breathing out her last breaths by the clearing in the forest. He imagined riding to Windemere and breaking Chester's neck with his bare hands. But of course he could not. The only way back to Windemere now was aboard the *Blackhawk*.

She was a handsome ship. If she had not been the means of his exile, he might have fallen in love with her. She was built for speed. Even tied to the wharf, she seemed to strain at her moorings like a greyhound on its leash. She crouched low in the water, flush decked, with sleek lines that tapered to a sharp bow. She also, Mungo noted, carried a dozen guns down each side, and a long twelve-pounder mounted on a swivel on her foredeck. A heavy armament, for a trading vessel.

He mounted the gangplank, breathing in the sights and smells of the ship. He had often thought that, in another life, he would have liked to be the master of a sailing vessel. He loved the sea, its endless shifting challenges and the freedom it brought. Even after all he had picked up on his voyages to and from England, he knew he had much still to learn. But he had a quick mind, and he feared nothing. He would adapt quickly.

Then a man stepped in front of him, blocking the view, examining Mungo like a piece of excrement that had dropped on the freshly scrubbed deck. Mungo looked into his face, and all his dreams of naval glory died. It was Lanahan, the man from the tavern: the same ugly face and hooked nose, and green eyes sharp with malice. The livid bruise spreading across his jaw, where Mungo had punched him, did nothing to improve his appearance.

"Off the ship," he said thickly.

"I am to sign on as crew," said Mungo.

He had heard the other gamblers referring to Lanahan as "mate"; he had never guessed he was the mate aboard the *Blackhawk*.

"Captain don't need more crew."

"I have a letter of introduction to Captain Sterling."

"Didn't mention it to me."

"Why don't you ask him?"

"He's ashore. Where you should be too."

Lanahan pointed to the gangplank. Mungo stood his ground, a lazy smile on his face to show he had no intention of leaving. The other men on deck, seeing a confrontation brewing, stopped what they were doing and started to take notice.

Now Lanahan could not back down without losing his authority. Mungo's smile broadened. The mate had a sailor's lean strength, but Mungo stood a head taller; his arms were twice as thick, and he had already knocked Lanahan down once. He tensed his muscles, ready to ride the first punch if it came. He would not start the fight, but he would happily end it.

He looked Lanahan straight in the eye, daring him to attack. Hatred flared in the mate's face, but he had learned his lesson well enough. He did not dare go for Mungo. He turned away.

"Mr. Tippoo," he said. "Remove this gentleman from the ship."

He stepped aside. Too late, Mungo realized that the mate had no intention of fighting him. The man who stepped forward was a different proposition entirely. He was a giant of a man, his clean-shaven head as round as a cannonball and criss-crossed with scars. The features were a mixture of Arabian and African, his smoke-colored eyes set deep in the recesses beneath his brows, and his flared nose as broad as it was tall. He stood at least four inches taller than Mungo, with broad shoulders and wide hips. His forearms were as thick as a woman's thighs.

Lanahan motioned with a flick of his wrist, and the bald-headed giant stepped forward. He shrugged off his high-collared tunic and folded his trunk-sized arms across his bulging chest, his golden skin gleaming in the sunlight. Some of the crew clambered on the rails and into the rigging to get a better view, while others gathered around the combatants. Mungo heard catcalls, and bets being placed on how long he would last before he pleaded for mercy and scampered back onto land.

Mungo refused to give them the pleasure of seeing his discomfort. He knew he would survive only if he managed to evade the grasp of Tippoo's monumental hands. He also knew that the crew would never permit him to escape the ring they had formed around him. The fight would stay on this patch of freshly scrubbed deck between the mainmast and the mizzenmast, with the polished brass capstan and two large hatches on one side, and the starboard beam on the other.

Mungo put up his fists and danced on his toes like the great English prizefighter, William Thompson, whose defeat of James "the Deaf Un" Burke for the All England Title Mungo had witnessed two years before in Leicestershire. The crew shouted encouragement as Tippoo advanced on him, head down and nostrils flaring. Without warning, the giant lashed out with a left jab, followed by a right hook. For a man so large, he was quick as a snake. As Mungo lurched backward, barely avoiding the blow, he tripped over the edge of the hatch and lost his footing. Tippoo pounced, but Mungo scrambled away, leaping to his feet.

Mungo circled, keeping his breathing shallow and staying light on his feet. Tippoo put out his arms and tried to corner him, throwing an occasional punch but always missing. Seconds passed without a landed blow, and the crew grew restless. Their jesting escalated into threats. Mungo was shoved from behind, and he stumbled forward, seeing Tippoo's fist a split second before it crashed into his jaw. He twisted his head and deflected the worst of the impact.

Half-stunned but reacting on instinct, he ducked and landed a sharp jab on Tippoo's ribcage, then threw a heavier punch at the giant's solar plexus. He felt the solidness of the impact. Tippoo grunted as the wind flew out of his lungs.

The giant seemed undeterred. He lashed out with his leg and caught Mungo on the calf, knocking him to the ground. Tippoo pounced, and this time he got a hand on Mungo's shirt. Bunching the cotton fabric in his fingers, he threw punch after punch at Mungo's head. Mungo struggled desperately to avoid the giant's fist and pummeled Tippoo's ribcage with counterpunches, but his shirt was a tether trapping him. Tippoo's blows sent shards of pain through his skull and made stars erupt in his vision. It wouldn't be long before one of the punches knocked him unconscious.

Out of the corner of his eye, he saw a glint of sunlight on polished brass. Instead of pulling against Tippoo, he leaned in and lowered his head like a battering ram, wrapping his arms around the giant and shoving him toward the capstan. Tippoo fought valiantly to stand his ground, but Mungo's weight and churning feet threw him off balance. Tippoo staggered backward and toppled over the capstan, taking Mungo with him. Tippoo's sprawling body protected Mungo from injury, but nothing cushioned Tippoo's head from the rock-hard deck. The transformation was instantaneous. The giant lost his grip on Mungo's shirt, and his enormous body went limp.

Mungo climbed woozily to his feet. His head felt ready to split like a piece of overripe fruit. He cast a glance at the fallen giant and gathered his wits, then turned to face the crew. Lanahan's face was screwed up in a furious, disbelieving rage. He had ordered Tippoo to fight, and now Mungo had made a fool of him.

Lanahan's hand began moving to the knife in his belt. Then, suddenly, he straightened. A heavy footfall sounded on the gangplank. The crew snapped to attention, so sharp it could only mean one thing.

The captain stepped on deck. He was not tall or particularly good-looking. His skin was leathery and worn after years facing Atlantic winds and the tropical sun. A pale, crescent-shaped scar inscribed an arc on his left cheek. But there was a devil-may-care arrogance in his gaze, and more still in the clothes he wore. His coat was a cutaway and tailored to his frame, his fine shirt and waistcoat brilliant white. His gold paisley cravat shimmered in the sunlight, while his sleek Italian boots were buffed to a shine. He looked as if he had just stepped out of his box at the opera.

Any man who dressed like that must either be a foppish buffoon, or supremely self-confident. And rich enough not to care. Not for the first time, Mungo began to wonder just how lucrative the voyage might be.

The captain took in the scene: Tippoo lying in a heap; Mungo with torn shirt and battered face; fresh blood on the holystoned deck. His face clouded.

"What the hell is going on here, Mr. Lanahan?" he snapped to the mate.

"We had an unwanted visitor. I told Tippoo to send him away."

"Without success, it seems." Lanahan squirmed. Sterling turned to Mungo. "Who are you?"

"Sinclair," said Mungo, giving his assumed name. "Thomas Sinclair. I have a letter here from my grandfather, Amos Rutherford."

He took the letter from his sea bag and handed it to Sterling. He watched the calculation on the captain's face as he read it. Whatever the letter from Rutherford might say, the decision to take Mungo was the captain's alone. Announcing himself by making an enemy of the first mate, and brawling with the biggest man on the ship, was not how he had intended to start.

But Rutherford's word must have carried considerable weight.

"Mr. Lanahan," Sterling said to the mate. "Fetch the muster book, and enlist Mr. Sinclair as a light hand."

"But . . ." Lanahan's face burned with hatred. "He is a troublemaker."

"That was an order, Mr. Lanahan." Sterling turned to Mungo. "I do not doubt your qualities. Any man who would go a round with Tippoo cannot lack bravery; and I do not think I have ever seen him bested in a fight. But remember this. On any ship, a captain is second only to God. And God has no interest in the *Blackhawk*. Do I make myself clear?"

"Aye, sir."

"Then welcome aboard." He picked up a holystone and tossed it to Mungo. "You may begin by clearing up the mess you have made of my ship."

On a bright August morning, the *Blackhawk*'s crew cast off the lines and sailed with the tide. The holds of the clipper were loaded with bales of cotton brought up from New Orleans, crates of cigars from Cuba and Richmond, lumber from the mountains of western Virginia, and mail destined for Europe. At all points of wind, the *Blackhawk* sailed with a speed that far exceeded the bulkier packet ships to which Mungo was accustomed. With guidance from the Maryland pilot, they made twelve knots of headway down the Chesapeake under topsails and mains, and crossed the bar at Old Point Comfort during the first dogwatch of the second day.

When they saw the blue horizon, the crew on the spar deck and high up on the yards let loose a cheer. The captain issued the command: "Make full the sails. Mr. Lanahan, take her out to sea."

By the time the sun sank into the western clouds, they had left the coast far behind. None of the crew seemed to notice the disappearance of the land as they were busy with their duties, but Mungo did. He was up the mast working on the topsail yard—Lanahan had wasted no time sending him as high as possible—and some premonition made him glance back just in time to see the gray shadow of his homeland wink out of existence as it crossed the horizon.

The ship heeled over in the breeze, so that when he looked down all he saw below him was foaming water. Gripping the mast one-handed, he took the locket from around his neck and held it in his fist. It hurt too much to look at the picture inside. He wanted to open his hand, let it drop into the sea and wash his pain away.

He held on tight. He would not let Camilla go. He would nurse the memory, let it sharpen his thirst for revenge until he had destroyed Chester Marion.

Something wet stung his cheek. He thought it must be a drop of rain borne on the wind, but when he wiped it away it was warm to the touch. A tear. He shook his head in disbelief. He had never cried in his life.

He put the locket around his neck again and let it drop inside his shirt. *Give me the keys of fortune*, he prayed, *and grant me vengeance*.

n the immense emptiness of the ocean, time was governed by the watch and whistle, and the weeks disappeared into the rhythm of night and day. There was occasional excitement when a sail was sighted, or when a quarrel erupted that the bosun had to break up. Otherwise the routine might be interrupted when the captain issued a call to quarters for a drill with small arms or cutlasses. Mostly, the hours at sea went by without event, the boredom broken only by the busyness of everyday tasks.

As a fo'c's'le hand, Mungo slept in the hammocks with the men and boys. Of all the challenges of the sailing life, it was the lack of privacy that he found the most difficult. Sleeping, eating, writing in his journal, even shitting in the heads, took place in the presence of other men. Mungo craved the free time he spent in the netting near the tip of the bowsprit, as the jib billowed above him, reading everything he could find on navigation and ship handling. He had thrown himself into the study of seamanship with a passion. At first it was to distract his mind from the thoughts of Chester and Camilla that weighed constantly, but soon his zeal caught Sterling's attention. The captain allowed Mungo to borrow books from his cabin, and let him practice reading the sextant and measuring their course. After his voyages to England, Mungo had thought himself a fairly competent navigator; now he realized how much he still had to master.

The men treated Mungo warily. A landlubber who took to the ship like an old salt; a gentleman who shipped as a common seaman; a fighter who did not pick fights: they did not know what to make of him. A few misinterpreted his good manners as weakness, and tried to bully him, but they quickly learned their mistake. So they mostly left him alone. Even Tippoo, the master gunner whom Mungo had fought, kept out of his way and showed no interest in prolonging the quarrel. If anything, he watched Mungo with a certain wary respect.

The only man on the ship who thoroughly hated Mungo was, unfortunately, the one best placed to make his life miserable. Lanahan, the first mate, had not forgiven Mungo for the card game, nor for embarrassing him in front of the men and the captain. He put Mungo in his watch, where he could give him the worst tasks, always ready with a rope end if Mungo's work was less than flawless. He saw Mungo's nautical studies as a personal insult, presuming it was an attempt to supplant him. If he ever caught Mungo reading a book, he would immediately invent some new chore for Mungo to do.

Mungo knew the mate was trying to goad him into insubordination. He could see it in Lanahan's eyes. One slip, and Mungo would be spread-eagled on the grating having his back ripped open with a cat-o'-nine-tails. Mungo would not give Lanahan that satisfaction. He took every humiliation and insult without complaint. He was obedient, hard-working, and relentlessly cheerful.

It did not help Lanahan's cause that Mungo proved to be a natural sailor. When Lanahan sent him aloft to work the sails in high winds, Mungo kept his balance on the yards like a cat. When he ordered Mungo to haul on some obscure line, or tie a complicated knot, Mungo was always able to oblige. Far from impressing the first mate, Mungo's ability only deepened his fury.

Mungo was not complacent. He knew that he was stoking Lanahan's anger, and that sooner or later it would erupt against him. All he could do was wait for it.

The weather remained fair through the weeks of September and early October. The wind blew steadily out of the southwest at twelve to sixteen knots, and there were only a handful of scattered squalls. These were just enough to top up the ship's freshwater stores, and allow the crew a bath in the lee scuppers to wash the salt off their skin. For long stretches of time the *Blackhawk* matched the pace of the wind, creating calm on deck, even as the arrow-shaped hull crashed through the waves and sent out geysers of spray.

On the twenty-first of October, a shout came from the foremast yards.

"Land ho!"

It was Mungo's watch, and he was on deck tending to the ship's compass. As soon as he heard the shout, he detached the spyglass his father had given him from his belt and went to the rail, leaning out over the water and searching the wedge of light between the lowest studding sail and its yardarm for sight of the land. He could smell it in the air—the richness of trees and soil mixed with the tangy brine of the sea—but he couldn't see it.

He ran to the mainmast ratlines and climbed to get a better view. The higher he went, the more he felt the rocking of the ship beneath him. The *Blackhawk* was rolling on a strong northern swell, and the mainmast was tracing a path through the air like the sweep of a clock's pendulum. He was ten feet past the fighting top when he heard a cry overhead. A second later, there was a crack of parting lines and the slap of buckling canvas. A sail had given way. Mungo arched his neck and stared into the clouds above him. A seaman was clinging to the bare pole of the skysail yardarm as it twisted free of its brace on the weather side. Meanwhile, the sail, shorn of its rigging, was flapping uselessly alee. Two other riggers were wrestling with the canvas on the yard below, but the first, whose clumsiness had most likely caused the accident, was scrambling to regain his footing one hundred and fifty feet above the deck.

"Secure the brace!" Mungo yelled, pointing at the severed line as it whipsawed about in the wind, whistling uncomfortably close to Mungo's head. "I'll see to a replacement."

But the rigger wasn't listening. He was clutching the yardarm for dear life, groping for a way to support himself. He could not find it. His whole weight dangled from the yard, and his cold fingers could not get a grip. Inexorably, he was sliding off.

Mungo let go of the ratlines with his right hand and reached out over the abyss, grasping for the trailing end of the brace. The severed line writhed like an angry snake. It was almost in range. Then the ship heeled over on a large swell, and the brace swung away from Mungo's fingertips. Mungo gulped in a lungful of air and waited for the ship to recover, his breathing ragged, his heart pounding in his chest. The brace swung back toward him, and he lunged again to grab it. This time his fingers touched it, but a gust of wind blew the line out of reach once more.

By now, Mungo and the rigger were both exhausted. Mungo knew it wouldn't be long before the *Blackhawk* hit a jarring wave and one of them—or both—lost his grip and fell. Mungo watched the brace jerk in the wind. It was tantalizingly close, but not close enough. He thought about giving up. He heard the seamen on the ratlines below, hauling up replacement rigging. When they arrived, they would fasten a new brace and steady the yardarm. But for the rigger above him, it would almost certainly be too late.

Mungo wiped his hands on his breeches and anticipated the motion of the ship as if it was an extension of his body, waiting for the moment when the mast swung past vertical in the direction of the brace. He coiled his muscles until every sinew was taut and—when the forces of wind and roll were just right—he leaped into space.

For an instant, he felt as if he was flying. He was so high above the sea that he could almost touch the clouds. Then the brace was in his hands, and his downward arc turned upward, the ship reached the end of its port-side roll, and brought him swinging back in the direction of the mast.

He knew he had only one shot to make this work. His hands

were about to slip and his arms had endured nearly all the punishment they could bear. He saw the ratlines flying toward him, the mast looming beyond them. His trajectory wasn't ideal, but it was close enough. Then, to his horror, Mungo sensed the yardarm turning above him as the weight of his body applied a torque on the brace. Instead of swinging toward the mast, he was now rotating around it. In desperation, he tensed every muscle in his abdomen and thrust his legs out toward the ratlines as they sailed past. His left foot caught the outer rope in the ladder and arrested his swing as pain exploded in his arm sockets. Suspended between the yardarm and the ratlines, his body had become a makeshift brace, his muscles now bearing the pressure of the wind on the untethered sail.

He wanted to scream at the seamen to cut the lines and let the canvas fall away, but the words escaped him. He wriggled his left foot into the netting and followed that with his right foot, establishing the anchor, as the ship reached the limit of its starboard roll and the forces changed again. He held the pose for long seconds, every nerve in his frame racked by agony. He felt as if he was being ripped in two. He could not hold on much longer.

Without warning, he felt a strong hand on his calf and another taking the fabric of his waistline. Through vision blurred by pain, he saw Tippoo's face looking over him. The strain on his shoulders slackened as the master gunner took the brace from his sweat-slicked hands.

"Hold on," Tippoo grunted. "I let you go now."

Mungo clasped the netting with trembling fingers and collapsed into it as if it were a hammock. Tippoo tied a knot into the end of the severed brace and took a fresh line from a seaman below him, lashing the tips together. The seamen below took up the slack, running the replacement brace through the blocks on the mizzenmast and lashing them to a cleat on deck. Only when the brace was secure did Mungo look up at the skysail yards. Now that the yardarm was no longer turning around the mast, the rigger had calmed himself sufficiently to find the foot-rope and regain his balance. His exhausted body was draped over the yardarm, his complexion pale.

Mungo turned to Tippoo. "I owe you a debt."

"If not for you, we would have to swab him off the deck. Now, he gets only the cat."

"The cat?" Mungo asked, finding his voice again, as strength flowed back into his body.

"He makes a mistake. He pays." Tippoo shrugged his mountainous shoulders, and the muscles below his neck rippled. "At least he is alive."

Sterling supervised the discipline with the rigor of a court martial, except that he was the sole authority charged with prosecution, judgment, and sentencing. He took evidence from the seamen on the watch, and, when all were satisfied with the rigger's guilt, he dispatched Lanahan to retrieve the cat o' nine tails from his stateroom and ordered the rigger to stretch out on the deck before the mainmast.

"A dozen lashes will make you more attentive to your duties," he said, catching Mungo's eye, "and spare Mr. Sinclair the trouble of having to save your sorry life again."

Mungo said nothing. When the first mate returned with the cat, Sterling took the fearsome instrument in hand and paced the deck in front of the rigger. He ran the nine thongs through his fingers while reminding all the crew of their obligations to preserve the safety of the ship. Then he handed the cat to Tippoo and went aft.

Tippoo removed his tunic and stood at the rigger's feet, while the man begged for mercy, his face to the ground. Tippoo brought the cat down on the man's bare back. In an instant, his white skin turned scarlet. The seaman yelped in pain and began to sob. Tippoo struck a second time, leaving welts in a different direction, then a third time with a backhanded motion that flayed the rigger's skin. Lanahan counted out the lashes until, on the ninth stroke, the rigger fell into unconsciousness. By the time Tippoo finished, the seaman's flesh was a grotesque mess, scored and blood-smeared.

"Get him to the infirmary," Lanahan barked, "and wash down the deck."

Mungo made his way aft. His nerves were still wound tight from his exertions atop the mast, along with the ache of strained and knotting muscles. The captain met him by the hatch, his eyes aglow with displeasure beneath the brim of his bicorn hat.

"Mr. Sinclair," he said, "you continue to astonish me. One minute I find you indispensable, and the next you act like an imbecile."

Mungo frowned. "I thought you would be glad I saved his life."

"By risking yours," the captain snapped. "And Tippoo's as well. If you had not been so lucky, I might have lost three men."

"Aye, sir."

"The fact that you succeeded does not justify what you did. You do not risk your life for anything, unless I give the order. On the high seas, chivalry is not a virtue and I did not take you on to be a hero. Do I make myself clear?"

Mungo nodded, his face as blank as it had been at the poker table. "Aye, Captain."

"Then see to your duties."

Camilla stayed locked in the tobacco store for three days. She lived on a knife-edge of hope and despair: terrified every time she heard the lock turn in case it was Chester or Granville coming to rape her again; hoping against hope that it would be Mungo.

They gave her a slop bucket, a cup of water and a plate. In the August sunshine, the storeroom became an oven. She was constantly parched; she couldn't even clean herself after Chester's assault. She had to live in the same tattered dress he had torn off her, his blood and fluids still crusted on her skin.

Then, on the third morning, one of Granville's men came for her. Without a word, he grabbed her by her hair and yanked her to her feet. He ripped her dress off her. She started to scream, then suddenly choked it off as a wave of water hit her body. She wiped her eyes. The man was standing by the doorway, a smirk on his face and a bucket in his hand.

"Boss said to clean yourself up," he said. "We're going."

He tossed her a clean dress. He stood by the door, his hand on the revolver in his belt, watching her as she wiped herself down and pulled on the new clothes.

She emerged, blinking, into the daylight and followed her captor to the big house. Carriages were drawn up on the driveway, half a dozen at least. At the front was one Camilla had never seen before, with gilded woodwork and a pair of fine black horses in harness. A jab from Granville pushed her toward it.

"Inside, quick," he ordered.

She stepped up and through the door. The inside smelled of new paint and fresh leather. Pulled velvet curtains draped the windows and made it dark.

"Don't make a sound," said Granville.

She perched on the edge of the plush seat, too frightened to sit comfortably. The curtains screened the outside world, but there was a small crack where they did not quite meet in the middle. She leaned forward and put her eye to the gap.

A group of men had come out of the house and were standing on the lawn in front of the portico. She saw Chester and Granville, and half a dozen others all very respectably dressed in top hats and dark suits, smoking cigars. None of them paid her any notice.

Old Tate, the butler, stood by them with a silver tray of drinks. Chester took one and toasted his companions.

"Congratulations," he said. "To the new owners of Windemere plantation."

The man opposite smiled. With a shock, Camilla recognized him. It was Jeremiah Cartwright, the militia officer who had captured Mungo and taken him to jail. Now she looked closer, she recognized the others, too. They were all old friends and neighbors of the St. Johns, men she had seen often as guests at Windemere.

Cartwright raised his glass to Chester in return.

"You are a man of your word, Marion, I give you that. When you told me you could deliver up Windemere, I confess I had my doubts, but you proved me wrong. You are one tough son-of-a-bitch."

"For a bankrupt estate, you drive a hard bargain," complained the man next to him—an older man with huge silver whiskers, named Horniman.

"Worth every penny," said Cartwright. "I know the Bible says thou shalt not covet thy neighbor's ass, but by God I have wanted this land for thirty years. I thank you for delivering it to me—even at the exorbitant price I have just paid you."

"This is the best land in the state," Chester assured him. "A fine investment."

"Then why are you selling it?" said Horniman.

"I have a fancy to move south. Tobacco is fine, but cotton land is cheap at the moment."

The other men made dubious faces. They were all old Virginia gentry; they did not trust cotton. Three years earlier, cotton had reached an all-time record high price and the plantations around the Mississippi River had changed hands for fortunes. Then the price had crashed, and all the speculators had been ruined. A lesson, the Virginia men all agreed, that farming was best left in the hands of gentlemen.

But Chester Marion was new money—nothing but a jumped-up lawyer, they thought. Let him burn his fingers on cotton if he wanted. They would be glad to be rid of him. True, he had his uses: it was he who had approached them with the audacious plan to seize Windemere from the St. Johns, and he who had executed it so ruthlessly. But he knew too much. And there was something about him—a fervid intensity, a lethal coldness—that unsettled them. If they would dare admit it to themselves, even these powerful men, pillars of society, were afraid of him.

They shook hands all round. Chester handed Cartwright a bunch of keys—the estate keys that had belonged to Mungo's father.

"Windemere is yours. All its fixtures, fittings, appurtenances and . . . ah . . . other property."

Horniman looked at the empty fields. "Where are the people?"

"I moved them to Cox's farm to keep them safe. You can retrieve them there, all safe and sound, at your leisure."

"What about the girl we caught with Mungo?" said Cartwright. "I heard you brought her back here to . . . ah . . . entertain you."

"I believe she comes with my portion of the estate," said Horniman.

"No, mine," said another.

"We're business partners," Cartwright reminded them. "No reason we can't all share her around."

Camilla froze. The gap in the curtain framed the ugly lust in their faces. Was this what Chester had saved her for?

But to her surprise, Chester shook his head.

"She is not part of the transaction," he said. "It seems I was a little rough in my use of her. She died."

Cartwright scowled. "Then you have overcharged me, you Jew. I paid you a thousand dollars for her."

"The contract excludes natural depreciation, wear and tear and suchlike," Chester said, and there was no missing the menace in his voice. His gray eyes stared down the assembled gentlemen, daring them to contradict him.

The men eyeballed each other. They were proud men, all jealous of their honor; in other circumstances, they might have settled matters with a duel. But they were also men of business—and there was no profit in a quarrel.

Cartwright shrugged as if he didn't care one way or the other. "Never try to argue with a lawyer. What's a thousand dollars more or less between friends?"

An uneasy silence hung over the group.

"I think that concludes our business," said Chester. "I wish you a prosperous future, and all success in your new property."

He tipped his hat. Without another word, he turned and strode to the carriage. Camilla shrank back behind the curtains, pressing herself against the carriage wall so that the other men wouldn't see her. Chester ducked in, slammed the door and removed his hat. Granville leaped up on the driver's box. With the lash of a whip, the carriage lurched into motion.

Chester stroked Camilla's hair. She tried not to shudder.

"Why did you tell them I was dead?" she asked.

"You heard that, did you?" A wolfish smile crossed his lips. "Because I did not care to haggle, and I wanted you for myself. A keepsake, so to speak, to remind me of an old friend."

Camilla did not understand anything that had happened, but she knew she was leaving Windemere forever. She turned and took a last look at the big house through the rear window. She did not romanticize it—she had been a slave there, and she lived with that fact every day. If Windemere had been good to her, it was only because the alternatives were so much worse. But even so, it was where she had been born, where she had grown up and where she had known Mungo.

Now that was all gone. She wondered where they were going. She wanted to ask, but she knew better than to try. She was a chattel, and possessions should keep their mouths shut.

A day after Mungo had rescued the rigger, the Welsh coast appeared in a shroud of rain that dogged the *Blackhawk* all the way to Liverpool. In spite of the dismal weather, the port was a hive of activity when they landed at Trafalgar Dock. Around them in the estuary of the River Mersey was a forest of masts belonging to at least forty tall ships. The wide wooden dock and cobbled lanes beyond swarmed with people. There were roughneck stevedores hauling lines and handling freight; costermongers hawking every kind of ware; street urchins running to and fro and leaving behind a trail of havoc; beggars praying for spare change from the shadows; and elegant gentlemen and ladies pretending to be above it all.

The crew went ashore with money in their pockets, and six weeks of pent-up appetites to fill in three days. The only one who stayed aboard was Tippoo. Mungo was not sure why. He could see on the giant's face that he wanted to go. He cast many longing looks at the waterfront; his thick neck was bowed and his shoulders stooped. But Sterling would not allow it. When Mungo asked, all Tippoo said was, "Someone has to guard the ship."

"I'll stay with you," Mungo volunteered.

"Truly?" Tippoo's face lit up with pleasure. Mungo shrugged it off.

"You'll need someone strong with you to guard the ship, in case you are overpowered."

Tippoo bared his teeth in a broad grin and laughed. In truth, Mungo had had a mind to stay aboard anyway. Many of his friends from Eton and Cambridge were of Liverpool families, and he did not want to risk being recognized. There was too much he would have to explain.

Also, the men would expect him to accompany them to the brothels, and Mungo was not ready for that. Whichever woman he lay with, he knew he would only see Camilla's face.

Instead, he spent his days with Tippoo, supervising the unloading of the cargo. The two men worked well together. They spoke few words, but there was an instinctive understanding between them as to what needed to be done. In the evening, they sat in the mess room, playing cribbage and drinking.

Mungo was curious about his companion. He tried to find out how Tippoo had come to join the *Blackhawk*'s crew—"I do not think you were born in Baltimore"—but Tippoo would not be drawn.

"Captain Sterling bring me aboard in Zanzibar," was all he would say, and then he would close up.

Though he was interested in Mungo.

"Why are you here?" the giant asked one night. "You were not born to be a sailor."

Mungo sucked on his pipe. "I had a fancy to see the world."

"Hah. I think it was a woman." Tippoo saw Mungo's expression shift and clapped his hands in triumph. "Yes. A man like you, always in trouble with a woman. Was she beautiful?"

"She was," Mungo allowed.

"I see in your eyes you mean to go back to her. You love her, yes?" Mungo said nothing. "Of course you do. And she loves you? Or perhaps she is with another man."

"She died," said Mungo. "Murdered by a man I thought I could trust. When I get back, I will kill him."

Tippoo nodded sagely. "That is wise."

As the hold began to empty, Mungo realized something peculiar about the *Blackhawk*'s cargo. The bales of cotton, crates of cigars, and packets of mail were stamped by customs agents and claimed for delivery and trans-shipment, but the stacks of lumber they had brought from Baltimore remained untouched. Most of it was planking, each piece six inches wide and twelve feet long, with some sturdier pieces that looked like fence posts. Stashed behind the lumber Mungo found a dozen unmarked crates. He hadn't seen them loaded in Baltimore, which meant they had been in the hold longer, perhaps since New Orleans. He asked Tippoo about them, but the gunner simply squared his shoulders and turned his back.

Mungo remained curious. At one point, when Tippoo was up on deck, he took a crowbar to one of the crates and levered the lid just enough to see the dull gray sheen of iron nails—scores of them. He knew from his time aboard the packet ships that surplus planking, nails and pitch were kept to repair damage sustained by a ship in transit. But the supply of lumber aboard the *Blackhawk* was more extensive than Mungo had ever seen. And if the other crates had nails in them—indeed, if even two of the crates did—then they couldn't be to mend anything. They were meant to build something. But what? And where?

Mungo was not naïve. He had a fairly good idea what the planks and nails were for, and why Tippoo did not want to mention it. But it was easier not to think about it, so he kept his thoughts to himself.

The *Blackhawk* took on a fresh cargo of trade goods for Africa. The raw cotton she had brought from Louisiana was replaced with cloth from the Manchester mills. Many stands of English muskets were brought aboard, as well as plentiful supplies of powder and shot. There were also many boxes of glass beads, and casks of tobacco. The smell wafting out of the barrels reminded Mungo of harvest time at Windemere.

At last the *Blackhawk* was ready to sail. But there remained one item unaccounted for: the second mate. Lanahan scoured every tavern and brothel in Liverpool, but he was nowhere to be found.

Sterling summoned Mungo to his cabin in a cold fury.

"Every day we sit in port costs me money," he said, staring out through the stern window. "I cannot wait for that drunkard to reappear."

He turned suddenly.

"When attaching a drogue, what kind of knot would you use? A clove hitch or a rolling hitch?"

The question was so sudden and unexpected Mungo almost missed the trap in it. But his hours of study, learning and observing had taught him well.

"Neither," he said. "The stresses on a sea anchor are immense. I'd use a bowline because it strengthens under tension."

Sterling grunted. "And if I asked you to establish a position by dead reckoning, from what point on the chart would you plot your new course line?"

"From the point of the last fix. Not from the last estimated position."

The questions continued for over an hour, a quick-fire interrogation that covered everything from points of sail to reckoning by the stars. Mungo answered fluently, drawing on his long hours of reading and learning. At last, Sterling seemed satisfied. He studied Mungo, his blue eyes as fathomless as the ocean. Then:

"I am appointing you as second mate."

Mungo stared, his thoughts racing. It was the last thing he had expected. He lacked experience, and almost every man in the ship had seniority to him. Some would not take kindly to being passed over.

But as mate, he would be due a greater share of the profits.

"Thank you, sir."

Sterling had evidently been hoping for a stronger reaction.

"You are not surprised?"

"A wise man once told me that the captain's word is second only to God's. I would not presume to question it."

"Ha." Sterling gave him a searching look. "You have a keen wit, Mr. Sinclair. Be sure you do not cut yourself with it. But you can read and write, which is more than most of these ninnies, and I have seen your navigation work."

"Yes, sir."

Sterling went silent again. Mungo wondered if he was reconsidering his decision.

Suddenly he said, "It will be a hard voyage to Africa and back. You may have to do things . . ." He broke off. "At all times, I expect you to carry out my orders without hesitation. Do I make myself clear?"

"Yes, sir."

Camilla's first impression of her new home was white—everything white. White sunlight from a clear September sky; a shining white house gleaming atop a round hill like a castle; fields of white cotton spread out around it, rolling with the contours of the land like snowdrifts. It dazzled her eyes and made her head ache.

"Bannerfield," said Chester. He half rose from his seat in their open-topped carriage, like a Roman general mounted in his chariot. His body swayed; his eyes reflected the sun and burned with triumph. "Five thousand acres of the best cotton land in Louisiana. Is it not magnificent?"

Camilla nodded. She had learned to keep silent in their five weeks traveling together: in the coach to Norfolk; aboard the ship that had brought them south and through the storms that had nearly wrecked them off Cape Canaveral; in the crowded streets of New Orleans; and now in the fields of Louisiana. The less she said, the less she gave him reason to hurt her.

And not just her. Camilla placed her hand on her belly and felt the taut skin through her dress. There was nothing to see yet, barely a bump to feel, but she knew it was there, growing inside her. Touching it was like sticking her hand in a fire, but she did it anyway. The child was a seed of rape, a living reminder of what Chester had inflicted on her. But it was also hers, and though she might hate it she had to protect it. She had not told Chester yet.

Then there was Mungo to think about. What would he do, if he returned and found out she was carrying Chester Marion's baby?

The carriage rattled up the long driveway. It seemed to take forever. As they passed, Camilla saw that the bright vision she had seen from a distance was not quite so pure as it had seemed.

There were specks of black in those brilliant white fields. Slaves stood stooped in the rows of cotton, picking balls of fluff from the plants and gathering them in baskets. Camilla tried to count the people, but soon gave up. There were hundreds of them, far more than there had ever been at Windemere.

Was that to be her fate? It looked like back-breaking work, but at least it would take her out of the house, away from Chester. Anything was better than that.

The carriage stopped at the head of the drive. The house was huge but not beautiful, Camilla thought. It had been built out of proportion, too tall for its breadth, like a weed that had grown too fast. It loomed over them, blocking out the sun and making the air suddenly cool.

All the house slaves had lined up to greet them. The men bowed; the women curtsied as Chester strode from the carriage. He did not acknowledge them, but bounded up the steps like a dog. Inside, the house was already fully furnished. Everything was spotless, yet a musty smell hung in the air as if it had not been used in a long time.

"The last owner lost it all in the crash of thirty-nine and blew his brains out," said Chester. "His heirs were so desperate to sell I bought it for a song." He giggled. "I hear there is still a bloodstain on the library wall where he shot himself."

He paced the hall, his footsteps echoing loudly off the cold marble. He looked around, like a child on Christmas morning who has found more presents than he dreamed of.

"We have arrived," said Granville, who had come in behind them.

He said it jubilantly, but it did not please Chester. He swung around, eyes alive with ambition.

"I have accomplished nothing yet. This—Bannerfield—is only a piece of grit in the oyster. I will make it such a pearl as this state has never seen."

He turned to Camilla, a chilling smile on his lips. Often he barely seemed to notice she was there, but then he would fix his gaze on her and it was as if she was all he saw.

"I am in the mood to celebrate. Go up to the bedroom, and make yourself ready for me."

Mungo's elevation to second mate caused less trouble than he'd feared. Even Tippoo toasted Mungo's success with a mug of rum, though he himself might have had a claim on the promotion. In some ways, the men found it easier to take orders from a gentleman than to work alongside him; it restored their faith in the order of things. After the incident with the rigger, they knew Mungo would watch out for them. The only discontents were a seaman named Keller—who'd had an eye on the promotion for himself—and Lanahan. Now that Mungo had his own watch, the first mate could not torment him the same way. Instead, Lanahan treated Mungo with studied contempt, and spoke to him only when Sterling required it.

The twelve-hundred-mile passage to Madeira was beset by headwinds and fraught with difficulty almost from the beginning. After passing to the west of the Isles of Scilly, the *Blackhawk* ran into the first of a series of tempestuous gales. The winds stripped the ship's foremast of canvas and overwhelmed the bilge pump, flooding the lower hold with brackish water as deep as a man's neck. What might have taken only a week had they been sailing in the opposite direction took three weeks of contending with the prevailing winds and the increasingly foul tempers of the crew. The only relief came when they passed the tip of Portugal and met the swift-flowing water of the Canary Current, which bore them steadily southward toward the coast of Morocco.

After twenty-three days at sea, the island of Madeira was sighted from the masthead. This sent the crew into a frenzy of excitement, which Mungo was at a loss to understand. He asked Tippoo the reason.

"Rum. Dancing. Whores," said the master gunner, as if the explanation should have been self-evident. "Every man's favorite port."

The *Blackhawk* entered the harbor and dropped anchor a short boat ride from the bustling wharf. Along with a handful of merchant ships, Mungo saw a British man-of-war tied up along the docks, its hull gleaming with new paint and its gun deck bristling with cannons. Her name was HMS *Fantome*, and by the way the crew whispered and pointed, Mungo guessed she was not unknown to them.

After the captain went ashore with Lanahan to greet the island's governor, Mungo tracked down Montgomery, the surgeon, in the officers' quarters and asked why the British warship had provoked such a reaction among the men.

The surgeon's lips squeezed into a bloodless line.

"We had an encounter with her off the African coast," he said stiffly.

"What sort of encounter?"

Montgomery hesitated, seemingly at a loss for words. Eventually, he said, "She gave us a shot across the bows, and forced us to heave to so her captain could check our papers. He was an arrogant bastard, but we saw him off in short order. We sail under the Stars and Stripes. We know our sovereign rights."

Mungo considered the information. There were only two reasons a British man-of-war would fire upon a merchant ship at sea. The *Fantome*'s captain must have believed that the *Blackhawk* was either a pirate, or a slaver.

As Mungo knew well from the debates at Cambridge, the British had adopted an unyielding stance toward the African slave trade. The government in London had negotiated treaties with the Netherlands, Portugal, Spain and France to permit the Royal Navy to search any vessel flying under those flags and to arrest any crew trading in human beings. Only the American government had not surrendered its rights to Britain. The Royal Navy was permitted to board a vessel to establish her identity, but if she proved to be American they could not venture below decks to explore her holds. Only an American naval vessel could do that—and though the slave trade had been illegal in America since 1808, her navy had little interest in enforcing the law so far from her own shores.

But what might the *Fantome*'s captain have found if he had been allowed into the *Blackhawk*'s holds?

Lanahan returned from his trip ashore with news.

"Looks like I'll be dining tomorrow night at the governor's mansion," he bragged. "It's the Mariners' Ball. The officers from all the ships in port are invited." His mood soured as he caught sight of Mungo. "That includes you."

Mungo was sitting on the hatch cover playing cribbage with Tippoo. If he had not been looking at the gunner, he would never have noticed the intense look of longing that flitted across the giant's hairless face. He looked so morose Mungo almost laughed. Yet the gunner seemed genuinely sad.

"What about Tippoo?" Mungo asked.

"Gunner's not an officer. He's not invited."

Tippoo pegged out his score on the cribbage board and said nothing. But Mungo could see an unaccustomed tension in him.

"He can have my place," said Mungo spontaneously. "The governor doesn't need to know he's not an officer."

"That is not your decision." Lanahan's face twitched with temper. "I am your superior—I say you go, and he stays."

Mungo put down his cards. "Then I will take up the matter with the captain."

But when Mungo found Sterling in his cabin, and explained the situation, Sterling dismissed it as brusquely as Lanahan had.

"Tippoo stays here."

"He saved my life when I was up the mast," Mungo reminded him. "I would like to discharge the debt."

"It's impossible."

"Why?"

Sterling rounded on him. "Because the governor doesn't allow slaves at his banquets."

Mungo stared. For once, he was at a loss for words.

"I did not know."

"Because it's none of your goddamn business," said Sterling. "Anyhow, aboard ship it makes no difference. When a dog's so tame, there's no call for a leash."

"Yes, sir." Mungo could see Sterling did not want to discuss it anymore—but there was one question he was still curious about. "How did you come to acquire him?"

"I won him in a card game," said Sterling. "In Zanzibar. Now, if you have nothing better to do, perhaps you could return to your duties."

The following evening, the *Blackhawk*'s cutter took the officers ashore for the ball. Sterling, Mungo and Lanahan sat in the stern, dressed in stiff coats and pressed shirts. Sterling was, as usual, resplendent in a plum-colored coat with gold embroidery, and a shirt that was almost invisible under clouds of lace. Lanahan, by contrast, was dressed all in black like a third-rate insurance clerk. Mungo, who had left all his fine clothes back in Baltimore, had had to borrow a coat from the surgeon.

The boat nudged against the wharf. Sterling and Lanahan got out. Mungo rose to follow, then suddenly swore.

"I left my cravat on board ship. I'll go back and get it and join you at the ball."

Sterling gave him a sharp look; Lanahan muttered something about poor breeding. But neither man wanted to wait.

"We will see you there," said Sterling.

As soon as Mungo returned to the *Blackhawk*, he went to Tippoo's cabin.

"Get dressed," he told the gunner. "You are coming to the ball."

Tippoo's ugly face screwed up in astonishment. "Captain changed his mind?"

Mungo grinned. "No. But once you are there, he cannot very well start a fight in front of the governor."

Tippoo stared at him, a torrent of emotions going through his head. Then he tipped back his head and laughed.

"He will throw you off the ship."

Mungo shrugged. "Rum, dancing, whores, you said. At least I'll have company."

The governor's mansion was constructed on a hilltop, in the style of a Portuguese villa. Its coral-colored walls rose to a roof of terracotta tile, with wrought-iron terraces draped with bougainvillea. Its elegant archways and spacious passages were arranged to channel the wind blowing off the sea into a broad cobblestone courtyard at its center. Here, the guests congregated, silver goblets of Cava in hand, listening to the strains of a *fado* guitar and awaiting the governor's appearance. Although it was only two weeks before Christmas, the early evening was as warm and dry as September in Virginia, scented with jasmine and brine.

Mungo and Tippoo stood by the fountain at the center of the courtyard. Tippoo looked as disconsolate as Mungo had ever seen him, squeezed into a frock coat that pinched his shoulders, and trousers that almost split across his thighs. The sailmaker had done what he could to run up a suit with a bolt of cloth he had brought from England to trade on his own account—but even his best efforts could barely accommodate Tippoo's enormous frame.

"I should not have come," said Tippoo.

"Are you worried about Sterling?"

Mungo had not seen the captain yet, but it was only a matter of time. In such a refined gathering, Tippoo stood out like a whale in a school of fish.

"Not the captain." Tippoo gestured to the Portuguese ladies making their entrances in swirls of taffeta and lace. "Them. How can I talk with them when they see only my size and the color of my skin?"

"Nonsense. Half of them are darker than you are."

Unlike the milk-complexioned maidens of England and America, the guests at the ball had skin like polished gold, with dark eyes and long tresses that had the sheen of exotic wood. Like tropical birds, they were robed in pinks and yellows, oranges and reds, their gowns as striking as the feathers they wore in their hair. Their eyes roamed as they mingled with the men, and many of them paused a moment longer when they saw Mungo and Tippoo.

"Besides," added Mungo, "I've seen Dahomey slaves as black as coal, and Virginia swells with skin like the driven snow. The color never told me a damn thing about the man inside."

His words had a curious effect on Tippoo—but Mungo didn't notice. His attention was on a young woman who had just entered the courtyard. Even among the dazzling company, she stood out from the rest. She was as tall as many of the men, though she moved with a feline grace that made every other woman in the room seem clumsy by comparison. Her almond-shaped eyes were radiant, but the look they carried was neither innocent nor naive, despite her youth. Mungo guessed her to be nineteen or twenty. Every man present could feel the energy radiating from her.

Including Captain Sterling. He had just stepped out of a doorway holding a glass of wine, and though he was entranced by the young woman he was not so blinded that he missed Tippoo standing head and shoulders above the crowd. He pushed his way through the throng, his face hot with rage.

"Let me." Mungo left Tippoo by the fountain and went to meet his captain.

"What the hell is he doing here?" hissed Sterling. His eyes glimmered with rage. "I will throw you off my ship for insubordination. You will work your passage home gutting sardines on a Portuguese fishing smack."

"Aye, sir. But if I go, Tippoo comes with me. And I've a notion you don't want to be without your strongest crewman approaching the coast of Africa."

"Are you threatening to steal my property?" The scar on Sterling's cheek throbbed with anger. "I told you, Tippoo belongs to me."

"I would keep your voice down," Mungo warned him.

"Do not presume to tell me—"

"There is no slavery on Madeira," Mungo went on, as if Sterling had not spoken. "The Portuguese outlawed it more than fifty years ago. The moment Tippoo stepped ashore he became a free man."

Sterling went silent.

"Shall I tell Tippoo his good fortune?" said Mungo. "Or shall we keep this between ourselves and allow him an evening of pleasure? The moment he returns to the ship, he becomes your property again."

Sterling's eye twitched. His finger clawed at the fabric of his collar.

"If you're so sweet on Tippoo's freedom, why don't you tell him?"

Mungo shrugged. "I respect a man's property. But I also respect a man's right to his pleasures—and I owed Tippoo a debt."

Sterling raised his glass and knocked it back in a mouthful. The red wine left a stain around his mouth, which he wiped away with his sleeve. He wanted to say something, but each time he opened his mouth the speech would not come.

At last, without another word, he spun on his heel and stalked away through the crowd. Mungo turned his attention back to the woman with almond eyes he had seen before. She captivated him, in a way that could not be explained by mere beauty.

A feeling began to rise in him that he had only felt once before, the summer he left for Cambridge—the summer he had spent with Camilla. The feeling struck him now so unexpectedly it left him dizzy.

He shook his head, annoyed with himself. At Cambridge, he

had never felt himself bound to be faithful to Camilla—they would be apart for years, and he was a young man with more-than-average appetites. Clarissa Manners, the girl whose irate brother had confronted him at the Union, had only been the last of many encounters he had enjoyed. He had felt nothing unusual for her, or any of the others, except the thrill of the chase and then the pleasure of their coupling. None of them had come near the place in his heart where he kept Camilla's memory.

So why should this woman prick his conscience now—with nothing more than a look?

You cannot be unfaithful to Camilla where she is, he chided himself. And a little harmless flirtation meant nothing.

"Do not get ideas above your station." Lanahan's voice broke in. "She is the Lady Isabel Cardoso da Cruz. Her father is the governor of Prince's Island."

"You know her?" said Mungo.

"She will be our passenger aboard the *Blackhawk*."

Mungo tried not to look unduly interested in the news.

"Whatever you are thinking, put it out of your head," Lanahan warned. "We are also taking her brother, Afonso. He has already killed three men in defense of his sister's honor."

"Where is he?"

Lanahan gestured toward a young man as tall as Mungo, with the broad shoulders of a wrestler and the upturned nose of an aristocrat. He caught Mungo looking at him; for a moment, their eyes locked. Afonso's gaze was cruel and condescending, filled with pride and jealousy. He stared Mungo down, waiting for the American to look away. Mungo did not oblige. He held the gaze, returning Afonso's contempt with an easy smile that made it clear he was in no rush to look away.

Afonso tossed his head. Then, very deliberately, he turned his back on Mungo.

"Stay away from him," said Lanahan. "He is a better man than you."

But Mungo was already in motion. He walked across the cobblestones to where the Lady Isabel stood gossiping with a group of female companions, gave her a smile and bowed.

"My lady, I am Thomas Sinclair. It is a great pleasure to make your acquaintance."

He held her gaze, ignoring the giggles of her friends and the look of jealousy from Lanahan a few feet away. Isabel glanced instinctively at Afonso. Mungo couldn't see him, but he could feel the heat of the brother's look on his back.

"Mr. Sinclair," Isabel said. "Do you speak any language other than English? I find it a most barbaric tongue."

"*Je parle français un peu*," Mungo replied.

He had learned the language at his father's insistence, on summer trips to Paris and Provence.

Isabel laughed, but she couldn't hide the hint of blush that tinted the skin at the base of her neck.

"You are much better than you think," she replied, speaking fluently. "There are times I prefer French even to Portuguese, but please don't tell my brother."

Mungo's French accent was stilted, but he was good enough to make himself understood.

"Your secret is mine, my lady."

The music from the guitar had stopped. A servant was talking, summoning the guests, but Mungo hardly heard. All his attention was on Isabel. When she smiled, it was as if she had suddenly thrown open the shade of a lantern and revealed a bright burning fire inside. Her skin shone, her red lips glistened and the tops of her breasts swelled from the neck of her gown. Mungo drank in the sight.

Then his view was blocked as Afonso stepped in his path. Afonso held out his hand to Isabel. She looked at it coolly but did not take it.

"What is it, brother?"

"We are summoned for the first dance."

He took her wrist and led her firmly away. Mungo considered stepping in, but thought better of it. If they were to be shipmates for the next few weeks, there would be other chances to continue their conversation.

The crowd sorted itself into pairs with bows and curtsies. The captains each took the hand of a Portuguese lady, guiding them through the entrance to the ballroom, while the officers competed for those ladies still unattached. Mungo picked out one, an auburn-haired girl in a gown of bright yellow silk who had somehow been left without a partner. For an instant, her gaze traveled to Mungo and she smiled at him.

Before he could approach, however, Lanahan bumped into him. He lowered his voice.

"Don't think for a moment that your interest in the Lady Isabel has gone unnoticed. I have spies everywhere on the ship. If you attempt anything improper, I will be the first to have you under the cat."

"What makes you think . . . ?"

But Lanahan was already stepping away and introducing himself to the girl Mungo had intended to partner. Her eyes fluttered between them, lingering on Mungo. He declined to intervene, offering her no path of courteous retreat from the first mate's invitation. She wrinkled her nose and accepted Lanahan's hand, proceeding with him to the dance floor in a sweep of yellow silk.

Mungo found Tippoo, who was standing on the fringes of the courtyard, aloof from the swirling crowd.

"What did the captain say?" the gunner asked.

"He sends his compliments and hopes you enjoy the evening," said Mungo. "Are you going to dance?"

Tippoo shook his head. "Who would dance with me?"

Mungo laughed. "I guarantee you, every woman in this room would jump at the chance. They are all looking at you from behind their fans, wondering if what you have in your trousers is as big as the rest of you. Also, they are not exactly spoiled for choice. Even Lanahan has found himself a partner." Mungo took a breath. "Assuming you can dance?"

The giant's head bobbed above his trunk-like neck. "I can dance."

Mungo understood. It was not the dancing that had unmanned Tippoo; it was the prospect of asking a well-bred woman to partner him.

"Come with me," Mungo said.

They moved through the dancers in the ballroom. Mungo saw Lanahan dancing with the girl in the yellow dress. Mungo walked over and stood to the side, trading looks with the girl, who smiled at him in relief. Lanahan tried to lead her away, but suddenly the music stopped.

As the band prepared a new piece, Mungo stepped forward and held out his hand, pretending not to notice Lanahan.

"May I?"

"Yes, of course," the girl replied. She curtsied to the first mate and sidled up to Mungo as the music resumed. "I am Catarina," she said, as they began to glide across the floor, their feet tracing out the dance.

"I am delighted to make your acquaintance." Mungo leaned closer. "But I am not the one you want. I have a friend whose company will quicken the blood in your veins."

The girl blinked in surprise, and she scanned the room.

"You mean the yellow-skinned giant?" she asked. "He looks as ungainly as an ox. I fear my toes would not survive an encounter with his boots."

"When the music is over, I am going to leave you," Mungo said, "and then you will be confronted with a choice—to submit to the attentions of Patrick Lanahan, or to give my friend a chance. I promise he will care for your toes, along with every other part of your body."

Catarina's shock nearly caused her to lose her footing, but she said, "What is your friend's name?"

"He is called Tippoo."

Lanahan, who had been lurking nearby, tried to interrupt the discussion with an irritable "Excuse me!" but Mungo shouldered him aside.

"I was just introducing the Lady Catarina to Tippoo."

By then Catarina's hand was in Tippoo's grasp, her fingers dwarfed by his own. Outmaneuvered, Lanahan's cheeks flamed as red as his hair.

"What is he doing here?"

"Sterling changed his mind," said Mungo. "Enjoy yourselves," he added to Tippoo and Catarina, appreciating the look of wonder in his friend's eyes. "My lady, you could not be in better hands."

He crossed the dance floor to where Isabel was dancing. She had shaken off her brother, and was now partnered with a gray-haired officer, the captain of the *Fantome*. Mungo kept to the edge of the room, striking up a conversation with the mate of one of the merchant ships while keeping his eyes on Isabel. When the song drew to a close, Mungo waited as the officer bowed and Isabel curtsied, then broke in.

"I doubt I can dance as nimbly as you, sir," he said to the captain, "but I would be obliged for the chance to try."

"By all means," the captain said with forced gallantry, "but only if the lady is willing."

Isabel played coy. "Captain Townsend was just teaching me a new variation on the cross-step."

The captain beamed with pride. "It's all the go in England."

"Is that so?" Mungo asked, feigning curiosity. He knew from watching them how badly Townsend had been leading her. He'd learned the dance at Cambridge, and he had danced it many times himself in the ballrooms of England. "In that case," he said, looking into Isabel's eyes, "perhaps you would rather the captain continue his lesson? I'm happy to defer."

"No," she said. "I think I have learned all I need. Thank you, Captain."

She gave Townsend a smile that he would never forget, and followed Mungo onto the dance floor. She leaned in close and switched from English to French.

"The good captain was an insufferable bore," she whispered. "I would rather learn whatever you have to teach me."

They danced through the rest of the evening arm in arm. Isabel was as athletic a dancer as Mungo had ever known, matching him move for move without a stumble or misstep. Her energy seemed inexhaustible, as did her appetite for motion. By the time her brother, Afonso, stepped in at the end of the final waltz and summoned her to a private supper with the governor, Mungo felt as if he had run ten miles.

"I think I have quite worn you out," she said. "But alas all our pleasures must come to an end. *Adieu.*"

"I think you mean '*au revoir*,'" Mungo answered. "I believe you are to take passage on my ship, the *Blackhawk*."

Was it his imagination, or did some flash of promise spark in her eye? Her lips were parted; a sheen of perspiration made her skin shimmer.

"Then perhaps our pleasure does not need to end just yet."

She left him in a swirl of silk and perfume as her brother led her away. Mungo watched her go, then caught himself angrily. *You are staring like some lovelorn booby*, he chided himself.

He still could not understand the way he felt about her—the way she had pierced so deeply into his thoughts. It made him unaccountably angry. Yet he wanted nothing more than to see her again.

"Camilla is dead," he reminded himself, so agitated he spoke the words aloud. He meant it as a rebuke, yet when the words came out they sounded more like permission.

He scanned the ballroom for Tippoo. Through an open door, he saw the gunner on a balcony overlooking the sea, half hidden in the folds of a yellow dress. He looked fully occupied; Mungo did not interrupt.

He made his way to the punch table for refreshment, wondering if Isabel would return, when a loud voice behind him said, "Mungo St. John!"

Mungo froze. There should not be a man within a thousand miles who knew him by that name. He turned slowly, before the voice could hail him again.

At first Mungo barely recognized the man who had spoken. Under the tropical sun, his fair skin had burned red and his sandy hair bleached to light gold. He wore the blue dress coat of the Royal Navy, with scarlet facings and a lieutenant's gold epaulets on the shoulders.

Then he saw past the uniform and the sunburn, to the young man beneath. It was Fairchild—his old sparring partner from the Cambridge Union—staring at Mungo with utter astonishment.

"You are a long way from Cambridge," Mungo said.

"So are you."

Fairchild stepped forward and shook his hand.

"I am commissioned as junior lieutenant aboard the *Fantome*. We are bound for Africa to catch slavers. I thought you had returned to Virginia."

"I did. There was a problem with my inheritance." Mungo lowered his voice. "I would be grateful if you could forget the name Mungo St. John. Here, I am Thomas Sinclair."

"What ship are you on?"

"The *Blackhawk*."

The delight at their meeting vanished from Fairchild's face.

"But . . . do you know what she is?"

"A merchant ship."

Fairchild leaned closer. "Damn you, St. John—Sinclair—

whoever you pretend to be. I know you too well. Do not play the fool—it does not become you."

"We are taking cloth and weapons to Africa," Mungo insisted.

"And what else is in her hold? Have you seen the nails and the lumber, or the great copper kettles she carries to cook for two or three hundred souls when they are crammed below decks? Have you seen the chains and the shackles that will bind them?"

"Are you suggesting the *Blackhawk* is a slaver?" said Mungo, as if the idea was completely preposterous.

"She is the most notorious slaver of them all." Fairchild shook his head. "I know you argued the slave cause at the Union, but I never imagined you would stain your hands with the vile trade itself."

"The slave trade is against the law," Mungo reminded him, as though that rendered the very idea impossible.

"And if the law were obeyed then neither of us would be here." Fairchild laid his hand on Mungo's arm. "I know you are a better man than this. For the sake of all that is holy, I beg you to leave your ship. Sign aboard the *Fantome*—we are short-handed, and I could vouch for you to the captain. A man of your strength and determination would be a blessing."

"I cannot."

Fairchild searched Mungo's face, as earnest and heartfelt as he had been at the dispatch box in the Union.

"If it is this matter of your inheritance—a question of income— you need not fear. There is good prize money to be had from the ships we capture."

For a moment, Mungo let himself entertain the idea. He imagined himself in a fine blue uniform, leading his men onto the decks of slave ships. He imagined heroic profiles in the illus- trated newspapers, hearty cheers from men like Fairchild.

Then he saw Camilla's face, and his father's, and Chester's. *You do not go against a man like that with only a half-dime in your pocket.* A naval officer might earn a comfortable living from his prize money, but it would not be the fortune Mungo needed to redeem Windemere. Whatever he needed to buy or sell, whatever the cost, the bargain would be worth it if it brought vengeance for Camilla and his family.

"It is impossible," he told Fairchild. "This is the course on which I am set."

Fairchild pulled back his arm as if he had been burned.

"Beware, Mungo St. John. You can change your name, but you cannot shed your guilt. If you stay aboard the *Blackhawk*, you are sailing on the path to the black heart of damnation."

His words struck Mungo with unexpected force. In an instant, he was back in the old observatory at Windemere, crouched over the body of a dying slave. *Beware the black heart, and the thirst that never quenches.* What had old Methuselah seen there in his death throes?

He shook it off. It was nothing but slave superstition and mumbo jumbo.

"I fear we are destined always to be on opposite sides of the debate," he said coolly.

Fairchild nodded. There was sadness in his face, but also steel.

"Be careful. This is not the Union anymore. Out here, debates are carried on with guns and blades, and the result is not decided by a vote. If the *Fantome* encounters your ship again, we will do more than put a shot across your bows."

"Then I shall watch out for you."

When the passengers came aboard, Mungo and Lanahan had to give up their cabins. They were on the same level as the captain's quarters and on opposite sides of the officers' wardroom, inside the hatch that led to the aft deck.

Mungo assisted Lanahan and two other sailors as they carried the baggage across the spar deck and into the shadows of the wardroom. The tiny cabins could not accommodate all the luggage the passengers had brought. The viscount considered which of his chests should be consigned to the hold, but Isabel merely waved her hand and said, "Any of them will do." She wandered into the starboard cabin and opened the ventilation port to admit a fresh breeze.

While Lanahan waited for Afonso's decision, Mungo slipped after Isabel.

"Is there anything I can assist you with?" he said in French.

"As it happens, there is." A smile played across Isabel's lips. She reached into the décolletage of her dress and pulled out a folded slip of paper. "I would be grateful if you could take this."

She looked like she wanted to say something else, but Lanahan reappeared in the doorway, calling for Mungo. Isabel's demeanor changed. She took hold of the sea chest in front of her and tugged hard on the brass latch, as if it was resisting efforts to open it.

"You see," she said in English. "It is always getting stuck."

"Allow me," Mungo replied. He made a show of struggle before sliding the latch and lifting the lid to the chest. "There you are."

"Thank you," Isabel said formally.

Mungo went onto the quarterdeck, the mysterious slip of paper clutched in his hand. The ship was lively with activity in preparation for departure, the bosun calling orders in every direction, riggers aloft preparing the yards and sails, seamen on deck making ready the lines, and the captain reviewing papers with a customs official by the capstan.

He unfolded the slip of paper. The words she had written were so small that he had to hold the paper up close to read them. He recognized the lines from a book of French verse he had come across in the library at Cambridge. They were from a poem by Marceline Desbordes-Valmore.

Vous demandez si l'amour rend heureuse /
Il le promet, croyez-le, fût-ce un jour.

Loosely translated, it meant: *You asked if love brings happiness /*
That is its promise, if only for a day.

"What is that?" Lanahan had come up. He must have rushed—his face was almost as red as his hair. "Let me see it."

He grabbed for the note. Obligingly, Mungo opened his palm as if to let him take it, but the moment he did so the wind snatched the paper out of his hand and blew it over the side.

"It was nothing," said Mungo. "Merely something I found in a chest."

Lanahan's face burned with suspicion.

"I am watching you, Mr. Sinclair," he warned.

Mungo could not forget the words Isabel had written him. He found himself muttering them through the night in his cot, his body tense with desire in a way he had not felt since he was eighteen years old. The locket around his neck weighed on his chest. Why did he feel so beholden to Camilla now, when it made no difference to either of them? Did he fear he might somehow turn fate against his revenge by taking another lover, that some immortal power might punish him for betraying her memory? That was a ludicrous idea. Nothing could stop what he would do to Chester Marion.

He was angry with himself. He did not understand how Isabel had got inside his defenses, but he would not lie there mooning like an adolescent. He rose, tore out a strip of paper from the logbook he kept, and hurriedly scrawled two lines of poetry from memory. It was by the Irish poet, Thomas Moore. He darted out of his cabin, slipped it under the door of Isabel's cabin.

If wishing damns us, you and I /
Are damned to all our heart's content;
Come, then, at least we may enjoy /
Some pleasure for our punishment!

He did not sleep any better after that. Next morning, he was tired and out of sorts. He avoided Isabel's eye when she looked at him, while studying her intently when her back was turned for any indication she had read his note. Isabel sat demurely on the quarterdeck reading her book, and gave no sign at all that she even noticed him.

But that afternoon, she asked to borrow his spyglass to examine a seabird flying behind the ship. When she returned it, there was another slip of paper carefully tucked between two sections of the tube. Mungo pretended he did not see it. But as soon as he went below, he extracted it and read the lines hungrily.

In order to know virtue, we must first
acquaint ourselves with vice.

Isabel and Mungo exchanged more notes over the days that followed, each with a snippet of poetry or prose, nothing that would identify them beyond the handwriting. Mungo enjoyed the game, choosing phrases that he knew would delight or amuse or scandalize Isabel. Sometimes he chose lofty passages from the Romantic poets, pure expressions of high sentiment; sometimes frankly carnal lines from the Marquis de Sade or the

Earl of Rochester. He enjoyed watching the little pink flush at her throat when she read them—and he enjoyed even more the verses she sent in return. She was, he discovered, surprisingly widely read.

At first the game amused him—a distraction from the routine chores of the ship. Then, like a hunt, it began to obsess him. The sly battle of wits; the glee in passing the notes right under Lanahan's and Afonso's noses; the risk of getting caught; and the thrill of the chase. Most of all, there was the hope of the prize at the end of it. At night, he lay in his bunk and dreamed of Isabel's body against his.

It began to intrude upon his duties. Once, when he was supposed to be checking the powder stores for moisture, Tippoo caught him daydreaming. Another time, while he was helping set the studding sails, he nearly lost hold of the brace when the canvas caught the wind. Captain Sterling complained that he was taking longer than usual to fix their position.

"If you didn't look so damn healthy," he said one day in his stateroom, "I'd swear you were ill. What the devil has gotten into you?"

Mungo knew it had become an infatuation, distracting him from everything else. He could not let it last. But there was only one way to cure it.

Finally, he thought of a plan. It was risky, but it could work if he enlisted a co-conspirator. There was only one man on the ship he trusted to confide in. He was hesitant, but when he asked, it was as if Tippoo had known the moment was coming.

"Have you forgotten the girl in the locket?" he teased.

Mungo did not laugh. "Sitting here like a monk will not bring her back."

"That is true. Every man has his needs. And I have seen how you look at the Lady Isabel," Tippoo said. "You are like a hot gun in battle. If you do not discharge your powder soon, it will blow up inside you."

If Mungo had given it thought, he might have wondered who else could have noticed his infatuation with Isabel. Certainly, Afonso and Lanahan were vigilant for any hint of impropriety. The first mate had attached himself to Isabel's brother, taking every opportunity to ingratiate himself with their illustrious passenger. But Mungo was too busy making his plan to think about that.

"Middle watch," Tippoo said, seeming to relish the prospect of bamboozling Afonso and Lanahan while repaying his debt to Mungo. "Make sure she is ready."

Three evenings later, at the stroke of midnight, Mungo heard the first bell signal the changing of the watch. He swung his legs out of his hammock and placed the soles of his shoes on the worn wooden planks. The lower deck was so dark he could barely see the outline of the other men sleeping around him. He retrieved his tobacco case from his chest, found the companionway and went up on deck.

Tippoo was already there. They made their way aft, guided by the glow of the binnacle light at the helm. The night was clear but moonless, the black sea roiling.

"All's quiet," said the bosun when they arrived, pulling on his pipe. "The wind's calming down. I reckon the Harmattan's giving way to the trades."

"Aye," said Tippoo with a nod. "I have the conn."

The bosun went below. With Tippoo at the helm, Mungo filled his pipe and lit it with a match. He studied the stars as he drew in the smoke. The sky was radiant with them, as if the blanket of night had been pulled over the sun then pricked ten thousand times, letting in the lost light of day. The stars were different this close to the Equator. The Dipper was hanging upside down; Polaris was a speck above the sea; and a new sky had opened up to the south—Scorpio rising beneath Libra, the Southern Cross shimmering beside the Centaur. Mungo had seen these constellations in books, but never so clearly with his own eyes.

He thought of Isabel lying awake on her bed mere yards from him, though separated by timber and planking, and felt a stirring inside him.

After Tippoo rang the second bell of the watch, Mungo leaned over the starboard rail. Unusually for a merchant ship, the *Blackhawk* had four ports cut into her hull, close to the waterline, to provide ventilation to the lower deck. In rough weather they could be closed, like gun ports, but in these calm waters they were kept open to alleviate the heat. One of them gave directly into Isabel's cabin, from where a light glowed out.

He went quickly to the stern and gathered one of the coiled painter lines used by the crew to tow a boat or an empty barrel for target practice. He lashed the painter securely to the base of the starboard rail, tucking in the trailing end so he could no longer see his handiwork in the darkness. He lowered the painter into the sea. He faced the helm again and waited for Tippoo's signal. This was the point of no return. Once he stepped over the side, he would be guilty of abandoning his post, a transgression punishable by a whipping or even the stripping of his commission. For Tippoo, conniving in the act and not even protected by an officer's rank, it could be more costly still.

The giant gazed across the deserted deck and angled his ear to listen. When he was satisfied that no one was about, he gave Mungo a nod. Mungo swung his leg over the rail, feeling with his toe for the protruding surface of the ventilation hatch. In the northeasterly winds, the *Blackhawk* was heeling heavily to starboard; the tilt and motion of the ship made Mungo's task much harder. He could see the sea rising and falling beneath him. If he slipped, the waves would snatch him away in an instant.

Under the ventilation port was a narrow batten of wood that ran around the hull. After that, there was nothing except a sheer drop to the sea. The batten was so narrow, Mungo didn't know whether his feet could get a purchase, but there was only one way to find out. He took hold of the line in one hand and the rail with the other, then swung his other leg over the edge, searching for the ledge with his toe. As he did, the ship hit a large wave, which sent the bow lurching sharply upward and caused the hull to heel over further. Mungo clung fiercely to the rope, as cold spray soaked his backside. When the ship righted again, he braced himself and tried again. This time, he found the thin batten.

Mungo waited until the ship rolled away, bringing the side up toward the sky, then he dropped his other foot to the ledge and slithered through the ventilation port, holding the painter until his feet were firmly on the deck inside the cabin. The floor was wet from waves that had splashed through the open window.

Isabel was waiting for him on the edge of the bed, the flickering light of the candle on the writing desk illuminating her body, clothed in a nightgown. She stood, and as the ship rolled back to starboard she fell into his arms. He felt her supple body against his, her cheek on his stubble, the squeeze of her breasts against his chest. She turned her face toward his, and he leaned down to find her lips.

There was no doubt about why he had come. He had made his decision; he did not think twice now. He kissed her hard, urged on by his desire, but she was his equal. She drew him close with ferocious strength. Her hands sought the belt around his trousers and unfastened the buttons, then her fingers slipped beneath. He was already fully erect. When she squeezed, he nearly groaned with pleasure, but he suppressed the sound in time. He hitched up her nightgown and felt the smoothness of her thighs and buttocks, the hollow of her back. She raised her arms over her head so he could lift the dress away. Pressing her hips against him, she leaned back and cradled his neck with her hands. Her breasts were round and full, with thick areolae and erect nipples as large as raspberries. He cupped them with his hands and took one nipple, then the other, into his mouth. She ran her fingers through his hair and began to thrust against his hips, whispering in his ear.

"Take me."

They stumbled toward the bed, as the ship rose on a wave and the creaking of the timbers masked their footsteps. She tugged off his shirt and trousers so that Mungo was as naked as she was. She pushed him down on the bed and straddled him in haste and hunger. He reached toward her, probing the soft cleft between her legs and guiding himself toward it. She shifted her hips to grant him entrance and touched his lips.

"Shh," she whispered. "We must not make a sound."

She began to move, undulating over him deliberately, then with urgency, until he felt something inside him about to burst. She shut her eyes and opened her mouth, giving herself entirely to the sensations. Mungo watched her all the way, thrilling at the sight of her body moving in the candlelight.

She climaxed with a shudder at the same moment he did, and collapsed onto him, her chest heaving as if she had climbed a mountain. She nuzzled her head into the crook of his shoulder and brushed the hair from her face.

"If I ever return home, I will let it be known that the men of Europe are nothing as lovers compared to an American sailor."

She traced a finger over his lips. "I think you have done this many times before."

Mungo didn't deny it.

Isabel propped herself up on her elbow. "Were there many women—or only one? Did you have a fiancée? A sweetheart? Someone special?"

"There were many women," said Mungo. "And with most of them it was the same. Some moments of pleasure that lasted an hour or a day or a week and served us both well, and afterward nothing."

Isabel fingered the locket that Mungo wore, the only thing he had not taken off.

"Then what is this?"

"A lucky charm."

She heard the note of tension in his voice.

"Is it a woman?" she teased him. "Do you think that I would be jealous?"

"It belonged to my mother."

"Then let me see."

She pried at the clasp, but it would not move. Mungo put his hand over hers and pulled it firmly away.

"Whose portrait would I find if I opened your little heart? What would she say, if she knew what we were doing this moment? Did you love her?"

"Love is a device for poets who have nothing more interesting to write about," said Mungo.

"Did you not feel it for your sweetheart?"

"I did not say I had a sweetheart."

"You did not have to. I can feel it in every muscle of your body." Isabel ran her fingers through his chest hair until her hand came to rest over his heart. "I do not doubt you mean the things you say about love. But I wonder if, deep in here, you truly believe it."

"You have no idea what is in my heart."

She shrugged her naked shoulder. A ripple went through her breast.

"It does not matter. We are not virgin lovers. We both know what we want."

"We do," Mungo agreed.

He had known plenty of women who could be voracious in the bedroom, but they had always dressed up their appetites in the pretty language of love and courtship. He had never met a woman as unapologetically direct as Isabel. He was grateful for her lack of sentiment. It made him feel less as if he was betraying Camilla's memory.

She adopted a little girl's voice, false and mocking. "Will you stay with me always?"

He kissed her forehead. "I can stay until the fourth bell."

She thought about this, as the ship rolled beneath them and the candle flame danced above its wax. She gave him an impish smile and ran her fingers down his hairy chest to his stomach, and beyond.

"Does that mean we have time to do it again?"

Mungo and Isabel met frequently as the ship sailed southward toward the Gulf of Guinea, as often as Mungo and Tippoo stood the night watch together. On deck, during the days, Isabel was more demure than ever. In her cabin, she was wild. As adventurous as Mungo was, Isabel had even more creative ideas. She took her pleasures greedily, and returned them with interest. When Mungo began to tire, she had ways of stimulating him until she had wrung every drop out of him.

He had thought that sleeping with Isabel would break the fever that had gripped him and cure him of his unwanted obsession. In fact, it only left him hungry for more. Every day, he thought constantly about what he wanted to do with her. Although he was in charge of making the watch lists, he could not doctor them every night without arousing suspicion. Each night that he could not get to her cabin felt like an eternity.

He could not understand it. It was only physical pleasure, as meaningless as scratching an itch. He had never been susceptible to the hypocrisies that afflicted the rest of society about the union of the sexes. At Cambridge he had had many women, and afterward given them no more thought than a good day's hunting, or a fine meal. But Isabel had a grip on his imagination he could not shake.

There was only one other woman who had ever burrowed so deep into him. And it was easier not to think about her.

Through all this, Isabel remained steadfastly unsentimental. There was no talk of love. Though Mungo might possess her body in deep and intricate ways, her soul remained always elusive. But a sort of friendship developed between them. In between their bouts of lovemaking, they lay entwined together and talked. She told him about her family and the world she had known: her upbringing in Lisbon; the years she had spent in Paris when her father was an ambassador in the court of

Louis Philippe; her travels between Portugal and Prince's Island during the count's tenure as governor. Wherever she went her beauty made her the center of attention—yet she felt detached from it, an outsider.

She spoke without reservation, hiding nothing and apologizing for nothing. Her father doted on her, her mother was dead, and her stepmother was an evil witch.

"And your brother?" Mungo asked.

She wrapped her finger in the corner of the bed sheet, twisting it until it was as tight as a noose.

"He is a perfect libertine. He acts the prude, but behind that mask he has appetites that would shock even you. Women, men, girls, boys . . . And if they resist, he takes them by force."

She had gone perfectly still, her voice low with emotion. A question hung between them, and Mungo knew he had to ask it.

"Even you?"

Isabel gave a bitter laugh. "He tried, once. I was fifteen, he was drunk. I told him if he touched me, I would cut off his cock and present it to the King of France. After that, he did not dare touch me. But the thought of any other man having me drives him to a rage of jealousy."

Mungo remembered what Lanahan had told him: *Afonso has already killed three men in defense of his sister's honor.*

Isabel rolled over. "I am bored of talking about myself. Tell me your stories."

So Mungo offered her a glimpse of the life he had left behind. He told her about Windemere, the galas and fox hunts, the joys of harvest and sailing on the James. He told her about his years in England, about coming of age at Eton, then returning to study at Cambridge after a season in Virginia. Isabel listened with interest, but there was mischief in her eyes.

"What is it like to own a slave, to possess another human being? Does it make you feel powerful?"

"It feels . . ." Mungo shrugged. "Normal."

"I think I should like it. To have a person completely under my control." She frowned. "Or perhaps you do not think the blacks are people at all."

Mungo remembered sitting on his father's knee at Windemere, a young boy watching the slaves at work in the fields.

"African souls are as much God's gifts as the souls of us white folk," Oliver had told Mungo. "They are inferior to us neither in intelligence nor in character—only in their education and religion. If we can teach them anything, it is to know the Scriptures, and to worship the true God."

"I never saw an ounce of difference between black and white," Mungo told Isabel.

"Then why keep them as slaves? Why should they not be free?"

Another memory came to Mungo, much later than the previous one. Mungo had been eighteen, just returned from Eton and cocksure with the arrogance the school instilled in its pupils.

"If you believe that black souls are gifts of God, why don't you set them free?" he had demanded of his father.

Oliver had blinked. "I give them every comfort I can afford. They are happy here."

"They are still slaves."

"And if I set them free tomorrow, what would happen to them? They would be put loose in a society that gives them no rights, with neither the means nor the aptitude to support themselves. They would starve." He had shaken his head. "They are children, and like children they need a loving father's firm hand to guide them."

"But white children are allowed to grow up and find their way in the world. Isn't that why you sent me to Eton?"

"That is different."

"Why?" Mungo pressed, using the same unrelenting style that his opponents had come to dread at the Eton debating society. "Because I am white and they are black?"

"No."

A sudden change of tack. "What if I said I wanted to marry a black woman?"

Oliver laughed. "That is absurd."

"Why? Are we not all equal before God?"

A sigh. "The world is more complicated than that. You see the world with the blazing eyes of youth—I see it with the clarity of experience. That is the difference between us."

Oliver had meant it in a kindly way. But the look he got in return from Mungo made a shiver go through him. When had his son become so remorseless?

"The difference between us," Mungo had said, "is that I am honest and you are a hypocrite."

Remembering the exchange now, in Isabel's cabin, he felt a rare pang of regret. He had hurt his father, who after all had been a flawed man trying to live a good life.

"My father made many compromises," Mungo said to Isabel. "I intend to live my life on my own terms."

s the days turned into weeks and the *Blackhawk* rounded Cape Palmas and sailed east toward the Bight of Biafra, Mungo began to stay with Isabel longer and longer into the watch. The fourth bell became the fifth, then the sixth and the seventh. Tippoo accepted these changes without protest, but the risk of detection increased. There were occasions when they heard footfalls outside Isabel's door and watched the handle, terrified that it might turn. To Mungo's knowledge, Isabel had the only key to the lock. But there was always a chance that Captain Sterling had kept a copy for himself. Each time the footfalls faded away, they rushed to finish their business before Mungo scrambled out of the ventilation port and up the painter to the deck, concealing the line at the bottom of the pile by the stern rail.

The sodden rope was the only evidence of their affair that survived the night, apart from Mungo's sweat on Isabel's sheets and the lingering scent of her perfume in his clothing. By sunrise, Mungo and Tippoo were asleep in their hammocks, and Isabel was alone in her stateroom. As far as any of them knew, neither Afonso nor Captain Sterling nor any of the crew suspected a thing.

It was a knock on the door that proved them wrong. It was late in the watch; the dawn light was already coming through the ventilation port. Isabel was lying naked in Mungo's embrace, when suddenly two sharp taps sounded from outside. Isabel and Mungo went still, silent, wondering if someone might have overheard the soft cries Isabel had uttered at the height of her pleasure.

Mungo allowed himself to hope he had misheard. The noise of the ship was all around them, the moaning of timbers and creaking of lines in tension, the luffing of sails not quite full, the whistle of wind through the yards and the jangling of dishes in the galley. But a minute later, he heard the squeak of a floorboard underfoot, and a second tap of a knuckle on the door.

"Isabel," said Afonso, "I heard you cry out. Is anything the matter?"

Isabel placed a finger on Mungo's lips. She let out a gentle moan, as if waking from a sleep.

"Afonso?" she said. "Is that you?"

"Are you all right?" replied the viscount. "Were you having a dream?"

"A dream?" Isabel paused. "Yes, that's right. I was dreaming. It was Mother again. Did I wake you?"

"No, it was a cry from the masthead. The lookout has sighted Prince's Island. Would you care to join me?"

Isabel glanced at Mungo. He nodded his head.

"A walk would be refreshing, but I need to dress."

"Of course. I will wait in my cabin."

As soon as they heard the viscount's retreat, Mungo threw on his clothes without a sound and left Isabel with a kiss. Reaching through the ventilation port, he took the painter and slipped through the opening. He heard the swish of the ship as it sliced through the water, the crackle of the sails as they flapped in the breeze. The wind had turned capricious in the Gulf of Guinea, sometimes blowing off the continent to the north, other times from the east or the south. Twice, it had stranded them in pockets of calm—for six hours the first time, then for more than a day. On this morning, the wind was steadier but still light, barely above seven knots.

The surface of the ocean was smooth, disturbed only by the western swell. When the ship rocked to port, Mungo hoisted himself onto the window ledge and reached out for the railing, holding fast as the ship rolled back and gravity tugged against him. He raised his foot to the batten beneath the rail and levered his body upward. He was so focused on maintaining his footing that he didn't see the shadowy figure waiting for him on the deck—or the blade balanced in his hand.

"A strange time to be inspecting the hull," rasped Lanahan's voice. Every word rang with triumph.

Mungo froze, glancing from the first mate's hate-filled face to the gleaming cutlass he was holding, and then to Tippoo, who was standing by the helm, his features transfixed by impotent anger. Mungo's instinct was to fight. His hand was still on the painter. He could lasso the first mate's wrist, knock the cutlass away, and pitch Lanahan over the side. Afterward, he could claim the first mate had been drunk and fallen overboard. Tippoo would swear it was true.

Then Mungo saw the rest of them. A knot of men stood by the mast, sailors Mungo knew were loyal to the first mate. All were armed, with pistols trained on Tippoo and on Mungo.

Mungo reassessed his plan.

"Did you intend to run me through, or shoot me?" he asked casually.

Lanahan laughed. "That would be too merciful." He spoke to Tippoo. "Master gunner, ring the bell and then come with me below. Both of you will answer to the captain."

The walk to Sterling's quarters felt like a march to the gallows. Tippoo went first, then Mungo, and finally the first mate, poking Mungo's back with the tip of his sword. The captain answered his door dressed in a white shirt and black trousers, his hair freshly oiled. He fixed his eyes on Mungo, his expression dark, and admitted them without a word.

Isabel was seated on the leather bench at the foot of the captain's bed. She was wearing a violet morning dress, her hair assembled in a hasty twist. Her brother stood beside her, a hand gripping her shoulder. When she saw Mungo, her lips parted slightly, as if in apology, but her almond eyes held no trace of regret. Her back was erect and her hands rested primly in her lap. She looked as regal as a princess. The viscount gave Mungo a glare of such fury and contempt that his eyes looked as if they might burst from their sockets.

Captain Sterling took a seat in his chair, whose gilt edges and velvet cushion reminded Mungo of a throne.

"Mr. Lanahan," he said. "The charges, please."

The first mate spoke. "With respect to Mr. Sinclair, dereliction of duty, endangering the crew, and immoral assault against a passenger. As for Mr. Tippoo, dereliction of duty, and conspiring with Sinclair in the assault of the passenger."

"On what evidence?" Sterling asked.

Lanahan laid it out. "A fortnight ago, Seaman Keller informed me that Mr. Sinclair had substituted himself for Mr. Keller in the middle watch. I made inquiries among the crew and learned that other substitutions had been made, always to place the second mate with the master gunner in the middle watch. I suspected something untoward and investigated the matter, enlisting the help of the Viscount da Cruz. On four occasions, I observed the spar deck under the cover of darkness and witnessed Mr. Tippoo alone at the helm, the second mate gone from his post. It was not until tonight, however, that I confirmed my suspicions. Mr. Sinclair has been carrying on a clandestine affair with the Lady Isabel. The viscount heard the sounds of their congress with his own ears, and I was on deck when the second mate scaled the line he used to reach her stateroom."

Captain Sterling turned to Afonso. "Can you corroborate this?"

The viscount nodded. "Sinclair is a snake. He preyed upon the frailties of my sister and brought dishonor upon my house."

Isabel pushed Afonso's hand off her shoulder and stood up.

"You may question my judgment, brother, but do not dare

accuse me of frailty. Mr. Sinclair did nothing to seduce me. He has proven himself a gentleman in all our engagements."

"Your mind was not your own. You allowed your feelings to overcome your judgment."

"I never let my feelings interfere with my judgment."

Sterling held up his hand. "As master of this ship, my concern is not the lady's choice of companionship, only the discipline of my crew. Mr. Sinclair, what have you to say for yourself?"

Mungo considered it. Sterling was not a man to be swayed by protestations of innocence or pleas for mercy, and Mungo was not the man to give them.

"I make no excuses."

Sterling nodded. "Then your punishment is decided. Forty lashes, and demotion to the rank of able seaman. For Tippoo, twenty lashes. To preserve the lady's good name, the charge will be falling asleep on watch."

"Is that all?" Afonso was livid. "My family's honor has been mortally insulted. The sins these men have committed are unpardonable. The penalty should be death."

"This is my ship, and my authority is absolute," said Sterling coldly. He glanced at Isabel. "Since the lady has admitted she encouraged her affair with Mr. Sinclair, the charge of assaulting a passenger is baseless. These men are being punished solely for putting my ship at risk."

That only made Afonso angrier. "My family are investors in this vessel. If you will not punish these men, I will take the matter up with my father. He will never do business with you again."

"And will you tell our father exactly what Mr. Sinclair did that disgraced me?" said Isabel. Her voice was quite calm, but again Mungo saw the gleam of mischief in her eye. "You were supposed to be protecting me. You will not go unpunished, if it becomes known that his daughter's honor is not so *intact* as he thought."

For a moment, Afonso stared at her in disbelief. Then his jaw tightened.

"I cannot accept this," he told Sinclair. "At sea I may be required to submit to your judgment, but on land you have no authority. I challenge Mr. Sinclair to a duel."

His words hung in the cabin air. Sterling looked at Mungo.

"What do you say, Mr. Sinclair?"

"I would like to know what the lady in question thinks of all these attempts to claim her honor," said Mungo.

All eyes turned to Isabel. Faced with a battle between her brother and her lover, with her reputation at stake, she might have been expected to burst into tears or plead for peace. But whatever was in her heart, her almond eyes gave nothing away.

"I do not need any man to protect my honor," she said. "But if you must prove your manhood with violence, do as you will."

Mungo looked at Afonso, the supercilious stare and smirking contempt.

"Then I accept the challenge."

The capital of Prince's Island was Santo António, a small town that supported a remarkable number of lavish mansions. Small boats crowded its harbor, just big enough—Mungo supposed—to make the short journey to the African mainland, and navigate the tangled river deltas beyond reach of the British slavery patrols.

A discreet distance away from the town lay a secluded cove, a crescent of pale white sand fronting a teardrop-shaped inlet of water fringed by coffee plantations. It was here, two mornings after the *Blackhawk*'s arrival on the island, that the ship's longboat rowed ashore carrying Mungo St. John, Sterling, Tippoo, Lanahan and the ship's surgeon.

The negotiation over terms had been brief. In a meeting in Sterling's cabin, the seconds—Lanahan for Afonso and Tippoo for Mungo—had had no difficulty agreeing on the weapons.

"Swords," Tippoo announced.

As the man who had received the challenge, that was Mungo's decision, but it was clearly not what Lanahan had expected. He had assumed Mungo would rather take his chances with a bullet than match blades with an accomplished swordsman like Afonso. He did not know that Mungo had practiced fencing since his earliest days at Eton. He preferred the French-made foil, or *fleuret*, for its light weight and perfect balance, but he and his friends had experimented with everything from the heavier military sabers to the punchier "court swords" that inspired the naval cutlass.

The choice pleased Sterling too, who had not hidden his distaste for the match. Honor could be served with less injury than if pistols were involved.

"The winner will be declared at the sight of first blood," he proposed.

"The Viscount da Cruz has no interest in a symbolic victory," said Lanahan pompously. He had leaped at the opportunity to serve as Afonso's second and ingratiate himself with the viscount further. "We will fight until one man pleads for mercy, or suffers a wound so serious he cannot continue." A sneer at Tippoo. "If Mr. Sinclair is willing to risk that."

Tippoo had bared his teeth. "No problem for him."

Now Mungo stood on the beach on Prince's Island. He was dressed as he would be for deck duty, the sleeves of his shirt unbuttoned at the cuff and folded back, the legs of his trousers rolled up to his calves, and his feet bare. He tested the balance of the blade Sterling had provided. It was made for dueling, with a long, thin blade sharpened on both sides, and a wide hand guard that protected fingers as well as wrists.

Across the coffee fields, Mungo heard the distant chime of a church bell striking eight. At that exact moment, a small procession appeared down the track that led from the town. Afonso, dressed in a scarlet frock coat, riding boots and a thin silk shirt rode in the lead on a black horse. Half a dozen soldiers accompanied him and, behind them, four glossy-skinned slaves carried a brocaded sedan chair. There, perfectly poised despite the swaying of the chair, sat Isabel.

Mungo had not spoken to her since their affair had been discovered. Afonso had all but imprisoned her in her stateroom, and Mungo had been confined below decks. Now their eyes met across the beach.

"You should not have come," said Mungo. "It may cause you distress."

Isabel looked at her brother. He had dismounted, and taken up his sword. The blade hummed as he made sharp, practiced strokes through the air.

"Your distress may be the greater," Isabel said.

The slaves placed her chair in the shade of a palm tree. The seconds and the surgeon joined her, while the soldiers lined up a little distance away. Isabel lifted a gloved hand and touched the soft spot at the base of her neck, then allowed her fingers to fall between her breasts. Mungo smiled, then focused on his opponent, ten feet away across the sand. Afonso had removed his coat. His shirt flapped in the breeze off the ocean, his white trousers and polished black boots gleaming in the morning sunlight.

Captain Sterling stood between them, his face hard. He checked that both participants were ready, then raised a handkerchief.

"You may as well get on with it."

He stepped back, letting the handkerchief fall onto the sand. Mungo held out the shining blade, pointing the tip at the middle button on the viscount's chest.

"I have no wish to do you harm," he called. "But if you insist on pressing this matter between us, then be warned. I will give you no quarter."

Afonso's eyes darkened. "I will soak the ground with your blood."

"So be it," Mungo replied. "*En garde!*"

The viscount put his free hand behind his back and bent his knees in preparation. Mungo did the same. They began to circle each other, their blades aglow in the slanting light, sizing each other up. Mungo saw a glimmer of surprise in Afonso's eyes as he registered Mungo's precise, well-honed movements. He had expected a clumsy sailor waving his weapon like a belaying pin.

The strike came with a speed that nearly caught Mungo off guard. He was saved by his instinct and parried the blow downward, then lunged into the gap, stabbing toward the viscount's shoulder. Afonso twisted away and lashed out with a backhanded slash that came so close to Mungo's ear that he heard the song of the blade as it passed by. Mungo danced to the side and aimed another powerful thrust at the viscount's shoulder. Afonso jumped backward and the blow fell short, then he leaped forward with a thrust of his own, which Mungo parried.

Since there was no time limit on the contest, the only constraints they faced were strength, stamina and courage. Mungo waited, conserving his energy. He backed off so that Afonso had to come at him, swaying out of the way of the attacks without reply. The strategy drove Afonso into a greater rage. He had expected a quick and easy victory, almost by right. Mungo's ability to prolong the fight insulted his superiority.

Afonso became careless. He slashed and cut and thrust and swung with such force that his face turned red. Mungo danced across the sand on the balls of his feet, waiting for the opening he knew was coming.

Afonso dropped the tip of his sword slightly as his wrist tired, and Mungo pounced, lashing out with a straight thrust that caught his opponent on the cheek and left a trail of bright blood. Afonso cursed and felt the wound with his free hand, staring at his scarlet fingertips in disbelief.

"You little cockroach," he said, rending the air where Mungo had just been with a vicious diagonal cut. "Stop prancing around and fight like a man."

"Like this?"

Mungo skipped forward, thrusting toward Afonso's face and drawing his opponent's sword arm higher. Without warning, Mungo dropped to his knees and whipped his blade underneath the viscount's, gouging the nobleman's side. Afonso cried out, clutching at the wound, and Mungo struck again, stabbing the viscount's shoulder.

In any other sword fight, these would have been disabling injuries. But Afonso da Cruz reacted like a man possessed. As his sword arm went limp, he grabbed the weapon with his free hand and lunged toward Mungo. Mungo jumped back a split second before the blade would have sliced through his cheek. The viscount's handsome face was a mask of pain, but he did not relent. He came at Mungo with renewed vigor, cutting and lunging with a power that seemed supernatural.

He put all his weight into a sweeping horizontal cut, as if aiming to sever Mungo's trunk from his legs. Mungo stepped back quickly, but his foot caught on a piece of driftwood buried just under the surface of the sand and he stumbled. As he threw out his arms for balance, he loosened his grip on the sword. Afonso caught the blade in the midst of its stroke and knocked it out of Mungo's hand. It cartwheeled through the air and landed at the water's edge.

The loss of the weapon stunned Mungo. Years had passed since he'd let go of a sword in the midst of a bout. Afonso took full advantage. He planted his feet and turned his blade into a spear, driving the point toward Mungo's heart.

Mungo threw himself on the ground, knocking the wind from his lungs and eating a mouthful of sand. The lethal thrust whistled over his head, missing his scalp by less than an inch. As Afonso gathered himself for another strike, Mungo scrambled away and launched himself toward his fallen sword. He landed in a flail of limbs, but his fingers clutched the handle as the viscount brought his blade down in a stabbing slash. Mungo twisted his blade to deflect the blow, used the strength of his wrist to whip his sword toward Afonso's face, hoping to drive his opponent back and give himself time to get to his feet. He was shocked when a geyser of blood exploded from Afonso's nose. The tip of his sword had sliced through skin and cartilage and exposed a strip of white bone.

Afonso howled and leaped backward, nearly tripping over his own feet. Blood drenched his beard, dripping from his chin, and he struggled to staunch the flow with the lapel of his coat.

"Halt!" cried Sterling. "That is enough!"

Afonso ignored him. Snarling and dripping blood, he shook off the pain and came at Mungo again.

Had he been in his right mind, he would never have thrown such a wild backhanded cut at Mungo's face. The momentum of the move left his upper body wide open to a counterstroke.

Mungo took his chance without thinking, so fast that Afonso did not even see it happen. The first he knew of it was when he looked down at his stomach, and saw Mungo's blade sticking through it almost to its hilt.

Afonso's fingers lost their grip on his sword. He watched as Mungo placed his hand on his chest and withdrew the blade. The world became a blur; he collapsed into the sand.

The surgeon rushed to Afonso's side. He tried to staunch the wounds, but the blood flowed like a flood tide. He felt for the pulse, then shook his head grimly.

"He will not survive."

Mungo stepped back and put up his sword, breathing hard. His shirt was drenched with sweat and spattered with Afonso's blood. He glanced at Isabel. She had not moved through the entire fight; even now, with her brother bleeding out his life into the sand, she did not go to him. Her almond eyes were impassive and unreadable.

Mungo turned to Lanahan. "I assume, as the viscount is unable to speak for himself, that he yields?"

A low growl escaped Lanahan's throat. He looked as if he would have liked to carry on the fight himself, if the rules had allowed it. He could not make himself say the words.

"Enough!" snapped Sterling. "This is finished. It is time for us to depart."

The soldiers who had been watching the spectacle were racing across the sand, weapons drawn. Mungo planted his feet and raised his blade, but Sterling grabbed his arm and tugged him away.

"We are on the sovereign territory of Portugal, and the governor—if you have forgotten it—is the father of the man you have just killed."

He pulled Mungo down the beach to where the longboat bobbed in the surf. The crew, alert to trouble, were already on their oars and pulling away. Mungo had to wade deep into the water to catch them up. Exhausted from the fight, he might not have managed to haul himself in, but a mighty heave from Tippoo behind lifted him over the gunwale and into the boat. Tippoo followed. As soon as all the *Blackhawk*'s men were in, the boat leaped away.

Mungo looked back. The soldiers had lined up on the water's edge, but they only carried pistols. The few shots they attempted fell well short of the longboat. Further up the beach, the slaves were wrapping Afonso's body in a sheet.

Beyond them all stood Isabel. She had risen from her chair and was staring out after the longboat. Her loose hair blew freely in the breeze; the palm fronds sent rippling shadows over her face. It was impossible to tell what she was thinking.

Mungo turned away and tried to put her out of his thoughts. So much had passed between them—she had aroused feelings inside him that he hardly dared to admit. Now, in all likelihood, he would never see her again.

That was for the best, he told himself. He could not let anything dull his thirst for revenge.

The burning felt like hot ash on Camilla's skin, yet its heat came from inside her body as if someone had set fire to the air in her lungs. She heard herself panting, desperate to slake her thirst, but water was nowhere to be found. Around her was gray light and dark shadow. She heard what sounded like human voices, an old woman and then a young man. They seemed familiar, but she couldn't place them. Her mouth opened and she tried to speak, but the words were trapped within her. Over and over, she tried to say them, but they were stuck. At last, the resistance gave way and the words tumbled out. She heard them but could not fathom their meaning.

She awoke with a cry, in her bed at Bannerfield. All was dark. A dull pain still throbbed deep between her thighs from Chester's visit before bedtime. She glanced out the window at the night and tried to recollect the words from the dream.

Beware the black heart, and the thirst that never quenches.

They were the words Methuselah had spoken to Mungo in the observatory. She wondered again what they meant. She had known since childhood that Methuselah had the power of second sight—all the slaves knew it. Perhaps she had inherited some of his gift.

The dream made her think of Mungo. Not a day had passed since she left Windemere that he hadn't been in her thoughts. He had been in her life since the day she was born—two years older and always ahead of her. As a baby, she had crawled after him while he toddled around the house. As a little girl, she had watched him climb trees and swim in the river, and thought she would never be so tall or so strong. In those days, she was so young she did not even realize what it meant to be a slave. She thought of him like a brother. They roamed all over the estate together, as inseparable as twins. Often, they stripped naked and swam across the creek to the island where Mungo's grandfather had built his observatory. Benjamin St. John was in ill health by then and seldom went there. They turned it into their secret castle, gathering nuts and berries for supplies, and fending off imaginary invaders with sticks.

Later, she would marvel that she had been allowed to be so close with Mungo. When she was older, she would wonder if Oliver St. John had permitted it simply because it flattered his illusions of himself, proof that he meant what he said when he claimed to treat his slaves like family. Maybe even a way of flaunting his liberal credentials to his scandalized neighbors.

But even under his ownership it could not last, of course. As they grew older, Camilla learned the immutable truths of her existence: black and white, slave and master. A tutor came and wrestled Mungo into the schoolroom, while Camilla was put to work in the laundry. They did not go to the observatory any-more. But whenever Mungo saw her, he still gave her the same smile he always had.

One day, Mungo's mother Abigail had sent Camilla to take a note to the neighboring estate. She went alone, which was not uncommon. The St. Johns often let their slaves leave Win-demere without escort. Oliver said it was because he trusted them to always come home. He seemed to forget the underlying truth—that they came back because any fugitive would have easily been recaptured.

Camilla was eleven years old and filled with the importance of her errand. She clutched the note close, wrapping it in the skirt of her dress so it would not get dirty from the road. She was so intent on her errand, she did not notice the other children waiting until she almost ran into them.

There were five of them, all white children from the sur-rounding plantations and all bigger than her. Their leader was Lucius Horniman, a surly boy whom she had never seen without a piece of candy in his mouth. He was sucking on one now.

"What you got there?" he asked.

She curtsied and showed him the letter. He did not move out of her way. Instead, he snatched the paper out of her hands and held it up out of reach, laughing as she jumped for it.

"Please," she said. "Mrs. Abigail said I was to deliver it safe."

"Then you'll be in trouble, won't you?"

Lucius held the letter out to her. Then, as she reached forward for it, he shoved it into her chest so hard she stumbled backward.

One of the other boys had come around behind her. He stuck out his leg, tripping her so that she sprawled flat on her back.

The boys were on her in a second. Some held her down, while others kicked and hit her. They were big enough to make their punches hurt, but Camilla did not move to defend herself. Whatever they did, she must not retaliate; she had to endure it. As much as Oliver St. John liked to boast how well he treated his slaves, she was old enough to understand that there were lines that could not be crossed. A black girl striking a white child was unforgivable. It would mean brutal punishment.

At last the children got bored of hurting her.

"We've had our fun," said one. "Let's go fishing."

Lucius shook his head. "I'm not done."

"What else is there to do?"

Lucius thought for a moment. A new and unpleasant look came over his face.

"You know that crazy preacher who came down from Boston, saying blacks and whites was all the same underneath? The one my daddy gave a thrashing to? Well, let's see if he was right."

He looked down at Camilla. "Get up. Show us what you got under that dress."

Camilla struggled to her feet. With trembling fingers, she unlaced her dress and pulled the sleeves down her arms. It dropped in the dust at her feet.

She was too young to wear stays. She stood there perfectly naked, her red-toned skin shining in the sunlight. The boys gathered around, gawking wide-eyed. One reached out and pinched her nipple.

"Ain't even got proper titties yet," he complained.

Lucius picked up a fallen branch and poked it between her legs. It hurt, but Camilla squeezed her eyes shut to hold in the tears. She would not give them that satisfaction.

She crouched down to pick up her dress, but Lucius rapped her hand with the branch.

"I ain't finished with you yet."

"Get your hands off her," said a voice from the top of the embankment at the roadside.

Camilla looked up. Mungo stood there, the sun radiant behind him and his white clothes gleaming. Since he'd been breeched, his mother had always dressed him in white—perfect miniature suits of white cotton and silk. "My little angel," Abigail called him, but there was nothing angelic about the snarl now on his face.

"We was just having some fun," said Lucius. "Didn't mean nothing."

Mungo jumped down the bank onto the road.

"She's mine."

"Sure. But you got plenty more niggers at Windemere. You—"

Lucius stopped talking. He doubled over, clutching his face as blood flowed through his fingers from the nose Mungo had just broken with his fist. The other children stared. One—Lucius's brother—picked up a stick and came swinging it at Mungo. Mungo grabbed it in mid-air, wrestled it out of his opponent's hands, and swung it so hard it broke over the boy's head. The boy turned and fled, followed by the others.

As soon as they were gone, Camilla collapsed into Mungo's arms. It was against all the iron-clad laws that ruled her life, but Mungo did not reject her. He held her close, stroking her hair gently.

At last she remembered who she was. She pulled away and put on her dress, ashamed of herself.

"Your suit," she said. "It's got blood on it. I'll be all week in the wash-house getting those stains out."

Mungo seemed not to hear her. He reached out, lost in thought, and retied the laces of her dress.

"If anyone ever hurts you again, tell me and I will kill them."

And though he was smiling, and it was an absurd thing for a white man to say to a slave, the fierce look in his smoky yellow eyes made her believe him utterly.

At the end of that summer he had sailed for England and Eton. He was gone five years. At first Camilla was heartbroken, then resigned. As the years went by, she grew into a young woman; there was more than enough at Windemere to occupy her thoughts. But she never forgot Mungo. Sometimes she wrote to him, little notes laboriously copied out by candlelight late at night, when the other slaves were asleep. She knew Abigail would not approve of a slave corresponding with her son—even to read and write was a crime for a slave—so she slipped them into Abigail's letters when she took them to the post office. Of course Mungo could never write back to Camilla, but sometimes Abigail would read aloud a passage from one of his letters— "Camilla would look very fine in the dresses that Lady Cavendish's maid wears" or "I went swimming in the Thames; it is much colder than when I used to paddle in the James with Camilla"—and Camilla would know in her heart he meant it for her.

Mungo's life in England sounded so different, she wondered if she would recognize him when he returned. Certainly, when the carriage pulled up outside the house one warm May evening, she hardly did. He had grown tall, his gangly adolescent frame had filled out with muscle, and powerful shoulders tapered to a slim waist. His hair was long, and his skin shone with a new luster. But the eyes were the same, smoky yellow and flecked with gold.

All the house slaves had assembled to welcome him back, but he picked her out of the crowd at once. He held her gaze for a moment, a smile curling his lips, before he stepped down from the coach and embraced his mother.

That night, Camilla left her quarters and stole out to the old observatory. She had received no message—she simply knew. Mungo was waiting for her. He had swept out the old building and filled it with dogwood flowers and beeswax candles. He had oiled the old machinery to open the sliding roof, so that the stars shone in and filled the room with light.

He put his hands on her shoulders and stared at her in the starlight.

"You've grown," he said, and kissed her.

That night, they discovered exactly how they had changed in the intervening years. They explored each other's newly swelling bodies, reveling in the novelty, unlocking delights Camilla had never imagined. When dawn came, she almost wept to be parted from him. But the next afternoon, she had found a dogwood flower left outside her cottage, and when she went to the island that night, Mungo was there again.

Mungo had rubbed the flower on her skin, then breathed in the scent.

"This will be our signal," he said. "The nights that I can come, I will leave a flower on your doorstep."

All that long, hot summer they met in the observatory as often as they could. Sixteen years old, she lived her days in a dream and her nights in a daze, thrilling every time she came home and saw a dogwood flower waiting for her.

Of course she knew it could not last. Even so, she was surprised how suddenly it ended. One morning, she went into Abigail's room to bring her breakfast, and found her mistress motionless in her bed. The doctor said she had suffered a heart attack.

That day, the light went out of Mungo's soul and a black mood came down. No more dogwood flowers appeared on Camilla's doorstep. Mungo spent his time sitting in the parlor with flocks of black-clad relatives, or arguing with his father. And then, as soon as the funeral was over, it was time for him to take ship for Cambridge.

The night before he left, she went to the observatory one last time. She waited until her limbs went stiff and the moon began to sink, and just as she had convinced herself he would not come she heard the rustle of branches, and his familiar voice calling her name in the darkness. When she embraced him, he felt as solid as one of the great trees soaring around them.

"I will come back for you," he whispered. "We were meant to be together—always."

She blushed. "That is silly," she said. "You know it can never be."

"Anything is possible," Mungo insisted. "When I was in London once, I saw a sea admiral walking with a woman on his arm. The admiral was an old man, but so dignified—tall and straight, covered in gold braid and medals and orders of nobility. You could tell he was a great hero. And the woman on his arm was blacker than you are."

He gripped her arm. "She was not his mistress or his servant. She was his wife."

Camilla could not comprehend it. All she could think to say was, "That is another country."

She did not romanticize what they might have had. She could not forget what she was, for the truth lived in every pore of her skin. She saw the evidence every time she caught her reflection in one of Windemere's grand mirrors. He was white, and she was black; he a master, she a slave. What future could they ever have had together?

Yet however many times she told that to herself, something in her soul had always refused to surrender to the remorseless logic. She had known, when she sent the letter to Cambridge, when she rubbed the dogwood petals on the paper, that Mungo would come. And she knew he would have come back for her again, if Chester had not snatched her away to Louisiana. But how would he ever find her here?

And the baby? She told herself that Mungo would love the child, because it was hers. But in the darkest places of her soul, where she feared to look, she wondered if he would dash its brains out.

Methuselah's words, made vivid by her dream, disturbed her. What was in Mungo's heart? She knew there was good in him—she had seen him do the noblest and kindest deeds for no reason at all. But she had also seen him be utterly callous. He was like the sun, set in its course: the same face bright and warming one moment, harsh and scorching another. Even though she loved him, she could not deny he frightened her.

Yet he was her only hope.

She placed her bare feet on the wooden floor and stood up. Through the window, she heard the calls of the night birds and the screech of cicadas in the grove of oaks that surrounded Bannerfield mansion. The bedroom was kept locked, but the lock was old and the spring was weak. Camilla had found some time ago that the blade of a kitchen knife, carefully inserted, could spring it quite easily.

She opened the door without a sound and slipped out.

As she descended the stairs, she saw a crack of light spilling under the door of Chester's study. The door was ajar. She almost lost her nerve and fled back, but desperation drove her on. Not even daring to breathe, she kneeled at the door and peered through the keyhole.

The room was empty. Chester had been working late—she could smell his cigar smoke still fresh—but he was gone now. He must have forgotten to douse the lamp. She hurried inside and crossed to the desk. She did not have a plan; she was driven by hope and instinct.

She found pen and paper and wrote as quickly as she could.

Chester Marion has taken me to a place called
Bannerfield. It is in Louisiana north of Baton
Rouge. Please come and rescue me he is a brute.

She blew on the ink to dry it. But what now? She could not send it to Windemere, not after its new owners had conspired to take it from Mungo. Where could the letter reach him?

She did not have much time. Chester might come back at any moment. Or one of the house slaves might find her. She knew they saw her as an interloper and a shirker—they would have no qualms turning her in to Chester.

She looked around the room in mounting panic. A pile of letters was stacked on the desk, ready to be taken away next morning. If she only knew what address to write, she could put her note in among them. Where was Mungo?

She was about to give up when the name on the topmost letter caught her eye. MR. AMOS RUTHERFORD, RICHMOND, VIRGINIA. She knew the name: Mungo's maternal grandfather. He had often visited Windemere when Abigail St. John was alive.

Camilla could not imagine why Chester would write to Amos, but that did not matter. Amos had always been fond of Mungo; he would know how to find his grandson. She cracked open the wax that sealed Chester's letter and slid her own slip of paper inside it. She pressed her thumb against the broken wax to warm it, trying to knead the fragments back together just as she had with Abigail's letters so many years ago.

"What the hell are you doing?"

The door swung open with a bang so loud it must have woken the whole house. Chester stood there, wrapped in a dressing gown.

The moment he saw her at his desk he flew across the room. He tore the letter out of her hand before she could hide it in the pile, and threw her against the wall.

"Did you read this?"

She shook her head, praying he would not open it. If he did not find the note she had put in, if it went back in the post, there was still a chance it might reach Mungo. That would be worth any punishment.

His eyes raked her with suspicion, but all he saw was a slave, and a letter that seemed to be sealed. He had not noticed the crack in the wax she had hastily smeared together.

"In any event, I suppose you cannot read."

He tossed it back onto the desk. Camilla dared to breathe again. Her secret was safe.

But he had thrown it too carelessly. The letter overbalanced the pile of correspondence; it toppled over, slid off the desk and dropped onto the floor.

The wax broke apart again. The letter flopped open, and as it did, her slip of paper fell out onto the floor.

"What is this?"

Chester picked it up and read quickly. His face went murderously dark.

"You treacherous little whore," he hissed. "I underestimated you. You not only read and write—you lie, too. Didn't I warn you what I would do if you ever spoke the name of Mungo St. John again? And now you try to bring him here?"

He grabbed her by both arms and threw her across the room. She fell, bruising her arm and cutting her head on a table. She scrambled to her feet and looked to the doorway, but there was no escape there. Granville had appeared, flanked by two plantation overseers.

Chester took a cigar from the box on his desk and jammed it in his mouth. He scrolled up Camilla's note, held it into the flame of the lamp until it caught fire, then touched it to the end of the cigar. The paper burned and crumbled to ash. He puffed on the cigar until its end glowed hot as an ember.

He walked slowly toward her. There was rage in his face, but not uncontrollable temper. It was the cold, deliberate fury of a man who knew exactly what he was doing. He stared at her pitilessly, as he might at a column of numbers that stubbornly refused to add up.

"This is for Mungo St. John."

He took the cigar from his mouth and, very slowly, pressed it against her right arm. She screamed in agony as he ground it into her flesh. The smell of charred skin filled the room.

"And this is for betraying me."

He sucked on the cigar until it glowed hotter than ever, then touched it to her left arm. She screamed again. Every slave in the house must have heard her, but no one came. They knew better than that.

Chester spat in her face.

"I have had my fill of this bitch," he told Granville. "Take her outside and do what you want with her. Then hang her as a warning to the others."

Granville moved in quickly, slavering like a dog in reach of a particularly succulent bone. He took a Bowie knife from his belt and thumbed the blade with cruel delight.

"We'll have some fun before we put the bitch down."

"Wait!" Camilla cried. The pain from the cigar burns was almost too much for her to speak, but she forced the words out through choking sobs. "If you kill me, you kill your own child."

Chester went still. Automatically, his eyes turned down to her belly. Ignoring the agony in her arms, she flattened her night-dress, pulling it tight across her hips so he could see the bump. It was still small, but on her slim frame it swelled out unmistakably.

His gray eyes, usually so fixed and remorseless, were suddenly filled with turmoil.

"Mine?"

"Who else's?"

He stared at her so long, the burning tip of the cigar began to dull. Even Granville became restless.

"Boss?"

"Shut up."

Chester breathed faster, thinking hard. The cigar began to glow once more. Camilla wondered if he meant to punish her yet again, if he would rather see his child die than let her live.

Chester tipped back his head and blew out a long plume of smoke that circled and eddied in the lamplight.

"Leave her be," he ordered. "We will put her to work in the fields. Maybe that will teach her obedience."

From Prince's Island, the *Blackhawk* sailed south along the fever coast, making eight knots of headway on a fresh northerly breeze. Their destination was Ambriz, a trading post midway between the Congo River estuary and the Portuguese settlement of St. Paul de Loanda. From the descriptions Mungo had heard from Tippoo, he knew that Ambriz was a "free port," not subject to the Portuguese governor at St. Paul de Loanda, and only occasionally patrolled by the British, who claimed trading rights further north. Ambriz's independence made it a hub of commerce and a magnet for unsavory characters from Europe and America—criminals, political exiles, mercenaries, even some gypsies—seeking sanctuary from polite society and a chance to make their fortune. There was a word for them in Portuguese: "*degrados*," which meant "outcasts," or "the degraded."

That afternoon, Sterling summoned Mungo to his cabin.

"Sit down," said the captain, waving to a pair of chairs beside the stern windows.

Mungo looked through the paned glass at the turquoise water and the swath of forest beyond. He took a seat opposite Sterling, wondering if this was an overdue reckoning for his duel with Afonso. Since they left the beach on Prince's Island, Sterling had acted as if the whole incident had never happened.

Nor did he mention it now. Instead, he asked, "What did Amos Rutherford tell you about the nature of our voyage?"

Mungo thought back to the day he had returned to Windemere. It was hard to believe it was only six months ago.

"He told me that the cargo would make my fortune."

Sterling nodded. "My partners are discreet. That is why our relationship has endured and made all of us rich. Let me ask you—what do you think we are doing in Africa?"

There was no point playing the fool. He had guessed it weeks ago. Even so, it required a certain steeling of his soul to say it—as if speaking the words aloud would make it real and irrevocable.

"I would assume we are here to take on slaves." Mungo cocked an eyebrow. "If the slave trade were not illegal, of course."

"Do you take issue with that?"

For a moment, Mungo was transported back to the debate at the Union. "Slavery is a crime against God," Fairchild had said—and Mungo allowed that might be true; he would not speak for God's thinking. But in the real world, slavery was a fact of life. Every man of distinction in the history of Virginia had been a slaveholder: George Washington, Thomas Jefferson, James Madison. The institution dated back to the founding days of the Republic when the first slaves had landed at Jamestown, and further still, to ancient times, defining the relationship between history's victors and their spoils. Societies like the Southern States, built on crops such as tobacco and cotton, could not exist without an inexpensive source of labor. The institution of slavery had secured that labor for generations.

"I have no argument with slavery."

"Slavery's different from the slave *trade*," said Sterling sharply. "It's the difference between killing a man in war, and sticking a knife in his ribs. One's legal and honorable, and the other ain't. So I'll ask you again—do you have any issue with the trade?"

Mungo considered the question. The transatlantic slave trade had officially ended before he was born, swept away on a wave of sanctimonious indignation. But Mungo knew his history. The men who banned the slave trade in America had thought that they were hastening the abolition of slavery itself—that without a fresh supply of slaves, the institution would wither. In fact, the restriction on supply had only made the slaves already in the country—and the children they bore—more valuable. An entire slave breeding industry had sprung up. Wealthy men had become even wealthier, their fortunes tied even more than before to the slaves they owned. And so the chains that bound blacks in servitude had become even tighter.

Mungo leaned back. "I will not play the hypocrite. If a man is happy to profit from the work of slaves, he cannot be too squeamish about the means used to enslave them." He paused for a moment. "Though all things being equal, I would prefer it if it were lawful."

Sterling pounded a fist on his desk. "There is only one law on this earth—the law that gives the strong and wealthy power over the weak and poor."

His words made even Mungo flinch. He hid his reaction. So far, the conversation had been conducted entirely rationally, two gentlemen talking to each other. But if Mungo gave Sterling cause to doubt his commitment, he had little doubt what would happen to him. Staring into the captain's eyes, Mungo had at last seen through to the man's essence. Though he dressed and talked as a gentleman, he was a predator whose only principle was self-interest.

For the moment, that self-interest was aligned with Mungo's.

"How do we obtain the cargo?" Mungo asked. "Do we capture them ourselves?"

Sterling seemed to relax a fraction. "Do you pick your own tobacco when you want to smoke a cigar? There's an American trader in Ambriz by the name of Alcott Pendleton. He's as crooked as a fork of lightning. Take your eyes off him for a second, and he'll have the shirt off your back. But he speaks Portuguese, he's friendly with all the native kings, and he can provide as many bodies as our hold can accommodate."

The color of the sea changed from sky blue to mud brown, the waves widened and the crests flattened. They were sailing along the length of the land, close enough to the coast to keep it in sight, when, suddenly, the shoreline parted along the hidden seam of a river. Sterling manned the helm as they made their approach, issuing orders to Lanahan, who relayed them with voice and fife. All those members of the crew not otherwise engaged stood at the rails with loaded rifles in hand, ready to repel any *mossorongos*—African pirate bands—who might mistake the *Blackhawk* for easy prey.

The harbor at Ambriz was a tidal lagoon south of the mouth of the Loge River. Most of the lagoon was deep enough only for fishing boats and dugout canoes, not a sailing ship like the *Blackhawk*, but the cove alongside the wharf had space for a ship to dock and two more to stand at anchor. Half the town seemed to be waiting for them on the quay: scores of mule carts, a large band of Africans in loincloths, and a moon-faced chief wearing a tribal headdress and a robe of many colors.

And one white man. The color of his skin alone would have made him stand out, but he had increased the effect still more by his dress: a purple frock coat, cravat, top hat and gilded cane. He could only be the American Sterling had mentioned, Alcott Pendleton. Mungo studied him from the quarterdeck as the ship sidled up to the quay.

After the gangplank was lowered, Mungo escorted Captain Sterling and Tippoo onto the dock. Sterling greeted Pendleton with a hearty smile and handshake and bowed to the African, who turned out to be the son of the local chief, the *Maniquitengo*, with the unlikely title of Lord Juan Pedro Kasavubu. The captain invited them both aboard for a glass of Kentucky bourbon in his cabin, and led them on a tour of the hold.

Pendleton examined their goods. He disparaged the cloth and beads, talked down the value of the firearms, and complained about the cut-throat practices of the Bakongo. His gaze never rested, Mungo noticed. His eyes roved his surroundings as if searching for danger; when a sailor accidentally dropped a crate of goods, he sprang around like a tiger. A tiny pistol appeared in his hand like magic. When he saw there was no threat, he simply tucked it back in his waistband and resumed his haggling with Sterling, as if nothing had happened.

Pendleton was a maddening negotiator. He talked around matters that were straightforward and debated points that should have been indisputable. Yet he was no match for Archibald Sterling. The captain spoke with authority, pushing the price higher until the American threw up his hands in exasperation and took Lord Kasavubu aside, conferring in a mixture of Portuguese and Kikongo. The African listened, his eyes on the captain. He nodded and spoke a string of words. Pendleton looked unhappy. Then he shrugged and held out his hand toward Sterling.

"His Grace is amenable. You have yourself a deal. All your trade goods, in exchange for three hundred and ninety-two."

The unit of currency was never mentioned. No one was so crass as to mention that they were accounting in human lives.

Sterling ignored the hand Pendleton offered. "It's not done until I see them."

"Of course," the trader replied. "I'm certain you will be pleased. But your journey was long. Let us celebrate tonight, and tomorrow I will show you."

From the flash in Sterling's eyes, Mungo knew he wasn't pleased with the delay. His manners made him concede.

"*Geribita?*" he asked.

Pendleton held out his hands. "For you, only the finest rum will do."

The next morning, Mungo awoke to hammering in the aft quarter of the hold, beneath his cabin. At Cambridge, he had been notorious for his ability to consume vast amounts of alcohol with no ill effects—but the sugary Brazilian liquor that Alcott Pendleton had brought on board the night before had addled his mind like nothing he had ever tasted. He buried his head in his pillow, but the ceaseless hammers echoed through the bunk and sent spikes of pain through his skull. Now that the hold was empty, the carpenters were busy with the timber and nails they had brought, constructing slave decks where their new cargo could be stowed as efficiently as possible.

Fighting back the ache in his head, Mungo rolled out of his bunk and dressed himself for an excursion into the bush—long sleeves, durable breeches, boots, Bowie knife and riding hat. He went on deck and found the captain holding court with the senior officers and the ship's surgeon.

"How is the work progressing on the slave decks?" Sterling asked Lanahan.

The first mate shot a glance at Mungo and narrowed his eyes. Since the duel on Prince's Island, his hatred of Mungo had simmered hotter than ever. Only the knowledge that Sterling would tolerate no more indiscipline among his officers had kept him in check.

"The supports are in place and the first planks are being laid in the bow. Give me three days, and I'll have her ready to load."

Sterling nodded. "Pendleton says the raids have been fruitful this spring. He claims to have over nine hundred darkies in his factory upriver. I'm taking Doctor Montgomery and Sinclair along with me to conduct the inspection and I aim to return by sundown. Mr. Lanahan, you will be in command in my absence. Drop anchor in the lagoon and keep watch for pirates. You have my permission to shoot anyone who strays too close."

The men departed to their duties. The captain unlocked the chest of arms behind the helm and extracted two Mississippi rifles and a flintlock pistol. He handed the pistol to Mungo, then passed him the rifles as well.

"Usually I'd give these to the porters," the captain said, "but I don't trust a single one of Pendleton's niggers to protect us."

Mungo gripped the stocks and followed Sterling and Montgomery down the gangplank to the dock where Pendleton stood waiting. The American was dressed in an ensemble more suited to a New York drawing room than a canoe trip up the Loge River, with a silk cravat and diamond studs in his cuffs. He greeted them heartily, appearing no worse for wear after consuming a bottle and a half of *geribita* in the captain's cabin the night before. Behind him the rising sun hung in the sky like a ball of fire. Mungo felt the prickle of sweat on his neck and shielded his eyes against the light, trying to ignore his pounding headache.

As soon as they were on the wharf, Lanahan ordered the gangplank raised and the lines cast off. Pendleton's launch took them along the south bank of the river to the shallows where the canoes were waiting. Each dugout was hewn from a single trunk and manned by Bakongo tribesmen in loincloths, holding paddles or muskets. Mungo studied them as he climbed aboard, searching their faces for a hint of deception. The Africans averted their eyes and shoved the boats off the bank, their skin glistening with sweat.

They took up the stroke with a sing-song chant that transported Mungo back to Windemere, the slaves singing in the fields as they brought in the tobacco harvest. Then he thought of Camilla, and Chester Marion, and the memories turned dark. He stared into the distance, his finger curling and uncurling reflexively around the rifle's trigger.

He smelled the barracoons before he saw them. At first, it was no more than a trace of putrefaction wafting downwind on the breeze. The stench increased until the air itself seemed infected with decay. Then came the cries, high-pitched and human, though male or female Mungo couldn't tell. He glanced at Sterling.

"Are they under attack?"

"Morning discipline," Sterling said. "It keeps the Quashies in line."

After a bend in the river, the Bakongo tribesmen landed the canoes onto a muddy beach strewn with driftwood and led them

up a winding path through a stand of overhanging trees reso-
nant with birdsong. As they walked beneath the shaded canopy,
Mungo saw a monkey staring at him through eyes ringed with
white. It scampered away in fright and disappeared into the tangled branches.

The trees gave way to a clearing of hardened clay pockmarked
with sprigs of grass. The smell hit Mungo like a punch in the
face. The noxious atmosphere of unwashed bodies and excrement was so overpowering he felt the urge to retch. He swallowed and tensed his stomach muscles as he took in the sight.

Pendleton's factory was as large as a village, with at least a
dozen barracoons erected in a circle around a central plaza,
where a muscular mestizo with yellow skin was whipping a
group of slaves tied to posts. The barracoons were fashioned out
of sturdy piles, driven into the earth and lashed together with
bamboo to create a barricade. The roofs were thatched, and
the floors were laid with rough-hewn planking. Hundreds upon
hundreds of Africans were packed inside the wooden fortifica-
tions. Mestizo guards paced with rifles at the edge of the forest.

The slaves' bodies were naked, oiled to make their skin seem
to glow with health. The adults stood jammed together, front to
back, and chained by the neck in rows inside the barracoons,
while the children were arranged shoulder to shoulder and
knees to chest around the outer walls. The floors were covered
in effluent. Some of the adults were moaning. A few were wailing in an unknown tongue. Most were standing silently.

Their heads turned as Mungo and the others emerged from the
forest, more than a thousand eyes drawn away from the "morning
discipline" taking place at the whipping posts in the plaza. The
eyes of the slaves jabbed at Mungo like daggers, accusing him
without a sound. His steps became leaden, his throat parched
despite the humidity in the air. He tried to tear his gaze from
them, but where else could he look? Their eyes were all around

him, their curiosity mixed with terror, their rage with sorrow and incomprehension.

He arrived at the plaza and stopped beside Sterling. Pendleton made his way to the whipping posts, taking the bullwhip from the mestizo.

"*Obrigado*, Carlos," he said, surveying the man's handiwork. "*Bom trabalho.*"

The slaves hanging from their wrists at the whipping posts were older. They would have been past their working prime even before Carlos went to work on them. He had taken the whip to every inch of exposed flesh. Their mouths hung open. The dirt at their feet was spattered with dark blood and urine.

Pendleton lifted the whip and laid into the old men again. When their screams faded and they slipped into unconsciousness, he returned the whip to Carlos and raised his voice, speaking in the language of the Bakongo. He held forth for a minute or two.

"They will do as you ask. There will be no trouble if you want to inspect them."

The mestizo guards pushed the slaves into a line, shouting in Portuguese and waving their guns. The inspection was painstaking and intimate. While Montgomery examined with his fingers and medical implements, Sterling peered into mouths and nostrils, checking teeth and squeezing muscles and breasts, looking under arms, in the crevice between legs, along the inner seam between buttocks, spreading eyelids, watching pupils dilate, and, finally, prodding the vaginal areas of the woman and the anuses of the men. The slaves that satisfied him were taken to a brazier, where a heated wire was used to brand Pendleton's initials onto the fleshy parts of their arms. Those who did not make the grade were chained together in a coffle by the whipping posts.

The marked slaves cried out to the heavens when parted from

their loved ones, especially the mothers separated from their children. A handful of women lashed out at the guards with their fists. Each was beaten to the earth with a rifle butt and shot through the chest. It made Mungo think of what Fairchild had said in their debate at the Union: *To keep innocent men and women in chains, to tear them from their homes and work them to death—this is a crime against God.*

But, as Sterling had said, God had no interest in the *Blackhawk*'s business. Mungo watched the captain carefully, studying his methods and trying to see the slaves through Sterling's eyes. He made a note of the attributes that Sterling prized, and those he did not: why he might reject one slave who appeared perfectly healthy, but accept another who seemed pale or feeble. On every decision hung a fortune. Each slave who reached Cuba alive would be worth over a thousand dollars profit. Any slave who did not survive the voyage was dead weight on the balance sheet. And one who brought a fever or a plague aboard ship could ruin them all.

By late afternoon, Sterling and Montgomery had worked through the population. The slaves selected were branded and herded into the barracoons closest to the river. Those who were left—the old, the sick and the smallest children—were segregated into their own barracoon on the far side.

"Delivery in four days," said Sterling. "One of my men will stay here to ensure that none go missing in that time."

Pendleton looked aggrieved. "A gentleman's word is his bond. By the time they see your hold, they'll be fattened nicely for the passage."

"What will happen to the others?" Mungo inquired.

A frown passed over Sterling's face as Pendleton dismissed the query with a wave of his hand.

"Not to worry. We'll find *something* to do with them."

• • •

The slave decks were completed in four days. Lanahan worked his crew of carpenters in eight-hour shifts around the clock, transforming the *Blackhawk*'s hold into a maze of floors, braces, subfloors and supports, and the foredeck into a slave pen with sturdy bamboo walls and a trellis for shade, all under the round eye of the cannon mounted on the main deck.

As soon as the construction ceased, Pendleton's porters lugged dozens of barrels of maize aboard, packing the stores with enough food to sustain the ship's crew and human cargo during the ten-week voyage to Cuba. Then came the casks of water, rum and cleaning lye. The seamen had to rearrange their hammocks on the berth deck to accommodate the provisions. Pendleton delivered the crates of ivory and containers of palm oil destined for New Orleans. These were jammed into the shell room in the stern, and the ammunition relocated along the ribs of the berth deck and in the forward magazine to distribute the weight.

Finally, the porters brought up the irons and coppers from the warehouse. The irons were light chains with manacles for wrist and ankle, and the coppers were huge cooking pots in which the maize would be boiled. The carpenters ran the irons along the slave decks and fastened the coppers in place near the hatch beside the capstan.

A week after they made landfall, the *Blackhawk* put to sea, sailing from Ambriz on the evening tide. All her sails were set full: to any watching eyes it would seem she was bound for home.

But in the moonlit hours of the middle watch she turned course and crept back into the Loge River estuary. On this night, all of the sailors were awake. The boat teams were on the water, the rest of the crew at attention on the spar deck, rifles and cutlasses in hand, while Captain Sterling scanned the dark waters with his spyglass. The signal came at half past two, as Alcott Pendleton had promised. A torch burned brightly in the middle of the river, and then disappeared quickly. Sterling lit the binnacle lamp and gave the order to Charles Morgan, who passed it along in a whisper to the crew: "Prepare to receive cargo."

One by one, the dugout canoes emerged from the shadows and glided quietly toward the ship, guided by the paddles of Pendleton's porters. The *Blackhawk*'s boat teams took turns escorting the canoes to the rope ladder hanging from the hooks that secured the gangplank, then held the canoes in place while the Bakongo tribesmen prodded the slaves up the ladder with muskets and spears, and the seamen on deck manhandled the new arrivals through the hatch by the capstan into the warren of decks below. Tippoo's carpenters checked the slaves for the captain's brand and lined them up along the planking on their sides, front to back. The carpenters secured the shackles in place by the light of a single oil lamp.

Despite the weapons all around, the slaves did not go quietly into the hold. They kicked and howled and tried to throw themselves over the side at the top of the ladder. One man succeeded, only to be speared by a porter as he thrashed in the dark water. Another slave, a young woman, tripped as she went over the railing and fell into the half-empty canoe, splitting her skull.

Tippoo caught the next man who lunged for the rail in his massive hands, lifted him off the deck by the neck, and drew his knife across the man's stomach, causing his bowels to spill out in a gush of bile and blood. Tippoo held the dying slave aloft until he stopped struggling, then propped his corpse against the capstan as an example to all those coming over the side.

It was Mungo's duty to record the cargo in the captain's logbook. He stood beside the binnacle, counting bodies as they climbed aboard, demarcating men and women and children. It meant he had to look at each one, gazing at their faces to guess their ages. Most lowered their heads, but some returned his gaze with wide, accusing eyes.

He had almost grown numb to the endless shuffling row of bodies, when he looked up from the ledger to see a face staring out of the line. It was a girl, sixteen or maybe less, for her hair had been shaved off like all the other slaves and it was hard to guess her age. She was pretty—beautiful, even—but that was not what caught Mungo's attention. She had softly rounded cheeks, bright eyes and flawless red-brown skin with a sheen like polished mahogany. She was almost the perfect mirror of Camilla.

Mungo stared at her, the pen and the ledger forgotten. He looked into her eyes, seeing her curiosity turn to fear. He wanted to comfort her, but there was nothing he could say.

Then Lanahan jabbed a musket at her and she vanished into the hold. Angrily, Mungo shook his head, made another note in the ledger, and moved on to the next slave.

The canoes departed as soon as they had deposited their cargo, returning upriver to gather another load. To Mungo's astonishment, it took under an hour to board all three hundred and eighty-nine slaves, the total agreed by Sterling and Pendleton, less the three who had died attempting escape. When the last African was stowed below decks, Tippoo's carpenters secured the hatch with a stout chain and three padlocks. The captain called the crew to muster on the quarterdeck, as the third-quarter moon dipped into the silvered swells, illumining the course they would take to the Indies.

"From now on, the watches will be four hours instead of eight, with double teams, one for the deck and one for the guard. Keep an eye on the hatch and another on the horizon. The only flag with any right to stop us is the Stars and Stripes."

Sterling turned toward Lanahan, who was standing beside him.

"Hoist the sails, Mr. Lanahan, and take her out to sea. The rest of you, except those on watch, get some sleep. You're going to need it."

The sails flapped from the yards and the ship's bow came around to the west. Mungo watched her course change on the compass with a grim smile. He had come halfway across the world, but at last he was heading in the right direction again. Back to America, to Chester and his revenge.

The morning after Chester had caught Camilla in his study, Granville took her out onto the estate. Dozens of hands, some as young as ten or eleven, were already at work, harvesting clumps of white cotton from flaxen stalks, to the rhythm of a bullwhip brandished by a young man on horseback. Granville handed Camilla a reed basket.

"Two hundred pounds by sunset. If you're short, you'll taste my whip."

She worked the rows as fast as her hands could move, gritting her teeth against the prick of the bolls, wiping her blood in the dirt. By late afternoon she was on the verge of collapse, her throat parched from the heat and the muscles in her back shrieking from the torment of ceaseless labor. But her basket was barely more than half full, while the baskets of the slaves around her were brimming. Hot tears spilled from her eyes and mixed with the sweat on her cheeks. She longed to rest her aching limbs and drink deeply from a flask of water hanging from the overseer's saddle, but the snap of the young man's whip kept her moving.

By the end of the day, she was near despair. Her fingers were lacerated and bloody, and her body more exhausted than she had thought possible. She tried not to think what it must be doing to the baby inside her. When the sky began to lose its light, she left the field with the other hands, wondering if her legs had the strength to carry her wherever they were going. She stumbled and fell, spilling her basket all over the ground. The other field hands filed by, but none stopped to help her up. Chester's displeasure had branded her just as much as the scars he had left on her arms: she was untouchable.

She pulled herself to her feet and gathered the cotton back into her basket. The white bolls were now streaked with gray dust. She joined the other slaves in a line that snaked into a cavernous barn, where they waited to hang their baskets on a scale. Granville made notations in a logbook, nodding when a slave met or exceeded the quota, scowling when they did not. On this day only two fell short—an old man whose skin seemed to hang from his bones, and Camilla, whose tally amounted to a mere one hundred and forty-five pounds.

Granville grabbed Camilla's arm and breathed into her ear, "There's a price a nigger pays for missing quota."

Camilla's body was numb from fatigue. She did not resist as he led her through the dusk toward the slave cottages that stood beneath the moss-draped oaks. Amid the cottages was a post buried in the earth with a crossbar nailed to it. The old man who had missed his quota was chained to the post and stripped of his shirt. This must have happened to him before, for the knot of scars on his back was almost like a second skin. He barely made a sound.

The field hands were made to gather around and watch. There was neither pity nor fear in their faces—this was simply a fact of life. Granville gave a brief speech about the perils of indolence, then unleashed a whipping so harsh that Camilla's skin tingled as if charged by lightning. The old man's cries rang out in the grove as the shadows deepened and lamps were lit in the big house. Camilla knew it would be her turn next.

The old man was unchained and taken away into one of the cottages. Granville pushed Camilla to the post. There was a savage hunger in his eyes and Camilla knew what it meant. Twice, he had been denied his chance to have her, and he had not forgotten it. This was his way of getting satisfaction.

He pulled her dress down to her waist and manacled her hands. He walked around her, ogling her naked breasts and snapping the whip in the air.

"One stroke for every pound you were short," he said.

Camilla gasped. Even the crowd of slaves seemed shocked.

Fifty-five lashes with that long, cutting whip was almost a death
sentence.

"What are you doing?"

Chester Marion's voice rang out around the punishment
square. With her face pressed against the post, Camilla had not
seen him walking down the path from the big house.

"What was her tally?" he asked Granville.

"Not even one-fifty."

Chester nodded. "Stow your whip. I'll handle her."

Disappointment flared in Granville's eyes, but he knew better
than to disobey his employer. He unchained Camilla. Chester
took her back to the house and made her undress in his bedroom
while a slave fetched a bath of hot water. He never took his eyes
off her as she washed the field grime and blood off her skin.

When she had finished, he said, "Stand by the window where
I can see you."

She did as she was told. He looked her up and down, his gray
eyes fixed on her with a savage purpose. She would almost have
preferred the touch of Granville's whip. His gaze seemed to flay
her flesh down to the bone. He looked at the taut skin over the
swell of her belly as if he could see the child growing inside—as
if he would reach in and rip it out. He seemed to be wrestling
with some emotion deep in his soul.

With a sudden flash of insight, Camilla realized what con-
flicted him. The child in her womb gave her a hold over him.
As long as she carried it, he could not hurt her without hurting
the baby.

But in the same moment, she realized it did not make her
safe. If anything, it only made her situation more dangerous.
He could not stand the thought that she had power over him.
If she used it, he would snap and then he might destroy both
her and her child.

With the intuition of someone who had been a slave all her

life, she understood that the only way to protect herself was not to show her strength. She must make him feel powerful.

She went to the bed and laid herself out on it.

"I am yours," she said humbly.

From then on, Camilla spent her days laboring beneath the glare of the sun, picking tufts of cotton from the bolls of Bannerfield and stuffing them into her basket. The Louisiana heat did not relent, even as the days moved toward Thanksgiving. Her delicate fingers, once employed to fasten corsets and mend gowns for Abigail St. John, were now calloused; her skin was stained with sweat and cotton dust. Her belly swelled beneath her simple housedress and she could only pray that the child growing inside her womb was not being harmed by her suffering.

The weeks of autumn became months, and Camilla mastered the ways of the cotton field. She learned how to conserve her energy and endure the hours under the sun; how to cleanse her mind of all distraction and turn her hands into engines; how to strip the plant of the white fibers and fill her basket to the brim. By November, she was one of the most productive pickers at Bannerfield, collecting between two hundred and thirty and two hundred and fifty pounds per day.

Chester was often away. He spent more and more time in New Orleans, and when he returned his talk was all of brokers and bankers and investors. Camilla did not know what it meant, but she could see the effects. Chester had a map of the county painted floor to ceiling on the wall of his drawing room, with Bannerfield's boundaries marked out in gilt lines. The estate was visibly the largest in the county, but it did not stop there. Every month, the painter was summoned again to extend the gold borders around more acres that Chester had acquired. The estate grew like a tumor, a malignant presence spreading over the heart of the county.

As the estate expanded, so did the house. Masons and carpenters came in their dozens to add new wings, porticoes, pediments and fountains. Engineers had to construct great earthworks to extend the hill on which the house stood so there was room enough for the foundations. When the buildings were done, craftsmen were summoned from all over the country to fill them with sumptuous furnishings. Furniture was ordered from France, curtains and upholstery from England, paintings from Italy. A pianoforte was brought up by barge from New Orleans and installed in the drawing room, though no one in the house knew how to play. Every morning when Camilla woke, she found a thin layer of gray-white dust covering her skin.

A new world took shape around her. Camilla's body changed. Her belly swelled plump; her breasts grew full. She could feel herself changing inside, too, like a tapestry being unpicked and then stitched back together in a new design.

Sometimes, out in the fields, she thought of trying to escape. But then the shadow of the overseer's horse would fall over her, and she would hear the whip slithering through his hands. She would never outrun him now, so heavy with child. And even if she did, where would she go? A lone black woman in Louisiana was effectively a thousand dollars' worth of lost property waiting to be claimed. Most likely, she would not even make it off the estate. Those golden lines on the map hemmed her in like the walls of a prison.

The Louisiana heat began to subside after the middle of December. The days turned pleasant and the nights cool, in the way that Camilla remembered from autumns in Virginia. But the fair weather could not ease the stresses of the cotton harvest. The production of cotton—the ginning, the pressing, the baling, and the transportation required to bring it to market—was intensive. Bannerfield's two hand-powered gins operated non-stop, night as well as day, until the last of the raw cotton was separated from the seeds and ready for pressing. Given the delicacy of Camilla's health, Chester Marion found her employment in the ginning barn. She spent her days amid a flock of old women and children, picking out by hand from the fluffy white fibers the seeds the machines had missed. It was mind-numbing labor, but it was easier on her fingers than handling the bolls, and at least she could sit down.

As her pregnancy advanced and her discomfort increased, Camilla worried that Chester would lose interest in her and revert to his abusive ways. To her surprise, he took delight in her ripening belly, running his hands over her distended flesh after intercourse and placing his ear against it to listen for the baby's movements.

"Isaac," he said, lying next to her in the bed one evening. "That will be his name."

Camilla glanced down the length of her body, past her rounded breasts to her stomach. She ran her hand over the bump in a circular motion, as if polishing a platter in the kitchen. She had no idea whether the child would be a boy, but if Chester wanted to speculate, she would not quibble.

"That's a good name," she said. "A strong name." She almost added, "My great-grandfather was called Isaac," but she caught herself. If she had learned anything in the months she had been at Bannerfield, it was Chester's hatred for her former life. If he could have erased every detail of Windemere and the St. Johns from her memory, he would have.

Chester reached out for her belly and rubbed it possessively, pushing her hand away.

"I'm going to raise him," he said. "The law may not recognize him as a free man, but here on my land he will be every bit a Marion."

Camilla tensed. She imagined how her child would be if he grew up seeking Chester's approval, seeing the pitiless cruelty of Granville's whip and hearing his snarling dogs hunting down the runaways. She longed to give her child a father with dignity and strength. But that was not possible. Not as long as Chester lived.

She took his hand from her belly and placed it on her breast.

"How is the harvest progressing?" she asked.

She had quickly learned that the one way to distract Chester was to talk to him about business. Early on, it had occasionally helped her deflect his intentions when he was in a particularly vile mood. Now, more and more, she used it to distract him from the baby.

"We're already at two thousand bales," he said with pride, "and we've still got a barn full of cotton to be pressed. We're going to fill half a steamship this year, I believe."

"Where will the bales go once they reach New Orleans?" she asked.

After drawing out Chester's private thoughts for months, she understood the commerce as well as any trader. She knew about the debt every planter carried into the harvest and the fluctuation in price per pound at the exchanges. She understood the way the great river served as an artery for every plantation from Baton Rouge to Arkansas, carrying hundreds of thousands of bales by steamship and barge down to New Orleans. She knew how the export houses acquired the bales from the planters, with floats from the moneylenders, and how the merchant ships then would carry them to the textile mills of the Northern States and England.

"The European market is strengthening," Chester replied. "The crop will probably go to Britain this year."

He seemed to grow bored of the conversation. He moved his hand from her breast over the hump of her stomach and down between her legs. She wanted to cry out and push him away, but she knew how vengeful he could be when his pride was wounded. She buried her face in the pillow and tried to think of the one man who might someday rescue her.

She had to find a way to bring Mungo to Bannerfield.

The morning dawned gloomy and gray, with heavy clouds and a strong storm swell that hit the ship on the port quarter and sent it rolling hard on her sides. The cries of the slaves drifted up from the hold, as did the sound and smell of their retching. None of the seamen who delivered the boiled corn mash to the suffering masses made it out of the hold without adding their own vomit to the slick on the floorboards. The first mate, who was officer of the deck, tried to lessen the misery of the slaves by dousing them with buckets of cold seawater. But he only managed to incite them to greater anger and desperation. A few of the hardiest Africans lashed out with their teeth. One sailor lost a chunk of flesh from his forearm. Another emerged in a wail of agony, missing a finger.

The once majestic Baltimore clipper was transformed into a dungeon. Mungo could find no place from the bowsprit to the stern where the noise and stench of human anguish were absent. He tried to block them out, but never did the time come when his stomach felt settled. This, he soon discovered, was the purpose of the casks of rum. The liquor was distributed liberally—consciences and finer feelings were anesthetized.

On the second morning out of Ambriz, before dawn, Mungo was on deck with Tippoo, observing the cook stir the ladles in the coppers as the maize boiled into a mash. The wind had picked up from the day before, cleansing some of the stink that hung around the ship like a cloud of toxic vapor.

A cry rang out from the foremast top: "Sail off the starboard beam."

Mungo whipped out his spyglass and searched the distant whitecaps for the sail. It came into focus: a sloop, hull down over the horizon. Its masts were visible against the pale blue sky, as was the Union Jack fluttering at her stern.

There were not many British men-of-war in these waters, and

Mungo had reason to remember this one. Even at that distance, he recognized her from the harbor at Madeira. HMS *Fantome*. Fairchild's ship.

The news spread through the *Blackhawk* like a fire in the hold, prompting seamen below decks to appear from the hatches for a glimpse of the British ship. Captain Sterling emerged from his cabin and studied the British ship through his own glass.

"There's no way to outrun her, not with our load. If she hails, we'll have to respond."

"She is downwind," said Tippoo. "She will smell what we are carrying."

"Indeed, Mr. Tippoo," Sterling replied, "but we have the law on our side. All he has is the threat of arms, which he cannot use without harming the very slaves he hopes to save."

His mouth tightened. "But ready the guns just in case."

Over the next thirty minutes, the two ships converged until they were so close that Mungo could make out the faces of the British officers lining the port-side rail through his glass. He looked for Fairchild and found him on the fo'c's'le, a spyglass to his eye, staring back at him.

When the sloop and the clipper had closed to within five hundred yards, the *Fantome* lit off one of its guns and shot a ball across the *Blackhawk*'s bow. At such close range, the boom of the cannon crashed over the *Blackhawk* like a breaking wave, rattling eardrums and silencing the cries of the slaves in the hold for a moment. When the echo had faded, the slaves raised their voices and shouted with inspired vigor, hoping that rescue was near.

"*Blackhawk*, this is the HMS *Fantome*," said Captain Townsend through his speaking trumpet. "We are carrying a writ from Her Majesty's government and its allies that entitles us to search and seize any vessel caught trafficking in slaves south of the Equator. Prepare your crew for boarding."

Captain Sterling replied, "*Fantome*, your confidence is misguided. Our papers are in order, and there is no treaty between

America and the British Crown that gives you the right to examine our cargo. You may board, but you cannot search."

Through his glass, Mungo saw Townsend drop his megaphone and lower his cutter. A crew of stout-looking sailors manned the oars. At the back of the boat, he saw Fairchild's telltale haystack of sandy-colored hair poking out from under his uniform hat.

As the boat approached, Sterling spoke to Lanahan and Tippoo, who passed the orders to their subordinates in muted voices. No one made any sudden moves, nor revealed weapons that might be visible from the *Fantome*'s deck. But by the time the naval cutter reached the *Blackhawk*'s ladder, Sterling's crew were prepared for a confrontation.

"Captain Townsend, welcome aboard," said Sterling, greeting the British master on the spar deck, as Mungo and the other officers fanned out behind him. "A pleasure to see you again."

"You would do well to hold your tongue, sir." Townsend surveyed the deck, his eyes righteous with the full dignity and power of the Royal Navy. "Anything you say here will become part of the record at your trial."

Sterling laughed. "You know the limits of your writ. If you wish to inspect our registry, I would be glad to produce it, but it hasn't changed since our last encounter. Beyond that, you have no authority to act."

The British captain replied, "The Congress of your United States has determined that the just penalty for such a loathsome commerce as slavery is death. I do not require a search to ascertain the truth of your crimes. The evidence is manifest to anyone with a tolerable sense of smell. On the authority of Her Britannic Majesty, I am hereby commandeering this ship for passage to New York. As soon as we escort you to safe harbor in your own country, we will deliver you up for prosecution."

The British sailors surrounding Townsend lifted their rifles and pointed them at Captain Sterling. He ignored them.

"By taking up arms against us without lawful authority, you

are committing an act of piracy and war against a vessel of a foreign nation." He waved his hands toward Townsend's men. "Put down your weapons, or whatever guilt you ascribe to us will become your own."

Mungo watched Fairchild. He was the youngest of the officers in the boarding party. He was also the only British officer armed with a sword instead of a rifle. His hand stayed on the handle until the moment his compatriots took aim at Sterling. He drew the sword and pointed it at Mungo. Mungo held still. Sterling's orders were clear. Any provocation the *Blackhawk* offered would give the British justification for reprisal. Negotiation was the better option, unless the *Fantome* compelled them to fight.

Silence gripped the deck as Sterling and Townsend and their men stared each other down. Neither captain was willing to concede. Whoever spoke next would be making an irrevocable choice.

Townsend broke the deadlock.

"Lieutenant Fairchild!" he said. "Take Captain Sterling and his officers into custody and lock them up in the brig. The rest of you, do not resist, or we will subdue you by force. From this moment onward, I am in command."

It was so quick that Mungo barely saw it. One moment there was a glint of polished metal in Tippoo's hands, and the next a knife was buried in Townsend's throat.

Sterling bellowed, "On me, *Blackhawk*!" and rolled behind a heavy chest. The rest of the crew, Mungo included, flung themselves flat on the deck.

A volley of musket fire exploded in their direction. But stunned by the murder of their captain, the British had fired a second too late. The bullets passed harmlessly over the *Blackhawk*'s crew—and now the British guns were empty. That gave the *Blackhawk*'s men time to produce the firearms they had hidden along the deck and take aim at the dense cluster of navy blue coats.

Unlike their enemies, they did not aim too high. The first volley of bullets cut down half the British contingent, sending bodies sprawling across the deck and blood gushing from ragged wounds. The survivors scattered, seeking an enemy to engage. A young seaman beside the capstan took a bullet in the stomach and slumped to the deck. Another ball caught a sailor above the eyes, blowing off the top of his skull. At the same instant, Lieutenant Fairchild plunged his blade into the bosun's side, yanked it loose and drove it through his heart.

Mungo took shelter behind the capstan and drew his Bowie knife. From the corner of his eye, he saw Tippoo pick up a British midshipman and hurl him over the side. The man screamed until the water choked him off. As bullets flew between them, Tippoo grabbed the long pistol the man had dropped and swung it like a mace, clubbing another officer to the deck.

Mungo moved toward Fairchild, skirting the lines at the base of the mainmast. They locked eyes. Mungo launched an attack that the lieutenant parried a moment before a series of blasts rocked the ship.

Somehow, even as battle raged on deck, Tippoo had managed to run out three of the guns and fire them. The sound left Mungo's ears ringing, but he could still hear the carnage they wreaked as the heavy balls crushed the hardened ribs of the *Fantome*. They sheared away swaths of her hull and mangled the sailors that stood in their way. As he listened to the screams, the thought crossed Mungo's mind that Sterling was insane, that the sloop would surely return fire and sink them in three hundred fathoms of water.

As the echo of the cannons died away, his fears were realized. The *Fantome* ran out her guns. Fairchild and Mungo both paused their battle and turned to watch. Light flashed; thunder rolled. Instinctively, every man on deck crouched low, though the *Blackhawk*'s thin bulwarks would be no protection.

But the balls did not strike the hull. The *Fantome* could not risk hitting her own men on the *Blackhawk*'s deck, and her commander would not endanger the slaves below. Instead he aimed high, at the clipper's rigging and masts. A few of the balls caught lines and tackle, but most sailed harmlessly overhead.

By then, Tippoo had driven his crews to reload their own cannon. The *Blackhawk* fired another salvo, and Tippoo had aimed miraculously true. The balls smashed into the sloop's hull, right on the waterline.

Mungo had no time to admire it. For Fairchild, the sight of his beloved ship being torn apart redoubled his anger. His blade swiped through the air, nicking Mungo's forearm.

"You'll not survive this!" cried Fairchild. He had lost his hat; his fair hair blew wild in the wind. "You will die on the gallows!"

Mungo leaped to the side, lunged forward and stabbed with his knife, missing the lieutenant's hip. He saw the wrath in Fairchild's eyes and the power of his hatred in every thrust and swipe of his sword. The two of them traded blow for blow, their feet dancing and their bodies ducking to evade the other's strikes. Although Mungo's blade was shorter, his reflexes were faster than Fairchild's, and his instincts leveled the field.

Suddenly Mungo heard the crackle of canvas above them. Sterling had managed to get men aloft and unfurl the sails. He felt the ship heel over to port and gather speed as she caught the wind. The British sailors still alive on the *Blackhawk* roared their frustration, and Lieutenant Fairchild put all of his strength into a retaliatory slash that might have cut Mungo in two had he not anticipated the move. Instead, the sword took a deep bite out of the starboard railing as Mungo twisted aside.

All Mungo had was his Bowie knife. The smaller blade was no match for the reach of Fairchild's sword, but if he could find the right angle, its maneuverability might yet prove an advantage. Fairchild was determined not to give it to him. Mungo dodged a thrust that speared the air beside the ratlines, evaded a swipe that parted one of the braces securing the royals on the foremast. As the ship plowed through a swell, throwing Fairchild off balance, Mungo took hold of a loose halyard and swung himself over the railing. The lieutenant pursued him furiously, stabbing at the ratlines, but by then Mungo was back on the deck on the far side, and Fairchild had to change direction again.

Mungo realized Fairchild was the last British officer still present on the deck. All of the others had been cut down or chased overboard. Behind Fairchild, the *Blackhawk*'s crew had gathered around Tippoo, their rifles leveled at the lieutenant's back.

"Should we shoot him?" asked Tippoo. "Or will you finish it?"

Fairchild heard the threat. Keeping Mungo at bay with the cutlass, he edged around to see what was happening. When he saw that he was the only Englishman left alive on deck, with his ship foundering and receding in the background, he gave a strangled howl of rage.

"We are not in the Cambridge Union anymore," said Mungo softly. "I do not think you will carry the vote with these men."

In reply, Fairchild swung his sword at Mungo. It was a clumsy stroke, born of impotence and desperation. Mungo dodged it easily. That got him inside Fairchild's guard and gave him the opening he needed. With his Bowie knife, he lashed out at Fairchild's sword arm, cutting his biceps to the bone. He drove his fist into Fairchild's solar plexus and heard the wind explode from his lungs.

Fairchild dropped his blade and doubled over, clutching his bleeding arm. Mungo stood over him.

"What are you waiting for?" Fairchild demanded. "Finish this now. Your soul is already condemned."

Mungo laughed softly. "No doubt you would die with the satisfaction of knowing that everything you think me is true. But we are not animals. We will put you ashore somewhere near the trade routes."

He saw the anguish on Fairchild's bloodied face: a mix of

gratitude for his life, and loathing at the thought of owing it to Mungo. But before Fairchild could decide which would win out, another voice spoke up.

"No." Lanahan strode forward from the knot of sailors. "Do you really suggest we should leave a witness alive? What if he testifies against us?"

"He'll testify that his captain attempted to impound our ship illegally, and we resisted in accordance with our rights," Mungo answered.

"*In accordance with our rights?*" Lanahan echoed. "This Johnny would say anything he could to send us to the gallows." He turned to Sterling. "Surely you won't tolerate this nonsense?"

Fairchild struggled to his feet. He had managed to tug up his shirtsleeve one-handed and bunch it over the wound, but the fabric was already so soaked through that blood oozed out of it. His face was white. Astern, the *Fantome* was already nearly a quarter of a mile away and listing badly to port, the water around her surrounded with debris and all of her boats deployed.

Fairchild spat on the deck and looked around at Sterling and Mungo and the rest of the *Blackhawk*'s crew.

"This is the Devil's ship," he said, "and all of you are cursed men. As God is my witness, I will make you pay for what you have done. Or you can slay me where I stand and perfect your crime."

"That sounds like a fine idea," said Lanahan.

"It would make a martyr of him," Mungo countered.

Lanahan's eyes narrowed. "What made you so soft on him? Man might almost get to thinking you had something in common. Man might wonder about Mr. Thomas Sinclair, who comes aboard this ship, no one knows where from, and so partial to niggers and Navy men."

"I work for the owners of this ship," said Mungo.

All eyes turned to Sterling. The captain said nothing. He took the pistol from his belt and rammed home a small bullet from his ammunition pouch. Very precisely, he fitted a new percussion cap and thumbed back the hammer. When that was done to his satisfaction, he held it out to Mungo.

"Mr. Lanahan has made certain allegations about your loyalties." He spoke in his usual drawl, but there was a black light in his eyes. "I would be obliged if you would prove him wrong."

Mungo stared at the pistol. It seemed to hang in the space between him and Sterling like the sword of Damocles. He had lost count of the laws he had broken since he walked out of the prison in Richmond: jumping bail, dueling, slaving, resisting arrest. None of it troubled him overly much. He had done what he had to do.

But to kill a British officer in cold blood was something different. A line would be crossed; he would be marked forever. Nor was this some anonymous victim he could easily forget. For three years at Cambridge, he and Fairchild had argued and sparred and studied together. They had never been friends, but they had enjoyed a certain familiarity. Now Fairchild was the last vestige of that more innocent world.

Mungo took the pistol from Sterling, turned and leveled it at Fairchild's breast. Fairchild nodded grimly, as if it was no more than he had expected.

"If I lose my life, so be it. It is for a higher cause. But you will forfeit something far more precious."

His blue eyes fixed on Mungo's face, no hint of fear but only defiant resolve.

"You are better than this," Fairchild said softly. "I know there is good in your heart, if you would only uncage it."

Mungo pulled the trigger.

The ship shuddered. The crew, unprepared for the impact, were thrown to the deck. Mungo himself barely kept his footing. He stumbled through the cloud of white smoke that the pistol had left behind and came up hard against the ship's gunwale. He looked out.

The echo of gunfire rumbled across the water. As the air cleared, Mungo saw what had happened. The *Blackhawk*'s helmsman had let her bow drift around a little, giving the *Fantome* a view of her side. The *Fantome*'s captain had accepted the invitation and got off one last desperate broadside to try and keep the *Blackhawk* from escaping. He would have aimed for the rigging, but the *Blackhawk* was too far away. The balls arced down through the air and hit the clipper low in the water, punching holes deep in her hull. Not enough to stop her, Mungo thought, but enough to cause chaos. Sterling stood on deck bellowing orders, sending men below to work the pumps and patch the holes. Others raced aloft to trim the sails, in case the pressure on the hull ruptured the ship more grievously.

In all the confusion, Fairchild stood exactly where he had before—still bleeding from the cut on his arm, but otherwise unhurt. Mungo's shot had gone wide.

Mungo was not the only one who had noticed Fairchild. Lanahan had seen him too. With a snarl of anger, the first mate charged across the deck to finish Fairchild with his cutlass.

Before Lanahan could reach them, Mungo wrapped his arms around Fairchild's chest and hoisted him off the planking. Holding the lieutenant like a disobedient child, Mungo carried him bodily across the deck to the side of the ship.

"Put him down!" Lanahan shouted behind him. "Put him down or I will run you both through!"

"You meant to miss," Fairchild hissed in his ear. "You could not do it."

"You have no idea what I can do."

In a single motion, Mungo lifted Fairchild over the gunwale and heaved him overboard.

Fairchild flailed in the air and landed in the water with a fountain of spray. Mungo wondered if he could swim at all, let alone with one arm badly gashed.

He did not have time to find out. He sensed a movement behind him and turned to see Lanahan rushing at him. The mate's lips were peeled back with fury, his eyes wild and the cutlass raised to strike.

"I knew you were a traitor!" he roared. "Now we've proof!"

Mungo was unarmed. Even if he'd had the means to protect himself, he had no time to react. The last thing he saw was the cutlass swinging at his neck. Then the world went dark.

amilla's baby was born on the third of May. Camilla was in labor for over twenty agonizing hours, the contractions building like a thundercloud until they blotted out the world. But the pushing, when it finally came, was mercifully swift. The midwife—a mulatto woman Chester had shipped up from New Orleans—spread Camilla's legs and probed with her fingers to widen the opening, urging Camilla to bear down. One push and the baby's head appeared; twice and it crowned; the third time and the child tumbled out on a current of blood-tinged fluid with a cry that pierced the night. The midwife cut the cord, cleaned the baby and placed it on Camilla's heaving chest.

"It's a boy," she said. "A firstborn son is a sign of blessing."

Exhausted as she was, Camilla felt relief flow through her. Chester's desire for a son had grown so intense that she had spent the last weeks of her pregnancy alternating between states of prayer and dread. She cradled the child in her arms and kissed his small wet head. She offered him her engorged nipple. She caressed his soft skin as he drew it in, whispering his name.

"Isaac . . . Isaac . . . Isaac."

It was hard to believe that he could be a child of promise. But Camilla wanted so badly to believe it was true. He was Chester's bastard, she couldn't deny it, but he was also her son.

"My blood runs in your veins," she whispered to the child. "I will not let you forget it."

"Rest," the midwife told her. "Call if you need me."

Camilla closed her eyes and slept. Soon, dreams came. She saw a bonfire, the tongues of flame that sent sparks into the sky. She felt the heat on her skin, warming her belly and giving courage to her heart. The bonfire was her friend, as were the souls gathered around it.

A hand tugged at hers. It was a boy about six years of age. His skin was paler than her own, but his proud nose and cheekbones and wide, walnut-colored eyes resembled the face she saw when she looked in the mirror.

There was another presence beyond the fire. A man was standing opposite her, staring into her eyes. Her heartbeat quickened when she saw him. Mungo St. John. His eyes were bright, his mahogany curls framing a striking and serious face. He turned, his expression gentle yet unfathomable.

The song of her dream began with a low hum that collected voices until the sound overflowed into words. She closed her eyes and joined the chorus, swept away by the moment. The words freed her from bondage, dissolving her chains. She listened for Mungo's voice, wondering if he remembered how to sing it, but he didn't open his mouth. He seemed perplexed. She didn't understand. He had always been so sure of himself, so confident of his place in the world. What had happened in his absence? What burdens had he brought with him on his return?

Something was different now. There was a distance between them, a life he had experienced that she could never comprehend. She followed his gaze through the dance of flames to the wizened face sitting at the head of the gathering. The song dropped off and Methuselah spoke, calling them forward as he had when they were children. She went first, holding her son's hand. Her grandfather was ancient now, his once lustrous skin shriveled and his hair white. He laid a bony hand on the boy's glistening head and called him by his name—Isaac. He spoke a prophecy over him.

"Light and darkness are entwined in your blood, opposing destinies that will collide in your youth. A sacrifice they shall demand, and a sacrifice they shall see. There is no other way."

"Yes, great-granddaddy," said the boy, clutching Camilla's hand with all his strength.

Camilla woke with a start. Little Isaac was still nuzzled against her nipple, but he was asleep. She looked out the window, searching the shadows of the night for a way to explain the vision. She began to whisper the Lord's Prayer. She repeated the last petition three times, once for herself, once for the baby in her arms, and once for Mungo St. John.

"Deliver us from evil . . . deliver us from evil . . . deliver us from evil."

Mungo opened his eyes to a headache that made his *geribita*-induced hangover at Ambriz feel like a tap on the shoulder. He was lying in a bunk, but not in his cabin. The smell of blood and lye told him it must be the sickbay.

He touched his skull and felt a thick bandage. It was dry, which was good.

A face peered down at him. Montgomery, the surgeon.

"You're up," he said brusquely. There was none of his usual cheerfulness, and no bedside pleasantries. "The captain said you were to go to him the moment you were awake."

When Mungo went on deck he found a different ship from the clipper that had sailed out of Baltimore. For a start, there was the smell. The slaves had been aboard for a week now, and the stench of so many people packed in chains below decks had permeated the whole ship. But that did not explain the mood of the crew. The faces Mungo passed—friends and shipmates he knew well—were surly and out of sorts. The sails flapped loose; lines lay uncoiled across the deck; there was play in the braces when they should be secured tight. The crew seemed to have lost all sense of discipline. Through the gratings that covered the hatches, Mungo heard the rhythmic squeak and rattle of the chain pumps.

They were alone on the open ocean. The coast of Africa had vanished, and as far as the horizon there was no sign of the *Fantome*. The damage from the battle had been patched up, though the workmanship was poor. Mungo wondered how long he had been unconscious.

"Mr. Sinclair!"

Sterling called him aft to the quarterdeck. Lanahan stood beside him, his face a picture of spite.

"I am glad to see you awake," said Sterling acidly. "I trust you enjoyed your rest. Now, you will answer for your conduct in the battle."

He could have done this in his cabin. Instead, he had chosen to do it on deck in front of all the men.

"If I recall correctly, I dispatched four of the British sailors who were trying to take our ship," Mungo said calmly. "Or it may have been five," he added. "I did not have time to ask for a coroner's verdict."

"You let their lieutenant escape."

"I tried to shoot him through the heart. Every man who was there will stand witness to that."

"You missed on purpose," Lanahan insisted. "You aimed wide at the last moment."

"I shot wide because the ship was hit by a broadside."

"That happened afterward. I saw it all."

"You have confused the matter," said Mungo. "The shock of battle has addled your memory."

"And afterward? Do you deny you threw him into the water so he could escape?"

"I do not deny I threw him in the water."

Lanahan turned to Sterling in triumph. "You see?"

"I was unarmed, the ship was damaged, and we had an enemy officer loose on our deck," Mungo continued. "I decided to remove him by the most immediate method to hand."

"So he could get away."

"Our ship had been hit and I did not know how badly. I feared the *Fantome* might overtake us. I thought if she had to pause to rescue her lieutenant, we would put more clear water between us. In any event, he was badly injured. He probably drowned."

"We saw the *Fantome* haul him out of the water. He appeared to be alive."

Mungo swept his arm across the empty sea behind them.

"And now we have lost her. My plan succeeded." He touched

his arm to his bandaged head. "Not that I seem to have earned much gratitude."

"You are lucky you still have your head," said Sterling drily. He had listened to the whole exchange, eyes fixed on Mungo, like a man puzzling over a book in a foreign language. "Mr. Lanahan would have taken it off your shoulders, if Tippoo had not deflected his arm. You felt the flat of the blade, not the edge."

Mungo sought out Tippoo's bald head in the crowd of seamen around them. The gunner gave him a nod.

"I am obliged."

There was a silence on deck. Lanahan glowered at Mungo, while Sterling stared at the mainmast and thought hard. The crew watched. Few of them liked the first mate, but they liked traitors less. Mungo could see in their faces that Lanahan's accusations had planted doubts, even among men he counted as friends.

Sterling reached his verdict.

"No one who saw Mr. Sinclair fighting in the battle can doubt his loyalty to the ship. As to the officer, it was a piece of quick thinking executed under stress when the ship was in grave danger. That is the end of the matter and I wish to hear no more of it."

He lowered his voice, so that only Mungo and Lanahan could hear.

"This is not the first time I have had to settle differences between my officers, but I trust it will be the last." He fixed his gaze on Mungo. "Do not forget that you are the subordinate here. It is your duty to obey your superiors."

He turned away. "We will have a hard enough time getting our cargo home without quarreling among ourselves."

The truth of those last words became evident when Mungo went below. The carpenters had fortified the damaged hull, taxing the limits of their skill and exhausting all the spare lumber in the hold. The patch they constructed was sufficient to keep out the sea, at least in ordinary weather. But the *Fantome*'s last broadside had snapped ribs and breached joints that were irreparable outside a shipyard. The *Blackhawk* was hobbled; she listed to starboard and lumbered across the waves.

Worse, the hole in the hull aft had allowed seawater into the food store and spoiled much of their supplies. There was barely enough left for quarter rations. The maize mash that was boiled up in the great copper kettles every day had to serve the crew as well as the slaves. Day by day, the men became more insolent and uncooperative. The cat o' nine tails came out of its bag almost every afternoon, but that only made the mood worse.

"I've never seen such sloth in a crew," Lanahan complained in a conference of the officers in Sterling's cabin. "It's as if they're under the influence of a foul spirit."

"It's hard to convince a man to work when his stomach is empty," said Mungo.

"You think I don't know that?" Sterling snapped. "I need you to tell me what to *do* about it."

"We're flogging men who've never given us trouble before," said Mungo. "We can't beat obedience into them. We should try inducements."

Sterling shook his head. "They're already receiving an extra ration of rum. We get them any more drunk, we'll lose control of them."

"We could threaten to withhold their wages," offered Montgomery, the surgeon.

"That would be a quick way to spark a mutiny."

Lanahan leaned forward. "I say we open the hold and let them have their pick of the girls. We'll handle it like they do at the bawdy-houses, all calm and orderly, no drama. It'll be a perk of the forenoon watch. While we're exercising the darkies, the watch crew can go below and have their fun."

"You want me to turn this ship into a brothel?" Sterling said.

"What could it hurt?"

Sterling drummed his fingers on the table, his thick brows furrowed in thought. Mungo could see he was considering it.

"I guess every man here knows how a brothel works," Mungo said. "But there are rules in such places that keep men in line. With this, it'll be an orgy. You let the crew loose below decks and who knows what they'll do. They'll pick favorites and argue over them, and soon enough there'll be violence. We'll end up worse than when we started."

Lanahan gave him a sneering look. "I always said you were soft on niggers."

"I'm soft on anything that turns this voyage to profit, and hard on whatever threatens that. A randy crew thinking with their cocks, and a boatload of beaten-up slave women with bellyfuls of mulatto babies—that does us no good. The Havana traders would rake us over the coals on margin."

For a moment, Mungo thought that his good sense had prevailed. Then the captain locked eyes with him.

"The crew and the cargo are my concerns, Mr. Sinclair. Are you suggesting that I am neglecting my duty?"

"My only concern is for the *Blackhawk*," said Mungo. "She is in a precarious way, and I believe Mr. Lanahan's idea is dangerous."

"These are dangerous times," said Sterling.

"Aye, Captain. But what purpose would it serve to imperil the ship further?"

"Your reservations are noted, Mr. Sinclair, but if this voyage has taught me anything, it is your talent for instilling discipline in the men. I am therefore putting you in charge of this scheme. You have full authority to maintain discipline while the crew take their pleasures with the darkies. Any sailor who transgresses your orders will receive ten lashes with the cat. The same goes for anyone caught quarreling over a lady. Let them have their fun, but let it be orderly. Otherwise, you will answer for it. Is that clear?"

Across the cabin table, Lanahan smirked at Mungo. "Every brothel needs a madam."

Mungo ignored him. He had heard the deeper challenge in Sterling's words. The incident with Fairchild was not forgotten. The captain was testing Mungo, reminding him he had no higher allegiance than obeying his captain's command.

Mungo shrugged, and gave a smile to show he did not care one way or the other.

"Yes, sir."

The crew called them "liberties," the term used during the leave they were granted at every port of call. They took to the idea with enthusiasm; their spirits and their discipline revived quickly.

When it was a man's turn to stand the forenoon watch, he waited for the nod from the helmsman and climbed down the ladder from the main hatch. There, he could browse among the slave decks like a trader in a market, picking out the choicest merchandise—though the stench and the filth did not encourage him to linger. When he had chosen, Mungo would undo the shackles that bound the girl to the big chains that ran all along the deck, leaving the leg manacles on. Then the man would lead or drag her to the alcove outside the magazine, and rape her. Some of the men were particular about the girls they selected, others took the first woman they saw. But the conclusion of the liberties was always the same—a man climbing back up the ladder with a sated smile on his face, and a woman stumbling back naked and weeping.

As Mungo had predicted, the crew developed attachments to the women they favored. Although there were over a hundred women in the hold, the men developed a taste for no more than a dozen of them. Tensions arose when two seamen standing watch together became aware of their mutual preference for a single woman. Seniority sometimes resolved the issue, but a fight often broke out when competing seamen were equal in rank. Mungo disciplined them with the cat but he could do nothing to quiet their raging jealousy. The hold was a primitive place, and the men were quick with their fists.

Mungo tried again to reason with Captain Sterling, to convince him to suspend the liberties for the sake of order.

"It's not just the women," Mungo said. "It's the effect it has on the male slaves." Men and women were kept on separate decks, but the sounds of the sailors taking their pleasure could be heard through the whole ship. "Some are brothers and fathers and cousins of those girls. There is a rage building on the lower deck, and one day it will explode."

"That is why we keep them chained up," said Sterling. "And as for the crew, I have never seen such an improvement in their work rate." He threw Mungo an ironic smile. "You are doing an excellent job."

The *Blackhawk* sailed past Guadeloupe and into the Caribbean, borne by the trade winds. Soon they would reach Cuba. The cargo would be sold, the extra decks broken down, the ship scrubbed clean ready to return to the United States. Mungo would not be sorry when the voyage ended. He had known the slave trade was not a pretty business—and it was a point of pride for him not to shy away from the horrors of the world. Yet the foul reality had been worse than anything he could have imagined.

Deep in his soul, it troubled him that he could not master his feelings. That had always been Oliver St. John's weakness. As much as Mungo loved his father, he had always sworn to himself he would be a better man. *I will not play the hypocrite.*

One more week, he told himself. Then the slaves would be gone and he would have money in his pocket. That was the only thought that gave him any consolation. At night he lay awake, planning how he might get his revenge on Chester Marion.

On a Friday afternoon, Mungo stood in the square of light beneath the hatch and waited for the first man of the day to come for his liberties. He heard heavy boots, catcalls from some of the crew. He knew who it would be even before he descended the ladder: Lanahan.

"Mr. Sinclair," said the first mate when he reached the base of the ladder. "The wheel of fortune has spun in my favor today." He sauntered forward. "Tell me—how many of these blackbirds have you fucked? I bet you've screwed so much pussy you find it hard to get your cock up, am I right?"

Mungo said nothing.

Lanahan laughed. "None? Is that just because you're a nigger lover, or because you're a sodomite as well?"

"If you only came to insult me, I can find another to take your place."

Mungo pointed to a girl that many of the men liked. Before the liberties had started, she'd been beautiful; now she was a husk of a woman, bruised and gaunt. She was perhaps sixteen.

"I've had her," Lanahan complained. He gestured to the knot of women cowering around the hatchway. "I've had all of these. I want something new."

"You'll get something new when we reach Havana."

"But I'll have to pay for that."

"And the more of these girls we keep undamaged, the more money you'll have in your pocket from the sale. It's simple good sense," Mungo explained.

"The captain said we should have our choice of all the girls."

A petulant tone had come into Lanahan's voice, eager for any opportunity to provoke a quarrel and assert his authority. It was an argument Mungo knew he would not win.

"Go and find one you like. Try not to hurt her too much."

The clearance on the decks was so low they had to crawl on all fours like dogs. The slaves were packed so tight together that in the gloom—to the white men—they became almost a single organism, twitching and shuddering and moaning. It was extraordinary for Mungo to think that each groan and motion represented an individual human being.

There were scores for Lanahan to choose from, but Mungo had annoyed him and he wanted to prove a point. He crawled all the way to the back of the hold.

"These should be fresh. No damaged goods back here." He ran his eye over the girls in the light that slanted in through the grating. "This one will do."

He pointed. "Get that chain off her so I can have my fill. Sterling will want me back on deck in a minute."

Mungo hadn't moved. The girl Lanahan had chosen was the one he had noticed coming aboard at Ambriz, with the rounded cheeks and mahogany skin that reminded him so much of Camilla. Although she had been one of the last to board, Mungo had rearranged the stowage so that she was placed at the bow, in the furthest place away from the hatches. None of the men had bothered to go there until now.

"She's not available." Mungo pointed to another woman, with wide hips and heavy breasts. "How about her?"

Lanahan leaned close in. As well as letting the crew have the women, Sterling had made good the shortage of rations with liberal doses of extra rum. Mungo could smell it on the mate's breath.

"She's too fat. This girl's the one I want," Lanahan insisted, with the whiny voice of a child being denied a sweet.

The girl looked between them, eyes wide and white in the gloom. She could not speak English, but she surely understood what the men were saying. Her gaze fell on Mungo, imploring him to save her. Even after six weeks in the hold, her face still bore bruised traces of the trusting innocence that had once been there.

"She's not for you," said Mungo.

"Keeping the best for yourself?" said Lanahan. "Or maybe

you're sweet on this one? Shall I go and tell Sterling you're disobeying his orders?"

Mungo thought for a moment. He knew how it would go. Sterling would support Lanahan, and the girl would suffer the same fate in the end. If anything, it might provoke Lanahan to be rougher with her if he thought it would hurt Mungo.

Mungo did not meet the girl's eye as he undid the lock that fastened her shackles to the heavy chain that all the slaves were bound to. There were only two more days to endure this, he told himself. He released her manacles and moved aside, allowing Lanahan to pull her back to the foot of the ladder. The girl's face trembled with terror; she looked as if she might try to bolt. But she had nowhere to go. There were bodies on all sides of her, the mate behind her, and Mungo blocking the way to the hatch.

Lanahan grabbed her around the waist, laughing, and yanked her by the arm toward the forward part of the hold.

"Looks like no one's had her yet," he said. "I guess I'll get to break her in. She'll be tight as a drum."

He caught Mungo staring at him, his yellow-flecked eyes tinged with something Lanahan had not seen before.

"What?"

Lanahan never knew what hit him. The point of Mungo's knife entered the soft hollow of his throat and cut all the way through to the neck, severing his spinal cord. He fell to the deck with a heavy thump, dead with barely a twitch. The girl was almost as shocked. One moment she was waiting for the next chapter of her ordeal. The next, Lanahan was lying beside her with a knife buried in his neck, and Mungo was looming over her like an avenging spirit.

She was too astonished to scream. She simply stared up at Mungo in terror.

Mungo's mind was already turning with the implications, racing faster than it ever had. He had acted on impulse, surprising even himself with the speed of his strike. Perhaps it had been a mistake—but if he had been minded to regret it, there was no time now. There would be another man waiting his turn after Lanahan, and he would be getting impatient. Mungo had to find a way of hiding the body, and then concoct a story as to why Lanahan had disappeared. If he was caught, Sterling would kill him.

He took the keys from his belt and slotted one into the lock on the chains that shackled the girl's feet. A look of wonder crossed her face as it sprang open.

Mungo pointed forward, to where the sail lockers and storage compartments were located.

"Find somewhere to hide until this has passed."

He had begun to form a plan. He would drag Lanahan's body deep into the slave hold and leave it there. When the first mate was found, it would be assumed that one of the slaves had done it, and impossible to prove which one. One or two might be whipped as punishment, but Sterling could not afford whole-sale retribution. Each life would cost him over a thousand dollars.

A voice came from the deck. "What in God's name is taking so long, Lanahan? Are you having a second run at her?"

Mungo opened the hatch to the lower deck, recoiling at the stench that blew out of it. Below, all he could see was a writhing mass of darkness. He put his arms under Lanahan's shoulders and lifted him, trying not to let any more blood spill on the deck.

The girl hadn't moved. She sat on the deck, still staring up at Mungo. Her face had changed. The last traces of innocence had vanished from her eyes for good; instead there was something hard and brutal there.

She had Mungo's keys in her hand, clutched tight as a child holding her mother's hand. She must have taken them from his belt while he was distracted.

Mungo went still. He let Lanahan's corpse drop to the deck and held out his hand.

"Give them to me."

Shyly, the girl pulled back her arm. Then she lobbed the keys into the air. She had thrown them too hard and Mungo had no time to react. The keys flew past him and dropped through the open hatch to the lower deck where the men were kept.

They never landed. A black hand snatched them out of the air. Mungo lunged down, but he was too late. From down in the darkness, he heard the snap of a lock, the jangle of metal as the keys were passed from hand to hand down the line.

A head popped up through the hatch. It was a fearsome face, a bald skull heavily tattooed with tribal scars. Mungo had noted the man before when the slaves were exercised on deck: tall and broad-chested, with large muscles and a princely bearing that had somehow survived all the humiliations of the voyage. Now that he was free, his face burned with fury. Before Mungo could stop him, he hoisted himself up through the hatch.

Mungo lunged for Lanahan's corpse. But the Bowie knife that had been stuck in the first mate's neck was not there anymore. It was in the girl's hands, and she was no longer cowering on the floor but standing upright, brandishing the blade with the confidence of a warrior. Mungo took a step toward her, and nearly had his arm cut off as the knife sliced through the air. The girl hissed something at him that he could not understand, furious words full of rage and vengeance.

Mungo was caught between two enemies. He looked back at the tattooed warrior. A manacle dangled from his hand, but it was not fastened anymore. The chain that had bound him had now become a weapon. He raised it up, and brought the curved metal cuff down on Mungo's forehead.

Stars exploded in Mungo's vision, and he reeled backward into the bulkhead, collapsing onto the deck. Through the haze of pain, he saw more Africans rising out of the hatch, a flood of black bodies bursting out of the hold and into the blaze of sunlight. He heard the screams of the crew as the freed slaves gained the deck. The Africans were unarmed, but their desperation overturned the odds. They wrestled away the crew's weapons, and turned them on their captors. Sterling's men fought back, but they were no match for the overwhelming tide of the Africans' rage.

Mungo struggled to his feet and stumbled toward the forward ladder outside the magazine. He shoved the fore hatch open and climbed the rungs to the fo'c's'le, his head throbbing as if cleaved with an ax.

He could hardly believe what he had unleashed. In a few short moments, the revolt had turned into a bloodbath. From the capstan to the stern rail, the deck was teeming with Africans—not only the band led by the tattooed warrior, but also the slaves who had been exercising on deck when the uprising began. They hacked with their captured blades until the deck ran slick with gore. The riggers aloft in the yards tried to hide among the sails, but the Africans scaled the ratlines and hunted them down. Bodies plummeted to the deck.

The *Blackhawk* was lost. There were not enough of the crew left alive to retake her, and those few that survived were being winnowed like wheat. Nor did Mungo think the Africans would show him any gratitude for having given them the keys to their chains. His only chance was to escape overboard. But he would not stand much chance alone.

Crouching behind the foremast, Mungo searched the melee for Tippoo. He saw the giant by the capstan, a saber in his hand, fending off more than a dozen Africans. They were having the better of it—the gunner was bleeding from many wounds where his opponents had already managed to land blows.

A cutlass lay on the deck where one of the crew had dropped it. Mungo picked it up, took a breath to gather his wits, then dashed into the fray, knocking slaves aside and carving a path to Tippoo.

"To the boat!" he shouted, waving for the giant to follow.

Tippoo swung his saber in a circular arc, driving all his

adversaries back. He turned to a pot of boiled maize beside him and, with the strength of three men, wrenched it off its foundation, pouring the cornmeal onto the blood-soaked deck. He raised the pot above his head and hurled it forward. The heavy pot felled two men at once, crushing limbs and sending them sprawling to the deck.

With his attackers in chaos, Tippoo cut down two Africans who stood in his way and ran to Mungo. The tattooed warrior tried to pursue, but the pandemonium was too great, and he found himself trapped by the mob.

Normally, a ship carried her boats inboard. But with all the space on deck given over to exercising the slaves, the cutter had been hoisted on the davits at the stern. Mungo was there. He swung at the falls that held the cutter but the blade was too blunt; the rope simply swung away, somewhat frayed but intact.

The Africans had seen what Mungo intended to do. Massing by the capstan, they raised their swords and rushed aft like a swarm of hornets. Mungo had no time to try hacking at the ropes again. Instead, he pulled out the pin that belayed the ropes.

The falls rattled through the blocks of the davits. The boat splashed down into the water. Mungo followed it, vaulting the rail and casting himself into the sea. He hit the water, clawed his way back to the surface and grabbed for the boat, which was already drifting behind the *Blackhawk*. His fingers grazed the gunwale, but he dropped into the trough of a wave and the cutter floated out of reach. He kicked with all his strength, knowing he would drown if he missed the boat. Above, he heard the Africans lined up along the rail jeering at him, peppering the water with belaying pins and anything they could throw to try and impede him. Thankfully, they had not found the powder store—or else they did not know how to use the guns.

The cutter was almost in reach. He kicked forward again. A swell buoyed him up, launching him forward; his hand closed around the transom. He hauled himself on board, just in time to hear a great splash ahead of him. Tippoo had followed him overboard.

But they were not free of the *Blackhawk*. With a jolt, the cutter stopped drifting back and started moving forward again, tipping into the waves side-on. The lines that held her were still attached to the davits, dragging the cutter along behind the ship.

The freedmen had now run out of blunt objects to throw. Instead, they turned their swords into javelins, hurling them toward the cutter twenty feet below. The fall lines were attached to the boat by hooks, but with the boat under tow the ropes were pulled so tight Mungo could not release them. The only way to detach the boat was to cut it free.

He picked up a sword that had landed in the boat and attacked the falls with all his might. The cords were as tough as oak saplings, capable of lifting five tons. He sawed at the heavy fibers, as the swords of the freedmen rained down around him. The wind spoiled their aim, blowing the blades wide, but the Africans discovered the value of pitching the weapons end over end, and their accuracy increased.

Suddenly, Mungo felt the cutter lurch and heard the sharp twang of the aft falls giving way. While he had been busy evading blades, Tippoo had climbed over the transom. One stroke from his blade parted the rear line at once, dropping the stern of the cutter into the sea. As the swells crashed into the boat, shoving it up against the *Blackhawk*'s hull and threatening to capsize it, Mungo scooped up another saber. Wielding the two swords like a pair of shears, he took a massive cut at the forward falls, putting all of his strength into the swing.

With a snap, the ropes split and spun away, and the cutter plunged into the waves. Water poured over the bow and the stern. Mungo threw out his arms to balance the boat. A wave smashed into him; the two cutlasses slipped from his hands and fell in the water, but the cutter stayed upright.

The little boat drifted away from the ship. The Africans let out a great cry. Their revolt had succeeded. Their bonds were broken, and the ship was theirs.

A growl like a wolf sounded behind Mungo. He turned—and though he was not a man to show his emotions, he could not hide his shock. He and Tippoo were not alone in the boat. Sterling had abandoned his ship. He must have thrown himself into the sea and grabbed onto the boat, then climbed aboard while Mungo and Tippoo were distracted freeing the fall lines.

The captain should have died at the hands of the men he had chained like beasts. Yet here he was—bruised, lacerated but alive—standing on the stern thwart watching his command disappear into the distance.

Sterling turned his stiletto eyes on Mungo.

"You did this to me, you son-of-a-bitch. You took my ship from me."

Mungo said nothing. Tippoo looked between the two of them. He pointed to the gash on Mungo's arm where the girl had slashed him with the Bowie knife, the bruises and cuts all over his body where he had run the gauntlet on deck.

"He bleeds like the rest of us."

Sterling grunted. "Anyone lets a pack of wolves loose, he's going to get bitten. Isn't that right?" When Mungo refused to answer, he went on, "The only nigger not in chains was the bitch Lanahan was fucking. What do you think happened, Tippoo? Did Sinclair take a nap? Did the girl overpower a man three times her size? And how did she get hold of the keys?"

Tippoo turned toward Mungo. "Is the captain telling the truth?"

Mungo shrugged. "He's not a captain without a ship."

"There's only one way this is going to end," said Sterling. "I'm going to cut out your heart and feed it to the sharks. And then Tippoo and I are going to bury the rest of you in the sands of Cuba."

He held out his hand to Tippoo, who still held the cutlass he had used to cut the fall lines. "Give me that blade."

Tippoo didn't move. He was looking at Mungo.

"Why did you do it?" he asked.

"Because Lanahan was right," said Sterling. "Because he's nothing but a nigger-loving traitor who doesn't understand the rights and wrongs of the world. Now give me that goddamn sword."

Mungo had lost his knife and there was no other blade in the boat. He was defenseless. Tippoo gazed at the sword in his hand, then gave a nod. He lifted the sword.

With a flick of his wrist, he let it go. It arced through the air and fell into the water point first. The blade barely made a ripple.

Sterling's weathered face contorted in a snarl.

"What in Hell's name are you doing?" he shouted.

"Fair fight," grunted Tippoo.

Sterling stared at him in amazement. Then, with a mocking laugh, he pulled off his sodden coat and shirt and curled his fists.

"So be it. I will do this with my bare hands if I must."

Mungo jumped onto the bench and spread his legs to absorb the motion of the swells. He feigned with a jab, then threw a hook toward Sterling's jaw. The captain avoided the punch and drove his fist into Mungo's ribs. As Mungo reeled and Sterling laughed, Mungo lashed out with a combination of jabs, followed by an uppercut. The jabs caught only air, but the uppercut struck Sterling's cheek at an angle as he tried to twist away. It was a glancing blow but it landed as the cutter pitched on a swell and threw off Sterling's balance. Arms wheeling, the captain fell back against the bench forward of the transom. Mungo closed in, but the captain levered his body against the gunwale and lashed out with his foot, sweeping Mungo's legs from under him.

Mungo landed hard on the thwart, badly bruising his side. As

Sterling scrambled to his feet, Mungo rolled into a crouch and lunged, driving his shoulder into the captain's stomach. The captain fell with a sharp crack, howling in pain and rage. For a fleeting moment, Mungo was certain Sterling's tailbone had broken. But Sterling shook it off and threw himself at Mungo with the speed of a much younger man. Mungo tried to dodge to the side but the captain caught hold of his shirt and spun him around, trapping his arms in a bear hug and arching his back as if trying to snap Mungo in half.

Mungo had always respected the captain's strength but he hadn't fully appreciated it until now. Sterling was as powerful as an ox. Mungo felt his lungs compressing, his ribs grinding, his spine flexing painfully. He tried to throw Sterling backward, but his feet couldn't find purchase. He had only one weapon left—his head. He whipped it backward and felt a burst of blinding pain as his skull collided with Sterling's. The captain howled in agony, but instead of releasing Mungo, he strengthened his grip.

The strain on Mungo's chest made it almost impossible to breathe. His mind raced. He wasn't strong enough to escape the captain's hold. His back was to Sterling, so he couldn't knee him in the groin. His hands hung uselessly at his sides. He tried to stamp on Sterling's feet, but he couldn't see to maneuver himself.

There was only one other force he could harness. As the boat rocked on a wave, Mungo collapsed one of his legs and flexed the other like a spring. With their combined weight suddenly unbalanced, they were pitched over the side before Sterling could react.

As soon as they hit the water, Sterling released Mungo and reached out for the boat, thrashing in the clutch of the waves. With a surge of joy, Mungo realized the captain could not swim.

He grabbed Sterling from behind and wrapped his arm around the captain's neck, dragging him under the surface. As they sank into the depths, Sterling bucked and struggled and clawed at Mungo's face and arm, gouging the skin with his fingernails. But Mungo steeled himself against the pain and held on tight. He pumped all his rage and contempt and loathing into this one single action.

The captain's body went limp and his lips parted, as if to swallow the ocean whole. Mungo released him and watched as he tumbled down into the deep. The water was so clear that Mungo didn't lose sight of him until his burning lungs forced him to move. He took a last look at Sterling's shadow, turned his face upward and swam toward the light.

When he broke the surface, he saw the cutter floating fifty feet away. Tippoo was doing his best to hold the boat stationary, but the swells were strong. Mungo floated on his back, enjoying the cool embrace of the ocean and allowing the sunlight to warm his skin. He swam to the boat and Tippoo hauled him over the transom.

Tippoo took up the oars and dug the blades into the water, pulling them toward the thin scrim of land visible over the south-west horizon. Mungo stretched out across the thwarts, realizing how exhausted he was.

"Your master is dead. You are free," he said to Tippoo.

The giant nodded. His bald face split open in a grin.

"Then why am I still the one rowing?"

II

THE *RAVEN*

Nobody saw Mungo arrive at the large house on the hill above Capitol Square in Richmond. He came after dark, wrapped in a long coat and with a wide-brimmed hat pulled down over his face. It was a wise precaution. The last time he left the city he had been wanted for slave stealing and bail jumping.

He laughed at the irony. Those were the least of the crimes he had committed. It would be a shame if they were the ones that snared him.

The walk up the hill was the last stage of a long voyage. After the loss of the *Blackhawk*, Mungo and Tippoo had rowed to Cuba, then traveled overland to Havana. There they repaired their finances—Mungo with cards, Tippoo with his fists in bare-knuckle prize bouts—until they had enough to buy passage on a French packet ship to New Orleans. More fights, card games and another ship had finally brought them to Baltimore.

The first thing Mungo did when they had landed was go to the courthouse and write out an affidavit that he, Thomas Sinclair and the lawful owner of the slave Tippoo, had manumitted his slave and given him freedom. The courthouse clerk produced a certificate, stamped with a crimson red seal that pleased Tippoo mightily. He ran his finger in circles over the wax, like some totem with magical powers.

"Truly, this makes me free?"

"As free as I am," Mungo assured him.

Tippoo stared at the words on the certificate, though he could not read them. His rough face shone with an almost beatific joy. If you looked closely, you might have seen tears forming at the edge of his eyes—though it would be a brave man to point that out to the bald-headed giant.

He wrapped Mungo in a hug that almost broke his spine.

"Thank you."

Mungo extricated himself from the embrace, smiling at his friend's pleasure.

"But keep the certificate close," he told Tippoo. "Free blacks are not safe in this state. There are any number of men who might want to enslave you again."

Tippoo bared his teeth. He had never lacked strength, but now there was a new confidence inside him that made him doubly formidable.

"Let them try."

Mungo had left him to enjoy his new freedom in the taverns and brothels of Fells Point.

"I will return in a few days," he promised, "but there is a family call I must pay."

Tippoo had flexed his muscles. "I can help?"

"I must do this alone."

Mungo had hired a hack and ridden south to Richmond. He had not sent advance word of his arrival. He wanted honest answers, not well-prepared lies and stonewalls.

Now, he mounted the steps of the big house and knocked. Carter, the white-whiskered butler, opened the door. At the sight of Mungo, he almost spat out his false teeth.

"Mr. Mungo," he stammered. "I didn't . . . Nobody said you was coming."

"No." Mungo pushed past him into the hallway. "Is my grandfather here?"

"Yes, sir."

"I will wait for him in the drawing room."

Nothing had changed since he was last there. Above the marble fireplace, Abigail St. John remained as beautiful and regal as ever in her gilded frame. Mungo poured himself a glass of whiskey from the decanter on the sideboard and tried not to think of all the things that had happened since he last stood in this room.

The creak of a floorboard behind him announced Amos Rutherford's entrance. Mungo put out his hand and his grandfather shook it, yet there was a coldness in the old man's eyes, a calculation that belied his inviting smile.

"I have been waiting these past two months for news from Captain Sterling," Rutherford said without preamble. "What happened to the *Blackhawk*?"

"She sank in a storm off Cuba."

Rutherford took the news impassively. "And Sterling?"

"Drowned. Along with the cargo and every other man."

"I guess you had an extraordinary escape."

There was a strange detachment in Rutherford's tone: neither particularly overjoyed by Mungo's miraculous survival, nor terribly distraught about the loss of his ship. He surveyed Mungo like a piece of merchandise he was examining for defects.

"I had hoped for a warmer welcome from my grandfather," said Mungo.

"Then you should not have brought news that you have lost my ship, and a cargo worth over a quarter of a million dollars."

"You mean the slaves?"

"Yes, of course the slaves," said Rutherford impatiently. "What else?"

"You were not so candid about the *Blackhawk*'s business before I sailed on her."

Rutherford rolled his eyes. "What difference would it have made? You were a fugitive and a felon. I did you a favor, putting you on that ship."

"So I could commit even more crimes?"

"You said you wanted a fortune. Well, that was the trade that made the St. Johns rich. I thought it would be in your blood—though you do not seem to have inherited your family's flair for the business."

Mungo stared. Whatever he had been expecting from Rutherford, it was not this. Everything he had said was an utter surprise.

"My family?"

"Your grandfather, Benjamin St. John."

"My grandfather was a plantation owner, not a slaver."

"Is that what he told you?" Rutherford chuckled. "Benjamin St. John was a practical man. He knew that if you want labor, it is cheaper by far to get it from the source."

"He went to Africa?"

"At the height of his career, Benjamin St. John was the most successful trader north of Charleston. Afterward, when he was rich enough, he used his fortune to buy himself Windemere. Respectability, a conscience. But most of the hands at Windemere, or at least their ancestors, first saw America from the holds of his ships. That old negro you used to keep around, Methuselah? He was the last of them."

Mungo had a sudden vision of Methuselah in the clearing, a dying man hastened to an ugly death by Chester Marion's bullet. He remembered Camilla weeping over her grandfather, and again he thought of the old man's last words: *Beware the black heart, and the thirst that never quenches.*

"Men tell themselves many lies about the world in order to preserve their way of life," Rutherford continued. "Your father's kindliness was his penance, I believe. It allowed him to maintain the illusion of distance from the indignities that made his own father so rich. I have no tolerance for such childish games. I accept that the forcible extraction of Africans from their homeland is not a pretty thing. It is violent. There are deaths. If it were not so unpleasant, there would be no profit in it."

Mungo knocked back his whiskey and stood, walking to the fireplace. He gazed up at the picture of his mother at Windemere, standing on the lawn in front of the house.

"How much did she know about all this?" he asked.

"It was how she met your father. Benjamin and I were in business together; I financed his early ventures. Of course I never shared the details of the trade with her, but there were incidents over the years—ships lost at sea and insurance claims my partners and I had to file. I'm sure she figured it out."

Mungo stared at the portrait. He had never noticed before, but now he saw it: the tobacco crop in the background was ready to harvest, but there were no slaves in the fields. It was a vision of Windemere as Abigail had wanted it to be, perhaps as she really did see it.

Everything he had ever believed about his family had been a lie. Abigail had known. Oliver had known. Mungo had thought he saw the world as it truly was, with none of his father's hypocrisies and evasions. Now he realized how contemptibly blind he had been. He felt as though Rutherford had ripped something out of his soul.

It must have showed on his face. But if he had expected any sympathy from Rutherford, he got none. Rutherford stood by the door, and though the old man was fifty years Mungo's senior and half a head shorter, his face was as unyielding as granite.

"I sent you on the *Blackhawk* to make you a man. I did not think you would come back a sniveling child, weeping over niggers like some kind of abolitionist."

He reached into his pocket and pulled out a creased piece of paper. "Do you know what this is?"

Mungo shook his head.

"It is an item from a Havana newspaper. It reports that a Baltimore clipper was salvaged in some distress two months ago, and on further inspection turned out to be manned entirely by negroes. It seemed they had overpowered the crew, seized the ship and got it in their heads that they would sail her back to Africa." He gave a contemptuous sniff. "Of course, they only ran her aground."

His eyes flicked up and caught Mungo's. "So now that we have dispensed with the fairy tales and the family history, perhaps you can tell me what really happened to the *Blackhawk*."

Mungo stared at him dully. "The slaves escaped and captured the ship. I got away in the cutter."

"So why the story about the storm?"

"I thought if I reported the ship sunk, it would be easier for you to claim the insurance."

"Indeed." Rutherford ran his eyes over Mungo. The coolness in his face had turned to something much darker. "Archibald Sterling was the finest captain in this trade I ever knew. He never lost more than the absolute minimum of his cargo, and in all his voyages I never heard he let any slave lay a finger on one of his men. So you'll understand how I struggle to believe that he somehow grew so careless that he allowed the slaves to escape their chains, gain the deck and slaughter the crew. Every man of them but you."

A taut silence stretched between them.

"Is that an accusation?" said Mungo.

"Sterling kept a tight ship. There was only one man aboard the *Blackhawk* who had not sailed with him before. And now that man comes telling me preposterous stories about what happened to his vessel." Rutherford gave a grim laugh. "I always thought your father's weakness was an aberration. I thought you were better than him, that you had inherited your mother's will and your grandfather's strength. Perhaps I was wrong."

"If you had seen the things I have done—"

Rutherford raised his head suddenly. "Why did you come here? To spin me lies? To beg my forgiveness?"

It was clear from his tone he did not expect an answer to his question. But there was a reason Mungo had come. The shock of Rutherford's revelation had almost driven it from Mungo's mind, but now it flooded back. The one thing that still mattered.

"I came to find out where Chester Marion has gone."

The change of direction caught Rutherford off guard. "Marion?"

"When I asked in Charles City, they said he'd sold Windemere and gone south. Some said it was to Louisiana, New Orleans way, but they did not know where."

Rutherford gazed in disbelief. "You cannot manage a cargo of chained slaves, but you still think you can go against Chester Marion? I would admire your determination, if it was not so laughable."

"Do not tell me what I can or cannot do." A hard edge came into Mungo's voice. "Where is he?"

Rutherford thought for a moment, then shrugged. "Even if I knew, I would not tell you. Instead, I will give you a piece of advice. Forget Chester Marion. He is more powerful than you will ever be. That chapter of your life is finished and nothing will bring it back."

He went to his bureau and pulled out a slip of paper. He wrote on it quickly and signed his name at the bottom.

"I will give you one other thing. Here is a check for one hundred dollars." He waved it at Mungo. "It is the last gift you will ever have from me. Use it to get yourself far away from here, because, by God, if I ever see you again I will have you thrown in jail."

The check was an insult. Mungo had no intention of accepting it. He could make the money easily enough with cards. But as Rutherford waved the paper at him, something caught Mungo's eye. He reached out and took the check, ignoring Rutherford's contemptuous sneer.

"You are just like your father. All you want is easy money."

Mungo did not hear him. He was staring at the check, his hands trembling.

"What is this?" he whispered.

"It is goodbye." Belatedly, Rutherford noticed the change that had come over Mungo. "What? Did you think you deserved more?"

Mungo ran his finger over the letterhead at the top of the paper.

"This is drawn on the Fidelity Trust Bank of Charles City."

"The check is fine, if that's what you're worried about. The bank is good for it." Rutherford chuckled. "I should know—I'm one of the partners."

Mungo gripped the check and slowly ripped it in two. The torn halves fluttered to the floor. Rutherford clicked his tongue impatiently.

"I suppose you think that was a very fine gesture. You will find in time you should have taken the money."

Mungo spoke slowly, controlling the rage that throbbed in his throat.

"That was the bank that repossessed Windemere. It was the bank that Chester Marion used, first to tie my father in a rope of debt, and then to hang him with it. The bank that Chester *owned*. And now you tell me you are a partner in it?"

For the first time that evening, a crack appeared in Rutherford's studied calm. He took a step back, thinking quickly.

"Perhaps you are not as dull-witted as I thought," he said. "Yes, I am a partner in the bank."

"You knew what Chester Marion was doing to Windemere? You let him do it?"

"I *encouraged* him."

For the second time that evening, Mungo's world had been turned upside down. He could hardly credit what he heard.

"Why?"

"Because after Abigail died, I had nothing to tie me to your father. All Oliver's foolish talk of emancipation, his notion of blacks as equals—it was an embarrassment to me. I became a laughing stock among my associates."

"You sold out your own family."

Rutherford made a deprecating gesture with his hands.

"I made a tidy profit from the transaction. Chester drove a hard bargain when he sold Windemere to your neighbors. They were all in on it too, of course."

Mungo's head reeled with the shock of revelation. Every word that Rutherford spoke demanded a thousand more questions.

"Then why did you help me? Why send me on the *Blackhawk*?"

"To save you from yourself. I thought you might make a new life and put all this behind you. I confess, I did not think you would give me quite so much cause to regret my generosity. I never imagined how naïve you truly are." He turned away dismissively. "Just like your father—unwilling to face the dirty reality of life. You—"

He broke off with a strangled cry. Mungo had closed on him and was gripping his neck with both hands, pressing his thumbs against Rutherford's windpipe. Rutherford struggled and tried to pull Mungo's hands away. But though he was strong and fit for his age, he was no match for his grandson.

"You have taken everything from me," Mungo snarled. His yellow eyes burned with fury.

Rutherford managed to lift his leg and stamp on Mungo's foot; for a second Mungo's grip faltered. Rutherford twisted away. He lunged for the bell-pull to summon his servants, but Mungo grabbed the collar of his coat and dragged him back, hurling him down onto the sofa. Pinning him down with his knee, Mungo snatched a cushion and pressed it down on his grand-father's face.

Rutherford struggled and fought; he jerked about, but he could not free himself. His movements grew weaker, the moans under the cushion fainter. Mungo did not relax his grip. His mind was absent, disassociated from his body. He did not notice when Rutherford stopped moving, or the damp patch that spread on the sofa. All he felt was rage.

The chime of the clock in the hall striking eleven brought Mungo back to himself. He lifted up the cushion. Rutherford lay there, eyes closed, showing no sign of the violent death he had suffered.

Quickly, Mungo stretched Rutherford out on the sofa and

laid a rug over him so that it would look as if he was asleep. He threw the pieces of the check on the fire. He folded Rutherford's arms across his chest, and put the empty whiskey glass in the dead man's hand.

He glanced at the bureau. What other secrets might he find in there? He was tempted to look, but at that moment a noise from the hallway reminded him of his danger. He had to get away.

He went out. Carter, the butler, was still standing in the hall, stiff in his frock coat. Mungo searched his face for any sign he had heard what happened. The old slave's features gave nothing away, but then slaves were well used to hiding what they knew.

Carter was the only man who knew Mungo had been there that night.

"Mr. Rutherford is taking a nap," Mungo told him. "He said he wasn't to be disturbed."

Carter nodded. Wordlessly, he opened the door to show Mungo out. As Mungo brushed past him, he thought how easy it would be to break the old man's neck, to end his life just as he had Rutherford's. Then there would be no witnesses to what Mungo had done.

"Goodnight," Mungo said.

He stepped out of the door into the night air. He could not say why he had let Carter live. Perhaps it was mercy—or maybe something in the butler's lined face and white hair had reminded him of Methuselah. After what he had done to his own grandfather, he could not believe it was conscience.

He hoped he would not regret it.

It was nearly midnight. There were no horses to be had at that hour, and Mungo did not dare linger in Richmond until morning. He set out on Baltimore Road, walking at a brisk pace that he could keep up for hours. The moon was high and the way was clear; if any robbers or cutpurses lurked at the roadside, they did not bother him that night. Perhaps they recognized in him the kindred spirit of a murderer. He was left alone with his thoughts.

He felt no guilt about what he had done. Rutherford had betrayed Windemere, he had let Oliver St. John be murdered, and he had bankrolled Chester Marion. Killing him had been the first blow struck for Mungo's revenge. If anything, Mungo felt a strange elation. Everything that had tethered him to the world was gone. Even the memory of his family had been torn down. He felt himself floating free, apart from the world, unrestrained by the considerations that bound lesser men. He felt in his heart there was nothing he was not capable of. The knowledge was liberating, like jumping off a cliff and discovering that you could, after all, fly.

The sun had risen in a soft pink dawn. Mungo was just starting to think about where he might find some breakfast when he felt a shudder in the road under his feet. Horses were approaching at speed. He turned, and saw them already coming around the bend. Half a dozen men in militia uniforms, the brass on their coats gleaming in the morning light.

There was no time to get off the highway and hide. He moved to the verge and stood aside to let them pass. But they did not ride by. Instead, they reined up in front of him. The horses' breath made clouds in the morning; their flanks steamed. They must have ridden hard.

The militia captain leaned forward in his saddle.

"Mungo St. John?"

Mungo nodded. They could not have found him by accident, and there was only one man who could have given the militia his name. He should have killed Carter when he had the chance. Now—against six armed men on horseback—he had no hope of escape.

"What is this?" Mungo asked, as casually as he could.

"We heard you might be on this road. Come with us."

"Is there a reason?"

Did Mungo imagine it, or did the captain's hand creep toward the butt of his pistol?

"It concerns Mr. Amos Rutherford."

"My grandfather?" Mungo's brow furrowed. "I left him a few hours ago. Has anything happened?"

"I cannot say any more at present. You will find out in Richmond."

They had brought a spare horse, so at least Mungo's legs were spared the return journey. He mounted up and rode in silence. What had taken all night to walk needed barely two hours to retrace. They rode into Richmond and back up the hill to the Rutherford house. It was now the middle of the morning, but all the shutters were closed and black crepe hung from the windows.

"What has happened?" said Mungo, acting as if he was surprised. "Who has died?"

"Come inside."

The militia captain ushered Mungo up the steps he had mounted only a few hours earlier. Carter held open the door, giving Mungo a hard, penetrating stare. Mungo returned it with a nod. A slave's testimony would not go far in a Virginia courthouse. But it might be enough to hang him.

Thankfully, they did not take him to the drawing room. Instead, a servant dressed all in black showed Mungo to Rutherford's office. A man was waiting there, sitting at the desk in front of a pile of papers. Mungo did not recognize him. He was a short dumpling of a man, with thinning hair and a drooping mustache. The handshake he gave Mungo was as limp as a dead fish.

"My name is Shelton. I am your grandfather's attorney. Do you know why I have summoned you?"

Mungo had a fair idea. But he had played—and won—enough bad hands in poker to keep bluffing to the end.

"Am I still wanted for bail jumping?"

Shelton's mustache twitched in surprise. "No, sir. Mr. Rutherford had me take care of all that a year ago. The charges of slave stealing were dismissed—and since there were no charges, *ipso facto*, there could be no issue with the bail."

"Then why did you bring me here? And why is the house decked in mourning? Where is my grandfather?"

Shelton looked at him sternly. "You were here last night?"

There was no point denying it. He had already admitted as much to the militia.

"I was."

"Mr. St. John . . ." Shelton clasped his hands together. "I am profoundly sorry to have to tell you this, but sometime after you left, your grandfather passed away."

Mungo bowed his head, as if the news was too much to bear.

"They found him on the couch. We presume he suffered a seizure or a stroke as he lay there."

Mungo's head jerked up so quickly he almost cricked his neck. "A seizure?"

"He had been drinking whiskey. His doctor had warned him of the consequences if he drank liquor, but evidently, he did not heed their advice."

"But . . ." The shock on Mungo's face was entirely real. Inside, his mind raced. "He seemed perfectly well when I left him. He complained he felt a little tightness in his chest—he was going to lie down." He bit his lip. "If only I had stayed longer with him."

Shelton put on his most sympathetic face. "I am sure there was nothing you could have done. The end must have been instantaneous, and surely without pain. Were you close?"

"He was almost all the family I had."

"Of course, of course. My condolences. The loss of a loved one . . ."

Shelton flapped a hand, as if the realm of emotions was entirely beyond his purview. Instead, he hoisted a large black paper-case onto the table.

"It seems callous to talk of business in the hour of your

grief. However, there are certain legal formalities that must be observed."

Mungo nodded. The attorney opened his case and pulled out a sheaf of papers.

"This is Amos Rutherford's last will and testament. He wrote it some years ago, but it is all valid and in order." He put the papers in front of Mungo. "As you can see, he names me as executor. The bulk of his fortune he leaves to his son in Charleston, but there is a significant bequest also to his daughter Abigail."

"She died four years ago," said Mungo.

"Indeed, indeed. But Mr. Rutherford had not updated the will since her tragic death. Therefore, as Abigail's sole heir, the bequest goes to you."

He snapped shut the paper-case.

"I am sorry I had to summon you back so abruptly. Since last August there has been a great deal of uncertainty about your whereabouts. So when the butler said that you had visited with Mr. Rutherford only last night, and that you might still be in the vicinity, I naturally felt I must seize the moment to get hold of you. I apologize if it seemed a little excessive, to send the militia after you, but I felt it was my only recourse."

He fell silent as he noticed Mungo's yellow eyes staring at him. The attorney shifted uneasily, discomfited by their gaze. He fiddled with the latch on his case.

"Is there something else?"

"You mentioned a bequest," said Mungo.

"Indeed, indeed." The lawyer's face brightened again. "Forgive me—perhaps I did not make myself entirely clear."

"What I meant to say is, you are now worth fifty thousand dollars."

For a month, Camilla was treated like a queen. She and Isaac were moved into the second-largest bedroom at Bannerfield. Isaac was given a crib carved from teak by a French cabinet maker from New Orleans, while Camilla spent her nights in the biggest bed she had ever seen. She could stretch out her arms full width and still not touch the sides. At night, she no longer had to fear for the sound of Chester at her door.

The baby was her joy. He had a button nose, and fat legs, and a little bow mouth that was always puckering up in search of the nipple. His skin was the color of almonds. Camilla worried he would be too dark for his father, but Chester proclaimed himself delighted.

"He can pass for a white man," he said. He was less enthralled with Isaac's frizzy black hair: "But we can iron that out when he is older."

Dressmakers came from as far away as Charleston and Savannah with bright bolts of silk and muslin. They sewed these into gowns for the baby, trimmed with lace and gold.

"It is a waste to put such finery on a baby," Camilla fretted. "He will sick up his milk on them and they will be ruined."

"Then we will make more," said Chester. "And you should not complain. You are doing very well out of this yourself."

The seamstresses did not just clothe the baby. They also dressed Camilla, running up beautiful dresses from the same fine cloths, artfully sewn so they could be taken in as her body returned to its natural shape after childbirth.

"What will I do with all these clothes?" Camilla wondered, eyeing herself in the long bedroom mirror. "I cannot wear them to pick cotton."

"You will not be going back to the fields," said Chester. He lay on the bed, eyes half closed, enjoying the sight of her in her finery. The neck was cut very low, accentuating her breasts, which had swelled plump from nursing. "You are destined for greater things. Undress."

Camilla turned away, letting the maid unbutton the gown. She stepped out of it and stood wearing nothing but her shift. She studied her figure in the mirror. She had already shed most of the weight she had put on during her pregnancy, almost back to the slender body she was used to.

"Pack that into a trunk along with the other clothes," Chester ordered the maid.

Camilla looked around. "Are we going somewhere?"

"I am taking you to New Orleans. There are some important men I want you to meet, and you must look your best."

"I did not know."

She tried to smile—she could see he wanted her to be pleased—but inside she was afraid. Amid all the joys of motherhood, she never forgot who she really was. And now that the baby was born, she had lost the only hold she'd had over Chester. If anything, the situation was worse. With Isaac in his power, he could hurt her in ways that whips and hot irons never could.

"Is it wise to go to New Orleans?" she asked. "For the baby, I mean. The air in the city is very foul. There are fevers and fluxes he might catch there."

"Isaac will stay here."

"But who will look after him?"

Chester reached out and pulled the bell-cord. A few moments later, a woman Camilla had never seen before walked in. She had red hair, full hips and a gap-toothed smile when she opened her mouth.

"This is Hattie. She will look after Isaac while we are gone."

Camilla looked at the woman with her crooked teeth and white skin, and wanted to claw her eyes out.

"So soon?"

Isaac started to cry, as if he could sense his mother's distress.

Camilla went to the cradle to comfort him, but Chester stopped her.

"Let Hattie take him. He will have to get used to his new nurse."

Camilla had to watch as the strange woman lifted her baby out of the cradle and pressed him to her large bosom. Isaac's nose twitched at the unfamiliar smell of the nurse's skin. He tipped back his head and began to bawl. The sound almost tore Camilla in two.

"Take him away," said Chester.

Hattie curtsied and waddled out. Camilla bit her lip and forced herself not to cry.

"Good milk," said Chester, watching her go. "He will grow into a strong boy suckling on her."

Camilla said nothing. Staring out the window at the cotton fields, she thought of all the times she had dreamed of flying far away to a place where Chester could not touch her. Now even that gave her no comfort. Isaac had made a bond of flesh and blood between her and Chester, an umbilical link that would keep her tethered to Bannerfield even when she screamed to be free of it.

There was only one man who could free her from this ordeal. But where was he?

Tippoo arched his back and pulled on the oars. With his strength to power her, the little dinghy leaped through the placid water of Baltimore harbor like a mayfly. In the stern, Mungo watched the port glide by: the red brick warehouses that lined the wharves; the chandlers and dry docks and shipyards. Schooners and sloops flitted across the bay, while a squat paddle steamer chugged her way south. Beyond, the spires and civic monuments of the city rose above the skyline.

"If you are so rich now, why can you not pay someone else to row?" Tippoo said. He was teasing—he had barely broken a sweat.

Mungo laughed. "Because I have better things to spend my money on."

He had remained in Richmond for a week after Rutherford's death, just long enough to cash in his inheritance. He did not go to the funeral. He knew it would cause a minor scandal in Richmond society, but he did not care. He was never going back.

He returned to Baltimore and found Tippoo passed out drunk in a brothel, with three whores wondering how to shift him so that the next client could have use of the room. Mungo had helped move the giant to more salubrious accommodation. When he came round, Mungo told him what had happened in Richmond, and the fortune he had inherited.

Tippoo, who had never had more than a few dollars to his name, had taken the news pragmatically.

"You can buy me a drink," was all he had said.

Now Tippoo leaned back on the oars. "When will you tell me why are we here?"

"There is something I want to show you." Mungo looked ahead. "Steer right a little, toward those slips."

"Sometimes I think you only like to watch me row," Tippoo complained. "Do we go all the way to New Orleans?"

The smile faded from Mungo's face as quickly as a cloud covering the sun.

"Not yet."

For the last week, there had only been one thought in his head. Rutherford had helped Chester seize Windemere, disgrace Mungo, murder Oliver and Camilla. Now Rutherford had given Mungo the means to get his revenge.

A small steam launch powered past, not far off their starboard side. Black smoke belched from her funnel, and the clatter of her engine drowned out every other sound. She was an ugly vessel, Mungo thought, a bulldog among the clippers and schooners whose white sails graced the harbor like swans.

The launch's bow wave rocked the little rowing boat.

"I have underestimated Chester at every turn," Mungo said. "I will not make that mistake again."

"Next time, take more guns," said Tippoo.

"I cannot defeat him with brute force alone."

All across the Atlantic and back on the *Blackhawk*, Mungo had had plenty of time to contemplate his revenge. A powerful man like Chester would be well protected—it would not be easy for Mungo to get close enough to put a bullet in him. And even if he could, that would not be enough.

He would repay his debt to Chester in full. Humiliate him, bankrupt him, reveal him to the world for the monster he was. It would not restore Camilla or Oliver; probably he would not even get back Windemere. But it would be justice.

And then he would kill him.

"His wealth is the source of his power. I must wait to move against him until I am rich enough to match him."

"You have fifty thousand dollars," Tippoo reminded him.

Mungo nudged the dinghy a little to starboard. "To a man like Chester, fifty thousand dollars is pocket change. I need half a million at least. A million would be better. So I am going back to Africa."

Tippoo crooked an eyebrow. He said nothing, but the expression on his face spoke eloquently: *You are going slaving again?*

Tippoo had never asked what had happened on the *Blackhawk*—how the slaves had managed to unlock their shackles and take the ship. But the giant was no fool. Mungo had no doubt he had worked out what had happened.

"I do not intend to follow in Sterling's footsteps," Mungo said. "The rewards of the slave trade do not outweigh the risks."

He said it as if it were a simple business calculation, the balance of entries on opposite sides of the ledger. Whatever might be in his head—the stench of the slave decks; the hiss of metal charring branded flesh; the heartbreaking wail of the captives; the look of terror on a young girl's face as she was brought out for Lanahan to debase—his yellow eyes gave no sign of it.

"But there is another cargo that fetches almost as high a profit, with none of the trouble."

Tippoo's face brightened with interest.

"Ivory. Demand is soaring in England—prices are rising. A man who could get his ship to Africa and fill her hold with ivory would make enough money that even Chester Marion would sit up and take notice."

"Then you need a ship."

"Indeed." Mungo grinned. "Look over there."

Tippoo shipped the oars and craned around. They had come out of the harbor basin and downriver a little way, where warehouses and wharves gave way to the shipyards. The slipways were full of ships in various stages of construction, from bareribbed skeletons to fully formed hulls that wanted only a gust of wind to slide into the water. And sitting at anchor in the channel beyond the yards was one ship so recently completed that the paint was still wet on her woodwork.

Even at rest, she seemed to be in motion. Her masts were raked so sharply back that she looked as if she was sailing into a gale. Her hull tapered to a sharp V at her bow that would cut the waves like a knife. Her yards stretched out like wings, wide enough to carry sails beyond all proportion to her size. Even in ballast, her hull sat low to the water.

"Not an ounce of fat on her," said Mungo proudly.

There were no decorative carvings to soften her lines—no figurehead at her bow and no ornament on her stern. Even the rigging had been kept to the minimum needed to handle the ship. Everything had been stripped down to its leanest essentials.

The rowing boat drifted close and bumped against her hull. Mungo reached out and stroked the planking on her hull. His hand came away black with fresh tar.

"She is the one," he murmured. His yellow eyes danced with delight. "She is the one to make our fortunes."

"You will buy her?" said Tippoo.

"I already have. She was commissioned by a cotton merchant. I visited the owner this morning and persuaded him to part with her."

Mungo grabbed the clipper's side ladder and climbed nimbly aboard. Tippoo made the boat fast and followed. Up top, she had a single deck that ran flush from her bowsprit to her stern rail, with as little as possible to clutter her working area.

"Was it hard to make him sell?"

"For what I paid, he will be able to replace her twice over. But she is worth it."

Mungo had brought up a bag from the boat. He pulled a bottle of whiskey from it and two glasses, which he filled to the brim. Tippoo wandered the deck, examining the ship approvingly. There was just one feature that displeased him.

"Only four guns," he observed.

"We do not need more. We will not be fighting off the Royal Navy, or putting down rebellions. Without cannon, we will sail faster and have more capacity for cargo."

Tippoo's face sagged miserably. "If you have no guns, you do not need a gunner."

"No. But I will need a first mate I can trust." Mungo handed him one of the glasses of whiskey. "Will you sign on?"

"Truly?"

At Mungo's offer, Tippoo lit up like a candle. He took the drink from Mungo's hand, knocked it back in one gulp, then hurled the empty glass against the cathead that stuck out from the ship's side. It smashed and fell into the water.

"I accept."

Mungo clasped his hand. "Then your first job is to scour the taverns and whorehouses of Baltimore and find me the finest crew you can muster."

Tippoo grinned. "And if they ask what ship they will join? What name do I say?"

Below the stern rail and the cabin windows, the ship's transom was blank. There was no name painted there yet. But Mungo already knew what it would be. With her dark hull and swooping lines, she put him in mind of a great black bird in flight. A bird that throughout history had been the messenger of the gods, foreboding doom and retribution.

"She is called the *Raven*."

Camilla and Chester set out for New Orleans—not by road, but down the Mississippi River, which flowed like an artery through the heart of Bannerfield. Chester had his own landing where the boats could tie up, and two huge warehouses fronting the river. After the harvest, the buildings had been filled to the rooftops with bales of cotton. Now, they were empty.

Camilla cast one last glance back at the big house on the hill, the monstrous palace that Chester had built. Somewhere inside it, her child was lying in another woman's arms. She felt an ache in her belly, as if the baby had been ripped out of her. Chester had not even let her say goodbye. She had not seen Isaac since the wet nurse carried him out of the bedroom the previous afternoon.

They boarded the steamboat that was to take them to New Orleans. Camilla had been on one of these boats once before, when she arrived at Bannerfield, but it still amazed her. It had no sails, but belched smoke and steam from a pair of chimneys; boilers on her bottom deck roared with the effort of turning the large stern wheel that paddled her through the water. It looked nothing like the boats she had seen on the James River at Windemere. Instead, it appeared more like a giant floating mansion: a flat bottom, a snub bow, and a white superstructure rising three stories from the waterline. It was painted brilliant white, like a plantation house, and decorated with ornate curlicues and columns.

"Do you own this?" she asked.

"There is no money in steamboats," sniffed Chester. "This is the packet line."

The inside was almost more spectacular than the outside. Their stateroom walls were covered in gilt mirrors, with a rich Brussels carpet on the floor and mahogany furniture upholstered in plush red fabric. The bed was wider than a carriage.

Chester sat down on the bed with an expectant leer that instantly made all the splendor of the cabin seem like nothing more than a tawdry brothel.

"It is a day and a half from here to New Orleans. I suppose we will find some way to pass the time."

They broke the voyage overnight, moored up at a landing, and reached New Orleans the following morning. A carriage greeted them at the bustling wharf by the levee and took them past a grand square, surrounded by majestic buildings and dominated by a towering cathedral. The bells rang in the air as they passed. The houses crowded in, their balconies decorated with ironwork and flowering vines. The only exception to the splendor was the smell. It hung around the city's neck like a wreath, blending the fetid stench of horse manure and urine with the sweet scents of tobacco and flowers, hanging moss and loamy earth.

"Welcome to the Crescent City," Chester said. "It's like no place on earth."

His town house was a marvel of imposing Georgian style. Standing three stories tall and fashioned out of red bricks, it cast a colossal shadow across the street, exceeding in height and width all the structures around it. Its gray-blue shutters, ornamental railings etched with fleur-de-lis, and entryway framed by accent windows carried an elegance that softened the sternness of the place.

A butler was waiting for them at the foot of the steps, dressed in a silk waistcoat. He welcomed them with a bow and escorted them from the carriage into a courtyard. Apart from the sand-laid bricks of the carriageway, the enclosure was laid out like a garden, with cast iron benches shaded by fruit trees in blossom, rainbow-colored peonies in window boxes, daffodils in patches of brown earth, and a circular fountain with water trickling from the mouth of a nymph-like creature.

The butler handed Chester a snifter filled with golden liquid.

"Brandy and bitters," Chester said, sipping it. He waved his hand at Camilla's curiosity. "Look around, look around. You will know it well soon enough."

Concealing her discomfort, Camilla went inside. She wandered through the rooms and halls, casting her eyes across the artwork—mostly martial scenes on land and sea—running her hands over the lines and weaves of the furniture, taking in the view of the carriageway and courtyard, and reading the spines of books in the library. Every surface was spotless, every piece carefully arranged. Yet for all its refinement, the place was empty and joyless. It felt as if someone had died there. When she felt Chester's touch on her shoulder, she almost jumped with fright.

"This is your new home," he said.

She blinked. "I don't understand. When are we returning to Bannerfield?"

Chester wrapped his arm around her and kissed her.

"You have given me a healthy son and this is your reward. No more labor in the fields. You will live like a duchess in this city, with liberties you could not dream of at Bannerfield. I will give you servants, and money to spend, and the freedom to come and go as you please."

She noticed he kept saying *you*. "Are you not staying?"

"I will visit often enough. My business regularly brings me to New Orleans. You will not have the chance to miss me too much." He smiled; a shiver of pain throbbed between Camilla's legs. "But Bannerfield demands the greater part of my time."

She hardly heard him. "What about Isaac?"

"He will stay at Bannerfield, of course." Chester looked surprised by the question. "The air in New Orleans is not wholesome for a child. He needs air and space to run around, and a father's firm hand to guide his growth. Also, I would not want this city corrupting his young mind with harmful ideas."

Camilla understood exactly what he meant. In New Orleans, blacks and whites mixed like nowhere else in the country. The color line was—if not exactly erased—at least blurred. Chester did not want Isaac growing up in a place where he might think that blacks and whites could be equal.

He is a colored boy, she wanted to scream. *He has as much of me in him as of you.*

But she knew if she said it, Chester would beat her. He might even kill her. He had decided that Isaac would be raised as a white child, and he would not allow anything that threatened that lie. No doubt that was why he had exiled her to New Orleans.

She wanted to curl into a ball and cry. But Chester had not finished with her yet.

"While you are here, you will play the part of a *femme de couleur libre*—a free woman of color. Also, I will expect you to . . . ah . . . *entertain* certain business associates of mine. Granville will stay to keep an eye on you. If you please me, I may allow you to return to Bannerfield on occasion to visit Isaac."

What "entertaining" meant became clear their second night in New Orleans, when Chester held a dinner. The table gleamed with silver and crystal; every servant in the house was enlisted to bring in an endless parade of wines and dishes. The unfamiliar food, rich and spicy, turned Camilla's stomach. It felt wrong to sit at the table being waited on like a white woman. She felt like one of the fish on the table in front of her, pulled out of the water to be gutted, richly dressed and served up for other men to enjoy.

But she was not the only woman of color at the table. All Chester's friends had brought women with them, ranging in hue from delicate ivory to dark coffee. These were not slaves—the men called them "*placées*." It seemed to mean something more than a concubine, but rather less than a wife.

Whatever they were, the women appeared well at ease with their situation. They ate and drank with gusto, laughed freely and teased each other constantly. They spoke confidently: about the latest fashions and dances; about the news from Paris and London; about the political situation in Washington and relations with Mexico. In their company, Camilla felt dull and wooden. Her skin was too dark, her manners untutored and she had nothing to say. She stared at her plate and ate too quickly.

Not all of the guests had brought partners. The man seated next to Camilla had come alone. He had a high forehead, and long sideburns that he had shaved to rakish points near the corners of his mouth. His eyes never stayed still, she noticed, but darted all over the table as if constantly looking for an opportunity.

"Are you recently arrived in New Orleans?" he asked Camilla.

She nodded, concentrating on not spilling soup down the front of her silk dress.

"My name is François," he introduced himself.

"Do you work for Chester?" she asked.

François smiled. "I think every man in this room works for Chester Marion, after a fashion," he said. "Chester's wealth is a great river, and we tend the fields that line it. When the river is so full it breaks its banks, we are ready to receive the overflow—and when the flood waters recede, we trust it will leave some residual deposits to make our own fortunes grow."

"I do not think I understand," said Camilla.

François leaned closer. His hand dropped from the table and rested on her thigh.

"Let me explain. That man over there, with the magnificent beard? His name is Jackson, and he is the president of the Bank of New Orleans. You would say he is one of the most powerful and influential men in the city. Yet he has extended Chester Marion over two million dollars in credit. If Chester were ever to default, his bank would be finished. So he must give Chester whatever he wants, to ensure that Chester's fortune increases and the bank's loans are repaid."

His hand slid further up Camilla's thigh. Camilla pretended not to notice.

"Or that man there, with the pointed chin and the long face like a basset hound. His name is Shaw—he is the commission agent for a Liverpool shipping firm. If anything happens to Chester's estate—if his fields catch fire, or his crop fails, or the ship carrying his cotton to market sinks—there will be nothing for Shaw to buy, no commission for him to earn and he will be ruined."

Camilla's head was swimming with all this information. Perhaps it was the wine. She had drunk far too much of it, trying to feel less awkward.

"You seem very well informed about Chester's affairs," she said. "What is your own business?"

"I own a factorage house."

"What is that?"

"I buy and sell things on behalf of my clients. The greater part of my business is with Chester Marion."

"Can he not buy them himself?" Camilla asked.

François seemed offended by the question. "He might try—but what would be the benefit? It would take all the time he has, and even then he would not be able to negotiate the prices I can get for him. It takes a million individual items to make a plantation productive—everything from seed for the fields and twine for the cotton bales, to a pianoforte in the big house. I purchase everything on Chester's behalf, and arrange for it to be shipped to Bannerfield. And when the harvest is in, I arrange for that to be sold for the most advantageous price, and shipped on to England."

Finally, Camilla realized who she was speaking to. She had heard Chester talking about his factor, in those long nights when she tried to distract him by talking about his affairs.

"You are de Villiers," she said.

He bowed. "François de Villiers, indeed."

"Chester often mentions your name."

He gave a self-deprecating laugh. "Only positively, I hope."

Usually, it was cursing him as a thief and a Jew who overpaid with Chester's money and then took an exorbitant commission. But Camilla did not think Chester wanted her to say it.

"He places all his trust in you," she said with a smile.

The dinner was over. The men rose to retire to the saloon, but François did not join them. Instead, he offered his hand to Camilla.

"The air in here is terribly close and I fear cigar smoke would give me a headache. Shall we go for a stroll?"

Camilla glanced across the room at Chester. He was deep in conversation with another man—the banker named Jackson—but his eyes missed nothing. He gave Camilla a small nod.

"I would like that," said Camilla.

The evening air was warm, scented with the flowers that hung off the wrought-iron balconies of the houses they passed. François escorted Camilla along Rue Bourbon and down to the levee, where they could see the vast panorama of ships moored in the river. He prattled on about the city and his affairs, and as he did his hand slipped lower down Camilla's back until it rested on her buttocks.

They stopped outside an elegant town house. New to the city, Camilla had lost all sense of direction and did not know where she was.

"My home," said François. He turned to face her, his arm holding her close. "Would you care to come in?"

Camilla hesitated. She had no doubt what would be expected from her if she went in.

"I do not know the customs in New Orleans," she prevaricated.

"I am sure Chester would not object," he said.

Camilla was not certain. Chester had told her to entertain his associates, and he had dressed her to show off her body. But had he really intended this?

She was a slave; François was white. She had no choice. François held the door open for her, the front of his trousers already bulging with anticipation.

She went in.

She woke next morning and did not know where she was. Then she felt François beside her, his hand squeezing her breast and his erect penis rubbing against her naked thigh.

Camilla shuddered. It was only a month since she had given birth. Her tender flesh was still healing, and de Villiers's attentions from the night before had left her aching inside. But of course she could not refuse him.

"What time is it?" she asked.

"What does it matter?"

"I should return to Chester."

"And I should go to work," he said. "I have a meeting with him this afternoon, and there are a great many papers to prepare." He rolled over on top of her. "But there is still time for this."

Almost without thinking, Camilla fell back on the tactic she had used so often with Chester.

"You must be very successful in your business. Chester thinks very highly of you."

François lifted himself up so he could look her in the face.

"I buy cheaply and sell dearly. It is not so complicated. The trick—my talent—is knowing how much a man is willing to pay."

The conversation did not interest Camilla. But she could see de Villiers's erection wilting as his mind turned itself to business. It was worth prolonging the conversation.

"Surely your customers are willing to pay what you charge."

He stroked her cheek. "My little negress, you would not understand. In any transaction, there are two prices that matter. What the seller is willing to accept, and what the buyer is willing to pay. My job is to find the most advantageous price."

Camilla furrowed her brow, feigning confusion.

"Let me give you an example. This morning, I am going to broker the sale of two hundred acres of land to Chester. I happen to know that the seller will take four thousand dollars an acre for it—but I also know that Chester can make a profit even if he pays seven thousand. I receive a commission as a percentage of the final price, so my job is to push him as close to seven thousand as possible, without him feeling I have taken advantage. That is why I am rich."

He chuckled. "I probably should not be telling that to you. But I suppose you do not understand a word I am saying."

Camilla gave him a blank smile. Not for the first time, she marveled at what white people would say in front of black people.

De Villiers ran his eyes over her once again. "You are far too beautiful to worry your head with business." He reached his arm around her and squeezed her buttocks. "I have told you my talents. Now it is time for you to show me yours again."

Camilla tensed. But at that moment, as if God had heard her silent plea, a riot of bells began to ring outside the window as all the churches in the city struck the hour. François frowned.

"Is that the time already? Alas, I should have liked to spend more time with you. But . . . business calls. I trust I will see you again soon?"

"I would like that," said Camilla.

She had hoped she would not be noticed returning home, but the moment she went inside the house on Rue Royale she heard Chester's voice bellowing, "Where is that little whore?"

The doorman gave her a pitiless look and ushered her into

the lounge. Chester was waiting for her, standing by the window smoking a cigar. The sight of it made the scars on her arm ache.

"Where have you been?" Chester demanded.

Camilla was still in her evening gown. Every pore of her body seemed to reek of wine and sex. Yet what could she say that would not drive Chester into a rage?

Silence was no safer. The vein on Chester's forehead pulsed with anger.

"Granville followed you last night. He said you went to de Villiers's house."

There was no point lying.

"I did."

"You stayed the night?"

"Yes."

"You fucked him?"

Even after everything Chester had done to her, the baldness of the question still shocked her. She blushed with shame. All she could do was nod.

The answer did not please Chester.

"I do not know if it was your ignorance, your stupidity or simply the lustfulness of your race. I brought you here to be a hostess, to charm my associates—not to play the whore. You have humiliated me."

"I thought it was what you wanted."

The answer seemed to enrage Chester even more.

"You are my property," he hissed. "Other men may look at you and admire you—they may even touch you. But they should never think they can possess you. Now they know how easily you can be had, you are worthless to me."

He rang the bell. Granville appeared at once.

"Take her down to the St. Louis Hotel and put her up for sale. Take whatever you can get, it does not matter how much. She has no value now."

It was so sudden; Granville had grabbed Camilla's arms before she even understood what Chester had said. She could hardly think with the wine from the night before throbbing in her head, with lack of sleep, with the deep pain between her legs. But one thing she saw clearly. If Chester sold her, she might be taken anywhere. She would never see Isaac again.

"Four thousand!" she cried, struggling against Granville.

Chester stared at her. "Four thousand what?"

"The land you are buying from de Villiers," she stammered. "The man who is selling will take four thousand dollars an acre."

Chester took five paces across the room, coming so close to her that spittle sprayed her face.

"How do you know that? How could you *possibly* know?"

"François told me. After we had . . ." She bit her lip. "He wanted to show how clever he was. He thought I was too stupid to understand."

Chester turned away. He stared out of the window, his mind busy.

"I was going to offer six thousand," he muttered. "And I was willing to go higher. If what you say is true, you have just saved me tens of thousands of dollars."

He swung around. "You should not have gone with François. What you did with him, it has displeased me very much."

Camilla remembered François's hand between her legs at dinner. She thought of the way the other women displayed themselves— their low-cut dresses, pouting, painted mouths and rouged cheeks. What was the difference?

"But . . ." Chester had not finished. "In your wantonness, you seem to have stumbled upon something of value."

Granville was still holding her arms as tightly as ever.

"Shall I take her to the St. Louis?" he growled.

"No." Chester looked Camilla up and down, her disheveled dress and unkempt hair and the make-up streaked over her face. "Go to your room and clean up," he told her. "I must go to a meeting with François. If what you have said turns out to be true, then maybe there is profit in keeping you after all."

He returned a few hours later and came up to her room in fine spirits.

"Four and a half thousand an acre!" he exulted. "You should have seen the look on François's face."

"Not four thousand?"

Camilla had never known Chester pass up the possibility of profit.

Chester stroked her cheek.

"My innocent little bird. If I had pushed it to the limit, François would have guessed I had inside information. He would have suspected you. At four and a half thousand, it does not occur to him what he told a black girl in bed. He puts it down to my hard bargaining instead."

Still Camilla was not certain what it meant.

"So I can stay?"

Chester looked surprised by the question. "Of course. I will send the chambermaid up presently to get you ready for this evening. I am hosting another dinner before I return to Bannerfield. François will be there, and I want you to pay him plenty of attention."

Camilla nodded, wondering if this new chapter of her life might not be even more of an ordeal than before. She felt no regret. She would suffer anything not to lose Isaac.

"And get some sleep," Chester added with an unpleasant smile. "From now on, I think you will be kept busy at night."

Commanding the *Raven* was like going to sea for the first time again. Mungo felt the same exhilaration, the same wild sense of freedom—only now it was all his own. He stood by the mainmast, his face dashed by the spray that came over her bow, feeling the ship surge beneath his feet on the wide ocean. He tipped back his head and laughed with delight.

Before he left, he had written a letter to Chester Marion. It had been brief and to the point. Not knowing where to send it, he had addressed it simply to *Chester Marion, New Orleans*. If Chester was as powerful as Rutherford had made out, it would surely find him. Mungo did not suppose it would make much difference—but he wanted Chester to know that he had not forgotten him while he was away on his long voyage.

Of course, the *Raven* was not perfect. She was a new ship, untested and unscarred; there were a thousand details that needed to be put right. Her rigging slackened and had to be made taut; her seams opened and needed caulking. Inch by inch, they tightened her up; they sanded, spliced, painted and polished until she flew through the water at the slightest breath of wind.

The same went for the men. In Baltimore, Mungo had taken on a whole new crew. He could not judge their competence as seamen until they went to sea, so instead he took the most hard-bitten, battle-scarred men they could find. All across the Atlantic he drove them hard, cursing and cajoling them into a well-disciplined unit who jumped to obey his orders.

They called at Prince's Island, though Mungo did not go ashore.

"The last time I was here, I killed the governor's son," he reminded Tippoo. "It is not the sort of thing the authorities are liable to forget."

Instead, he sent Tippoo to find out what he could.

"There is a new governor," the giant reported back. "Da Cruz died of a fever."

"And his daughter, Isabel? Is she on the island?"

Mungo tried to keep the interest from his voice, but he did not fool Tippoo. The mate bared his teeth in a grin.

"I think you want to know that. I ask, but she is not here. They say she moves to New Orleans."

Mungo's memories of New Orleans amounted to little more than taverns and brothels, and Creole women dressed in a riot of colors.

"I'm sure she will thrive there."

He was annoyed with himself how disappointed he was that Isabel was gone.

You are not some lovelorn adolescent mooning over his first sight of a girl's boobies, he told himself.

"There is more," Tippoo went on. "The English officer we fight against? The man you throw off the ship?"

Mungo was jerked back from his memories of Isabel. "Fairchild?"

"He lives. I think you make him a hero. He has his own ship now, the *Maeander*. He is in these waters. He call at Prince's Island two weeks ago."

Mungo swore. "Fairchild has the right to come aboard any ship he encounters. If he finds us, it will count for nothing that we are engaged in lawful commerce now. He will not rest until he has us both in irons."

"Then best to keep away from him."

"His ship will be patrolling off the coast. We will plot a course well west of there." Mungo thought for a moment, his yellow eyes gazing into the far distance. "And see if you can buy any guns before we leave."

As soon as they departed Prince's Island, Mungo doubled the lookouts at the masthead. They sighted dozens of ships in the waters south of Cape Verde, but most were miles away, and only a few came close enough to hail. They kept special watch for the red, white and blue of the Royal Navy ensigns. Once, they sighted a double-masted ship lying hull down over the horizon to the east, with what looked like a red naval ensign at her stern. But it vanished into the haze, and they did not see her again.

They put in at Cape Town for supplies. In a tavern by the waterfront, Mungo found a weather-beaten Dutchman, a hunter. A bargain was arranged—an excessive quantity of gin in exchange for everything the man knew about elephants.

"Can they be killed with a bullet?" Mungo wanted to know.

The old hunter leaned forward, slurring his words from the alcohol.

"Of course," he said, "but it ain't easy. There's a spot on the neck, a hollow behind the ear about two thirds of the way down. That's where to aim for."

By the time they had finished, Mungo had a first-class education on the subject of hunting elephants—and the hunter was snoring face down in a pool of gin on the table.

From Cape Town, the *Raven* doubled the tip of Africa and turned north-east. Mungo had heard many tales of the terrible storms that mariners often encountered around the Cape, but the weather stayed fair and kind, as if fate herself were smiling on his venture. They passed without difficulty. There, at last, he could relax a little. Fairchild's ship was part of the Western Preventative Squadron—he would not enter the Indian Ocean.

They followed the coast, keeping a wary distance. For hundreds of miles the shore rose in steep shelving cliffs, waiting like black teeth to snap up any ship that strayed too close. They saw nowhere to land, and Mungo did not dare go too close for fear of the wild currents and unpredictable winds that swirled around them.

Further on, the cliffs shrank down to a low shore of mangrove swamps and golden beaches. Even these were not so placid as they looked. Sometimes, Mungo would see the bleached ribs of wrecked ships poking up through the sand, evidence of the dangers that still lurked beneath the blue waves.

They sailed past the settlements at Durban and Delagoa Bay, and on into the Mozambique Channel. Still they could not find a place to land. Mungo wanted to avoid the established ports, where the ivory trade was controlled by middlemen and prices would be inflated; he was looking for somewhere they could land unobserved. But the further north they went, the closer they came to the more inhabited parts of the Swahili coast.

"This is near your part of the world, is it not?" Mungo said to Tippoo.

For all they had done together, the times they had saved each other's lives, he still knew almost nothing of the mate's life before the *Blackhawk*. Tippoo never mentioned it, and Mungo knew better than to ask. Yet here in the Indian Ocean, he was reminded of something Sterling had said: *I won him in a card game in Zanzibar*.

Mungo pointed to the chart spread out by the binnacle, where the island of Zanzibar was marked.

"Is that your home?"

He did not really expect Tippoo to answer. But perhaps being in these waters, so close to his past, had shaken something loose in the giant. Instead of changing the subject, he stared out over the rail and said, "Yes, Sterling won me in a card game. But my father was a king."

It sounded like a preposterous boast, but Mungo did not laugh. There was something in Tippoo's proud bearing that made it seem strangely plausible.

"The king of Zanzibar?"

"The Sultan of Oman. Zanzibar is part of his kingdom."

"Then you are royalty."

Tippoo shook his head. "My mother was a slave girl. A man cannot be half-free. So I was a slave."

"How did Sterling find you?"

"He came to Zanzibar to speak to my father. America sent him to tell my father to sign a treaty against the British. Sterling saw my mother and asked if he can buy her. My father offered him a bet. They play cards. If Sterling wins, he takes my mother. If he loses, he takes me."

It was impossible not to sympathize—to be wagered against your own mother in a card game, knowing one way or another you would be torn apart.

"Sterling was a real son-of-a-bitch."

Tippoo shrugged philosophically. "I was a slave. And if I not go with Sterling, I not find you. Not find you, not be free now."

"That is true."

Mungo could see that Tippoo was growing uncomfortable with the conversation. He had revealed more about himself in the past few minutes than he had perhaps to anyone since leaving Zanzibar. Mungo gave him a reassuring grin.

"With any luck, by the time you have finished this voyage you will be richer than a king."

That was a hollow piece of bravado. Every day decreased the chances they would find somewhere to land. All the men knew it. The mood on the ship grew sullen; Mungo became snappish and short-tempered. And still the continent of Africa denied him.

One day, they came to a bay lined with reed banks. Mungo examined them with his telescope, but there was no break in them as far as the eye could see. It would have been another disappointment—except he had hardly any hopes left to dash.

"We will not get in that way."

Virgil Henderson, the bosun, stirred himself. For some time

he had been studying the shore; now he turned and said in his Georgia drawl, "Looks a lot to me like the Sea Islands back home."

"What of it?" asked Mungo.

"From a ways off, those swamps seems like a solid wall. But close in, you find there's river mouths you never guessed would be there."

There was nothing to lose.

"Lower the boat," Mungo ordered.

They took the cutter in to shore. Henderson had been right: going closer, they saw mazy channels opening up, so tight and circuitous that they vanished among the reeds. Mungo chose the largest, and steered the cutter in. Hope rose in his heart, more than he had felt for days.

It did not last long. After a few bends, the channel split into half a dozen little rivulets too narrow even for a canoe. They retraced their course and tried another one of the inlets. That too yielded nothing. The men sweated on their oars under the hot sun; the moment they paused, flies swarmed off the reeds and attacked them.

"Even if there is a way through, we will never find it this way," said Mungo.

Henderson leaned over the side and scooped up a handful of water. He tipped it in his mouth, then hastily spat it out with a sour face.

"Salt."

"What did you expect?"

"Water should be sweeter where the river flows out." He looked around. The reeds about them were deep in the sea, waving gently in the water as the current ebbed and flowed. "Tide's high. When it goes out, we might be able to find where the river is."

They waited. As the tide receded, the reeds seemed to rise

out of the water. Some of the channels dried up; others, deeper, remained in a delicate skein of shining water between the mud-banks. Long-legged birds emerged wading through the shallows, while insects skittered across the mud.

Mungo took the cutter to the deeper water, studying the glassy surface for any ripple that would betray a current.

"There."

It was not much—barely a pucker on the face of the bay. But when they rowed over to it, and Mungo put his hand in the water, he felt the pressure of a current on the back of his hand.

He tested the water, as Henderson had. It was much less salty than the sea.

"There must be a river near here."

They followed the current as best they could, navigating around clumps of reeds and mudbanks that blocked their way. Sometimes the channel was so shallow they had to get out and haul the boat across. Soon all the men were plastered with filth, stinking to high heaven. But always there was a trickle of water leading them on.

"If there is a river, it cannot be more than a brook," Mungo muttered, heaving the heavy boat forward over the sucking mud.

With a splash, the bow tipped forward and slid down into deep water again. Mungo had been so busy concentrating on his task, he had lost sight of his surroundings. Now he looked up, and his spirits leaped. They had come through the swamp, and were looking into a broad lake behind it. In the distance, the unmistakable course of a great brown river led lazily into the interior.

The men gave a cheer. They piled back into the cutter, smearing her thwarts with mud, and took up their oars with new strength. Once they were out in clear water, Mungo hoisted the sail so that the men could rest. They marveled at their new surroundings, while Mungo steered into the river mouth.

"If we could get the *Raven* through the swamp, I reckon we could bring her up here as easy as the Patapsco River in Maryland," he said.

He studied the riverbanks, which teemed with wildlife: deer and antelope in herds of thousands; crocodiles basking on the mud; brightly feathered birds squawking from the trees. There was no sign of human habitation.

A fierce joy rose in Mungo's heart. The fates had tested his resolve, but he had come through.

"This is where we will make our fortunes," he declared, to more cheers from the men.

As the sun sank, they turned back downriver to return to the *Raven*. By now, the tide was flooding in again, making their passage through the marshes much easier. They dropped buoys to mark the approach so they could find their way back, and put a man in the bow to take soundings with the lead line. As Mungo had suspected, at high tide there would be just enough draft for the *Raven* to slip through the channel into the river estuary.

That night, he broached a cask of rum and let the men celebrate. The next morning, nursing their hangovers, they worked the *Raven* through the reeds and into the river delta. Nosing cautiously upriver, Mungo was pleased to find they could sail several miles inland before the water grew too shallow. They anchored in the stream, went ashore and set a rough camp in the shade of some high-spreading trees. The first thing Mungo had them do was to rig a furnace where they could cast bullets. The reason for it became clear when they unloaded a huge case that had been stowed in the weapons locker, so heavy it took three men to carry. Mungo summoned Tippoo and flung it open. The smell of gun oil wafted out. The giant stared in wonder.

"*Jenna al-mootfah*," he murmured in Arabic. He lifted out the biggest gun any man there had ever seen. Its barrel was so wide you could fit a plum down it. "Did a rifle mate with a cannon?"

"I had it custom-made in Baltimore," said Mungo.

He had had no idea what it might take to bring down an elephant, and neither did the gunsmith. Mungo had told him to err on the side of caution, and the gunsmith had embraced his instructions with enthusiasm. The gun was a smooth-bore monstrosity that could take a quarter-pound ball and ten drachms of the strongest powder. The gunsmith had nicknamed it "Goliath."

Tippoo lifted it out of the box and cradled it in his arms. The weight made even his biceps swell with the effort.

"And what do you use?"

Mungo took another gun out of the chest. Set beside Tippoo's weapon it looked as slender as a beanpole, but that was misleading. It was a double-barreled gun, Damascus steel, smooth-bored so that the oversized balls would not be slowed by the rifling. The bullets were smaller than the Goliath gun's, but with a narrower muzzle and a strong powder charge they should fire with more power. Mungo hoped it would be enough to penetrate the elephants' thick hides.

There were guns for the rest of the men too, the latest Hall rifles with breech-loading mechanisms and percussion caps instead of flintlocks. Mungo was not sure how much damage they would do, but at least the men would be able to reload quickly. Perhaps with rapid fire they could make sufficient small wounds to bring down an animal, or at least enough noise to scare it away.

For a week, the men practiced their shooting on the herds of game they found everywhere around them. The sailors were unaccustomed to hunting on land, but Mungo had grown up stalking deer with his father at Windemere. He taught them how to read the breeze and stay downwind of their prey, how to sight their guns on moving targets, how to creep stealthily through the long grass.

Often, he despaired of them. They were men of the sea; even

walking on land was something they did but rarely, and awkwardly. But gradually they improved, and the game was so plentiful that every night they dined on freshly butchered venison.

Elephants never came down to drink at the river—Mungo guessed they feared the crocodiles—but once or twice he saw a herd on the horizon. The sight quickened his heart. He begrudged each day he had to spend training the men. As soon as he thought they were ready, they shouldered their guns and struck out in that direction. He had never hunted such great beasts before; he had little idea what to expect.

Every tusk you take is another coin to buy your revenge on Chester, he told himself.

He touched the locket around his neck. It was a beautiful country, so different from anything he had known. He wished he could have shown it to Camilla.

They reached the rise where he had seen the elephants previously. Smashed trees and stripped leaves showed where they had passed, but of the animals themselves there was no sign.

"What now?"

Tippoo didn't answer. Instead, he pointed to a mound of huge, round turds dried out by the sun.

"Follow the shit."

Once they had found the spoor, it was not hard to read. They traced it for miles, through high grass and thorn trees. The hard ground made it difficult to tell how many beasts they were chasing, or how recently they had passed—but the piles of dung grew ever fresher.

After about eight miles, the grassland gave way to thicker jungle. The elephant tracks split up, meandering in different directions.

"Which way?" Tippoo asked.

Mungo peered through the foliage. The jungle was mostly tough acacia trees, with curving thorns as sharp and strong as fish-hooks. A man who entered it would soon find himself caught on those spikes, unable to move without tearing his clothes to shreds. Or if they caught in his flesh, he might never move again.

It was too dense. Choosing at random, he turned left and began skirting around the edge of the jungle, looking for broken branches that would reveal the elephants' way in. He had expected to find it quickly, yet two miles later the jungle wall remained as impenetrable as ever.

They had been out for hours. The sun was sinking toward the horizon, and in these tropical latitudes night would fall quickly. They would not make it back to camp before dark. They would have to bivouac where they could, and risk whatever predators lurked in the jungle.

Mungo's thoughts darkened with frustration. The plan he had formed to bring Chester down relied on acquiring a fortune. Every dollar that he had inherited from Rutherford had been sunk into this venture to make the profit he needed. Yet even now, with evidence of the elephants' presence all around him, they remained tantalizingly elusive. Had fate brought him to this place simply to taunt him?

He knew he should turn back, but some stubborn part of him could not admit defeat. He carried on, leaving the others trailing behind. Through a cluster of bushes, around a stand of trees, and . . .

There they were.

Two elephants, old and gray and huge, with long heavy tusks jutting from their faces. They stood at the edge of the jungle, stripping leaves from the trees and chewing them noisily.

They had not seen him. Mungo stared, frozen in the surprise of the moment. Then he reached for his gun. Silently, he slipped it off his shoulder and raised it to fire.

A breath of a breeze disturbed the still air. So faint, it barely tickled the hairs on the back of his neck, but it was enough to betray him. He was upwind of the elephants—the air carried his scent straight to them.

With a frightened blast, they charged forward into the jungle. Boughs snapped; branches scattered. Saplings were uprooted and trampled to the ground. Before Mungo could even get off a shot, they had vanished into the jungle.

With a curse, he took three steps after them—then stopped. Reason asserted itself. The elephants had made a clear path through the jungle, but he would never catch them if he followed it. The wind would be behind him, always giving him away before he could get close enough to fire. The only way he would have a chance was if he could get in front of them, downwind.

Tippoo came into view, sweating hard under the weight of his enormous gun. Without explaining, Mungo started to run again, following the edge of the jungle as it curved around to the north. Sweat ran down his eyes; a stitch throbbed in his side. Still the jungle continued unbroken. Perhaps it never ended, he thought, and he would keep running until he reached the far shore of Africa.

He paused, panting. The breeze blew over the sweat on his cheeks and cooled him. No longer from behind, he realized, but straight into his face. Glancing at the low sun, he saw that he had come right around the far side of the patch of jungle.

If the elephants had come out this way, there should be signs where they had broken through. He saw nothing. They must still be in the jungle, taking refuge among the dense vegetation and thorn bushes.

Earlier, Mungo had thought the jungle was impassable. Now, the knowledge that the elephants were in there made him reckless, heedless of his own safety. He plunged in, crawling on his belly to avoid the worst of the thorn bushes. Even so, he could not entirely escape their hooks. They plucked at his clothes and scratched his skin. One wickedly curved spike came so close he felt it brush his eyelash. A fraction closer and it would have blinded him. Still he went on, pausing every so often to listen for the elephants. It was impossible to imagine such huge animals being silent, yet he heard nothing except the chatter of insects, the calls of unfamiliar birds, and Tippoo struggling along behind him. The loyal giant had followed Mungo into the forest, though his bulk meant he took more of the brunt of the thorns. When Mungo glanced back, he saw Tippoo's face had become a mask of rivulets of blood.

A deep sigh whispered through the forest. It sounded so human, Mungo thought it must be Tippoo—but he could hear his friend breathing hard over his shoulder. The noise had come from somewhere ahead.

It sounded again, guttural and low. And something else—a slapping sound like a sail filling with wind.

There could only be one thing in the jungle large enough to make that noise.

The elephants must not be far away—a few paces at most. Yet the jungle was so thick it screened them entirely. Checking that the wind was still against him, Mungo wriggled forward and stared.

A large gray shape stood amid the foliage, barely ten feet away. It kept so still Mungo could hardly be sure if it was an animal or simply shadow. Only its ears moved, flapping against its side to make the slapping sound he had heard. It was straining to listen.

It could not smell Mungo, but it knew he was there. Where was its mate? Mungo searched the undergrowth. As his eyes adjusted to the patterns of the jungle, he realized there were more gray shapes behind the first one. Not just the second elephant he had seen earlier—there seemed to be a whole herd, perhaps twenty of them.

He was so close, if they took fright now and stampeded toward him he would be crushed under their massive feet. Hemmed in by the thorns, he would not even be able to roll away.

He did not move. He did not make a sound. Even that was not enough. Whether he was close enough that they smelled him, or if it was simple animal intuition, the elephants took fright. One moment the jungle was almost preternaturally still; the next it exploded into motion and chaos. The ground shook; cries echoed through the jungle.

He could not let them get away again. Thorns tore his skin and ripped his flesh as he pressed forward; in ordinary times he could not have stomached the pain, but now he was oblivious to it. With a final push that left a chunk of his hand hanging from a branch, he broke through into the clearing that the elephants had trampled.

It was like stepping into a giant, deadly game of ninepins, where every piece was ten feet high and weighed six tons. Terrified elephants blundered about, knocking into each other and braying desperately.

Through the dust clouds that swirled around, Mungo sighted his weapon on the largest animal he could see, aiming for the hollow behind the ear. The left barrel of his gun belched fire; the bullet struck. But in the chaos, it was not accurate enough. The ball penetrated the skin but not the heart. All it did was enrage the animal and frighten his companions. They fled from the noise of the gun, bunching together at the far end of the clearing. The thorn trees grew so thick there even the combined mass of the elephants could not get through. They pressed against each other, like a mob heaving on a door that would not yield.

Mungo knew that only a shot to the head or neck stood any chance of making a kill. But at the moment, all he could see were the beasts' hindquarters, packed tightly together in a gray wall. He edged sideways, trying to get around their flanks.

The elephants were still failing to break down the barrier of trees. It surely could not hold much longer. Mungo could already hear branches begin to snap. At the front of the phalanx, one of the elephants grabbed a bough with his trunk and ripped it away. The movement turned his head sideways, so for a moment it was exposed.

A deafening blast shook the clearing. From the corner of his eye, Mungo saw Tippoo, spinning back and dumped on his backside, the Goliath gun smoking in his hands. The elephant Mungo had seen bellowed in agony as a half-pound ball of lead smashed into his shoulder.

The sound, and the smell of blood, drove the herd to a new pitch of terror. The trees gave way; the path opened. The elephants stampeded away. In the tumult, Mungo could not see what had happened to the animal Tippoo had shot.

But one beast did not run away. At the back of the group stood a big bull elephant that dwarfed every other animal in the herd. His ears were ragged; his mighty tusks were as thick as anchor cables, and scarred by uncounted years of fighting. He had never lost a battle. Now he turned and saw Mungo—an impudent ape—standing before him.

He charged.

Mungo stood alone. Tippoo lay on the ground, clutching his shoulder—only a few yards away, but it might as well have been miles. The big gun was empty, he had no time to reload, and against the mighty bull elephant even a man like Tippoo was no better than an insect. Nor could Mungo run. The elephant would overtake him in seconds. Either he would be gored on the end of those mighty tusks, or trampled under the huge pounding feet.

So Mungo stood his ground. It was the hardest thing he had ever done—keeping firm in the face of six tons of elephant bearing down on him—but he knew it was his only hope. The animal put back its ears and lowered its head, so that its tusks almost grazed the ground. A haze of dust surrounded it as it drove forward. Fifty feet away.

Mungo raised the gun. Without rifling, it could not be accurate over any great range in the best of circumstances. Against a moving target, with the whole world shaking around him, he would have to wait until he could be absolutely certain.

Now the elephant was thirty feet away and gaining speed. A calm overtook Mungo. Though the ground trembled under his feet, the arms that held the gun did not waver. The cards had been dealt and could not be changed. Either he or the elephant would die. At least if it was him, he might see Camilla again.

Twenty feet away. So close, Mungo could taste the dust of its charge on his tongue. He drew a breath and held it, just as he had hunting deer at Windemere. He sighted the gun on the old bull's lowered head, in a little swelling in the center of the forehead. He fired.

It was a shot born of desperation—and ignorance. If Mungo had known more about hunting elephants, he would never even have tried it. In the course of his life to come he would bag hundreds of the beasts, but never again with a direct shot to the front of the head. Later, with more experience and when he had seen the thick bone of an elephant skull, he would know that the odds were a million to one against.

But—this time—they fell in his favor. The shot worked. The bullet struck home, and the elephant collapsed so suddenly Mungo did not even have to move out of its way. It lay on the ground, a few feet away, unmoving. A trickle of blood ran out from the hole in its forehead, which looked far too small to have taken the life of such a great beast.

A wave of exhilaration swept through Mungo and left him giddy. He had cheated death; he had secured the first down payment on his revenge. In the morning he would be in agony from the thorns, but for now the thrill of the hunt and success flooded his veins and muted the pain. He scrambled up the dead beast's flanks to stand on its mighty shoulder, tipped back his head and howled a scream of victory to the darkening sky.

Down in the clearing, Tippoo had lifted himself off the ground. His face was a mask of astonishment. By now, more of the *Raven*'s crew had managed to find their way in, cutting through the jungle and following the sound of the guns. They stared at Mungo with almost superstitious awe, as if looking at a god. His clothes had been cut to such ribbons he was virtually naked. Almost every inch of his long body was smeared with blood—either his own, or the elephant's. Yet he was invincible.

"There must be near to five hundred pounds of ivory in those tusks," he exulted.

"And more," said Tippoo.

He gestured to the gap in the jungle that the elephants had battered down. Most of the herd had escaped, but the animal he had hit with the Goliath had not gone far. She lay dead, a little way down the path. Two more tusks.

"Then let us get to work."

In the months that followed, the barrels of their guns were rarely allowed to cool. The *Raven*'s crew became adept hunters, finding the elephant spoor and tracking it, sometimes for days at a time. They learned how to position themselves against the wind so that the elephants would not smell them; how to find the spot behind the shoulder, about two thirds down the body, where a single bullet could get the kill. They dug pits, and filled them with sharp stakes to trap the elephants; they made hides from where Tippoo could use his great gun to blast through the elephants' chests into their vital organs. Most of all, they learned how to strip the ivory from the skull without breaking it, extracting each tooth intact to be added to the store of their plunder.

It was not easy. The longer they stayed, the further they had to range inland to find the huge herds that would give them the most ivory. They strayed into inhabited lands, meeting local tribes whom they befriended with gifts of glass beads and cloth, in exchange for food. And still they kept going.

After six months, they had enough ivory to fill the ship's hold. So much, Mungo had to hire porters from the tribes to carry it back to the coast. Their caravan stretched almost a mile, hundreds of men and women with elephant tusks stacked on their heads. Thirty thousand pounds in weight, according to the meticulous tally Mungo kept in his account book. By the time he had sold it in New York or Baltimore, it would be worth nearly half a million dollars.

"Then I will be able to go after Chester," he told himself.

The plan he had devised, in those long nights in his cabin aboard the *Blackhawk*, was not much different from what Chester had done to his father. He would ruin Chester's fortune, acquire his debts, and then call them in until Chester was bankrupt. The money that those ivory tusks represented would allow him to achieve it.

At last the ivory was stowed tight in the hold. The *Raven* weighed anchor, nosed out of the river mouth, and set her course for home.

Never in her life had Camilla known such freedom as she enjoyed in New Orleans. She could go anywhere in the city without asking permission. In the sea of Creole faces that thronged the streets—every shade of black and white, slave and free—the color of her skin attracted no attention at all. The only looks she drew in the street were on account of her beauty. At home, she was mistress of the house. Even the other slaves deferred to her. That horrified her—but when she told them to go away, that she could dress and feed and wash herself, she saw the fear in their eyes. If they did not earn their keep, Chester might sell them, or send them back to the fields at Bannerfield. So, reluctantly, she let them lace up the fine dresses Chester had given her, and brush her hair and bring her breakfast on a silver tray in the mornings.

Her life in New Orleans settled into a routine. Early each morning, she went to the Cathedral of St. Louis on Rue de Chartres and prayed. That was the happiest moment of her day—in the dim hush of the sanctuary, she could feel clean and safe. It was also the only time she could be free of Granville, who found the atmosphere inside the cathedral disagreeable. Once he had visited a few times and assured himself that the only other clientele so early were priests and nuns, he stationed himself by the door and waited outside. Camilla was left by herself, to pray for Isaac and Mungo and, for a few moments, to feel close to them.

Isaac was the reason that Chester could allow her so much freedom. However far she ranged, she would always come back. However great the delights of the city, she would swap them in a moment to be back at Bannerfield with her son. It was the wound inside her that could never heal. As weeks became months, she could only imagine how her boy was growing: bigger, stronger, weaning, babbling, crawling. In her mind, he was still the tiny baby she had cradled in her arms. Would she even recognize him? Would he remember her?

She hated what Chester had made her. At Windemere, even at Bannerfield, she had been a simple laborer. They might own her body, but never her soul. Here, though her bed was softer and her clothes as fine as any great lady's, he had made her his whore.

But as the months passed, she found herself doing more than simply making herself beautiful for white men, and performing for them in dining rooms and bedrooms (for de Villiers was not the only man she was forced to entertain). It happened so gradually she barely noticed it, but more and more she found herself taking an interest in Chester's business dealings.

The first time was a month after she had arrived in New Orleans. Chester was back in town. His book-keeper, a wizened old man named Sullivan, found them at breakfast to ask if he should pay an invoice to François.

"Ask Camilla," Chester said through a mouthful of toast. "She knows all the tricks François is up to."

Sullivan gave her the paper. The look on his face said he could not imagine what a slave girl might make of it. Camilla ignored him and read the bill slowly. It was for flour that had been sent to Bannerfield.

"François has charged you at New Orleans prices," she said, pointing to the relevant lines.

"What is wrong with that?"

"Because he had his agent buy the flour in Louisville, where it is cheaper, and shipped direct from there."

Chester snatched the paper from her and stared at it. He was so rich, and so busy keeping rich, it was easier for him to pay François's inflated prices than examine them too closely. Yet if ever he found out he had been cheated, his anger was a fearsome thing.

"He told you this?"

"I happened to see the letter he had written to his agent."

Chester gave her an appreciative nod.

"Tell the foreman at Bannerfield to inspect the flour sacks and see where it was milled," he told Sullivan. "If what Camilla says is accurate, inform François that he has made a mistake with his invoice."

"He tried to cheat you," Sullivan grumbled. "You should take your business elsewhere."

"Not at all." Chester gave a malicious grin. "I know every factor in this city will try to cheat me. The difference is, with François I can now find out *how* he is doing it."

After that, every time a bill came from François, or an order had to be placed, Chester would tell his clerks to ask Camilla. Soon it became a habit for them, even when Chester was not there. Without any formal authority or position, she became indispensable to the running of his affairs.

To her surprise, she discovered she had an aptitude for it. She liked totting up the columns of numbers, the order they represented, the feeling of control when they obeyed her. When she did not understand something, she applied herself to learning it until she had it perfect. She found books in Chester's library—on maritime insurance, stock markets, and a hundred other topics—and smuggled them up to her room, poring over them by candlelight until her eyes hurt. It became an obsession. The more useful she could make herself to Chester, the more chance she would be allowed to see Isaac again.

Sometimes, if there was something she wanted to know, she would visit François's office and flirt with him until he explained it to her.

"I only see you when you want something," he complained, but that was not true.

He saw her in the evenings, when she dressed up in her finery to attend the soirées and dinners where the *beau monde* of New Orleans entertained their mistresses; several nights a week he saw her undress from that same finery and take him to her bed.

She supposed François knew what she was doing. He must realize that everything he said was reported back to Chester. Or maybe he did not—she knew men could be blind to things they did not want to see, and it was easy to dismiss a black woman. Perhaps he did know, and accepted it as the price of her company. Or perhaps he did not care. Chester's business was so vast, and growing, that however much Camilla found out, François would still make a fortune. And enjoy the pleasures of her body while he did.

"How much would it cost to buy a steamboat?" Camilla asked him one night, curled against him in bed.

He laughed. "That is a funny question."

"Chester said he was considering getting one. For Bannerfield."

That was not true; Chester had no idea about it. But François believed her. He propped himself up on one arm and looked down at her.

"He said that?"

"I overheard him talking to Granville." She lay flat on the bed, her eyes wide and innocent.

"It is a very foolish idea," said François, frowning. "It would cost fifty thousand dollars at least to buy a steamboat. Then there are the costs of fuel, the crew, to say nothing of the hazards of navigation. And if Chester kept it purely for Bannerfield, it would be sitting idle more than half the time."

"Perhaps I should not have mentioned it," said Camilla meekly.

François smiled and kissed her. "It is lucky you did. Now, with a few tactful words, I can save Chester from making a big mistake. Much better for him to leave it to me to arrange shipping as and when he needs it."

And take ten percent of the price. François did not say it, but he did not have to. At that moment, unbeknown to him, Camilla was thinking exactly the same thought.

The next thing he said put it out of her head.

"I will not see you for some time after this. Chester has asked me to sail to Africa."

Camilla tensed. "To Africa?"

"He is buying a plantation in Havana, and he needs people to work it." He sighed. "I told him the markets in Havana are perfectly adequate, but he insists he will be cheated there. So he has asked me to go and choose them myself."

"I thought the slave trade was illegal."

It should not have shocked her that Chester could do such a thing, but it still did. She had been born a slave; no other life had ever been possible. But for ordinary people who had known freedom to be wrenched from their lives, simply because another man's greed demanded it—the injustice burned at her. How could anyone justify such a thing?

It did not seem to trouble François.

"The navy patrols are the least of it. Storms, shipwreck, fever . . . It will be a miracle if I return." His face brightened. "Though if I do, I will be considerably wealthier."

"How long will you be gone?"

"Six months, at least. More, if the weather is against us." François stroked her hair. "But do not worry. I will not forget you."

"François is up to something," said Chester.

He and Camilla were walking along the levee, near the Bannerfield warehouse. They looked like a pair of sweethearts, Chester in a handsome suit and Camilla wearing a purple dress that accentuated every curve of her body. She held his arm, and smiled, and tried to forget all the things he had done to her.

"I dined with François today, and all he could talk about was the ruinous cost of steamboats," Chester continued. "Is he planning to charge me more for our shipping?"

"He is already overcharging you for the shipping," said Camilla. "What worries him is that while he is away in Africa, you might realize how much he makes from you and buy your own boat."

"Why would he think that?"

"Because that is what you should do," said Camilla. "I have looked at your accounts. Everything that Bannerfield uses or produces travels by the river. You spend nearly a hundred thousand dollars a year on it. For that money, you could buy and operate *two* steamboats of your own and still save money. If you used spare capacity to carry goods for the other plantations, it would even be a source of income."

Chester stopped dead. He stared down at her, his face caught between suspicion and surprise.

"How did you work that out?"

"I got the idea from you," she said humbly. "Do you remember, at dinner last month, you were complaining how much it cost to bring the crop down river? I simply added up all the shipping costs in the ledgers, and then asked some of your friends how much a steamboat might cost. It was not very difficult."

Never let him see what you are capable of. Never become a threat.

She saw the idea taking root in Chester's mind. Without him noticing, she had been steering him along Front Levee to a jetty near the Union Cotton Press. At crop time, the wharf would be jammed with steamboats unloading cotton bales at every hour of the day. Now, it was mostly deserted. Only a single steamboat was moored up at the wharf.

"Why don't we take a look at her," said Chester, as if the idea had just occurred to him spontaneously.

A man with a weather-beaten face and a wiry frame strode down the gangplank. He offered Chester a hand that was as gnarled as old tree roots.

"Ezekiel McMurran," he introduced himself. "Master of this vessel."

Chester did not bother with formalities. "Is she for sale?"

McMurran nodded. "She was built last year for a consortium, planned to run a packet line service up to Louisville. But one of the partners died, and the others fell out, and now they want rid of her."

"Is she reliable?"

"I can show you."

Chester and Camilla followed McMurran aboard. He showed them the machinery: the great boilers mounted on the main deck, the furnaces that fired them and the long mechanical arms that took their power to the stern-wheel. He showed them the cabins on the deck above—confusingly, known as the boiler deck. They were not as luxurious as the stateroom that Camilla had had on the voyage down from Bannerfield, but that did not matter.

"You do not need passenger quarters," she told Chester. "You can rip out most of these cabins to create more room for cargo."

Finally, McMurran took them up to the hurricane deck, the topmost deck where passengers could promenade. The only structure here was a cabin for the crew, known as the Texas, surmounted by a small glassed-in structure that held the ship's wheel.

"The pilot house," McMurran explained. "That is where we steer the ship."

They stood on the hurricane deck looking out over the length of the ship, and the broad crescent of the river and the city beyond. The captain waited expectantly. Camilla wanted to say more, to nudge Chester toward a decision. But she sensed it was not the moment to pressure him.

Chester slapped the side of the Texas.

"I will take her," he declared. "And you too, if you will stay on as her captain."

McMurran grinned and shook his hand. "Honored."

"You will not regret this," Camilla promised him. "Now it

will be easier for you to come and go between New Orleans and Bannerfield whenever you like. And I will be able to visit you more often."

"Indeed," said Chester. The thought of the money he could save had put him in a merry mood. "We will make the inaugural trip together. Isaac will be so surprised when he sees what we have bought."

In that moment, Camilla knew the nearest thing to happiness she had felt since Isaac was born. She threw her arms around Chester, a gesture that was only half contrived.

"Thank you."

Did it trouble her, that all her efforts only served to increase Chester's fortune? That he would use the money she saved him to buy more land, which would need more slaves to work it? That the boats would be used to carry those slaves to Bannerfield, along with seed for them to plant and whips for the overseers to lash them with?

All that passed through her mind. But every day was a battle for her life. She might lie awake at night yearning for Mungo, dreaming of the day he would step through the door and rescue her—but as the months passed, that dream slowly died. She had to rely on her own wits to survive; guilt was a luxury she could not afford. All that mattered was getting back to Isaac.

"I will rename her," said Chester with a sweep of his arm. "She will be the *Windemere*. A memory of happy times."

Camilla wasn't sure how he wanted her to respond.

"I had almost forgotten Windemere," she murmured.

Footsteps sounded on the boiler deck below. The joy of the moment was ruined as Granville's head appeared at the top of the stairs that led up to the hurricane deck. His face was flushed, his breathing short.

"A letter came from Virginia," he said. He passed it to Chester. "You ought to read it."

Chester took it in surprise. The seal was unbroken.

"How do you know what is in it?"

Granville pointed to the sender's address scrawled on the back above the seal.

"There."

All the warmth of the day seemed to drain from the hurricane deck as Chester read aloud.

"Mungo St. John, Baltimore."

He snapped the seal so hard it tore the paper. As he read, his face went white.

"I must return to Bannerfield at once."

"What has happened?" said Camilla.

At the sight of Mungo's name, that familiar handwriting, her heart had lurched sideways. He was alive. He had not forgotten her after all.

Chester turned away without answering. He seemed oblivious to Camilla as she peered over his shoulder and read the letter.

I have returned from my adventures a considerably richer man than before. I have a few affairs to attend to, but rest assured I know where to find you and I have not forgotten the debt I owe you. I shall join you presently to settle the matter with interest.

Chester turned to Camilla, his gray eyes burning into her.

"Did you know?"

"How could I?"

The utter shock in her voice was enough to convince him. He was more agitated than she had ever seen him. His face was gray, the muscles in his cheek twitching as if he was having a seizure.

"He means to kill me."

Camilla did not think she had betrayed any emotion, but perhaps she had allowed a trace of hope to flash across her face. Perhaps Chester, in his turmoil, simply assumed it. He shot out his hand and grabbed her by her throat.

"Do not think Mungo is coming like some kind of white

knight to save you," he hissed. "I would kill you sooner than let him have you. And as for Isaac . . ." He gave a grim laugh, though Camilla thought she saw a stab of pain in his eyes. "You know what he would do to the boy to hurt me."

Camilla gripped the rail of the hurricane deck. She wanted to tell Chester he was wrong, that Mungo could never hurt the child because Isaac was Camilla's flesh and blood.

Of course she could not tell him that. Partly because it would only enrage Chester further—but also, partly because deep in her heart she could not be sure it was true. Would Mungo's love for her be greater than his hatred for Chester?

Chester balled up the paper and threw it over the side. It flew down to the water and disappeared into the river.

"I will return to Bannerfield at once. When Mungo comes, I must be ready."

Once again, the Cape of Good Hope was true to its name; the *Raven* passed it in benign weather, re-provisioned in Cape Town and made for home. The fastest route would have taken them straight across the South Atlantic, but storm season was near. The alternative was to beat up the west coast of Africa into higher latitudes, and then turn west toward America.

That brought the risk of another encounter with Fairchild. But in thousands of miles of coastline, Mungo was willing to take the risk. Probably, he thought, his old adversary had returned to England by now anyway.

As they entered the tropics, the sultry heat reminded Mungo of the last time he had sailed these waters. One night, he dreamed he was in Isabel's cabin on board the *Blackhawk*. He felt her warmth as she fell against him, the press of her body on his. He watched as she pulled the nightgown over her head and leaned back, allowing his eyes to feast on her nakedness. Her hand slid down his chest and into his breeches; he saw her lean over him on the bed, an angel bathed in candlelight, and draw him into her. He buried his head in her breasts.

Then he looked up, and it was not Isabel but Camilla. He put his arm around her and hugged her to him; he felt himself begin to climax. But before he did, she melted away in his arms like mist in sunshine, and he was left alone in the cabin.

He woke feeling soiled and uneasy. Isabel had been a distraction, a way to amuse himself on the *Blackhawk*'s long voyage. Why was she even in his thoughts now?

A knock on his cabin door brought his attention back to the ship. Belatedly, he realized the ship was rolling much more heavily than when he had gone to sleep. The wind had risen; so had the sea. He could feel the forces shivering through the *Raven*'s timbers.

Virgil Henderson, the bosun, put his head around the door. A Georgia native, he was used to Atlantic weather and the hurricanes that sometimes battered his home state, but now even he looked troubled.

"It's going to be bad."

Mungo was already out of bed and pulling on his trousers. In the short time it took him to get on deck, he felt the wind strengthen.

"Why did no one wake me earlier?" he shouted furiously.

The sea was high; clouds as black as tar rolled in from the west, covering the dawn. A high wind thrashed the *Raven* with spindrift and spray.

"Furl the mainsail and the foresail. Double reef the topsails!"

The men raced to obey, clinging to the yards for their lives as the ship tossed them this way and that. The storm clouds rose and the gale-force winds set upon them like a pack of howling wolves. The waves were already like mountains rolling across the surface of the ocean. They tried to ride out the storm under topsails, but the battering sea nearly capsized the ship, forcing Mungo to strip her down to bare poles and run before the wind.

There was something elemental about the terror inspired by a gale. As Mungo clung to the binnacle stand, bracing his feet against the bucking of the rain-slick deck, he saw the ocean beyond the rail as a force of supernatural malevolence, as if the Angel of Death had taken up air and water as weapons against them. There was nothing to do but pray for mercy, though it had no effect. The storm's violence increased until the rain came at them sideways, the waves rose up like monsters from the deep, and the wind filled the sky with the sound of its rage. It dragged on for a night and a day, pummeling the *Raven* so relentlessly that the cook gave up trying to feed the crew, for none of them, including Mungo, could hold anything down. The only rations issued by the kitchen in the midst of the maelstrom were water and rum.

Sometime in the small hours of the second night—what time Mungo didn't know, for the watch officers had stopped ringing the bell—the ship lurched upward with such violence that everything not fixed to a bulkhead crashed to the deck. For a terrifying moment, the ship hung suspended as if the sea had tossed it into the air. Then it rolled over like a felled tree until the ocean greeted the hull with a fearsome slap. Mungo heard the mizzen mast give way. The sudden splintering of hardened wood rent the air like an explosion, drowning out the screams of the crew. The *Raven* floundered on its side, until another wave gave counterbalance to the keel and turned the ship upright.

Bracing himself against the heaving sea, Mungo scaled the ladder and crawled onto the spar deck, holding fast to the safety tether Tippoo had lashed to the port-side rail. The night was so dark and the air so thick with rain that the deck was almost invisible. By some miracle, the knockdown had not doused the binnacle lamp. In the dim halo of light cast by the flame, Mungo saw Virgil Henderson lying on the quarterdeck, a rope binding his waist to the base of the helm. The wheel was now untended, turning aimlessly with the random motions of the rudder.

Mungo followed the tether to the rail and the rail back to the helm. He cast a glance at the broken mizzen mast, which was hanging over the starboard rail, its parted lines writhing like snakes in the currents of water on the deck. Henderson lay still, but as another wave broke over him Mungo saw him cough reflexively to get the water out of his lungs. He was alive.

But he could not get up. With so much water pouring over the deck, he would drown, or else be dashed to pieces if he stayed there.

"Somebody take the helm!" Mungo shouted. "We need to get him below!"

The seamen behind Mungo were wiry and slight, useful on the yards, but no good when it came to lifting at least two hundred and twenty pounds of dead weight. Mungo untied the rope from Henderson's waist and threw the bosun's arm over his neck, heaving with all his strength. He managed less than three feet. He called for help, as rain whipped his back and his face. The load on his shoulders lightened. He saw Tippoo beside him.

"One, two, three . . . pull!" he cried.

The bosun moved. Two more sailors crowded around, grabbing Henderson's belt and legs, while another wrestled with the helm. They trundled the bosun to the aft hatch and down the ladder to the berth deck, where they somehow managed to hoist him into a hammock. Mungo collapsed, exhausted. He wiped his eyes and tried to clear his mind.

With every pitch of the deck, the ship groaned. The wind had sheared away the topgallant and royal yards on the mainmast. Half of the netting on the bowsprit was gone, and twice a breaking wave had knocked the *Raven* down, driving her masthead into the turbulent sea, parting braces and stays from stem to stern, and sending unwary seamen over the side. Somehow the main mast had absorbed the beating, but unless the gale relented there was no way that luck would hold.

It was pointless to attempt repairs in the storm, but the crew managed to cut the broken mizzen mast free and restore order to the tangle of lines around it. Henderson emerged from the sick bay, bandaged but unbowed, to supervise the work. By the time they had finished, the wind had begun to taper off, softening from a shriek to a howl. Mungo watched as a sliver of purple sky appeared, turning slowly pink. The appearance of the sun was so dazzling that he had to shield his eyes against it. After over forty-eight hours of night, the world turned into a sudden kaleidoscope of color. The ship was flaxen and brass, the sea a greenish blue, the clouds flecked with gold.

A cry rose upon the lips of the sailors.

"Land ho!"

Mungo thought he had misheard. There should have been no land within a hundred miles. But when he looked forward, he saw a line of white foam emerging from the purple clouds of dawn, and the forested coast of Africa beyond. The storm had driven them further east than he had ever imagined.

And now they were in even greater danger.

"That is a reef!" Henderson hollered into his ear. "It will smash us to pieces!"

Mungo looked for a gap in the boiling surf but there was nothing. It stretched unbroken as far as he could see. Even if there had been a way in, the *Raven* was so damaged they could never have steered her through it. Nor could they beat away. The wind and current were dead behind them, driving the *Raven* toward the reef at terrifying speed.

"We have to lighten the ship!" Henderson shouted.

Mungo wasn't sure he had heard right.

"What do you want me to do?"

"Put the cargo overboard!"

"The ivory?"

Mungo stared at him wildly. It was an impossible suggestion. Without the cargo, he had nothing. No profit, no money, no revenge.

"There must be another way. We cannot lose that cargo."

Tippoo pointed to the reef. "Lose the cargo, or lose the ship."

He was right. Resist it as Mungo might, he could not deny the sickening truth. The current was carrying them straight onto the reef. If the *Raven* was caught there, she would be smashed to pieces. They would lose the ship, the cargo, and most probably their lives. Their only hope was to reduce their draft and pray the waves lifted them above the rocks.

There would be no revenge if he was dead.

Still he could not give the order.

Suddenly he was swept off his feet into the air. His first thought was that a wave had seized him, or that they had struck the reef already. Then he realized that Tippoo had lifted him off the deck, gripping his arms like a parent trying to shake sense into a child. For the first time in his life, Mungo saw real fear in the giant's face.

That, more than anything else, made him realize he had no choice.

"Do it!"

He stood by the wheel, hardly able to watch as Henderson organized the crew to bring the bundles of ivory up from the hold. One by one, they went over the side. Each one seemed to take a part of Mungo's soul with it. He had poured everything he had into the hunt—the whole fortune he had inherited from Rutherford. Every tusk was a battle he had fought with the mighty animals, a wager he had made with his life and won. For nothing.

The waves rose. They were nearly at the reef. Still the ship seemed too low in the water. Tippoo's men untied the cannons from their mountings and heaved them overboard. The furniture from Mungo's cabin followed it, a trail of flotsam bobbing in their wake.

Mungo gripped the wheel, though it was only an illusion of power. He was in God's hands now.

Sterling's words came back to him, dripping with sarcasm. *God has no interest in our business.* Was that how he would die, sucked down into the depths like Sterling? Was that justice?

"Here we go," said Henderson.

The men grabbed onto whatever fragments of the ship they could hold. The deck bucked; the waves surged around them. The roar of the surf drowned out everything. White water foamed around the *Raven*'s bow; something scraped her keel.

"We are not light enough!" Henderson yelled.

Mungo looked back. The day seemed to have gone dark again. Then he saw why. A giant wave, some last remnant of the storm, was racing in behind them. It reared up beneath them, lifting the *Raven* high on its crest. For a moment, Mungo could look down and see the naked reef exposed below, a forest of razor-sharp rocks.

The wave broke in a torrent of foam. There was no way they could survive this. The *Raven* was thrown forward, and Mungo braced himself for the impact that would destroy his ship.

It did not come. The *Raven* scudded across the surface of the sea, still afloat and unbroken. When Mungo looked back, he saw the line of foaming water receding behind them. The wave had carried them clean over the reef, into the calm waters beyond. In the shelter of the lagoon, the waves eased. The wind dropped. The *Raven* slowed, then came to rest in a few feet of water. A little distance ahead, golden sands stretched up toward a thick forest.

"Allah is merciful," said Tippoo.

"Is he?"

Mungo's voice was desolate as he gestured to the *Raven*'s broken decks. The beautiful vessel he had fallen in love with in Baltimore was no more. Her graceful lines had been smashed in, her masts broken off and her canvas wings snapped.

And that was not the worst of it. When he went below, the hold was four feet deep in water. He waited for his eyes to adjust to the darkness, but that did not make it any better. There was nothing to see. The hoard of ivory that had been packed so carefully was gone. All that remained were strands of the dried grass that had been used to pack them, floating on the bilge-water.

"Did none of the cargo survive? None of it?"

Henderson licked his lips nervously. "We'd never have got over the reef otherwise. We'd have been smashed to pieces and drowned."

"None of it?" Mungo repeated, as if he had not heard. "There was half a million dollars in that hold."

He had been on deck for three days straight. He had not eaten or slept. He felt dizzy and nauseous; his body had become a clumsy thing he could barely control.

Without warning, Mungo spun around and unleashed his fist at Henderson's head. The bosun had no time to protect himself. Mungo's punch hit Henderson's jaw so hard it almost broke the bone. The bosun was thrown back, stunned, into the bilge-water.

"That ivory was everything I had in the world. Everything!"

Henderson picked himself up out of the water, looking at Mungo like a puppy that has felt the first kick of its owner's boot.

Mungo barely saw him through the curtain of rage that had descended. This was the third time in his life he had lost everything. Chester had robbed him of Windemere, Camilla, his family. The share he should have had of the *Blackhawk*'s profits had been snatched away, when all he had done was try to stop a girl being raped. And now the storm had destroyed his last chance of revenge. He could almost hear fate laughing at him, grinding him under its heel.

"The things I have done . . ." He thought of the slaves screaming in the *Blackhawk*'s hold; Rutherford's staring eyes as Mungo choked the life out of him; Sterling's body sinking into the depths of the ocean. "And this is my reward?"

Camilla was dead. The *Raven* was lost. Chester had won. Mungo's body could not contain his rage. He balled his fist to lash out again; Henderson cowered. But before Mungo could strike, an enormous pair of hands grabbed him from behind. That only drove him to new heights of fury. He tried to rip himself free, twisting and pulling like a caged animal. But Tippoo's hands were stronger.

"Let me go, damn you! This is mutiny!"

"This is not his fault," said Tippoo calmly. "What we do, it is the only way to save the ship."

"Save the ship?" Mungo gave a wild laugh. "What is the point of saving the ship if we have nothing left? The food is spoiled and the water casks are breached. Our cargo is gone and we are bankrupt. The *Raven* is a cursed ship, a ghost ship, and we are all dead men."

Many of the sailors crossed themselves and spat into the water when they heard that. As desperate as their situation was, they did not want their captain making it worse by calling down evil forces. But Tippoo remained impassive.

"We find water. Hunt food."

"And the cargo?"

Tippoo shrugged. "Still in Africa. Still have guns."

"The elephants are three thousand miles from here."

Few elephants were left on the west coast of Africa, and the ivory they produced was hard and brittle, not suited for carving and worth a fraction of the price of what they had jettisoned. It would take years to replenish what they had lost here. Mungo could not wait so long for such meager returns. Nor could he risk his ship going back around the Cape in this condition. She needed a complete refit that would cost thousands of dollars. How could he afford that?

Another wave of despair broke over him. He tried to wrestle free of Tippoo's grip. He needed to hit something, someone—anything—to release the fury that boiled in his heart. But Tippoo was stronger and would not let him go.

And as he felt Tippoo's giant hands locked around his wrists, as strong as iron, a door seemed to crack open in his mind. A sliver of light—another possibility.

A terrible possibility. A door he knew he should not open. A cargo that would fetch almost as much as the ivory, but could be had in a fraction of the time.

He would not go down that path. He slammed the door in his mind shut.

The choice calmed him. Tippoo felt Mungo's arms go slack as the rage left his body. The giant let go of Mungo, though keeping a wary watch on his captain. Mungo offered his hand to Henderson.

"My apologies," he said. "I was not myself before. You saved the ship, and I am grateful for it."

Henderson shook his hand and mumbled something.

"What now?" said Tippoo.

Mungo looked around. "We do what we can."

They lowered the boats and towed the *Raven* to the water's edge. When she was as shallow as she could go, they fastened thick hawsers to her bow, wrapped the lines around tree stumps, and hauled her out of the water up onto the beach.

They felled trees and planed them smooth to replace the masts. They found termite nests in the ground, where the earth was so thin and brittle you could step through up to your knee, and dug them out to make saw-pits. They built a makeshift forge where the carpenter's mate could melt down iron and forge nails. Hunting parties were sent out into the bush, and they came back with fresh venison, which they cured over the fires. Mungo drove the men like a demon, working them from dawn to dusk. At night he barely slept, but prowled the beach with a gun in case any natives found them.

Henderson examined the repairs they had made.

"Should do for getting us back to Baltimore." He sounded doubtful.

"We are not going to Baltimore," said Mungo. "We are going back to the hunting grounds in East Africa."

Henderson stared at him. "But that'll be another year. Maybe two. The men didn't sign on for that."

"Any man who doesn't like it can stay here." Almost the only items that hadn't gone overboard were the rifles. They had been locked in the weapons store, and in the chaos of the storm no one had been able to find the key. "I will not return to Baltimore empty-handed."

Tippoo slapped the ship's hull with the palm of his hand.

"If we go to hunt, we need more. Rope. Better canvas. Powder. Food for the voyage."

"I have been thinking about that," said Mungo. As much as they had patched up the ship, he knew she was not strong enough to risk around the Cape of Good Hope. "I have fixed our position. By my reckoning we are only fifty miles south of Ambriz."

Tippoo spat on the beach. "Pendleton?"

"He is the only person for five hundred miles who can get us the stores we need."

When the repairs were finished and the tide was high, they hauled the *Raven* back into the water and floated her off. She was a sad shadow of the proud vessel that had sailed out of Baltimore. Patches of bare wood spotted the dark timbers of her hull like mold. Some of her sails were fresh from the hold; others had been sewn together from fragments. She listed slightly to port, where they had not managed to balance the ballast. But she was afloat, and when they took her out to sea her canvas held together as they sailed north.

As before, a smear of smoke on the horizon told them they were approaching Ambriz. They crossed the bar of the Loge River again, where two years earlier the *Blackhawk* had sailed in, and moored in the lagoon. They were the only ship there this time; the village seemed almost deserted. Mungo wondered if the navy had raided it, but when he and Tippoo went ashore a gaggle of children emerged from the huts, chattering and pointing.

"Pendleton," he said. "Where is Pendleton?"

They led him up the beach. In a clearing fringed by trees, a cluster of mud huts made a rough compound around a thatched house. The children waited at the perimeter, pointing and giggling, while Mungo approached. It was mid-afternoon, and a sleepy haze hung over the place. The only sound was the buzz of flies, and a pig-like grunting coming from the house.

A wooden terrace overlooked the sea, shaded by a palm awning. A white man stood there, leaning on the rail and staring out over the beach and the breakers to the distant horizon. At first Mungo thought it must be Pendleton, but as he came closer he saw the man was more slightly built, with a high forehead and sharp sideburns.

The man heard Mungo's approach and turned. At the sight of another white man his face broke open in a smile; he raised his left hand in greeting. His right hung across his chest, tied up in a sling.

"Greetings," he said. His accent was American. He studied Mungo, as if trying to make sense of him. His nervous eyes never seemed to stay still. "You're a long way from civilization."

"And even further from Virginia," Mungo answered.

The man laughed. By the skin of his face, burned red-raw by the sun, Mungo guessed he was not long arrived in the tropics.

He nodded toward the *Raven*'s masts, just visible above the trees that screened the harbor. "You come on business?"

"We put in for repairs. My ship was caught in a storm."

The man grimaced. "Mine too—though we were not so lucky as you." He half-lifted his broken arm. "The ship was lost. I was fortunate to come away with nothing worse than this."

Mungo was about to ask more, but at that moment there was a loud halloo. Pendleton emerged from the main house, wearing nothing but a colorful cloth like a kilt around his waist. An African woman, wearing even less, followed behind carrying a bottle of *geribita* and three crystal glasses.

"I was not expecting visitors so late in the season," said Pendleton, squinting suspiciously at Mungo. His pupils were small, dulled with a narcotic haze. "Who the hell are you?"

"I was here with Captain Sterling two years ago," Mungo reminded him.

Sterling's name seemed to placate Pendleton. He threw himself into a chair and gestured Mungo to sit.

"Is Sterling with you now? I was surprised he didn't come this year."

"Sterling died on the return voyage." A flash of memory, choking the life out of Sterling underwater. "I have my own vessel now. But she was damaged by the storm."

The African woman uncorked the bottle of *geribita*. She poured three glasses of the liquor and handed them around. Her bare breasts hung low as she bent over to give Pendleton his drink. He gave them a squeeze, then sent her away.

"My house appears to have become a home for castaways," Pendleton said. "You've met my other guest, Mr. de Villiers?"

"Just now."

Pendleton flapped a hand in their direction. "Mr. de Villiers, Mr. Sinclair."

Mungo started at the sound of the false name he had taken aboard the *Blackhawk*. He was surprised Pendleton had remembered it. He thought about correcting his host, then decided against it. There might yet be advantages in hiding his real identity.

Swilling the poisonous liquor around his mouth, Mungo told the story of his elephant-hunting expedition, the success he had had, and the disaster that had struck.

"I need stores and supplies to refit my ship," he said.

"And then to Baltimore?" said Pendleton.

"Back around the Cape. I must make good the cargo I lost."

"You could load a cargo here," said Pendleton casually. "That would save you a deal of time."

"Do you have that amount of ivory?"

Pendleton exchanged a wink with de Villiers.

"It was a darker shade of ivory I had in mind. Black ivory."

Again, Mungo felt the door in his mind crack open with possibility. Again, he forced it shut.

"I am set on an easier line of work."

"A pity. You could have turned a profit, and helped François here get home to New Orleans," said Pendleton.

That drew Mungo's interest. "You are bound for New Orleans?"

"That is where I was headed when the ship was caught by the storm."

"Terrible," Pendleton added. "Took three hundred of the best people I had to offer. Lost all of them—he was lucky to survive."

Lost all of them. Three hundred men and women chained to a sinking ship, unable to escape as the sea sucked them down, screaming until the sea filled their lungs. Mungo refused to think about it.

"Still, his client can afford to replace them," Pendleton continued. Another wink. "They say Chester Marion is the richest man in Louisiana."

The name hit Mungo like a bullet. It was all he could do to keep hold of his glass.

"You work for Chester Marion?"

He had let too much emotion show. De Villiers gave him a curious look.

"Is he a friend of yours?"

"We have never met," said Mungo. "But I knew his reputation. In Virginia, before he moved south."

"What a happy coincidence," said Pendleton.

He glanced between the two of them, as if trying to work out how he could use this turn of events to his advantage.

Mungo ignored him. His yellow eyes were fixed on de Villiers.

"If we ever return to New Orleans, you could introduce me to him."

"Of course." De Villiers sipped his drink. His nervous gaze darted this way and that—Mungo, Pendleton, the palm trees and the breaking surf. Like a cornered dog, he could sense Mungo had him at a disadvantage, but he could not work out how or why. "Though Mr. Marion is not in New Orleans so often anymore. Most of the time he is at his estate at Bannerfield. He leaves much of the business in town to his mistress."

A thought struck him. "I wonder if you'd heard anything about her. The rumor is he brought her with him from Virginia." He chuckled. "I did not know they were so liberal up north as we are in New Orleans."

Mungo had never heard of Chester having a mistress at Windemere, black or white. That sort of gossip would not have interested him.

"What is her name?"

"Camilla."

The glass of *geribita* slipped from Mungo's hand and smashed, exploding across the hardwood floor in a spray of sharp glass and liquor. He sprang to his feet, crunching shards of crystal underfoot, with a cry as if his heart had been ripped out.

"*How?*"

Pendleton and de Villiers were staring at him. Mungo fought to control his emotions—but how could he? His world had been upended like a ship in a storm. The one fact he had built his entire life around turned out to be a lie. Camilla was alive. All this time, she had been in Chester's possession—and he had left her there.

He mastered his feelings enough to speak. He could not let de Villiers anywhere near the truth of who he was.

"My apologies." He rubbed the spilled *geribita* with the toe of his boot. "This must be stronger than I remembered."

Both men watched him uneasily. De Villiers tried to make light of it.

"If you had seen Camilla, you would certainly not forget her. She is an irresistible beauty. Chester likes it to be thought that she is a free woman of color, but I happen to know she is still in bondage." He grinned uncertainly, still tense from Mungo's sudden eruption. "Chester does not keep her charms to himself. He spreads them around, very generously I may say."

It was all Mungo could do not to snap the man's neck like a chicken. Instead, he forced a ghastly smile.

"He must have changed. Chester Marion was not known for

his generosity in Virginia. Indeed, I heard that when he moved South he left a great many debts owing."

De Villiers frowned. "That is a poor thing to say of a man like Chester Marion."

Mungo had to leave. "Perhaps I misremembered." He put his hands to his head, trying to keep it from spinning. "I fear the liquor has gone to my head. Perhaps some air . . ."

He spun on his heel and walked away, heedless of the two men's gazes following him. He strode out of the compound and down to the beach. His feet crushed the shells that littered the soft sand.

At the water's edge, he stopped. He squatted down on his haunches, staring into the breaking surf.

For only the second time in his life, tears came to his eyes. He had cried when he thought Camilla was dead; now he cried again at the knowledge she was alive. If it was tears of joy, or anguish that he had left her so long in Chester's possession, he did not know. The crushing impotence he had felt in the *Raven*'s hold, confronted with the loss of his cargo, was nothing to what he felt now.

He needed to go to New Orleans. To rescue Camilla and destroy Chester. He could not wait.

You do not go against a man like Chester Marion with just a half-dime in your pocket.

He had nothing. He did not even know how he could pay Pendleton for the stores he needed to get home. And he could not go back to East Africa and spend another year hunting elephants, looking up at the moon every night and knowing that Camilla was in Chester's bed.

You could load a cargo here. That would save you a deal of time.

Once more, the door in his mind edged open, offering him another path. This time, he did not slam it shut. Staring out over the water, he saw the *Raven* swinging at anchor in the river estuary. He imagined her hold fitted with new decks. He imagined men and women loaded in, packed head to toe as tight as the ivory had been. He imagined a thousand dollars for each of them.

Could he do it—rip three or four hundred souls from their homes and transport them to a life of misery, simply so he could have his revenge on one man? The pictures in his mind changed. He imagined the Africans locked in this black hole, skin rubbed open by their chains, trapped in pools of their own vomit and blood and excrement. He imagined the stench and the screams that would accompany them all the way across the Atlantic.

I accept that the forcible extraction of Africans from their homeland is not a pretty thing. It is violent. There are deaths. If it were not so unpleasant, there would be no profit in it.

He thought of Chester Marion. He thought of the profit to be made in the slave markets of Havana. He thought of the money it would take to bring Chester to justice, and the satisfaction of making him pay for everything he had done. He thought of Camilla.

I will not play the hypocrite and weep false tears for the choices I have made.

If he could eat food served by slaves, bought with the labor of slaves, in a house built on the fortunes his grandfather had made in the slave trade, how could he blanch at this? He would be no better than his father, ringing his hands about equality while keeping his slaves in their chains. Better to be a villain than a hypocrite.

Sterling's voice came to him, seductive and sure: *There is only one law on this earth—the law that gives the strong and wealthy power over the weak and poor.*

A part of Mungo had flinched when the captain said it; now he saw the naked truth. If there was justice in the world, Camilla would not be Chester's captive. Windemere would not be lost. The ivory he had worked so hard to gain would not be scattered over the African seabed. Rutherford had been right: Mungo had been unforgivably naïve. Now, with every illusion stripped away, he saw the world as it truly was—a heartless place, infinitely indifferent to the sufferings of man. There was no such thing as fate. A man could make of his life what he would; the only thing that could stop him was chance or his own inadequacy.

Mungo would not be weak. If his conscience protested, that was merely the dying voice of a morality he had left behind, like a snake shedding its skin to grow. He would do whatever he had to do.

His tears had stopped. Now that he knew his course, he was filled with light and strength. All the bitter energy that had knotted his soul was suddenly loosed to a single purpose. It felt so good and pure, like the time he had punched Lanahan in the bar in Baltimore.

He walked back up to the compound. Pendleton and de Villiers were still there, now well into the bottle of *geribita*. Mungo knew they had been watching him, wondering about his extraordinary behavior. He offered no explanation. He no longer had to justify himself to any man.

"You wanted three hundred slaves for Chester Marion?" he asked de Villiers. "I will carry them for you—for a price."

He had stepped through the door in his mind, not even noticing as it slammed shut behind him. He had made his choice. There would be no going back.

But it would not be easy.

"There is no rush," said Pendleton. Night had fallen and they had moved inside the house. "De Villiers emptied my barracoons with that last shipment. Now the season is over, the natives will not bring any more captives for months."

"I cannot wait that long," said Mungo.

Pendleton shrugged. "You cannot whip up niggers from river

clay either." He pointed to one of his serving women, a girl of about fifteen. She was naked, except for a thin strip of cloth around her hips. "You will find ways here to pass the time."

Mungo ignored him. "Where do the slaves come from?"

"Upriver. Inland."

"Have you been?"

"Of course not." Pendleton made it sound an absurd suggestions. "The traders bring them to me. Why do you ask?"

"If the slaves will not come here, then I will go to them."

Pendleton banged his cup down. Liquor slopped out of it.

"That is a bad idea."

"I have no choice. I must get back to America."

"I don't think you understand how things are here." Absently, Pendleton traced a pattern with his finger on the table. "They've been buying and selling slaves in this country since the ink was wet on the Bible. There is a web of rules, customs, allegiances and debts that surrounds this trade, and it runs so deep in the land it's practically bedrock. So if a white man comes into it thinking he can have it all his own way just because they're savages, he's in for a rude awakening."

"I don't underestimate the dangers."

"How many men do you have? Maybe twenty? The local kings can muster thousands of warriors."

"Would they go to war because we took a few hundred of their people?"

"They don't give two shits about their people!" shouted Pendleton. "They'd go to war because you'd be muscling in on their trade and they don't care for competition."

He took another sip and shot Mungo a crafty look. "The only way you could do this is if you had local help. Someone who appreciates the intricacies involved."

Mungo understood him perfectly.

"Perhaps I have not been clear about my intentions," he said.

"I never imagined I could do this without your help. I rely on you completely to guide me."

"Why should I do that?" Pendleton asked, and though he slurred his words there was no missing the avarice in his voice.

"Because I will give you ten percent of the slaves I take."

Pendleton looked horrified. "If we are to be partners in this venture—true partners—then the division should reflect that. Half each."

Mungo settled back, took another mouthful of *geribita* and settled in for a negotiation.

They finally agreed on thirty-five percent. It was more than Mungo wanted to pay, but he had little to offer. He would need gunpowder, supplies, shackles, food for the slaves—everything, in fact, except the manpower. He did not mind being out-haggled. All it meant was that they would have to capture more slaves. Whatever else happened, he would make sure the *Raven's* hold was full when they left.

Pendleton hadn't finished.

"We cannot take the slaves here," he said. "We must go up the coast, to the Nyanga River."

"Why? You know people there?"

"The opposite. Because I know people *here*." Pendleton sighed. "Didn't you ever hear the expression 'don't shit where you eat'?"

They loaded up the *Raven* with shackles, copper kettles, maize and rice, and a new anchor. Then they sailed north.

As the months stretched out in New Orleans and the year turned, Camilla found she thought less and less of Mungo—her whole life at Windemere was like a dream she could remember only in snatches. Losing Mungo had hurt, but there was another, deeper wound that drove out every other thought. Each night she fell asleep weeping, her body aching for the embrace of her son. Sometimes, she would receive a letter from Bannerfield with news—"Isaac has started to walk"; "Isaac is chattering like a little bird"; "Isaac is a proper little lord"—and thought her heart would break.

She hardly ever saw Chester. He did not come to New Orleans anymore. Since the letter from Virginia, he had retreated to Bannerfield and stayed there, locked behind his gates. Camilla did not know what he was doing there, but there were clues in the manifests of the *Windemere* as she made her runs upriver. Two hundred boxes of Mississippi rifles; three dozen casks of gunpowder; cavalry saddles; one hundred dragoon swords; four hundred rifle cartridge boxes; fifty percussion pistols; one thousand cases of .54 caliber rifle ammunition.

Then one day a note arrived from Chester summoning her back to Bannerfield. She feared it meant that she had done something that displeased him—that it had been reported back to him and he wanted to punish her—but even that would be bearable if it gave her the chance to see Isaac.

She boarded the *Windemere* at the wharf by the Bannerfield warehouse, down on the levee. It was a lonely journey; apart from Granville, she was the only passenger, and she spent the voyage locked in the only stateroom. All the other cabins had been removed, on her instructions, to make room for cargo. The spring rains had come at just the right time that year, and the summer had been warm—Bannerfield was expecting a record cotton harvest. It would take all the space available on the

Windemere to bring it down to New Orleans. For miles before she reached the landing at Bannerfield, the ship steamed past acre upon acre of cotton fields gleaming white in the sunshine. It reminded her of the first time she had seen it.

But something had changed. Wooden watchtowers had been erected in the fields, manned by men with guns. There were more armed men at the landing when the *Windemere* docked, and still more around the huge warehouses where the crop was being piled up. Dressed as soldiers in blue uniforms and forage caps, they made Bannerfield look more like an armed camp than a plantation.

That impression only grew as Camilla disembarked. One of the soldiers, sporting a sergeant's stripes, was waiting for them. He saluted Granville, and gave Camilla a derisive glance.

"Been expecting you," he said. "We'll take you to the judge."

A troop of soldiers escorted them to the main house. The gardens around it had been dug up. In their place were broad ponds that almost made a moat around the house, while the excavated soil had been piled up in high embankments like levees. More men paced the earthen ramparts.

Camilla barely noticed any of it. All she wanted to see was Isaac. She scanned the windows that were now covered with iron bars, the paths that had been trampled to mud, looking for her son. He would be nearly two years old now. Would she even recognize him? Hope and worry swelled inside her until she thought she would burst.

Chester received her on the rear piazza, a wide terrace populated with marble statues overlooking the ponds and the ramparts. He sat at a table laid for lunch, already well into a bottle of wine. A little distance away, a small boy charged up and down the terrace with a wooden toy rifle.

Camilla cried out at the sight of him. He was so big, a little man dressed in white trousers and a dark blue jacket exactly like his father. The little puckered mouth that had suckled her breast was now broader; the tightly curled dark hair had grown out and was worn long, tied back with a ribbon. They must have used irons to straighten it.

He pointed the wooden rifle at her.

"Who that lady?" he said.

"That is Camilla," said Chester. "She is . . ." He paused, searching for a word. "One of our people."

"Oh," said the boy, with a dismissive shrug that stabbed Camilla right in her heart.

At two years old, Isaac already understood what "our people" meant. It meant she was a slave, and that meant she did not matter.

She approached Isaac slowly, forcing herself to smile.

"I hope that we can be friends."

The boy retreated behind his father's legs.

"My name is Camilla," she said slowly. "Can you say it?"

"Milla," he said.

"That's right." Her smile widened, but only so that he would not see her holding back tears.

"Can we play?" he asked.

"Not now," said Chester. "Camilla and I have business to discuss."

A black woman in a white bonnet came out and ushered Isaac away. Camilla bit her lip, and took a seat at the table. Servants set out the meal—brown oyster stew and beef collops—but she did not touch anything.

"Why did you bring me here?"

Chester sawed into his beef with gusto.

"Have you heard anything of Mungo St. John?"

"Nothing."

He looked up from his meal. His eyes fixed on her, making her feel exactly as she had when he had her naked in the little room upstairs.

"Do not try to hide anything from me," he warned. Blood from the meat oozed onto his plate. "I have not forgotten how he thinks of you. If he comes to New Orleans asking after me, he will soon get to hear of you."

"If you think you cannot trust me, then keep me here," said Camilla quickly. "Let me stay where Mungo cannot find me."

Chester rolled his eyes. "I think not. I cannot afford to bring you back from New Orleans—you are far too useful to me there. For one, François de Villiers should return soon from his little trading voyage. You have that little rat eating out of your hand, and with the cotton harvest coming in I will need all your wiles. I have accumulated a great many debts against that crop, so I shall need to wring every cent from the sale."

"Then I could come here after the crop is sold?"

"No." Chester gave her a cruel smile. "You are my little bird. I will leave you free to sing in the garden, so that when the cat comes you can fly up and warn me."

He reached across the table and held her hand, so tight she thought her bones would crack. "You will warn me, will you not?"

Camilla nodded, gritting her teeth against the pain.

"Isaac is turning into a bonny little boy," he said.

The change of tack caught Camilla off guard. She had to fight back the tears that sprang unwanted from the corners of her eyes.

"You miss him?"

"Yes." She did not trust herself to say more.

"Of course you do. What mother would not?" Chester took another mouthful. "I cannot risk having you here, corrupting him with false ideas about his heritage." Every one of his words was like a blade twisting in her gut. "But . . ." His gray eyes narrowed. "If you did something to prove your worth, perhaps I might reconsider. I might allow you to visit, to spend time with Isaac. You would like that? I might even—if you deliver me what I want—give you your freedom. That is more than Mungo St. John ever promised you, is it not?"

He let the possibility dangle in front of her. Camilla stared, a thousand thoughts racing through her mind.

"Think on it," said Chester. "Your freedom and your son, in exchange for Mungo St. John."

They sat in silence for a little while. The only noise was the sound of Chester chewing his meat.

"Why do the men call you 'Judge'?" said Camilla.

"I had myself elected County Judge a few months back."

"What for?"

In all the time she had known him, Camilla had never seen Chester interested in titles or offices. He did not care about society's opinion; all he wanted was real power.

"It gives me a certain influence on affairs with my neighbors. Property disputes, business suits . . . But more than that, it gives me the authority to call out the militia." He waved at a group of blue-jacketed soldiers marching along the path. "As you can see, that is exactly what I have done."

"It looks as if you have raised a private army."

Chester drained his glass and held it out for the servant to refill.

"My agents made inquiries back east. Apparently, Mungo bought a clipper ship and fitted her with a crew of the most notorious cut-throats in Baltimore. He loaded her full of enough weapons and shot to start a revolution, they say. Then he sailed out of Baltimore and vanished."

"Vanished?"

"This was more than a year ago. He has not been heard of since. But I am certain he is coming."

"Maybe the ship sank at sea."

"Maybe," said Chester. "Until I see his body laid out before me, I will not believe it. That man is capable of anything."

He sliced off the last of his beef collop—but instead of eating it, he picked it up and tossed it over the edge of the terrace. It sailed through the air and landed with a splash in the pond.

No sooner had it touched the surface than the water erupted. Camilla saw an upthrust snout, the snap of glistening jaws, and a long scaly body writhing amid the foam. It streaked away, its back rippling the water, and disappeared into the shade at the edge of the pool.

"What was that?" she cried.

"An alligator."

Camilla stared. "You put alligators in the garden?"

"They found their own way in, not long after we dug the ponds. I did not discourage them. If Mungo St. John tries to swim the moat, he will get a nasty surprise."

"But Isaac must play near there. What if he fell in?"

Camilla could hardly bear to imagine it—her little son and those bright flashing jaws.

"I have put a high wall around it, as you can see. They cannot get out. And his nurse sees that he does not go where he should not," said Chester nonchalantly. "She knows what I would do to her if anything happened to the boy."

He put down his knife and fork and glared at her. "Or what will happen to you, if you displease me."

Tippoo called out the soundings as the *Raven* cruised under quarter sails toward the mud-stained mouth of the Nyanga River. The rise of the sea floor was gradual, with no obvious reefs or sandbars. The waves broke evenly along the beaches on either side of the estuary, crashing down with a muted thunder that put Mungo on edge. In a life spent under sail, there was little as terrifying—and exhilarating—as the last minutes of an approach to an unmarked shore.

Mungo guided the ship around the tip of a coastal peninsula and into the calmer waters of the river's current. He ordered the sails stowed and the anchor dropped, and left de Villiers with three men to guard the ship. With his broken arm, the American factor would struggle through the jungle and be no use in a fight. Mungo needed him to stay alive, to bring him to Chester.

"Keep the flag flying day and night," he said, pointing to the Stars and Stripes hanging from the masthead. "As long as we show those colors, no navy patrol can search us."

He embarked in the cutter with Tippoo, Pendleton and the rest of the crew, armed with rifles and machetes. They landed on a broad mudflat that stretched along the river's edge to an embankment. At the top of it, they found the head of a path through massive, seven-foot stalks of grass. Tippoo hacked away with his machete, widening the opening, and sent two seamen ahead with orders to chart their course.

They followed the grassy track until the savannah ended at the edge of a vast forest. The trees reached high into the hazy sky, their vine-draped limbs overlapping like the thatching of a roof and blocking out the light of the sun. Through the tangle of underbrush, Mungo saw the sweep of the river bending away into the distance, shaded by trees whose trunks stretched over the swirling water like the buttresses of a cathedral.

They stopped beneath the branches of a tree whose girth

exceeded the arm-span of two men. They took swigs of water from leather flasks and swatted away the flies buzzing around them, as sweat oozed from every pore in their skin. It was only nine o'clock, but the air was so dense with humid heat that inhaling it felt like breathing underwater.

Mungo examined the great tree. Its bark was mottled white, like the sycamores in the forests of Virginia, but its exposed roots were alien to him. They extended outward from the trunk and stood as tall as a man in some places. He gazed into the canopy of leaves and saw a black object in the highest branches. Had its shape not changed, he would have guessed it was a bird's nest. But an arm snaked out and he realized it was a monkey, with almond-colored fur around its nose and chest, and a pair of stumpy legs beneath the bulge of a fat belly. The creature was staring at him. He returned the creature's gaze until it let out a fearsome screech and swung off its perch, crashing through the upper storey of the forest.

"Chimpanzee," Pendleton said, as the men glanced around in fright. "They are rare to spot and impossible to hunt. Believe me, I have tried. There are animals in this jungle that no one but God has ever seen. The Portuguese call it *o Jardim de Éden*— the Garden of Eden."

The air was as stagnant as a millpond, not a breath of wind to relieve the heat. A bird took flight and vanished into the trees. Mungo wiped a drop of sweat from his eye and tuned his ears to listen. The forest was quieter than he expected. He heard crickets chirping and the low warble of a songbird. There was the faint murmur of the river, the current so lazy it hardly made a sound.

"Move out," ordered Pendleton, and the sailors swung their machetes against the long grass. Mungo stayed put, which drew Pendleton's attention. "What is it?"

Mungo put a finger to his lips, unslung his rifle and pointed it into the trees. He had caught a flicker of movement—not much more than the twitch of a leaf, but when he looked closer he saw a shadow that had materialized at the edge of the river. It looked like the prow of a dugout canoe.

"Someone's out there," he whispered.

"Some*one* or some*thing*?" Pendleton whispered.

"A boat."

The *Raven*'s crew were at a disadvantage. With their backs to the tall grasslands and their eyes more accustomed to the sun than the shadows of the forest, they couldn't see far enough into the trees to make out an enemy, let alone bring them down. With hand gestures, Mungo ordered the men to fan out in an arc. Meanwhile, his eyes began to adjust. As well as the prow of the canoe, he could now see its gunwales and arrow-shaped stern, along with the handle of a paddle. The canoe was smaller and sleeker than the dugouts that had ferried them to the barracoons in Ambriz, and tiny by comparison to the huge craft that the Bakongo porters had used to deliver the slaves to the *Blackhawk*. Mungo searched the riverbank for more canoes but saw none.

"Cover me," he told the others. "I'm going to take a look."

He set off into the forest, avoiding dry twigs and leaves on the ground. He kept his rifle trained in front of him, moving the barrel from tree to tree as he advanced. When he passed through a curtain of leaves as wide as lily pads, he startled a family of birds, which flew off in a mad beating of wings. He nearly stepped on the head of a snake lying in a spray of foliage, but lunged out of the way in time, the serpent slithering into the hollow of a log.

It took him ten minutes to reach the canoe, which was resting on a bank of mud beside an eddy in the river. Three paddles lay propped against it, the blades still wet, but no sign of the men who had wielded them.

The cocking of a musket broke through the sounds of the

bush. Mungo swiveled around and saw a gun barrel pointing from a thicket of leaves. Outnumbered, cursing himself as a fool for walking into the trap, he raised a hand in surrender.

Three men emerged from the brush. They were Africans, with dark skin and proud faces. Two carried spears, while the third carried the antique-looking musket Mungo had heard being cocked.

Portuguese was the only European language they were likely to understand. Mungo spoke almost the only words of it he remembered.

"*Bom dia.*"

The man with the musket examined Mungo. He was the youngest of the three—younger than Mungo—but he had a fierce energy that the others naturally deferred to. His face was smeared with white clay, tracing the outlines of his mouth and cheeks. He had flat features: a straight nose, sharply cut cheeks and bright eyes that surveyed Mungo like a falcon tracking her prey.

He said something, though whether it was his own language or heavily accented Portuguese, Mungo couldn't tell. It did not sound friendly.

Mungo laid down his rifle.

"*Amigo,*" he said.

Did that mean *friend*? If it did, it had no effect.

A branch snapped behind him. Pendleton walked up, making no attempt to hide himself. His arms were spread wide, with a bottle of *geribita* in one hand and a string of brightly colored beads in the other.

He spoke rapidly to the Africans in Portuguese, underscoring his words with extravagant gestures and beaming smiles. He handed the bottle to the Africans and mimed drinking. They sniffed it suspiciously, but did not drink. They conferred among themselves.

"What are they saying?" Mungo asked impatiently. He hated not knowing what was going on, almost as much as he hated putting his life in Pendleton's hands.

"These men are Punu warriors. The one in the middle is called Wisi." The man in question glowered to hear his name spoken. "His father is the Nganga, a kind of local king."

"And?"

"They're going to take us to see him."

"There is no need—"

Pendleton put a hand on Mungo's arm. He never stopped smiling, but his eyes flashed a warning.

"You cannot go slaving in the Nganga's lands without his permission. It would be . . . impolitic."

Over his shoulder, Wisi had noticed the exchange. The prince's eyes narrowed in distrust. Pendleton waved the bottle at him again.

"Also, now that he has found you, he will expect payment," Pendleton went on to Mungo.

"But I have nothing to trade. That is why we came here ourselves in the first place."

Pendleton beamed at Wisi, a picture of innocence.

"Then you'd better think of something to offer before we reach the Nganga."

After loading the *Raven*'s men, the Punu tribesmen took up the paddles of the dugouts and propelled them upriver in single file, staying close to the bank and out of the mainstream, except to avoid submerged rocks and brambles. They chanted as they rowed, their strokes guided by the rhythmic beat of a drummer. They reminded Mungo of the Africans he had grown up with at Windemere, the hands who had harvested and cured the tobacco and loaded the carts for sale at market.

He wondered if Methuselah had come from this part of the

world, if some of their blood flowed in Camilla's veins. He touched the locket at his throat, and tried to forget the old man's dying words. *Beware the dark heart, and the thirst that never quenches.* Heading upriver on this terrible mission, it was hard not to think of what the prophecy might mean.

The blistering sun rose in the sky and fell again toward the ocean they had left behind. The forest crowded around them, the trees still but never silent, the eyes of many creatures watching as they glided by. Mungo saw white herons and kingfishers with brilliant blue breasts, and river terns that darted about as if dancing on the water. Occasionally he saw monkeys scampering in the treetops, and elephant and buffalo ranging along the shoreline. Sometimes snakes swam by, their heads poised above the water. On a rocky beach, Mungo saw a giant lizard sunning itself. It eyed the canoes, as if gauging the threat, then fled into the forest at such a pace it seemed simply to vanish.

Toward the end of the day the Punu warriors in his canoe wrinkled their noses and passed a word around that sounded like "*ibubu.*"

Mungo shook Pendleton awake from where he had been dozing in the bow of the canoe.

"What does *ibubu* mean?"

Pendleton turned to the nearest tribesman and said something in Portuguese. The African pointed with two fingers to a cluster of giant trees across the river whose boughs were draped with vines as thick as a man's arm. Pendleton used a hand to shade his eyes and searched the trees.

"*Ibubu* means great ape," Pendleton said. "They are the lords of the forest, as dangerous as lions when provoked. The ancients called them gorillas."

Although Mungo could see nothing in the shadows, the gorillas could see them. A scream rent the air, then another. The shriek was almost human, like a man on the torture rack crying out in agony. All the Punu ceased their chanting and peered into the forest. The sailors glanced around in fright, as if the sound had been uttered by a demon.

Mungo retrieved his spyglass, training it on the giant trees. He saw the silverback, sitting on one of the low-hanging branches like a king perched on his throne. He was a majestic animal, black except for the silver around his knees and neck and the bronze on his forehead. He had a broad, hairless chest, as muscular as a blacksmith, shaggy hair that hung from its arms like a shawl, and a craggy face that seemed to carry the wisdom of a thousand years. It was shocking to Mungo how closely the gorilla resembled a man. It was as if they were cousins, that somewhere in the forgotten past their ancestors might have been brothers.

He watched the gorilla until the canoes rounded a bend and he could see it no longer. He stowed his spyglass and listened as the Punu warriors took up their chant and carried on up the river. As the orange sun descended into the trees, they ran the dugouts onto a sandy embankment and Wisi ordered everyone to disembark. The tribesmen started down a path into the forest, singing all the way. The sailors from the *Raven* followed them with hands on their knives, eyes wide with fear, as the shadows extended and swallowed the light.

They reached the edge of the forest as the first stars began to appear. Beyond the trees was a wide savannah with a village at the center. The glow of torches formed a halo around the encampment, beckoning them like a hearth. The sound of distant chanting came through the air, along with the beat of many drums. Closer to the village, the music was louder, and the noise seemed to take on a physical dimension, as if it was the pulse of the earth itself. There was a density to the air, a presence that Mungo couldn't name.

He saw the bonfire and the dancers encircling it, stamping their feet on the dirt and twirling about with burning fronds in their hands. All of them were men, bare-chested, faces covered by elaborate white masks, their loins wrapped with blood-red cloth. The drummers were also men. The women of the village stood on the periphery, clad in skirts of grass, their breasts bared. Their hair and skin gleamed as if oiled, and their long necks and arms and legs glittered with jewelry.

In their midst, surrounded by young women, sat the Nganga. Like the dancers, he was wearing a carved white mask, but his was embellished with a crown of feathers and a beard of scarlet cloth. Around his wrists and ankles were bangles of polished gold, and hanging from his neck was a bejeweled necklace with a golden pendant, inlaid with a huge rose-colored diamond. Most extraordinarily of all, his throne was not African but European—a high-backed chair of gilded wood and brocade upholstery, the sort found in the courts of Lisbon and Paris.

He leaned forward and peered at the new arrivals. Behind the mask, Mungo saw two eyes alive with the same predatory intelligence he had seen in Wisi.

"Tell him we have come to help him fight his enemies," said Mungo.

He had spent the long hours traveling up the river thinking over Pendleton's warning. *The Nganga will expect payment.*

"And to make him rich," Mungo added.

Pendleton translated. The Nganga was unmoved. He said something offhand; the women around him laughed.

"He says he is at peace with all his neighbors. The only people he doesn't trust are the white men."

Mungo nodded. "That's wise. White men come, they steal his people and they hunt on his land." He saw Pendleton hesitate. "Say it," Mungo ordered.

He could not be sure what Pendleton said. But the words made the Nganga sit back thoughtfully.

"I know the Nganga wants to protect his people," Mungo continued. "But how can he do that with spears and sticks and rusted guns?"

Pendleton looked appalled. A curt command from the Nganga forced him to relay the message.

"What do you have to offer?"

Mungo held up his gun. It was one of the Hall rifles they had brought from Baltimore, stamped with the mark of the arsenal at Harper's Ferry.

Wisi stepped forward and spoke, waving his musket.

"He says they have guns."

"Not like this." Mungo looked at Pendleton. "Tell him I am going to give a demonstration."

"If you think you can intimidate these people—"

"I am not trying to intimidate anyone. But if you do not warn him what I am about to do, he may very well get the wrong idea when I open fire."

Reluctantly, Pendleton relayed Mungo's words.

"Tell him I challenge Wisi to a contest. You will time one minute, and we will see which of us can let off more shots in that time."

Pendleton translated. The Nganga nodded in approval, while Wisi hefted his musket defiantly. The Punu warriors cheered. A tree, about a hundred paces away, was chosen as a target. Mungo and Wisi loaded their weapons and laid out their powder and ammunition, while Pendleton pulled out his gold pocket watch.

"Ready?"

Mungo and Wisi nodded.

"Begin."

The two guns fired almost simultaneously. Both men were good shots—splinters flew from the tree as both balls hit the target. Mungo and Wisi did not pause to admire their marksmanship. Both were already reloading. Wisi tipped powder down the barrel from a flask, then took the long ramrod and rammed home the next ball.

He was still ramming it when Mungo fired his second shot. At the sound, Wisi looked up in disbelief. He was less than halfway through reloading, but Mungo had hit the tree a second time and had already begun to prepare for his next shot. Instead of loading the ball down the full length of the muzzle with the unwieldy ramrod, the Hall rifle had a second lever in front of the trigger guard that lifted out a short chamber from the stock. You could load the ball in there with your finger, slam it shut and it was ready to fire. While Wisi poured powder into the pan of his flintlock, Mungo simply placed a small percussion cap onto the steel nipple that stuck out for the hammer to strike.

Both men sighted their rifles again and fired. It was Mungo's third shot, but only Wisi's second, and while Mungo's ball hit the target yet again, Wisi's went wide.

"Fifteen seconds left," said Pendleton.

The Punu prince's face darkened. He grabbed his powder horn and, without pausing to measure the charge, tipped it down the barrel. He dropped the ball in and snatched the ramrod, nearly taking out the eye of one of the watching warriors. With the briefest tap that could barely have touched the ball, he extracted it again, primed the rifle and pulled the trigger.

There was a soft crack as the flint struck skin and bone. Wisi looked up in shock, turning to rage as he saw that Mungo had put his hand over the frizzen, stopping the flint from striking a spark.

He threw the rifle aside and pulled a knife from his belt, bellowing a stream of obscenities. Everyone was shouting. The warriors around him took up their spears and beat their hafts on the ground, closing around Mungo. The Nganga rose from his chair.

"What have you done?" said Pendleton in a panic.

Mungo remained perfectly still, his hand bleeding where the flint had struck it.

"Tell Wisi he put too much powder in his gun," said Mungo. "And he did not ram the paper wadding down after the ball. If he had pulled the trigger, the blowback would have taken his head off."

As Pendleton translated, the look on Wisi's face turned from fury to embarrassment. The Nganga leaned forward and spoke curtly.

"He demands that you prove it."

Mungo spread his hands in impotence. "I could not prove it without doing myself a mortal injury."

The Nganga nodded. But it did not seem to have satisfied him. He beckoned one of his warriors forward and gestured him to pick up Wisi's gun.

"I would not do that," Mungo cautioned.

The warrior shouted out a defiant battle cry. He took the gun, aimed it at the tree and pulled the trigger.

The weapon exploded. A tongue of flame shot back out of the touch-hole, sending fire and shards of flint straight into the eye of the man who had fired it. He dropped the gun and stumbled away, clutching his face and screaming. One of the women went after him. Otherwise no one moved.

Wisi sheathed his knife, his face almost as gray as his war paint. The warriors put down their spears and shuffled back.

Behind his mask, the Nganga stared at Mungo with something more like respect.

"There is no shame in losing to me," said Mungo. "I did not want to prove I was the better man. I wanted to show I have the better weapon. And that is why I have come here," he went on. "To give the Punu these weapons."

"You don't know what you're doing," Pendleton said, aghast. "If you give these niggers modern weapons, proper guns, it changes the balance of power."

"You're underestimating them," Mungo retorted. "They will use the guns against their own neighbors, just as men do the world over. And when they have won their battles you will have an even richer seam of captives to mine for slaves."

"What if they turn the guns on us?"

"Then they will soon find they have nothing to shoot." Mungo did not lower his voice, or change his tone; outwardly, he kept smiling at the Nganga. "Didn't you see how I primed it. The rifle is useless without a percussion cap, and I guarantee you there is nowhere within a thousand miles of this place that will provide them. So any man who can supply the caps will always be someone the Punu will do business with."

Pendleton shook his head. "You're the damnedest son-of-a-bitch I ever met," he said.

Mungo ignored him. He went forward to Wisi and presented him with the Hall rifle. Wisi took it reverently, examining the mechanism.

"*Amigo*," said Mungo.

Wisi nodded. For the first time since they had met, his face broke into a broad smile.

"*Amigo*."

The Nganga stood up and opened his arms in welcome. Tippoo and rest of the *Raven*'s crew joined the party around the throne. A group of women dispersed to one of the huts and returned with garlands of dried leaves. They handed a pair of these to each of the sailors and showed them how to fit them over shoulders and under arms to form a crosswise sling. Other women brought around baskets of dried roots to be chewed. Mungo hesitated.

"What is this?"

"They call it *iboga*," said Pendleton. "It'll open your eyes to visions you've never seen." He lowered his voice conspiratorially. "It'll also make you rock hard and ready to fuck like a bull in heat."

Mungo hesitated. It looked like nothing more than a pile of wood shavings. He took a small handful and chewed.

"I don't feel anything."

"Give it a few minutes," said Pendleton.

The men of the village resumed their dancing and drumming. Wisi took Mungo's hand and led him toward the fire, bringing him into the dance. The other sailors joined in. Mungo's feet began to move without conscious thought, as if he were a marionette and someone else was handling the strings. The universe in all its vastness shrunk to the space of his body as he whirled and pranced and stomped and swayed.

He realized the drug must be taking effect. His body seemed to lighten, as if partially liberated from gravity, and the world around him began to undulate. The sparks of the bonfire coalesced into shapes as they climbed into the starlit sky. He saw the shadowy faces of animals and humans, images he recognized and others he had never seen, at once inviting and terrifying. He felt a stirring in his loins, the power of it making him forget everything else.

When the women came for them, Mungo experienced neither inhibition nor control, only the pure compulsion of desire. A girl led him to a hut, so dark he couldn't see her. But he felt her when she pressed herself against him, her hands and mouth and breasts and buttocks, and he felt her heat when he entered her and the wave of ecstasy as she drew him toward climax.

In the dark, in the grip of the drug, he suddenly realized who she was. It was Camilla—she was alive, he had found her, and they would never be parted again. The wave inside him crested and crashed with such force that he cried out as if in pain.

He slumped against the girl, and fell into a trance-like sleep.

Mungo woke at first light with the vision of Camilla so fresh in his mind, he reached out and pawed the straw mattress next to him, expecting to find her there.

Of course he was alone.

He had dreamed of her before—many times—but the *iboga* had made it so vivid that even now he half thought he might see her duck under the door and come in, smiling that shy smile he loved so much.

Then, with a twist of guilt, he remembered the girl from the night before.

Two weeks ago you found out Camilla was alive, and this is what you do?

Had he betrayed her? What if fate took notice, if it deemed him unworthy of the task he had set himself? What if he never rescued Camilla?

He rubbed his eyes and told himself he was an idiot. The *iboga* root had addled his mind. There was no such thing as fate, he reminded himself, and the only limits on what a man could do were those he placed there himself. Conscience was merely a disguise for hypocrisy. If the encounter had meant anything, it was to stiffen his resolve for what he had to do that day. In order to free Camilla.

He dressed slowly and stumbled out of the hut. There were pigs and goats in pens, chickens and dogs wandering about, roosters strutting, children scampering around the legs of their mothers. Women sat by cooking fires, making flatbread and stirring broth for stew, while old men brought in fish from the river. The young men were taking no part in the domestic chores. They were sitting by the embers of the bonfire, painting their faces and preparing themselves for war.

Wisi was with them, as were Pendleton and Tippoo, checking the weapons and powder stores, and showing some of the young men how to handle and load the Hall rifles. The traditional weapons of the Punu were knives, short swords and spears, forged out of iron they had acquired from the Portuguese and the French, usually in exchange for slaves.

"What are they doing?" Mungo asked.

Unlike alcohol, the *iboga* left no headache or nausea, but he felt as if his head were stuffed with cotton.

"I spoke to the Nganga this morning." Pendleton was all smiles and good humor—the *iboga* had put him in an ebullient mood. "He is so pleased with the gift you have offered him, he has decided his men will join our expedition."

"That is not necessary," said Mungo. "Tell him we have enough people already."

"I will tell him no such thing." Pendleton lowered his voice. "Your gift of the rifles has fired the Nganga with a certain entrepreneurial zeal. He sees opportunities that were not there before—the chance to extend his power and become rich. In short, he has decided to join our venture as an equal partner."

"That will mean fewer slaves for us."

"But with more men, we can take more slaves," said Pendleton. "And there is nothing we can do about it. We are on the Nganga's land—we accept his terms. I told you there would be a price."

"It seems to go higher and higher," Mungo muttered.

But his mind was already moving on. There was no denying that with more men, it would be easier to get the captives back to the ship. As long as the ship's hold was full when she sailed, it did not matter how many people he had to take to pay his debts.

Wisi had been appointed as the leader of the Punu war party. He was the firstborn son of the Nganga, and when he issued orders, they obeyed without hesitation.

"They make a good army," said Mungo, admiring their weapons drill. "And he is a good commander."

After filling their bellies with the morning meal—rice, yams and stewed fish—they gathered their weapons and provisions and marched out of the village toward the rising sun, deeper into the wilderness. The jungle was dense with animal life and snakes hiding among the leaves, including a fat one with brown and black diamonds on its skin that Wisi identified as "the king of vipers" before putting a lead ball through its head.

In an ancient grove of the massive wing-rooted trees—according to Pendleton, they were called *ceiba* and were held sacred by the Punu—Mungo heard Wisi's men using the word *ibubu* again. He took a breath and caught the whiff of a pungent odor. He craned his neck for a glimpse of gorilla but saw nothing but leaves and branches. The tribesmen waited in silence, their eyes roving the forest. One of them pointed and Mungo saw a miniature black form descending from the heights on a pair of thick vines. Mungo thought it was a monkey until it climbed onto a hunched shadow at the base of the tree. The mother gorilla turned toward them for an instant, then crashed away into the underbrush. A great roar split the air, sending Mungo's heart pounding. Of the silverback he saw only a flash before it, too, vanished into the trees.

"Have the Punu ever killed one of them?" Mungo asked Pendleton.

"They do not hunt the *ibubu*. But there are times when they must fight to protect themselves. That happened to Wisi when he was a boy. He was with his sister when they came across a family with babies. The female *ibubu* attacked Wisi's sister and tried to rip off her face. That is what they do." Pendleton shaped his hand into a claw and pulled it down from his forehead to his chin. "Wisi drove his spear through the creature's heart. But he could not save his sister. She lost too much blood."

The next day they turned north, across swathes of savannah and forest. Occasionally, they had to ford swift-flowing rivers. The pace they kept pushed many of the sailors to exhaustion, but they carried on with only mumbled complaints.

Late in the afternoon of the second day, they spotted a hippopotamus among the reeds of a quiet bend. A few minutes later, they surprised a crocodile taking in the sun on a beach. It brandished its fearsome teeth, then threw itself into the muddy water, disappearing below the surface. After sighting the monster, some of the sailors refused to cross the river.

"The village is that way," Mungo said, pointing back the way they had come. "Good luck finding your way there."

That cut short the mutiny. The men decided they were more

frightened of the jungle—and Mungo's anger—than the croc-odiles. They crossed the river without mishap, and carried on until evening. They made camp in a patch of forest a short walk from a clear stream. While the sailors tended to their bruised and blistered bodies, the Punu tribesmen speared fish and built a fire, cooking the fish on a spit. They served it whole, and pre-pared their plan of attack for the following morning.

Pendleton translated. There was a village, Wisi said, a little distance away, populated by a rival clan. They would make their approach in the hour before dawn, circling the settlement like a noose. On Wisi's signal, they would fire their guns into the air and raise an alarm, while converging on the village from all sides and driving the people into a herd at the center. Anyone who tried to escape would be killed. The rest would be lashed together with the rope and sticks, and marched back to the Nganga's abode. Wisi and Pendleton described the process so simply that it sounded to Mungo more like a ritual than a raid.

The night descended like a curtain over the forest. The sailors found it difficult to sleep. The sounds of the nocturnal forest were foreign to their ears—the calls of the night birds and the rustle of animals in the underbrush. When a leopard let out a screech, they pushed their bedrolls as close as they could to the fire. The Punu warriors, on the other hand, spread piles of leaves into padded beds and slept soundly.

Exhausted after two days of marching, Mungo turned in early and fell into slumber. But though his body shut down, his soul drifted without rest through the world of dreams.

He was asleep, and then he was awake in a land of shadow. Running. He heard the pounding of his feet, felt the jarring impact in his bones. He was panting, his lungs aflame, sweat streaming down his face. But the place was freezing, like the sunless void of a winter's night.

He heard a scream. It reached like a blade through his rib-cage, transfixing his heart. The pain was greater than anything he had ever imagined. He tried to shriek, but no sound came from his throat.

He glanced over his shoulder and saw the shadow among shadows. It was the *ibubu*. The pain inside him grew as the monster closed in. He heard the rough snort of animal breathing, the gallop of the monster's knuckles on the ground. He spent the last of his strength in a mad dash, but the beast caught him with ease. He was flying through the air, hurled by powerful hands and arms.

The gorilla emerged from the shadows and stood over him, its rancid stench like a cloud in the air. He saw the flare of its nostrils, felt the crush of its paws on his shoulders.

Then the vision changed. There were snakes writhing in a pit and an old man in their midst, his withered body punctured by fangs. The man was Benjamin St. John. Then the old man was gone, replaced by one much younger, his face shrouded by a mane of dark hair. His body had fewer wounds, his neck and chest were still unmarked. But the snakes were hissing at him, sensing his vulnerability. They came for him in a wave, driving their fangs into his throat and cheeks.

A shake from Tippoo shocked Mungo's eyes open, and the dream was gone.

"It is time."

It was still dark. As the men gathered, Tippoo distributed rations of dried fruit and salted beef. One of Wisi's lieutenants handed out small *iboga* roots. Mungo waved off the basket and forbade his men from touching it.

"Only a fool would refuse *iboga*," sniffed Pendleton. "You don't want them shitting their breeches, do you?"

"My men will stand up under fire. And if a man has a gun in his hands, I prefer him to have a clear head."

"As you wish."

Pendleton made a show of taking the largest root from the basket.

After dousing the fire with water from the creek, they threw coils of bark rope over their shoulders and decamped under an order of silence. Wisi and his men took the lead. As Mungo moved through the darkness, he felt the grain of the rifle stock in his hands, the cold touch of the trigger. He saw stars peeking through gaps in the leaves and traced the head of the Dolphin not far from the feet of the Eagle. They reminded him of his grandfather. It seemed a lifetime ago—the nights he had spent as a boy with Benjamin St. John, studying the planets through the lens of the telescope in the observatory at Windemere. The rings of Saturn, the moons of Jupiter, the blue orb of Venus, the nebula of Orion, the trio of Alpha Centauri . . . His grandfather had told him that they demonstrated the grandeur of God, but that was not what Mungo saw. To him, those cold and distant spheres said—if they deigned to speak at all—that he was a speck of dust in an infinite universe, beneath notice.

Later he had seen those stars again, through the open roof of the observatory, lying on his back with Camilla naked beside him. On those nights, he had almost felt some trace of his grandfather's reverence. Now, the memory was too painful to touch.

His foot caught on a root; he stumbled, and almost discharged his rifle by mistake. He should watch his footing, he told himself angrily, not stare at the stars.

When they reached the border of the plain, Mungo saw the outline of the village. The sky in the east was beginning to brighten; by the dawning light, Mungo could see at least a hundred wattle-and-daub huts clustered together on a low ridge that rose above the plain. Wisi had estimated the population at three hundred inhabitants, including children, but Mungo reckoned there must be double that number.

The war party moved silently across the grass, fanning out until they encircled the village. Wisi waited until they were all in position before he mimicked the warble of the songbird and the men raised their guns to the sky, rending the tranquil morning with an explosion of gunpowder and shouts of bloodlust.

Even though he was prepared for it, the sudden thunder of so many guns sounded to Mungo like the beginning of the end of the world. He scrambled to his feet and ran toward the village as the noose the Punu had made closed around it. The wattle fence that ringed it was no protection. The Punu smashed through it like charging elephants.

Still the villagers had not woken to their danger. The Punu warriors were among the huts now, working through the village with practiced efficiency—breaking open wicker doors, jamming their guns and spears through doorways, shouting their war cries and letting off shots to terrify their victims.

But something was wrong. Instead of emerging with prisoners, they came out of the huts shaking their heads in confusion. The huts were empty. Even the women and children had gone. Had the village been abandoned? But no—there were goats and chickens in their pens, and the fires that Mungo had seen the night before still smoldered. Where was everyone?

It was a trap. Mungo realized it a split second before it sprang. Somehow, the villagers must have seen the Punu coming. They had abandoned their homes, letting the raiders in unopposed while they waited in the jungle beyond the village. Instead of being surrounded, they had surrounded their attackers.

Now they struck. Mungo heard the whistle of air as a spear flew past his shoulder, and the wet crunch of the sharpened point burying itself in the Punu warrior beside him. The man screamed, but it was drowned out by the war cry that rose from the tribesmen who were suddenly racing toward them with spears and knives and shields.

Bullets flew and bodies fell, but still the attackers came, throwing their spears with deadly accuracy. A Punu warrior took one through the neck. Another slumped to the ground with a shaft protruding from his stomach.

"Keep in among the houses!" Mungo shouted.

Wisi's men and the *Raven*'s sailors were vastly outnumbered.

If they fought on open ground, they would be slaughtered. Instead, they ran to one of the larger huts, near the middle of the village, and took up a defensive position. Mungo's men fought with their backs to the wall, firing their rifles at the oncoming villagers, while Wisi and his warriors guarded their flanks. The surrounding buildings gave their enemies cover—but they also broke up their attacks. Instead of rushing at the war party and overrunning them, they were forced into narrow approaches where the Hall rifles could hold them off.

In Baltimore, Mungo had hand-picked the *Raven*'s crew to be hardened fighters. Wisi's men were warriors. The villagers, by contrast, were farmers and laborers. They were fighting for their freedom, for their village and their families—but nothing had prepared them for the ferocity they faced. The Hall rifles cut them down with devastating effect. Some of the villagers took balls through the heart, others through the head, their skulls exploding on impact.

The attack faltered. Some of the villagers fell to their knees in surrender. A few disappeared into the forest.

"Don't let them get away!" cried Pendleton. "Those are the men we came for!"

The *Raven*'s crew charged forward after the fleeing villagers. Some of the Punu followed them. But they had gone too soon. Unseen in the melee, a group of villagers had crept around the rear of the house where the raiding party had made their stand, to attack from behind. They burst out now from around the corner, catching the remnants of the Punu unawares. Half a dozen warriors went down before they even saw their attackers. Others turned, but too late.

Mungo had already started to follow the fleeing villagers when he heard Wisi's war cry. By the time he looked back, only two of the Punu remained alive—Wisi and one of his lieutenants, caught in a swarm of villagers. The two warriors stood back to back and cut down every man who assailed them. One villager lost his hand; another took a blade through the throat; a third fell after being struck in the head with Wisi's spear. But there were more, and they kept coming. They fought with abandon, knowing that capture would be worse than death.

Mungo saw Wisi's lieutenant fall, stabbed by a sword from behind. Wisi let out a blood-curdling yell and swung his spear like a mace, striking the attacker with a blow to the head. A second man lashed out at his exposed flank. One of the blades pierced Wisi's leg. Another spear flew past his neck, missing his throat by an inch. To Mungo's amazement, Wisi shook off his wounds and struck out with his short sword, slicing the arm of one of the men down to the bone. The man howled and stumbled backward, as blood erupted from the wound.

But Wisi's strength was flagging. The last three attackers thrust their blades at his stomach and head. With twists of his body, he managed to evade all of them, but the effort left him winded, his leg coated with blood and buckling where it had been stabbed.

Mungo ran in. He swung his rifle like a club, knocking the attacker nearest him off his feet, then drove his knife into the side of the next man. That gave Wisi precious moments. He feigned an attack with his sword, and as the last villager twisted away he exposed his legs to the sweep of Wisi's spear. The man went down in a tangle of limbs. With a fearsome cry, Wisi raised his sword to plunge it through the man's spine. He would have killed him, had Mungo not shouted, "He's worth nothing to us dead!"

Although Wisi knew no English, he seemed to understand. He wiped the blade on his loincloth and used it to prod the fallen man's buttocks. Doubled over, the man crawled toward the circle at the center of the village.

The battle was over. The survivors—those who had surrendered, or been captured—were herded back to the central square. Soon Wisi's men found their women and children, who had been hiding in a clearing in the forest nearby. The Punu warriors dragged them back to join their menfolk. Some were sobbing and babbling in their indecipherable tongue. Others stared vacantly at the ground, faces set hard in defeat. Wisi's men bound them by their necks with the bark ropes, while the *Raven*'s crew guarded them with their rifles.

Pendleton stepped forward and grabbed a young woman by the arm. A man beside her lunged toward him, but one of Wisi's men struck him with the butt of his knife and put his boot on the man's neck, while aiming his weapon at the crowd. The villagers recoiled, their pleas turning to sobs. Pendleton dragged the girl away, toward the nearest hut.

"What are you doing?" Mungo asked.

Pendleton paused. The *iboga* root had had its usual effect, putting a grotesque bulge in his trousers.

"Sampling the merchandise," he said with a smirk.

Mungo leveled his rifle. "You don't touch any of them."

The chill command in Mungo's voice cut through even the *iboga* daze. Pendleton took one step forward, saw Mungo's finger tighten on the trigger, and stopped.

"I thought we were partners," he complained.

"And that is why we will do nothing to spoil our cargo. Let her go."

With a sour look, Pendleton released the girl. She ran back to the crowd and squeezed in among them.

Pendleton spat on the ground. He took up a coil of bark rope and thrust it into Mungo's hands.

"Tie them up—by the neck, mind you, not the waist. That way they won't pretend to fall. And you'd better make sure the knots are tight. If there is a shortfall, it will come out of your share."

A dawn mist rose off the mouth of the Nyanga river, blotting out the sun and turning the world gray. Birds sang and monkeys screeched from the trees, but the sound was muted; the river surface was still and glassy. The only ripples that disturbed it came from the prow of a longboat cutting through the water, and the sixteen oars that drove it forward.

In the stern of the boat, Captain Edwin Fairchild of HMS *Maeander* peered through the mist for the dark shape of the ship he knew must be moored nearby. It had been a poor year for him. Either the war against the slave trade had had more success than he dared hope, or—more likely, he feared—the slavers were getting better at avoiding the Royal Navy. In the months the *Maeander* had been sailing these waters, they had barely caught anyone. Then there had been the storm—which the *Maeander* had barely survived—and more fruitless days patrolling the coast. It was late in the season, and pickings were slim, but Fairchild had driven his crew relentlessly. He was convinced there might still be ships in the area, and would not give up the chase.

"If there is any hope of saving even one poor African from bondage, we owe all our best endeavors to save him," he had lectured the crew.

Even so, he could not keep the ship at sea forever. With provisions running low, Fairchild had been about to turn back to their base at Freetown. Then his prayers had been answered. All his weeks of searching and doubt had simply been the Lord's way of testing him. Coasting north, looking to take on water, an eagle-eyed lookout had spotted a masthead in a river estuary. As soon as they were around the point, hidden by a thickly wooded peninsula, the *Maeander* had dropped anchor.

Fairchild's officers had counseled caution. Better to wait until she sailed, when the evidence of her crime would be incontrovertible. But Fairchild was impatient. The shame of his last voyage aboard the *Fantome* still burned in his breast. He had stood on the slave ship's deck and failed to save her captives. Worse, he had only escaped with his life thanks to Mungo St. John. True, the London papers had lionized him as a hero for standing alone against the slavers, and he had earned a promotion from the engagement. But that was hollow praise. What he needed was redemption.

"Besides," he argued, "once the slaves are loaded aboard, we will not be able to use our cannon without risk of hurting them. Better to take the ship at anchor, when she has no chance of escape."

And that was why, at first light, Fairchild found himself leading a boarding party of three boats up the river. His scouts had reported that the slave ship appeared lightly manned, but he was taking no chances.

"There."

He saw a dark shadow ahead and altered course. The mist hid their approach until they were almost under her stern. Even when they were close enough to read the name picked out on her transom—*Raven*—no one saw them. The crew had not bothered to post a guard.

The longboat sidled against the *Raven*'s hull. The coxswain—a sturdy man whose preferred weapon was a boarding ax—made to climb her ladder, but Fairchild waved him back.

"I will go first," he whispered. He would lead by example.

His heart raced as he climbed the ladder. He kept waiting for shouts or shots, any sign that he had been seen. But none came. He reached the top, paused a second to draw his pistol, then vaulted over the side.

"In the name of Her Majesty Queen Victoria, I am taking possession of this ship!" he announced.

No one heard him. The deck was empty. More of his men swarmed over the side, weapons ready.

"Search her!" Fairchild snapped the order.

His confidence had begun to waver. Perhaps she was a simple merchantman that had put in for water. Perhaps the ship had been abandoned. But her rigging was in good order, and though she had suffered damage recently it had been repaired.

Then all his doubts were laid to rest. The coxswain emerged from below decks shepherding four disheveled men who stank of rum. They must have been rousted from their hammocks. They looked around in shock, rubbing their bleary eyes in disbelief at the crew of Royal Navy men aboard their ship.

"Which of you is in command?" Fairchild asked.

After a pause, one shuffled forward. He did not look like an officer. He had a prominent forehead, sharp sideburns and a terrible sunburn. He looked around like a cornered animal, fixing his eyes anywhere but on Fairchild.

"Are you the captain?" Fairchild asked.

"Only a passenger."

"And what is your purpose here?"

The man looked at the masthead, as if for inspiration from above.

"Fishing," he tried.

"Where is the captain? Where are the rest of the crew?"

"Gone hunting."

"Hunting for what?"

He did not answer, though it made no difference. The coxswain had finished his search and emerged from below carrying a set of iron shackles. He threw them down on the deck.

"There's hundreds of those. They've even built the slave decks."

"Then this ship is forfeit," said Fairchild.

Whoever the captain might be, he was clearly an amateur. Most slavers took great care not to carry any of the tools of their evil trade until the slaves were ready to come aboard. Chains, shackles, copper kettles—even timbers and nails for building extra decks: possession of any of these things meant the Royal Navy could seize the ship. The *Raven* proclaimed her guilt on every count.

The only protection she had was the American flag fluttering defiantly at her masthead. It should have given her immunity from being searched by a British officer; Fairchild had overstepped his authority. But there were ways around that.

He crossed to the mast and severed the halyard with his saber. The flag fluttered to the deck. Fairchild threw it over the side and watched it disappear in the muddy river current.

"You will record the ship was not flying any colors when we boarded her," he told his men.

They nodded happily. They all stood to gain a share of the money if the *Raven* was sold by a prize court.

But where were the rest of the crew?

Fairchild surveyed the shoreline.

"There are no barracoons here. They must have gone inland to capture the slaves themselves."

He had never heard of such a thing—usually, white captains and crews touched African soil as little as possible—but it was the only explanation. The captain was not just a novice; he must have been desperate. Fairchild thanked the Lord again for the opportunity he had been given.

"Secure the ship," he told his men. He pointed to the embankment beyond the mud flats that lined the river. The trees grew thickly around its edges; the only path led up an earthen gully toward the higher ground. That would be the way the slaves would come.

"When this ship's captain returns, we will give him a warm welcome he does not expect."

A thought struck him. He turned back to his prisoner.

"What is the name of the man who commands this unholy vessel?"

De Villiers considered not answering, but it would make

no difference. They would surely find the name written in the logbook.

"Thomas Sinclair."

Fairchild had heard the name before, though for a moment he could not think where. It was not a man he had captured before. Someone he had read about?

Then—with a rush of surprise so hard he almost had to sit down—it came to him. A warm night in Madeira, the Mariners' Ball and the last man he had expected to see.

I would be grateful if you could forget the name Mungo St. John. Here, I am Thomas Sinclair.

He gripped the rigging, staring out at the mudflats and the land beyond. As the shock receded, he saw this for what it truly was. The Lord had answered his prayers. He had given Fairchild the opportunity to atone for what had happened aboard the *Blackhawk*.

When Mungo returned, Fairchild would be ready for him.

Mungo crested the brow of the hill and looked down into the river delta. There was the *Raven* riding safely at anchor. His spirits rose to see his ship again, and the promise of the open sea. The journey back had been long and difficult. The slave coffle—almost three hundred and fifty people—moved agonizingly slowly. Back at Wisi's village, the Punu had yoked the captives together with forked branches tied fast around their throats. Even if one escaped, a six-foot branch hanging off his neck meant he could not run far. It was a wise precaution, but it did not help their speed—and Mungo could not drive them too hard, for he needed them in good enough condition to survive the passage to Cuba. Normally, they would have had weeks or months being fattened up in the barracoons, but Mungo did not have that luxury.

He was desperate to get aboard—to be free of Africa, the

flies and the heat. Yet now he hesitated. Looking down on the *Raven*, he felt a prickle on the back of his neck that something was wrong.

There was no one on deck. That angered him, though it didn't surprise him. De Villiers and the others were probably below decks, out of the sun, sleeping off their hangovers.

Then he saw it. The masthead was bare; there was no flag flying.

Mungo pulled out his spyglass and studied the scene more carefully. The edge of the riverbank had been churned to mud, as if a great herd of animals had come down to drink. But what animal would choose to drink so close to the ship? Beyond, he saw tracks in the soft earth. From a distance they could have been animal tracks, but magnified by the glass they looked decidedly more human. He followed them with his telescope, across the mud flats and up an embankment until . . .

There.

It was well camouflaged, but Mungo already had an idea what he was looking for. In a grove of trees, almost hidden by thorn bushes and long grass, he saw the black muzzle of a gun pointing out.

He ran back to the main column and gestured them to halt. The slaves collapsed to the ground, groaning. The branches tied around their necks had made sores that were beginning to suppurate in the heat. Flies clustered on the wounds, and with their hands bound the captives could do nothing to stop them.

All because of Mungo. He was the reason they had been torn from their homes, watched their families slaughtered. Sometimes when he looked at them, he felt a pang of something almost like sympathy. He knew—too well—what it was like to lose everything. Was it right to visit the same misery on them in pursuit of his revenge?

You are starting to sound like Fairchild, he scolded himself. God could judge him. Chester had given him no choice.

There is only one law, Mungo reminded himself. *The power of the strong and wealthy over the weak and poor.*

He could not let himself be weaker or poorer than Chester. He had to rescue Camilla.

And now he had more urgent things to worry about than the pangs of conscience. He summoned Tippoo, Pendleton and Wisi and explained what he had seen.

"How many men?" Tippoo asked.

"I did not see any. But the ships of the Preventative Squadron are mostly corvettes and sloops. There could be upward of a hundred men."

Mungo tried to imagine what the British officers—they must surely be British—might have planned. Clearly they were expecting him to bring his slave coffle down the track and across the mudflats to the ship. They had prepared their ambush on the embankment so that when he came out on the mudflats, he would be directly under their fire.

But if he were the British officer in command, he would not have stopped there. The Royal Navy had obviously been aboard the *Raven* to strike her colors. Presumably they had captured her skeleton crew as well. Why leave the ship abandoned? Why not hide a detachment of men below decks, ready to burst out on Mungo's men when they arrived? Out on the flats, Mungo would be caught between the sailors on the embankment and the sailors on his ship. He would be utterly at their mercy.

"What do we do?" said Tippoo.

They could not retrace their steps to Wisi's village. It would take the best part of a week overland; slaves would start to die. Even if they reached it, what then? The Nganga had no more men to spare. And while they were gone, the British captain might get bored of waiting. If he sailed the *Raven* away, Mungo would be marooned.

But to march out onto the mudflats would be as good as surrendering. Even with Wisi's men and the *Raven*'s crew combined, he barely had forty men. They would be outnumbered more than two to one.

Tippoo, Wisi and the rest of the men were looking at him, waiting for a decision.

"The only advantage we have is that the British do not know that we have seen them," Mungo mused.

"So?" said Tippoo.

"So we will give them what they expect."

Mungo explained his plan. It took some time to translate it for Wisi, and even longer to persuade him to accept it.

But there was no other choice.

Fairchild crouched at the top of the embankment and peered out through the brush that disguised their position. A fly crawled over his face, but he did not swat it away. He had waited three days in this infernal heat, being eaten alive by insects and scratched by the thorn bushes that surrounded them. Some of his men had started to mutter that they should give up. They had more than enough evidence to seize the ship. They could take her to the Mixed Commission Court and claim their prize money, and leave her crew to rot on the coast.

Fairchild had silenced all such talk. He would wait here until Judgment Day, if necessary, for Mungo St. John. The man was the Devil incarnate. Fairchild had to stop him. And yet, even now, he thought of the look in Mungo's yellow eyes in that moment he had pointed the gun at his head aboard the *Blackhawk*. He was convinced he had seen a spark of goodness there, a moral qualm buried deep that had made him spare Fairchild's life. If Fairchild could capture Mungo—confront him—he could surely redeem him.

There is more joy in Heaven over one sinner who repents, than ninety-nine just men, he told himself.

That was why he had endured three days in this horrible place, deaf to the pleas of his men, and of reason, rather than simply sail away with his prize. He would save Mungo St. John, and when they returned to England, Mungo would be able to testify with the full power of the convert about the abhorrent practices still rife on the coast of Africa. His testimony might even force the American government to withdraw the immunity their ships enjoyed, and allow the British squadron to intercept them. That would be a hammer blow against the slave trade.

On the hill away upriver, where the Nyanga disappeared around a bend, a movement caught his eye. Keeping his telescope carefully shaded, lest any flash of the glass betray him, Fairchild examined the ridge. A man had appeared. He paused, scanning the river basin ahead. Fairchild held his breath, but evidently the man saw nothing to alarm him. He lifted his arm in greeting to the *Raven*, lying at anchor, and began descending the hill. More men followed, armed with rifles. Fairchild counted a dozen of them, escorting a column of about twenty Africans who were bound together at the neck by forked sticks. It had not been a productive raid. Twenty slaves, even prime healthy young men such as these, would not even cover the cost of the voyage.

They would never see the inside of the ship's hold, Fairchild promised himself. He wriggled back and found his second in command.

"Ready the men," he ordered.

Of the *Maeander*'s total complement of one hundred and eighteen men, he had brought one hundred ashore.

"If the *Raven* escapes, that does not leave enough men to work the ship to pursue her," his lieutenant had warned, but Fairchild dismissed that risk. Mungo would not get aboard the *Raven*—and if he did, he would find forty of the *Maeander*'s toughest men waiting for him. Sixty more were with Fairchild at the top of the embankment.

Everything was ready. Fairchild loosened his sword in his scabbard, checked the priming on his pistols, and prepared to give the command to attack.

Mungo led his men across the mudflats, forcing himself not to look at the guns hidden in the thicket to his right. He felt almost naked, walking into a trap he knew was waiting for him. What if he had misjudged? He doubted the British would open fire at that range for fear of hitting the slave coffle, but there was always the possibility that they had a marksman with a rifle trained on his head.

He held himself upright and showed no fear. He had made his choice, making the best of the hand he had been dealt. Now all that remained was to see how the cards fell.

The boom of a gun sounded from the embankment, echoing across the flats. Smoke puffed from the thicket, and a flock of red-breasted birds flew into the air. Mungo turned, as if he was surprised, to see a group of check-shirted British sailors charging out of the trees, armed with pikes and boarding axes. An officer led them, sword raised, blue coat unbuttoned and flapping around him. A mop of sandy hair blew back from his weathered face.

He halted his men about fifty yards from the slaving party.

"You are surrounded and your ship is taken!" he shouted, his booming quarterdeck voice carrying easily over the flat ground. "Surrender yourselves to Her Majesty's justice!"

Mungo stared. This time, his surprise was entirely unfeigned. Now that they had stopped, he could see the officer clearly.

"Fairchild?"

"Mungo St. John!" There was no surprise in Fairchild's voice; he had anticipated this moment. They stared at each other across a hundred and fifty feet of mud. "In the name of all that is honorable and good, I implore you to surrender!"

Mungo had no time to wonder what trick of fate had brought his old adversary here. The die was cast.

"We surrender!"

He threw down his rifle. The other men did likewise. The Africans in the coffle looked around as if they could not believe what was happening, while Fairchild advanced with his men. Mungo met his gaze head on, no sign of defeat in his yellow eyes.

"You did the right thing," said Fairchild.

"You did not give me much choice."

Mungo nodded to the men surrounding him, then back to the *Raven*. Dozens more sailors had appeared on her deck, muskets at the ready.

"But you have a choice now." Fairchild's men spread out, making a ring around the slave party. "God has given you one last chance. Give up this life you have made for yourself."

He thought he saw a shadow of regret cross Mungo's face.

"I did not choose this life," Mungo said softly.

"But you may choose to change it."

"No."

Fairchild thought he had misheard. Before he could think, a cry from beside him drew his attention away.

"The ship!"

His lieutenant was staring beyond the captives, across the flats to the river where the *Raven* was moored. Or rather, Fairchild saw, where she should have been moored. Instead of lying fast at anchor, she had somehow slipped her cable and was drifting downriver toward the sea.

It took her prize crew completely by surprise. They dropped their weapons and scrambled for her rigging, trying to find the sheets and halyards on the unfamiliar ship so they could regain control. The mainsail dropped, but that only made the situation worse. The wind was coming from off the land, so that as it caught the sail it only added to the ship's momentum downstream. Away from Fairchild.

Fairchild turned to Mungo in horror. "What—?"

In the few seconds he had been distracted, everything had changed. The slaves were no longer bound in a coffle. They had pulled off the sticks that yoked them together—which were not sticks at all, Fairchild realized, but rifles with bark tied to them. They brandished the guns at their erstwhile rescuers.

"Don't you understand?" Fairchild shouted. "We are here to rescue you!"

Of course they could not comprehend him. In a split second, something he had said to Mungo that night at the Cambridge Union flashed back in his memory. *Arguing with you is like arguing with the Devil himself. White is black, and black is white.* And how else could you explain the terrible sight he saw now? Blacks, armed with modern rifles, turning them on the white men who had come to save them.

The Africans fired. The *Maeander*'s men were taken completely off guard. Eight or nine of them went down, clutching wounds, or killed outright. Before the others could respond, Mungo's crew grabbed the weapons they had thrown down and added a second volley.

Fairchild's numerical advantage had evaporated. Instead of a dozen men, he was now facing three times that number, all armed. The reinforcements on the *Raven* were drifting helplessly downriver. And the sudden onslaught from the Africans had leveled the field still further.

One man was responsible for this. One man alone who could make Africans turn against their saviors, who could ruin Fairchild's triumph yet again. With his sword in one hand and pistol in the other, Fairchild sought him out through the smoke and dust that swirled on the battlefield.

The guns had fallen silent. There was no time to reload, even with the rapid Hall rifles. Some of the Punu used the stocks of their guns as clubs, while others pulled out the knives they had hidden under their loincloths, or revealed spears hidden as coffle sticks. Wisi picked up a boarding ax dropped by one of the dead sailors and whirled it over his head, driving back any man who came near.

But British reinforcements were arriving. The men Fairchild had left on the embankment ran down to help their comrades. That gave the Royal Navy men a numerical advantage once more. Mungo and his fighters had to give ground, retreating toward the river. Soon they would be trapped against its banks.

Fairchild saw Mungo's broad figure and lunged toward him. One of the slavers—a white man in an extraordinary purple coat—tried to block Fairchild's way, but Fairchild leveled the pistol and shot him in the face. The sound of the gun warned Mungo. He spun around, just in time to see Fairchild's blade coming at him. He swayed out of the way, bringing up his own sword to parry. The blades rang together.

The two men faced each other.

"I will kill you, St. John!" shouted Fairchild.

"So you keep saying."

Mungo put up his guard—but at that moment, one of Wisi's men leaped back to avoid a cutlass thrust. He knocked hard into Mungo, pushing him aside. Fairchild saw and went for him with his knife. By the time Fairchild had beaten him back, Mungo had disappeared again in the confusion.

A dripping figure rose out of the reeds that fringed the water. With his hairless head and giant bare shoulders, he looked almost like a hippopotamus emerging from the river. But this was a man, with a heavy cutlass in each hand. He strode out of the water where he had been hiding and threw himself into the fray. Three of the *Maeander*'s sailors came at him with boarding pikes. He beat the points aside, decapitated one man with a swing of his massive arm, punched another in the face so hard it shattered his nose, and ran the last through left-handed. More men followed him out of the water. They were the men who had slipped downriver unseen and cut the *Raven*'s anchor cable.

Only five of them, but they came at the British sailors from their flank where they were unprotected. They made a bloody impact, and when the sailors turned to meet the new threat they exposed themselves to a fresh onslaught from Wisi's men.

Downriver, the *Raven* had stopped moving. She had drifted onto a sandbar and run aground. The men aboard looked to the boats, which had been tethered to her side, but their painters had been cut and the boats were no longer there. With no alternative, some of the crew leaped in the water and tried to swim across to help their shipmates from the *Maeander*. They paid for their bravery. The river looked placid, but its current was strong and its channel deep. Soon the water rang with the screams of men being carried away out to sea.

Their shipmates on the mudflats heard them. Veterans of the Royal Navy, they were no strangers to close combat. They had fought in boarding parties, against slavers and pirates, many times. But those were on cramped quarterdecks, where the fighting arena was tightly circumscribed. This was new and frightening, not knowing where the next attack might come from.

There was another difference, too. On a ship, you could not run away. Here they had that option. Mungo's men pressed them hard, contesting every inch of the riverbank. The sailors had been told they had come to rescue the Africans, but now those same blacks were fighting and killing them with shocking efficiency. More and more, the British sailors decided that the battle was not worth it. They broke and ran, back across the mudflats toward the trees at the top of the embankment. Back toward the *Maeander*, moored on the other side of the peninsula.

Mungo was not stupid enough to think that the battle was won. If the sailors managed to load their muskets and form a line, they would have a clear shot at the men on the flats. He ran after them, swerving wide, scrambled up the embankment and into the copse where they had lain in wait.

The position was abandoned. All the sailors cared about was

getting back to their ship. From the heights, Mungo could watch them running into the forest. He did not try to stop them. They were too few to do him any harm now.

Except one.

Fairchild was the last to give up the battle. He was no coward; he would gladly offer his life to his cause. But there was no point fighting on when his men had deserted him. Surrender was unthinkable. So he ran. Better to fight another day, than die for nothing on this godforsaken patch of mud.

No one followed, or offered any parting shots. The victors were exhausted, and though they had plenty of rifles, none could find the ammunition to load them. They let him go. Fairchild reached the shade of the embankment, grasping roots to pull himself up, and set out after his men. Once he was in the trees, he would be able to lose any pursuers.

A shadow moved in the forest. A man stepped out of the shade that had hidden him and planted himself on the path, directly in front of Fairchild.

Fairchild shook his head in disbelief.

"Mungo St. John. It seems the Lord is determined to put you in my way."

Mungo leveled his sword. Fairchild laughed. He pulled back his coat and there, in his belt, sat a second pistol, untouched. He pulled it out and aimed it at Mungo.

"This time, I have the advantage."

Mungo went still. "Even at the Union, you were a hard man to beat."

Fairchild ignored the compliment. He had fought against a rabble of slavers, outnumbered them more than two to one, and still lost. The rage and the shame of it burned in his breast. But there was one thing that hurt most of all.

"How did you do it?" he asked. "How did you persuade those

blacks to fight against us? Against their own interests? Against *me*?"

Mungo shrugged. "You are a good man," he said. "But you cannot see past the color of a man's skin."

"I will not take lessons in morality from a slaver," spluttered Fairchild.

"You see a black face, and all you see is a saint or a victim. I see weakness and strength, greed and hope, value to be exploited and potential to be harnessed—just as I do when I see a white face. In short, I see a man I can do business with."

Fairchild shook his head in incomprehension. "But what will it profit you, if the cost of that business is your own soul?"

"The good Lord, in His wisdom, left me with no other capital to work with."

Fairchild tightened his grip on the pistol. Mungo was a monster, an unrepentant sinner. To kill him now would be doing God's work. A chance to salvage victory from this disastrous battle.

Yet his finger hesitated on the trigger.

"The last time we met—aboard the *Blackhawk*—you could have killed me, and you did not."

"I threw you in the sea for the sharks," said Mungo evenly.

He took a stride forward. Fairchild stepped back, maintaining the distance between them.

"You saved my life. Something in you rebelled at the path you have taken and offered you a glimpse of the light."

He looked into Mungo's eyes, the golden flecks so impenetrable. Was that a hint of doubt he saw? Mungo stepped forward, hand half raised as if offering it in friendship. Fairchild wanted to believe it was sincere, but he was not so gullible as to trust Mungo. Again, he took a step back so that Mungo would not get too close.

"Come with me. Bear witness against the evil things you have seen and done. Redeem yourself."

"You think you could make an abolitionist of me?" Mungo was still advancing, forcing Fairchild to retreat.

"You proved at the Union you can be a fearsome advocate for any cause you choose."

"I am not cut out to play the hero."

"A man like you can play any role in life he chooses."

"It would be a life of poverty."

"A life of virtue," Fairchild countered.

Mungo sighed. "I cannot afford that."

All the time they had been speaking, Mungo had kept edging Fairchild backward. Now, Fairchild noticed how far he had gone. Was Mungo trying to take advantage of him somehow? It was time to remind his opponent who had the upper hand.

He stiffened his pistol arm, and planted his back foot firmly behind him to show he would not be moved any further.

And suddenly the world went askew. His boot did not land on the hard ground he was expecting. Instead, the earth gave way beneath him. His leg plummeted through a thin crust of dry soil and stabbed downward, until with a sudden jolt it stopped dead. He felt a snap, and a stab of excruciating pain.

Quick as a snake, Mungo darted forward. Two strides brought him to Fairchild. He twisted the pistol out of the Englishman's grasp and took it for himself, stepping back before Fairchild could respond.

Fairchild hardly noticed. He lay on the ground, writhing and clutching his leg, which had been swallowed almost thigh-deep by a hole that had opened in the ground.

Eyes watering, he gazed up at Mungo with a look of such fury it would have made a lesser man flee. Mungo only laughed.

"What . . . ?" Fairchild could hardly speak through the pain.

"A termite nest," said Mungo. "You must be careful of them. They can be quite treacherous."

Keeping out of range of Fairchild's grasp, he peered over into the hole. Fairchild's leg hung at a horribly unnatural angle.

"I think you have broken it."

Fairchild clenched his teeth. He tried to haul himself up, but the moment he put weight on his leg the pain was so great he bellowed in agony. He slumped back down. Mungo stood over him with the loaded pistol.

"So this time you mean to kill me?"

Fairchild tried to put a manly face on it, to meet his death with dignity. But the pain was so intense he could not manage it.

Mungo's eyes were unreadable. Perhaps he was considering killing Fairchild; perhaps he was simply savoring his victory. Then he smiled.

"I think, for the moment, I will keep you where you are."

Leaving Fairchild cursing and groaning, he returned to the beach. He dispatched two men to go and stand guard.

"Do not harm him," he told them, "but see he does not go anywhere."

The battle had been brutal. More than half of his men were dead or wounded, including Alcott Pendleton. Mungo did not mourn the old slave trader's loss for a second—it would save him a thirty-five percent commission—but it did mean he had lost his interpreter. And he needed to speak to Wisi.

"I have a proposition for you," he said.

Fortunately, one of the Punu warriors had once served a French slaver at Bangalang, and spoke enough of that language that Mungo could communicate through him. He waited patiently while the interpreter translated.

"I have a ship, and a cargo—but not enough crew. I want you and your men to come with me."

The slaves they had captured were all safe in their coffle, behind the ridge where they had been left during the battle. But Mungo had too few men to keep them under control on the long voyage, let alone to handle the ship, even if they could float her off the sandbar.

Wisi looked doubtful. "Black man goes on white ship, not come back."

"I will see to it that you come back." Mungo saw doubt in the prince's eyes. "I saved your life," he reminded him. "And you saved mine. Surely that is reason to trust each other."

He could see the Punu prince was not convinced. He pointed to one of the captives, a broad-shouldered young man of about eighteen or nineteen.

"See him? Where we are going, he is worth a thousand dollars. A thousand dollars will buy ten rifles."

Now he had Wisi's attention.

"I will offer you one tenth of all the profits from the venture," said Mungo. "Enough to buy two hundred rifles. When you come back, you will be the most powerful king this country has ever seen."

A slow grin spread across Wisi's face. He nodded.

"And the English ship?" said Tippoo. He jerked his thumb toward the promontory. "She is still waiting."

"She will not attack us," said Mungo confidently.

As many men as he had lost from his crew, the *Maeander* had suffered worse. He guessed they barely had enough men to get underway, let alone to man the guns in a fight. And he had their captain.

"Send a message to them under a flag of truce," he said. "Tell them we will release Captain Fairchild, as soon as we have loaded our cargo and put to sea."

"Will they accept those terms?" asked de Villiers doubtfully. They had freed him from the *Raven*'s hold, embarrassed but unhurt. When he saw the slaves they had brought, he had looked at Mungo as if he were a magician.

"The *Maeander* must have been patrolling this coast for weeks," said Mungo. "I guess they do not have the stomach for another fight. They will take any excuse to go home."

Wisi had not followed the conversation, but now he spoke up. A short question, punctuated with jabs of his finger at the *Raven*.

"He says, 'Where do we go?,'" said the interpreter.

Mungo stood and pointed down the river, out beyond the estuary to the far western horizon. The sun sank into the sea behind a haze of clouds, a red orb that laid a bloody path across the waves.

"That way."

III

BANNERFIELD

S hafts of sunlight lanced through the glass dome that crowned the great rotunda of the St. Louis Hotel in New Orleans. They shone down through the cigar smoke and sweat haze that filled the air, playing over the marble pilasters and carved garlands that adorned the walls. A traveler who had been to Rome might have recognized a resemblance to the Pantheon, or St. Peter's Basilica—but this was a temple to less exalted gods. Half a dozen wooden lecterns stood on the floor, and at each one an auctioneer was going about his business. Anything could be bought. The auctioneers spoke rapidly and at the tops of their voices, each trying to outdo the other, while the well-dressed crowds moved about so constantly that an unschooled observer could not be sure if a man was bidding on a piece of fine art, or furniture, or a consignment of tobacco or a brace of young slaves.

On that morning in October 1844, François de Villiers arrived at his customary time. He moved slowly through the crowd, greeting acquaintances, exchanging a few pleasantries and good mornings with familiar faces. Most of the men and women there knew that he had recently returned from Africa, and were keen to hear of his adventures.

But equally interesting to them was his companion: a tall man with long, flowing raven-dark hair, who said little but watched everything with his smoldering yellow eyes. His coat was expensive, the watch chain dangling from his waistcoat was gold, and the bulge in his pocket seemed to speak of a very full purse.

"Allow me to present Mr. Thomas Sinclair," said François. He was speaking to a cotton broker, though a dozen other people were listening to his every word. "He is the master of the *Raven*."

Everyone nodded. The ship's arrival the previous afternoon had piqued their curiosity, for she had never called in at New

Orleans before. She seemed to be crewed mostly by negroes, with a giant bald golden-skinned man as her first mate. She had made no move to unload any cargo since she arrived, nor take any aboard. The only thing anyone had seen come off her was a large iron-bound chest, so heavy it had taken four men to lift. With a great deal of effort, they had carried it up the levee to the Bank of New Orleans.

"A pleasure to make your acquaintance," said the broker. "Do you intend to stay long in New Orleans?"

Mungo flashed a smile that for some reason made the merchant shrink back a little.

"Only until I have completed my business."

He spoke absently, only half paying attention. His eyes were scanning the crowd, searching for Camilla's face. His heart raced at the thought she might be in the room. Would he recognize her?

On the auction block, an African girl no older than fifteen was being presented. She was entirely naked. Her hands moved to cover her breasts and pudenda, but the auctioneer batted them away to expose her bare flesh.

Casually, Mungo asked, "Chester's mistress—the black woman you spoke about—is she here?"

De Villiers gave Mungo a look of surprise. "Camilla would never come here. You cannot send a slave to buy a slave."

"Fine breeding stock," the auctioneer called, squeezing the girl's young breast. "Her mother bore a dozen sons, and every one of them strong as a horse. Do I hear seven hundred dollars?"

A man in a wide-brimmed gray hat raised his hand to bid. Immediately, another woman countered with a wave of her fan.

De Villiers nudged Mungo. "You are not tempted to bid? I guess there's no need, when you can get them wholesale."

Mungo didn't answer. He was staring across the room at the woman who was bidding. She wore a long dress of shimmering blue silk, and moved with feline grace. Her dark hair was pulled back under a hat that shaded almond eyes and a flawless complexion.

François followed Mungo's gaze. "She is a beauty, is she not?"

"You know her?" Mungo's voice was faint with disbelief.

"She is the Marquise Solange de Noailles," said François, delighted to show off his knowledge yet again. "She arrived in New Orleans some months ago and has caused quite a stir. She is a cousin to Louis Napoleon of France, and to Prince Achille Murat, who once lived in this city."

Mungo neither knew nor cared that members of the French royal family had ever resided in New Orleans. He very much doubted that the woman in the carriage was related to them. Certainly, she had never mentioned it in those long nights when Mungo had lain naked with her in her cabin. But then she had been Isabel Cardoso da Cruz, not Solange de Noailles—and certainly not a marquise. Perhaps many things had changed.

On the auction block, the girl's price was now up to over nine hundred dollars.

"Is the marquise married?"

"She is the most eligible lady in New Orleans," said François. "Of course there are rumors . . . but I think they say more about the hopes of her suitors than their expectations. She keeps her favors to herself."

"Is she one of your clients too?"

"Alas, no."

From the tone of de Villiers's reply, Mungo guessed he had had his hopes disappointed in more than matters of business.

"Sold!"

The auctioneer's hammer came down. The bidding had finished; Mungo saw the slave girl being led across to Isabel.

"She always gets what she wants," said François, with a trace of envy.

"I'm sure she does."

Mungo's eyes never left Isabel, though if she had noticed him at all she gave no sign of it.

He shook François's hand.

"I have business to attend to. But we must meet again soon. You have told me so much about Chester's mistress, I feel I have to meet her."

"That is easily arranged," said François. "She will be at the Toussaint Ball at Coquet's ballroom this Saturday."

"What is that?"

"A masked ball. But beneath the masks . . ." He winked. "I promise you will never have seen anything to compare."

"I have been to balls before."

"But not like this." François licked his lips. "This is a place where white men gather to dance with colored women. Does that shock you?"

"Not particularly."

François looked surprised. "You do not think it offends the natural order of the races?"

"There is no natural order. Only rules that one race invents to make the other serve its uses."

François stared. His mouth opened as if to say something, but the thought could not express itself. At last he managed, "Your opinions would make a cynic blush."

"I do not deceive myself with the masks people wear."

Again, François was lost for words.

"In any event," he stammered at last, "Chester's negress Camilla will be there."

"I would not miss it for my life," Mungo assured him.

He left quickly. Lingering glances from many of the women in the room followed him out. He emerged onto Rue St. Louis just in time to see an elegant carriage pulling away. It was fashioned like a sleigh, with a royal blue canopy, gilded trim and a chassis as white as the sidewalls on the wheels. The horses were also white—Andalusians from Spain by the look of them. Isabel sat upright in the back, with the slave girl she had purchased beside her.

In the busy streets, the carriage could not move quickly. Mungo was easily able to follow it on foot, up the street and then east along the cobblestones of Rue Royale. The crowds were thinner here—he worried he might lose the carriage—but almost at once it turned through an arch into the courtyard of a handsome mansion.

Mungo examined the house. Constructed of lime-washed brick, it stood three stories above the street, its wide cast-iron galleries rimmed by decorative railings. The shutters were closed across the ground floor windows, but those on the upper floors were thrown wide to admit the breeze. He imagined Isabel standing at the highest railing, watching the sun set over the city.

There was nothing to gain by seeing her again—and many good reasons to avoid her. She was the one person, other than Tippoo, who knew his real name and who could expose him for who he really was. He could not risk letting Chester Marion learn that he had arrived in New Orleans before he was ready to reveal himself. Also, he reminded himself—and then was angry he had needed reminding—he should be focusing all his energies on Camilla. The prudent choice would be to keep well away from Isabel.

But the sight of her had sparked a desire in him he could not account for, the same inexplicable longing he had felt aboard the *Blackhawk*.

He walked up to Isabel's front door and rang the bell.

"Thomas Sinclair, to see the Marquise de Noailles," he announced himself to the doorman.

"Do you have a card?"

Mungo had not had time to have them printed yet. He took a scrap of paper from his pocket—a bill of sale from Havana—and scribbled a few lines on it.

"Give her this note."

The door closed. Mungo waited. A few moments later it opened again, and the doorman stepped aside to usher Mungo in.

"Mungo St. John," said a familiar voice—cool, condescending, but shimmering with amusement, like the rainbow veneer on mother-of-pearl. "Or is it Thomas Sinclair?" She spoke in French, just as they always had. "I confess I have a terrible memory for names."

Isabel stood at the top of a grand staircase, silhouetted against a bright window. She wore a gauzy dress, and the sun shone through it so that she seemed to glow. It made the fabric almost transparent, revealing every curve of her body beneath.

"Mademoiselle da Cruz," said Mungo. "Or is it the Marquise de Noailles? It has been so long I am certain many things must have changed."

She waved her hand. "Names and titles are so inconstant. We take them on and off like clothes. Now, I am Solange, and I would be grateful if you would use that name. But some things have not changed."

As she descended the stairs she came into focus. Her dress took substance; her face was no longer shaded. She had grown up in the years since he last saw her. Her face had taken on a strength that made her even more beautiful; the eyes that had watched the world with girlish amusement now surveyed it with the full knowledge of her power.

She was holding the note Mungo had sent. On it, he had written the same lines that she had given him the day she came aboard the *Blackhawk*.

> You asked if love brings happiness /
> That is its promise, if only for a day.

She tossed the paper onto a console table.
"You have not forgotten how to make an impression."

"I was not sure you would receive me," said Mungo. "After the way we parted." He thought back to the beach—Afonso's blood staining the sand while the *Blackhawk*'s boat pulled away through the surf. "I am sorry about your brother."

She arched her eyebrows. "Truly?"

"No." There was no point lying to her. Of all the people he had ever met, she was the only one who made him feel that she could see straight through him. "He was a fool to challenge me to the duel. He got what he deserved."

"I agree. The greatest favor you ever did me was ridding me of my brother." She laughed at the expression on his face. "Do I shock you?"

"Nothing you do could shock me."

"He was a brute. He had already tried to rape me once and he would doubtless have tried again. Even my father did not mourn him."

They eyed each other for a moment, like a pair of wolves sizing each other up. For the first time, it occurred to Mungo that she might actually have told Afonso about their night-time encounters herself, or helped him discover them, purely so that Mungo could remove an obstacle from her path.

After all the things he had done, he could hardly judge her.

"How did you come to New Orleans?" he asked.

"Not long after we arrived on Prince's Island, my father died of the fever. With my brother dead, all the inheritance passed to me. I could not stay one day longer in that place—but nor did I want to go back to Europe. A dreary marriage to some dim-witted titled buffoon was all that awaited me there. So I came to America."

"Why here?"

"You know I find American men irresistible. And I thought the New World would be a place where a woman could reinvent herself."

"That is how you became the Marquise Solange de Noailles? They say you are related to Louis Napoleon."

She shrugged. "People believe what they want to believe. In a new city, it is useful to be talked about. It opens doors."

"You have not married?"

"I am waiting for the right man."

"The man you are in love with?" Mungo teased her.

She clicked her tongue impatiently. "A man who is at least as rich as I am, and too stupid to stop me doing as I wish. Or too clever to try. I will not spend the rest of my life in the sort of gilded cage that Afonso tried to put me in."

"I pity the man you make your husband," said Mungo.

"Do you?"

The house was silent; all the servants had vanished. Mungo and Solange—that was how he had to think of her—faced each other in the marble hallway. The only thing that moved were the dust motes caught in the air.

Solange stepped toward him and put her arms around his waist. He felt the heat of her body glowing against him like a hot coal.

"Why did you come to my house?"

"I wanted to see you."

"Really?" She put her hand to his chest, feeling the bump of the locket under his shirt front. "Have you given up trying to avenge your lost love?"

She leaned forward and kissed him, pushing her tongue into his mouth. Her breasts pressed against his chest, while her hand reached for the button of his trousers. The smell of her perfume overwhelmed Mungo's senses.

He pulled back. "Camilla is alive," he blurted out.

Solange recoiled as if she'd been burned. Her almond eyes glowed like a cat's.

"You told me she was dead."

"That was what I believed. Now I know otherwise. She is here in New Orleans."

Solange's cheeks were flushed, and there was a patch of red at the base of her throat. It was the first time Mungo had ever seen her angry. She stepped away and pulled a little bell-cord that hung from the ceiling. As if he had read her mind, a slave appeared at once, carrying a tray with two glasses of wine. Solange took one and drained it in a single gulp.

The alcohol seemed to calm her.

"I am happy for you."

"She is a slave to the man who murdered my father."

"So you are going to kill him." She said it as a matter of fact, not even a question.

Mungo gave a grim laugh. "That would be too kind. I am going to destroy him. I will dismantle every brick of the edifice he has built his fortune on, until he is left naked in the ruins of his life. I want him to look on his desolation, and know that I have taken away everything he cherished, just as he did to me. And then I will kill him."

Solange nodded. A lock of hair had come loose and fallen over her face, making her eyes unreadable.

"I hope you get what you wish for."

Camilla did not want to go to the ball. She was tired, her head hurt and she missed Isaac. All she wanted was to return to Bannerfield and cradle her son in her lap. But the cotton harvest was approaching, and Chester would be hungry for information: prices, shipping rates, warehouse fees, new officials who could be bribed, properties that might go up for sale. She would keep her ears open, and perhaps afterward Chester would let her go to Bannerfield to tell him what she had heard.

Also, François would be there, and he would expect to see her in the new costume he had sent her. It was beautiful, and she hated it. The dress was made of shimmering blue and green silks, cut low around her breasts and oversewn with brightly colored feathers. The mask that accompanied it was made from two crossed peacock feathers, with holes for her eyes at the center of the whorls. When she looked in the mirror, she did not recognize herself.

Chester's coachman took her to the ballroom. Not so long ago, she would have tripped at the first step down from the carriage, trying to manage the bustling skirts of her dress; now she moved with easy grace. There were many things she had learned since she came to New Orleans.

Inside, the chandeliers were bright and the room filled with smoke. The air throbbed with conversation and laughter, and strains of an orchestra playing a *contredanse*. All the guests wore masks—some simple black-and-white affairs, others as colorful as birds of paradise. Their fantastical masks hid the even more extraordinary range of their different skin colors beneath—the Toussaint Ball was a place where, for a few hours, blacks and whites could pretend they were something other than what they were.

Camilla's fabulous dress made her the most striking woman in the room, but she did not enjoy the attention. Behind those masks she could feel men looking at her, undressing her with their eyes. With her plumage, she felt like a rare bird in a room full of cats.

She made her way around the room, trying to smile at the men who stared at her. Despite their costumes, she recognized several of Chester's business associates: Jackson, the president of the Bank of New Orleans; Shaw, the commission agent; Levack, the cotton merchant. She flirted with one, danced with another and leaned forward eagerly to listen to what they had to say, giving them fine views straight down her low-cut bodice. She came away with a thorough knowledge of when the biggest plantations would be shipping their cotton to market, and how the prices were likely to move.

She went to the punch table, took a full glass and drained it. It did not help her headache. She wanted to go, but she had not spoken to François yet. He had told her the day before that he had a new client for her to meet, a man he had brought back from Africa who wanted to do business with Chester.

She took another drink, and had just raised it to her lips when she heard the crowd behind her go silent. She turned. François had arrived, but that was not what had transfixed the room. Rather, it was the man who had come in with him.

Camilla stared. Indeed, the whole room had stopped to stare at him. He stood half a head taller than any of them, dressed in an immaculately tailored black coat that made everyone around him seem gaudy. But it was his mask that attracted most attention. It was made in the shape of a sharp-beaked bird—a crow or a raven—but it was not black. It appeared to be made of solid gold, hammered so that the light from the chandeliers rippled over its surface like water, as if a sun had suddenly blazed into existence on the dance floor.

The golden mask hid the man's face, but his silhouette was so familiar it made her heart almost stop. He looked exactly like Mungo. He was the same height, with the same broad shoulders and finely tapered waist, even the same confident bearing and tilt of his head.

Surely it was impossible.

Camilla had to go. The resemblance was too perfect, bringing back memories and unbearable hopes she thought she had buried forever. Suddenly, her thin dress felt like a lead shroud; the ribs of her corset squeezed her chest, and the mask weighed on her head like a millstone. She turned on her heel and ran to the back of the ballroom.

A door led her onto a small balcony, overlooking the courtyard where coachmen and postilions were playing cards and talking. She tore off the mask and breathed in the night air, sucking it greedily into her lungs, trying to ease the pressure on her chest.

"Are you unwell?"

It was François's voice; she'd hoped he hadn't seen her. She gripped the iron rail and stared down into the courtyard.

"My apologies," she said, drawing on a well of strength deep within her. "I took faint. It is passing now."

"The air is very close in there," François sympathized. "I will ask them to open some windows."

"That would be kind."

She wanted him to go and he did, calling for servants and brandy. She heard the door close behind him.

But she was not alone. Someone else was there, standing behind her. He made no sound, but stood so close she could feel the heat coming off him on her bare shoulders. She gripped the railings tighter. There was no point resisting. He must be a white man—all the men at the ball were white—and to be a black woman, alone with a white man, meant only one thing.

She could feel his eyes running over every inch of her body. Though she had been born into slavery, and so never had to stand on the auction block, this was how she imagined it must feel.

Still he did not touch her. Instead: "I said I would come back."

Time stopped. The world changed. Her whole life—everything

she had forced herself to think and believe for years—collapsed at the sound of those six words. The voice she had longed to hear through so many terrible nights and lonely days. The voice she had never expected to hear again.

Even then, she refused to believe the evidence of her ears. What if she was wrong? What if she had misheard, or misremembered him. She did not dare to look. To have her hopes crushed again would kill her.

A firm pair of hands grasped her arms. Gently, he pivoted her around so she was looking at him, up at the shrouded face looming over her. The raven mask hid his features—but watching her from behind it she could see a pair of smoky yellow eyes flecked with gold. The only eyes in the world that looked at her like that.

"Camilla," he breathed.

"How . . . ?"

She was not even sure how to finish the question. Mungo did not give her the chance. He pulled off his mask, bent down and kissed her on the lips—softly at first, then with gathering force. His mouth was so hot she thought he would scald her.

She pulled away, frightened that François would come back. Mungo stiffened. He let her step back, but did not let go of her arms.

"I thought you were dead," he said. He shook his head, angry with himself. "I should not have believed it."

"Chester kept me for himself. It was part of his triumph over you."

Her head was so full of wonder she could barely think. But the moment she said Chester's name, the tender look on Mungo's face transformed into something so savage that Camilla trembled.

"He fears you." She gripped Mungo's arms, as if afraid he might melt into the air like a ghost. "He knows you are free—he is convinced you will come for revenge. He has made himself the most powerful man in the state to stop you."

The door behind them banged open. Mungo and Camilla sprang apart as François stepped out on the balcony. His eyes darted between them; his mouth—visible below his half-mask—pursed in a sour expression.

"I see you have already met my *petite amie*, Mademoiselle Camilla," he said. "I had been hoping to make an introduction."

His eyes flicked around the little balcony, trying to understand what was happening. The night was warm, the music inside was boisterous, the dancers were enjoying themselves—yet out here, the atmosphere felt charged with lightning. And he did not like the way Mungo was staring at Camilla.

François offered her his arm. "Perhaps you would care to dance?"

Before she could respond, Mungo said, "She is still too faint." Through the windows, he saw a pair of slaves taking the punch-bowl away to the kitchens to refill it. "She needs another drink."

"I do not think that is wise," François countered. "If she is faint, alcohol will not help her."

"Please." Camilla touched his arm, wishing she still had her mask on. "I would be grateful. And afterward we can dance."

François bowed, cast one last cautionary look at Mungo, and went inside. As soon as he was gone, Mungo wrapped Camilla in an embrace so tight he threatened to smother her.

"I cannot breathe," she whispered.

He didn't relax his grip.

"Come away with me," he whispered. "I have a ship in the harbor ready to sail—by dawn, we could be far out at sea. We can go to England, or Canada, or Africa, or India—anywhere in the world. You will be free."

The vision he offered was like a shining door, opening in the prison walls that had confined her since she was born. More than she had dreamed of.

But not if it meant leaving without Isaac.

"Chester has men all over the city," she said. "If they suspected

I was running away—or who you are—they would kill us before we could reach your ship."

Everything had happened so fast, Camilla felt as if a dam had burst, as if a torrent of water had swept her off her feet and down into a future she could not control. She had to find a purchase.

"We must go somewhere we can talk in private," she said. "There are so many things I must tell you."

"Where do you live?"

"Rue St. Louis."

"I will come there."

"No." Her eyes were wide with fear. "It is Chester's house. All the servants are his. He would hear of it."

"Then come to me. I am on Rue Bourbon."

"I would be seen. Chester is a jealous master. He has me watched, always."

"What, then?"

She saw impatience glowing in Mungo's eyes. His fingers curled into fists. He had changed since she last saw him. When she held his arms, she felt muscles that the Eton schoolboy and the Cambridge undergraduate had never had. There were scars on his face, and lines around his eyes that spoke of experiences she could not guess.

In the precarious world of slavery, he had always made her feel . . . not safe, exactly, but protected. Now, he frightened her.

"Go to the cathedral tomorrow at sunrise," she told him. "Wait in the confessional—the priests do not use it so early. I will come to you."

Mungo nodded.

"Now go." Still he didn't obey; she had to peel his fingers off her arms. She hoped the bruises would not show the next day. "François is coming. We cannot give him any more cause for suspicion."

The door opened again. François stepped out carrying two fresh glasses of punch. It had taken longer than he expected, but he was pleased to see that Mungo and Camilla were standing a respectable distance apart.

He handed one glass to Camilla, and kept the other for himself.

"I trust you enjoyed a profitable conversation?" he said, still wondering what had passed between them.

"Indeed," said Mungo. "I believe that Chester and I will have plenty of business to take care of."

"Excellent." François offered Camilla his arm, and this time she took it. "Now let us go and enjoy that dance you promised me."

The next morning, before the bells chimed six o'clock, Camilla entered the Cathedral of St. Louis. She dipped her fingers in the cherub's cistern, crossed herself with holy water and took a seat in one of the pews. She knelt to pray. She was not Catholic by upbringing—the St. Johns were Presbyterians. But New Orleans was a Catholic city, and the cathedral was the only place outside the town house where she could be sure she was alone. She had come to love the ritual of Catholic devotion: the sign of the cross; the kneeling and the standing; the Eucharistic bread and wine. Familiarity was security.

She waited in the pew, mouthing a silent prayer, until she heard the creak of hinges in one of the wooden booths in the side aisle. Her pulse began to race. She knew the priests were busy in the sacristy, preparing for morning Mass. The confessionals should be empty. No one else would bother them, so long as they kept their conversation brief.

She crossed herself again, strode to the rear of the sanctuary and slipped into the confessional.

The divider slid open and she sensed his presence. She could make out the shape of his face through the screen, the yellow hue of his irises and the throaty tenor of his voice. When he spoke her name, she held her hands together to keep them from trembling. The sound of her name on his lips after so long sent the blood coursing to her head.

"Where have you been?" she asked. "How did you come here?"

A cloud seemed to pass across Mungo's eyes. All the terrible things he had done had been for Camilla. But now they were face to face, he could not bear to tell her.

"A long story. Too long. Tell me about yourself."

She closed her eyes and collected her thoughts. She told him everything, from the moment she had been dragged away from the observatory and locked in the tobacco store; the trip to Louisiana and Bannerfield; her time picking cotton in the fields; and finally, her life as Chester's mistress in New Orleans.

There was only one thing she left out.

Mungo took in every word in silence, save a sort of hiss through his teeth every time she spoke Chester's name.

"You did not try to run away?" he said when she had finished.

"Bannerfield is so large, I would never even have got off Chester's land. Even from New Orleans, a slave on her own in Louisiana will not go far. Have you seen what they do to runaways?"

And I could not leave Isaac.

That was the one thing she had omitted, the truth she could not tell. She had never kept a secret from Mungo before. But she feared what he would do if he learned about her son. She remembered the savage look that had come over Mungo's face at the ball, even at the mention of Chester's name. Could he accept a child who was Chester's flesh and blood?

You are not the same boy who left me at the end of that summer, she thought, looking at the scarred face. She did not know him—not all of him. She did not know what he was capable of.

For now, Mungo accepted her explanation of why she had not run away.

"But you can come with me now," he said.

Camilla started. "Now?"

"My offer last night still stands. My ship is ready. And this time, there is no François to see us go."

"What about Chester?" She whispered the name so quietly it was like a breath of wind, as if even in this sacred space the Devil might hear.

"I will come back for him later."

Mungo had lain awake all night thinking about it. He had spent years planning his revenge, dreaming of Chester's downfall. To walk away from it now would be like a monk renouncing his God.

But until he met François at Ambriz, the one thing he had never considered was that Camilla might be alive. That changed everything.

"You said he knows I am looking for him. Let him rot in the palace he has built himself, waiting every day in terror of my return. Let the guilt and fear gnaw away at him, until he is a husk of a man. Then—maybe—I will return to deliver the *coup de grâce*."

Camilla didn't know what to say. She twisted her hand in the skirts of her dress until it made a tight knot.

"I cannot."

"Why?"

"I cannot just walk out of my life. Even this life. There are . . . some things of mine." It sounded so feeble.

"I am wealthy. Whatever you need, I will buy you." He pressed his hand against the wooden grille that divided them. "Come with me."

Camilla did not move. Her mind was racing, weighing truths and lies on which a life might hang. How could she explain it? How could she *not* explain it?

Out in the cathedral, the service had begun. A priest was reading from the huge leather-bound Bible mounted on an eagle-headed lectern. The words were in Latin, unknowable to Camilla. They would not have reassured her if she had understood them.

Then Abraham bound his son Isaac, and laid him on the altar, and took up the knife in his hand to sacrifice his child.

"There is something I left out of my story," she began. "I have a son."

On the far side of the grille, she heard a sigh like a blade rasping over a whetstone.

"A son?"

"Born two years ago."

"Who was the father?"

"Chester . . ." The fury on Mungo's face made her stumble over her words, hardly able to breathe. "Chester's overseer. You remember the man at Windemere—Granville. He . . ." She broke off for a moment. "Chester let him have me. Many times. The baby was born nine months after."

On the other side of the grille, Mungo had sunk back into the shadows. She could not see his face, only the two shining points of his eyes.

Did he believe her?

"Where is the child?" Mungo asked.

"Chester keeps him at Bannerfield."

"That is why you cannot escape?"

She nodded. Already, she could feel the lie about Isaac's paternity eating away at her soul like acid.

"And you love him?"

"I know he is the child of violence. But he grew in my womb, and my blood flows inside him. I could not leave him, any more than I could leave you."

Mungo's fingers curled through the holes of the grille. With a sudden jerk of his arm, they tightened around the slats and ripped them away, leaving a splintered hole in the partition.

Camilla looked around, terrified that someone would have heard. Mungo's arm shot through the hole and grabbed her chin, forcing her to look at him.

"This could be your only chance."

"You are hurting me."

Mungo's fingers gripped her so tight she thought he would break her jaw.

He unbuttoned his shirt and drew out the silver locket. He opened it. In the dim light, she saw the sketch of her he had made that summer before he went to Cambridge.

I look so young, she thought. Before Chester, before Bannerfield, before childbirth and motherhood. *Am I the same person?*

"I wore this in some of the darkest places on earth," he said. "I will not give you up now."

"And I suffered things a man can never know," she answered. She saw her words strike home. "I have more reasons to flee than you will ever understand. But I will not leave the one good thing God has given me from this nightmare."

There was a pause, broken only by the distant sound of the choir singing the psalm.

"Can you bring the boy here?"

Mungo's eyes still glowed with that inexpressible menace, but behind them his mind had started to turn itself to practicalities.

Good, Camilla thought. Better that than more questions, more lies.

"Chester would suspect something. He never lets Isaac leave Bannerfield." She thought quickly. "Do you have a riverboat?"

"I can get one."

"There is a landing at Bannerfield where they load the cotton onto Chester's steamboat. Come to that place at midnight in four days. If it is safe, if I can get Isaac away, I will show a green light and you can dock."

"If you cannot?"

"I will not show the light."

"And if that happens? What should I do then? Sail away and leave you to Chester's mercy?"

She reached through the partition and clasped his hand between hers. What would the priests think when they saw the hole he had torn?

"We will find a way."

When François arrived at his office that morning, he found Mungo waiting for him.

"Did you enjoy the ball?" François asked. "I did not see you go."

"I left early. I had had my fill."

"You seemed to enjoy your conversation with Miss Camilla. I should warn you," François went on, "that Chester Marion is a jealous master. You should tread carefully."

Mungo nodded, and changed the subject. "I wish to give you some money."

François forgot Camilla. His face lit up. "How much?"

"Enough to buy a steamboat. Can you arrange it?"

François took on a pained expression. "Of course. But I must tell you that steamboats are not as profitable a proposition as . . . ah . . . *other* vessels you have commanded. You will earn pennies on the dollar—if she does not sink. A boat depreciates very quickly—then there are the costs of insurance, fuel, the crew . . ."

He might as well have been talking to himself. He could see by the look in Mungo's eyes that his mind was set. And François had not forgotten that when he gave Camilla the same advice, she had simply taken her business elsewhere. At least if he brokered the sale, he could expect a commission.

"I will find you just the ship you need."

Mungo had never been aboard a steamboat before. He had seen them chugging around the harbors at Norfolk and Baltimore on their runs down the Chesapeake, and in New Orleans they were always on the river. Compared to the grace of ships like the *Raven* and the *Blackhawk*, they were squat and ungainly things. Yet he could not deny that the intricacy of their machinery intrigued him. Once, in Norfolk, he had stood on the dock looking down at the boiler, watching the great arms grind into motion as the pressure rose. He had been amazed by the raw power that could be generated by nothing more than wood, fire and water.

Now he stood on the deck of the *Nellie Mae*, a hundred feet long, with four boilers mounted on her main deck powering a large wheel at her stern. Two funnels rose near her bow, like vestigial masts.

"A bastard contraption," Mungo muttered to himself.

Standing on her deck, he felt none of the thrill that he got from the *Raven*. Even so, there was grudging admiration in his voice.

"She does not draw much draft?" he asked the captain.

"Eight feet, loaded to the guards. Not much more than two feet when she's empty."

"Speed?"

"She's the fastest boat on the river. With a fair wind she can make twenty knots."

Mungo ran his hand over the boiler. The iron was cool to the touch, but he imagined it throbbing under full steam, the metal burning red-hot.

Tippoo had gone to the prow and was peering at a small six-pound cannon mounted there.

"Does it work?" he asked.

"We use her for salutes, signaling and suchlike."

"But she would take a ball if necessary?" Mungo prompted.

The captain looked astonished. "What for?"

"Pirates," said Tippoo.

"There are no pirates on the Mississippi," said François.

"She will do handsomely for my purposes." Mungo turned to the captain. "How much do you want for her?"

The captain chewed his wad of tobacco. "Thirty thousand dollars."

"That is so high you should arraign him for theft," objected François. "You could build a brand new boat for that, with change to hire a crew."

"Thirty thousand dollars is fine," said Mungo. "And I would appreciate it if you could fill the bunkers with coal. I hear it burns stronger than wood."

Tippoo handed him a pen and ink. Balancing on a bollard, Mungo wrote out a draft.

"You may cash this against my account at the Bank of New Orleans." A thin smile. "They are always happy to oblige."

"And the crew?"

Mungo gestured to the rest of the men he had brought. Tippoo was there, and Virgil Henderson; also Wisi, and a number of his warriors. The Punu had taken to life aboard the *Raven*, and had not complained when Mungo explained there would be a delay returning to their homeland.

"I have my own crew."

The captain stared at them disbelievingly. "You think you can crew this boat with niggers?"

"I'll trouble you not to speak about my crew that way," said Mungo. "They are free men, and the equal of any sailor in New Orleans."

The captain looked as if he was about to object more, but something in Mungo's eyes made him think better of it.

"Have it your own way," he muttered.

Stepping through the gates of Bannerfield made Camilla a different person. In New Orleans, she could live with the illusion of being free. At Bannerfield, that was gone. Whatever Chester might permit her out of his sight, in his house she could only be one thing. She took off her fine city clothes and put on a simple white house-slave's dress. She undid her hair and let it hang down under a simple cap. She ate dinner with the other servants in the kitchen, barely touching her food. Upstairs, in the dining room, Chester and Isaac would be dining off fine china and silver cutlery.

At least she was there. She had thought it would be hard to find a pretext to persuade Chester to let her come to Bannerfield. But chance, for once, had smiled on her. Chester had summoned her himself, without explanation, the morning after she had seen Mungo. A day to prepare herself, and then two days upriver, had brought her to Bannerfield on the exact day she had set. A part of her worried that it was not a coincidence, that someone had seen them together, but even that fear could not completely quell the hopes that she allowed herself to feel. She would take Isaac, join Mungo, and escape this life forever.

Chester would not let her see Isaac straight away. Instead, he sent her to the little room in the attic. Being there, trapped in that close space, peeled away her hopes. It could have been her first night at Bannerfield—or even further back, in the tobacco store at Windemere. She was utterly helpless.

She did not know how long she had waited when she heard the footstep on the stair. Just like in the old days, but heavier now. Her muscles clenched. The handle turned, the door opened. Chester surveyed her from the doorway.

Even in the few months since she had last seen him, he had grown more terrible to look at. His hair had thinned to the point where he could not hide it. Instead, accepting the inevitable, he had shaved his head bald. He had grown even fatter, his stomach sagging over his waist and his arms as fat as a cow's haunches. Another man might have looked pathetic, but Chester carried the weight with a natural strength. He was no longer the feeble attorney others had overlooked; the great mass of his body seemed like an emanation of the power that had grown within him. Or perhaps the power had always been there, and no one had noticed.

There was no mistaking what he wanted. He wore only a silk dressing gown with nothing underneath. His belly pushed open the folds of the gown.

"What is the news from New Orleans?" he asked, as if they were sitting in the saloon taking tea.

Was this why he had summoned her? Camilla was so surprised she struggled to answer his question.

"New mills are being built in Manchester, in England. They have bid up the price of cotton, and at the moment there is not the supply in New Orleans to meet the demand. The sooner you can get your crop to market, the better you will profit from it."

Chester nodded thoughtfully. "Good. Undress yourself."

Camilla unlaced her dress and stepped out of it. She shrugged off her petticoat, then lay back on the bed.

Think of Isaac, she told herself.

"There is something else," Chester said. "Mungo St. John."

Camilla went still. She wanted to roll over and bury her face in the bedclothes so her emotions could not betray her, but she could not. Chester's gray eyes were as hard as glass as they stared down at her. His whole body seemed to throb with a desire that had nothing to do with Camilla's body.

"Have you found him?" Camilla asked.

"No," said Chester. "Not yet," he added. "But there is a man recently arrived in New Orleans who calls himself Sinclair. Granville saw him on Rue Royale—he is convinced it was St. John."

He took a step toward her. His body was damp with sweat, so that he looked like an enormous slithering snail. "Have you seen this man—Sinclair?"

What could she say?

"He was at the Toussaint Ball."

"And?"

She tried to remember all the people who had been there. Would anyone have seen them together? François, of course. If Chester spoke to him, he would quickly find out how long Camilla had spent on the balcony with Mungo. Or perhaps he already knew, and was toying with her, testing her loyalties.

She had to say something. She remembered the offer he had made her before: *Your freedom and your son, in exchange for Mungo St. John.* If she admitted that she had seen him, would Chester honor that bargain?

But staring up at him, she did not think he knew the truth. He had spent the last year and a half in terror of Mungo. If he was sure that Mungo had returned, he would not be able to hide it.

"It could have been Mungo," she said doubtfully, as if struggling to remember.

"*Could* have been?"

"He wore a mask—I could not see his face—and it has been years since I saw him. But . . . he was the right height."

"Did you speak to him?"

"No."

"Did he see you?"

"I do not think so. I spent most of the evening dancing with your friends. And I was masked as well."

Chester pulled the dressing gown closed around him. He sat down on the edge of the bed, deep in thought.

"Tomorrow you must go back to New Orleans and find out everything you can about this Mr. Sinclair. If he is Mungo St. John, he will come to you."

"He probably does not even remember me," said Camilla.

Chester laughed, a cold laugh that filled her heart with dread.

"I am certain he does."

After he had finished with her, she dressed and waited until the clock in the hall struck half past eleven. She did not need to pack—there was nothing from this life she wanted to take. The fine clothes and jewelry Chester had bought her were nothing more than chains of taffeta and cotton and gold. She needed none of it.

She lit a lamp, closing the shutter so that only a tiny bar of light escaped. She found the green shawl she had brought especially from New Orleans and wrapped it around her head as a turban. Then she stole out of the room.

Isaac's bedroom was next to Chester's, separated by an adjoining door. By the dim light of the lamp, Camilla saw the door was open. She could hear Chester's loud snoring coming through it.

As quietly as she could, she crept to Isaac's bed. She touched his face, stroking his cheek gently to wake him.

His eyes fluttered open drowsily.

"Milla?" He still hadn't mastered her name; part of her hoped he never would.

"Shhh," she hushed him. "Come with me."

"Why?"

"To go somewhere."

"I want sleep."

His voice was too loud. Through the open door, she heard Chester stirring.

"It's a surprise," she whispered. Isaac liked surprises.

"What s'pry?"

"We're going to see a boat."

That persuaded him. He got out of bed. There was no time to dress—she took him in his nightshirt, barefoot. The door squeaked as she closed it, but she did not dare wait to see if she had been heard. She was committed now.

The night was warm. As they hurried down the road that led between the fields, she could smell the aroma of cotton oil from the seeds that had been broken during harvesting: earthy and faintly sour, like mildew. It took her back at once to those back-breaking days picking cotton while her pregnant belly swelled. She clutched Isaac's hand tighter.

"Where's Daddy?" he asked.

"Your daddy's coming later."

"Daddy likes s'pries," he said happily.

He was going too slowly. Camilla swept him up off his feet and carried him in her arms. He was a heavy boy, and the comforts of life in New Orleans had sapped some of the strength she had had during her stint in the cotton fields. But she did not slow down. She was almost at the top of the rise, and beyond that, she would be at the river.

On the far side of the Mississippi, the *Raven*'s cutter lurked in the shadow of the trees that lined the bank. Mungo sat in her stern, his telescope trained on the dock opposite. He had been watching for over an hour, utterly motionless, like a hunter in his hide waiting for the game to appear.

They had come upriver that afternoon in the *Nellie Mae*, just one more steamboat on a busy waterway. As they swept past Bannerfield, Mungo had studied the docks and the warehouses built along it. A huge steamboat was tied up at the wharf, swarming with workers who were loading it with bales of cotton. Mungo tried to calculate how much the boat could hold, the value of the cargo she carried. It must be a fortune.

They had carried on past Bannerfield without stopping. Tippoo and the crew had spent a day—and two bunkers' worth of coal—shuttling around New Orleans harbor, learning how to stoke the boiler and throttle the engines, how to handle the ship and the big sternwheel. Wisi, who was used to navigating the treacherous rivers of his own country, made a natural pilot, scanning the waters ahead to warn them of sandbars and hazards to navigation. Tippoo supervised the boilers, stripped to the waist, while Virgil Henderson took the helm. In three days, they had become a more than competent crew.

Near sunset, they turned around and lowered the *Raven*'s cutter, which they had brought with them. Mungo, Tippoo and a dozen of their men rowed the cutter downstream to a place opposite the Bannerfield landing, while the *Nellie Mae* moored up just downriver, around a bend from the plantation. The cutter hid in an inlet, where tree branches and the long beards of Spanish moss hung over them. Mungo took up position with his telescope, though it was only nine o'clock and he couldn't expect Camilla for hours. Tippoo serviced the little swivel gun they had mounted on the bow and loaded it with a small quantity of powder and loose shot.

Then they waited.

Tippoo pointed to the steamboat moored at Bannerfield, a hulking monster that dwarfed the *Nellie Mae*.

"What does it carry?"

"Cotton," said Mungo.

"Valuable?"

Mungo made some calculations in his head.

"There's probably about quarter of a million dollars sitting on that boat. More in the warehouses."

Tippoo spat over the side. "That is why they can afford the slaves."

"Mmm . . ."

Mungo stared out into the darkness. He hadn't told Camilla how he had come by his new fortune. Maybe he never would. But he knew he would have to find another way to live now. Perhaps he could return to his original attempt, trading ivory with Africa and the Indies. He imagined living aboard the *Raven* with Camilla, letting the wind and the currents and the chance for profit guide them.

Tippoo broke into his thoughts.

"Many guards."

Mungo nodded. He had seen them, patrolling the decks of the barges and around the warehouses. He had counted over three dozen of them, but they did not seem particularly alert. They clearly did not expect any danger.

He touched the Hall rifle that lay propped against the gunwale beside him. All his men had them. They had seen off Fairchild's crew of Royal Navy sailors—Chester's ragtag militia should pose no problem.

"What's that?"

The river was almost half a mile wide. The light was little more than a pinprick in the darkness, like a distant star, but Mungo saw it. He studied it with his telescope. Even through the glass, the flame was a tiny flicker, but he could see two figures standing by it, silhouetted on the ridge against the starry sky.

"On your oars," he called.

They could not risk approaching Bannerfield in the *Nellie Mae*. The fires in her boiler and the noise of her engines would alert the guards before they were even underway. Instead, they would take the rowing boat in silently, then meet up with the steamboat afterward.

The current was strong, pushing them two feet downstream for every foot they moved across it. The men pulled hard, while Mungo sat at the tiller trying to hold their course. He gazed ahead. Camilla had said she would show a green light if it was safe to land. Squint as he might, the light he could see was definitely only a yellow flame. But it would take so long to cross the river, he had to be in position when she showed it.

He stared at the light until his eyes hurt, willing it to turn green.

Camilla stood at the top of the embankment that looked down on the river. There was no moon. Below, she could hear the water eddying and rushing as the river flowed by, as vast and unstoppable as fate.

She held Isaac's hand tighter. She knew the power of the river. She had seen it take whole trees and spin them around like blades of grass. Once, in flood, she had watched a wooden cabin float by, its inhabitants sitting on its roof as if they could not believe what had happened to them. If Isaac slipped here, he would be carried away and drowned.

But would he be any safer if he got in Mungo's boat? She had lied to Mungo about Chester, but Isaac knew who his father was. He would surely reveal it sooner or later. What would Mungo say then? Would his love for Camilla save her son?

It was too late for doubts. She had made her decision. She let go of Isaac's hand and unwound the green shawl from her head. The lantern had a little snout, like a teapot, so that its light would only be visible from a narrow angle. All she had to do was let the shawl hang in front, and the light would show green.

She checked around her one more time. There were guards at the landing and on the boats, but she was two hundred yards upriver from them. They could not see her in the darkness.

"When's the s'pry?" said Isaac. He yawned. "I want my bed."

"In a moment," Camilla promised.

Something jabbed her in the small of her back, so hard she nearly lost her balance. She might have tumbled down the riverbank, but at the same time a hand grabbed her hair and pulled her back. She felt the press of steel against the base of her spine.

"Strange time to be out with my son," rasped Chester.

"Mighty strange," added Granville's voice. "Especially for a slave."

"Daddy!" Isaac threw his arms around his father's legs. Then he looked up. "Why are you holding a gun?"

"It's dangerous to be out at night." Chester kneeled down. "Why did you come here?"

"Milla said it was a s'pry."

"Did she?" Chester looked up at Camilla, keeping the pistol trained on her. "This evening I told you Mungo St. John may be in Louisiana, and now this very same night I find you on the riverbank with a signal lantern and my son. What am I supposed to think?"

He looked out at the river, sniffing the air. "Is he here?"

Camilla did not trust herself to answer. Her hesitation only fed Chester's suspicion. She felt him tense; for a second she thought he might shoot her that instant. Instead, he mastered himself and stepped back thoughtfully.

"Think carefully," he said. "You asked what I would do if you brought me Mungo St. John. I am willing to honor my promise.

Freedom." He let the word hang in the darkness. "The chance to be with Isaac every day." He ruffled the boy's hair. "Would you like that?"

"I like Milla," said Isaac.

"What is it to be?"

Camilla did not know what to say. Her heart was stretched to breaking, pulled between Mungo and Isaac. The river flowed at her feet, and she had the sense that whatever choice she made would have terrible consequences.

If she had only been choosing for herself, it would have been easy. But she was choosing for Isaac, too. For all the terrible things Chester had done to her, she could not deny he was a loving father. Would Mungo be as kind to the boy? The question that had gnawed in her breast since the day Isaac was born now threatened to consume her. How far would Mungo go for his revenge on Chester?

He loved her, she reminded herself, and she had to believe that the love in his heart was greater than his hatred for Chester. At the ball, he had been willing to sail away that night and abandon his revenge on Chester so he could be with her. Surely he could not hate the boy.

She had to believe that.

She still had the shawl in her hand. If she threw it over the lamp, Chester would have no time to stop her. Mungo would see it. She could feel his presence, just like those nights at Windemere going to the observatory, knowing he would be there.

If he saw the signal, he would come. He had not told her his plan, but she knew he would not come alone. He would come with men; they would have guns. However many of Chester's men opposed him, he would fight his way through. Nothing would stop him.

Could she keep Isaac safe if it came to a battle? She looked down at him, rubbing his eyes. She imagined a bullet flying out of the darkness and putting a hole the size of a dime through his forehead—blood dribbling down his face. She could not risk that. Not even for Mungo.

She let the cloth fall to the earth and turned the lantern away from the river.

"He is not here. I only brought Isaac to look at the steamboat." She shivered. "I am cold. I would like to go to bed."

She could tell Chester was not satisfied. She could hear the scrape of Granville's fingernail scratching the haft of his knife; the creak of the pistol spring as Chester thumbed the hammer. There was no telling what he might have done to her, if at that moment Isaac had not sat down on the grass, given an enormous yawn and begun to cry.

"Please, Daddy," he said. "Can we go home?"

Camilla kneeled down and swept him up in her arms, cradling him close. The touch of his small body against hers dissolved any doubts she had about what she had done.

It broke the spell. Chester grunted and turned away.

"Double the guards and tell them to be vigilant," he told Granville. "Light lamps on the boat. I do not want anyone coming within five hundred yards of the landing."

He glared at Camilla. "As for you . . . we will speak more of this later."

Out on the water, Mungo saw the light vanish. He held his course, waiting for it to reappear. It must be a shadow blocking the light, or maybe Camilla had turned to look at something.

It didn't come back. Instead, new lights flared up on the decks of the steamboat. Mungo saw men raising lanterns all around the upper decks. More of the militia came out from the warehouses, roused from sleep. They spread out along the boat's rails, staring out over the water with rifles raised.

"Back oars," Mungo hissed.

The cutter was almost on the edge of the orb of light that the lanterns cast. If they were seen, they would make an easy target.

Tippoo let go of his oar and picked up one of the Hall rifles. He aimed it at the barge, then turned and gave Mungo a quizzical look.

"Yes?"

Mungo hesitated. He looked back to where he had seen the light on shore. The glare of the lanterns on the boats ruined his night vision and made it hard to see, but so far as he could tell the figures who had been there before had vanished.

"She is not coming."

Tippoo lowered the rifle. He nodded slowly, acknowledging the anguish on Mungo's face.

"What now?"

Mungo put the tiller over and pointed the cutter's bow downstream, back toward the *Nellie Mae* and away from Bannerfield. Away from Camilla. The rowers shipped their oars and let the current take them.

Mungo looked back, trying to master the frustration that threatened to boil over inside him. Camilla had been there, he was sure of it. He had felt her presence. Why had she not shown the green light? Had she been discovered? If so, what would happen to her? A hundred possibilities raced through his mind, each worse than the last. If the current had not already carried them so far downstream, he would have ordered them to turn back and attack, the odds be damned.

He sat back against the transom and waited for his anger to cool. There was nothing to gain by being rash. There was only one way he could help Camilla now.

On the bench in front of him, Tippoo was still waiting for an answer to his question. *What now?*

"We will bring Chester Marion to New Orleans. Then we will destroy him."

Camilla spent three days in her room. Twice a day, a servant brought her food and emptied her chamber pot; otherwise, she was left alone. It almost drove her mad. Sometimes, she looked at the hook on the roof beam where the lantern hung, and at the bedsheets, and terrible thoughts came into her mind. She told herself to stay strong—for Isaac, for Mungo—but knowing that they were out there only made it harder to bear her captivity. Occasionally, she heard Isaac's little voice drifting in from outside, and then she would press herself against the barred window until her head hurt, trying to get a glimpse of him. He sounded so happy. That was what hurt most.

On the third afternoon, Granville came and took her outside. Chester met her in the garden, walking along the gravel path beside the ponds he had dug. She did not wait for him to speak.

"I should go back to New Orleans," she said. "It's crop time. You need your eyes and ears among the traders and the factors."

Chester eyed her as if she hadn't spoken. He kept perfectly still—except for his head, which jerked back and forth like a cobra ready to strike.

"Do you have anymore to say about what happened the other night?" he asked.

"Isaac couldn't sleep. I took him out to see the boat and the river."

"Isaac said you woke him."

"I heard him cry in his sleep."

"I was in the room next door and I heard nothing."

She shrugged. "Sometimes a mother's ears are more sensitive."

Chester scowled. "Granville thinks there was a boat out on the water. He is convinced you were signaling to it."

"Granville sees dangers everywhere."

"Because that is what I pay him for!" Chester kicked out in a sudden flash of fury. A spray of gravel flew off the path, over the wall and down into the pond. "I sent word to my agents in New Orleans. They say that the mysterious Mr. Sinclair has not been seen there this past week."

"I would not know."

"Do not play the fool with me." His eyes drilled into her. "Has Mungo St. John returned? Is he in New Orleans? Did you think you could bring him ashore to murder us all in our beds?"

With each question his voice grew more hysterical. Specks of spittle flew out of his mouth. He was so frenzied, Camilla did not even dare to protest her innocence in case her denial provoked him more.

"I will have the truth from you," he hissed.

He grabbed her by the arms and shoved her onto the wall that lined the moat. On the elevated path the wall was only knee-high, but on its far side it dropped six feet or more straight down into the water. Chester held her down on the wall, forcing her head out over the edge. In the commotion, her bonnet came loose and dropped into the water.

It barely made a ripple as it landed—but it did not go unnoticed. On the opposite side of the pond, three alligators moved off the shore where they had been sunning themselves and began swimming toward her.

"You know what these creatures can do." Chester pushed her further out over the water. The alligators were almost halfway across. "I will let them have you. They will devour you, inch by inch, until I have the truth."

The monsters were coming closer, spiny backs surging through the water. Camilla wanted to scream, but that would do no good. What could she tell Chester? She could not admit that Mungo had been there. But nothing else would satisfy him.

The alligators were nearly there. Chester rolled her over onto her stomach so she was face down, staring straight at them. One of the creatures, faster than the others, was upon her. It rose out of the water in a splash of spray, wide open jaws lunging for her. She saw black eyes, a gnarled face like tree roots, and more teeth than she had ever imagined.

The jaws snapped shut—but they closed on thin air. At the last possible moment, Chester jerked Camilla back off the wall and threw her onto the path. The alligator, unable to scale the barrier, fell back in the water with an enormous splash while Camilla lay sobbing on the ground at Chester's feet.

"Maybe you are telling the truth," Chester conceded. He beckoned Granville over from where he had been loitering nearby.

"Ready the coach. Camilla will be returning to New Orleans this evening."

Granville looked surprised, but he knew better than to question Chester in this mood.

"Find out everything you can about this Thomas Sinclair." Chester was speaking to Camilla now, though he did not deign to look at her. "Let me know whatever you learn—and be sure I will hear of it if you lie to me."

He had finished with her. He walked on, his face calm again. Camilla fled gratefully, but Granville waited.

"You trust that black bitch?" said the overseer.

Chester puffed on his cigar and smiled. "Of course not. But I can still use her to my advantage."

"Not if she betrays you."

"No," Chester agreed. "That is why you will accompany her to New Orleans again. Stick to her like her own shadow, see who she speaks to. Keep a particular watch for our friend Mr. Sinclair."

"And the girl?"

Chester stared at the pond. "She is no use to me if I cannot trust her. Do nothing until I arrive."

Granville licked his lips. "And then?"

"You can do what you want with her."

Mungo was dining with François at the house on Rue Bourbon, talking of the upcoming presidential election, when the doorbell rang. From the hallway, Mungo heard the door open, a hushed conversation, and then the click of the latch closing again. A moment later, François's valet appeared.

"A negro girl brought this for you," he said to Mungo.

He was holding a single flower, four white petals tinged with pink around their edges. Each petal swelled out from the stem, then curved back to a small notch in its tip to give it the shape of a heart.

"Is it a geranium?" asked François, who had no interest in gardening.

"A dogwood flower," said Mungo.

He cupped it in his hands, as reverently as a priest holding the communion wafer, and breathed in the scent.

"A lady brought this?" François raised a coquettish eyebrow. "I think you have an admirer, sir."

He had not expected the reaction he provoked. Mungo looked up from the flower, and the look on his face was almost murderous. François recoiled; his stomach lurched.

Then Mungo's habitual smile returned. He handed the flower back to the valet.

"Put it in water," he said. He picked up his knife and fork and, with a single sharp motion that made François wince, sliced open the fish on his plate.

"Let us return to the topic of the election."

The next morning, Camilla rose early. Her maid brought her breakfast, but she didn't touch it. Her stomach was a knot of emotions. Had Mungo received her flower? Had he understood what it meant? Would he come? And if he did, would it be safe—or would they be discovered?

Granville was waiting for her at the front door, already dressed and with a knowing leer on his face. He looked her up and down, and Camilla tried to not imagine what he was thinking.

"I am going to confession," she said.

He gave a mock bow and opened the door for her. As soon as she stepped out, she heard his sharp footsteps fall in behind her. They followed her down Rue St. Louis, around the corner onto Rue de Chartres and all the way to the cathedral—like the beat of a drum marching a woman to the gallows.

The clock on the central tower already showed past six. She left Granville to take up his customary position outside the front door, and went straight in to the confessional.

She didn't notice Granville slip inside after her.

The confessional was empty. They had repaired the grille Mungo had broken on their previous visit, replacing the wood with iron bars. But there was no one behind them. Even before her eyes adjusted to the dark, Camilla could feel Mungo's absence.

She waited. Five minutes, then ten. Her hope faltered; fear began to pile on fear. He had not understood the message. He could not come. Chester had found him and he was dead. Or he was angry with her for not showing the lantern on the dock at Bannerfield and had abandoned her.

She was about to leave, when suddenly she heard the squeak of hinges on the confessional door and a man stepping inside. She sagged forward onto the kneeler and closed her eyes in relief.

"Thank God you came," she breathed.

"'Forgive me, Father, for I have sinned' would be a more customary way to start," said a voice. Not Mungo's, but high, petulant and heavily accented with French. "And no doubt you have a great many sins to confess."

Camilla's eyes snapped open. Behind the iron bars, she saw the outline of a fat, bald-headed man whose face was covered in sweat.

"Who are you?"

"Father Michel. I have this for you."

With his lips pursed in distaste, he pushed a small slip of paper through the bars to her. Normally, he would never have demeaned his holy orders and the sanctity of the confessional by passing a note—surely scandalous—from a man to a woman. But the man had been uncommonly persuasive, and he had donated a thousand dollars to the Church, and that surely was to the greater glory of God.

Camilla read the note. *I could not come. You are being watched.*

At that moment the door of the confessional was torn open. The priest squealed in alarm as a fist reached in, dragged him out and threw him onto the cathedral floor. Granville's terrifying figure stood over him, pistol drawn.

"What are you doing?" the priest yelped.

"You're not St. John."

Granville looked as if he might shoot the priest in frustration. Fortunately for the priest, he mastered his anger—though he did not holster his pistol. He swung around, scanning the cathedral. Apart from a pair of Ursuline nuns, it was empty.

The priest got to his feet and drew himself up.

"Monsieur," he said in a voice of holy outrage. "What is the meaning of this?"

"What were you doing?"

"He was hearing my confession," said Camilla. Inside she was trembling, but she channeled her fright into angry indignation.

While Granville had been distracted with the priest, she had had the presence of mind to hide Mungo's note. "Am I not allowed to confess my sins?"

"Depends what you've done."

Granville stared at her with naked suspicion. Camilla met his gaze with—she hoped—righteous innocence.

"If you have finished frightening this lady, perhaps you would be so kind as to leave the house of God," said Father Michel.

With a final, withering look at the priest, Granville stalked away. But not far. He took up position at the cathedral door, watching Camilla with unblinking eyes.

The priest dusted himself off.

"Mademoiselle," he said stiffly, "I do not know what sins you may have committed, but I think it is more than is in my power to absolve."

A thousand dollars was starting to seem like a poor bargain for nearly being killed.

"God forgives everything," Camilla reminded him.

"Then you may take it up with Him directly."

With a sniff, the priest left for the safety of the vestry. Camilla moved reluctantly toward the door. Even with Granville there, the cathedral was the one place in the city she had ever felt safe. Where could she find Mungo now?

She walked down the central aisle. One of the nuns had risen from her prayers and fell into step beside her.

"If you wish to pray in peace, you could always visit our convent," she said, with a pointed glance at Granville. "Men are not allowed there."

"Thank you," said Camilla absently.

"I find when I am troubled, it helps to pray to the saints," the nun continued. "St. Louis, of course. Or sometimes St. John."

Camilla stared at her, wondering if she had heard right. Before she could ask, the nun turned toward the altar, crossed herself and scurried away. Perhaps she had been frightened off by Granville, who was closing in as if the diminutive nun might somehow be Mungo in disguise.

"I wish to go and pray at the Convent of the Ursulines," Camilla told him.

It cost more to bribe a nun than a priest, Mungo discovered. Also, a dash of melodrama. He needed all his charm to persuade the Mother Superior of the Ursulines that Camilla was his half-sister, a freedwoman who had been kidnapped from their home in Maryland and sold into slavery in New Orleans; that he had come to take her back from her evil and rapacious master.

"If I could only have half an hour with her," he pleaded. "I could assure myself of her well-being, and make arrangements to bring her back."

Although she had lived most of her life behind the convent walls, the Mother Superior was neither innocent nor a fool. She could see Mungo's story was most likely a preposterous fabrication. Still, if it were true, it would be uncharitable to deny his request. And (she admitted to herself) she wanted to help him. Although she had pledged herself to God, she was still a woman, and the tall, shapely gentleman with the smoky yellow eyes and long dark hair aroused in her feelings for which she would surely have to do penance later.

Also, there was the matter of the five thousand dollars he wished to donate to the convent school.

Which was why, when Camilla arrived a short while later, she was welcomed into the convent, while Granville was made to wait outside the gates. The Mother Superior brought Camilla up to an empty cell.

"You will leave the door open," she said. "I will wait outside."

Camilla went in. The room was plain and bare: whitewashed walls, a desk and stool, a bed, and a crucifix on the door. And there, sitting on the bed leafing through a Bible, was Mungo.

She ran to him and threw her arms around him, almost crying with relief.

"Sister," said Mungo, with a significant nod toward the door. Camilla understood at once.

"Brother." She sat down beside him, keeping a demure distance in case the Mother Superior looked in. "I did not think I would see you again after what happened on the dock."

"You were discovered?"

"Chester found me. His men would have slaughtered you if you'd come ashore," she said in a low voice. She reached out as if to take his hand, then remembered the Mother Superior.

"He let you come back?"

"He suspects you have returned. He thinks he can use me as bait to trap you. That is why Granville was watching so closely at the cathedral."

"But he stayed at Bannerfield? And your son too?"

Camilla nodded, her head bowed as if in prayer. Silence fell on the little cell.

They were alone; they had escaped Granville. Mungo could not help thinking how easy it would be to get her aboard the *Raven* that moment. In half an hour they could be sailing away to a new life. If not for the boy.

"Chester will never let my son go," said Camilla. "Not while he lives."

She looked up at Mungo. A moment of understanding passed between them.

"All those years I thought you were dead," said Mungo, "I had only one thought in my heart. To destroy Chester. To strip him of everything he holds dear—his fortune, his reputation, his honor—and confront him with the wreckage of his ambition. And then to kill him."

His voice was hard as diamonds. Camilla did not flinch.

"How did you plan to do that?"

"The same way he ruined my father. Acquire his debts, then call them in."

Once, Camilla would have needed nothing more than the cold certainty in his voice to convince her that he would do as he said. Now, she was not so easily carried away.

"It is not straightforward," she warned. "What Chester did to Windemere took years—and he was in just the right place to manipulate and deceive your father."

"But Chester has debts?"

"They are enormous." Camilla spread her arms as wide as she could. "Chester's appetite for land and slaves is insatiable. To buy more, he has mortgaged everything he has. But it is hard to turn them against him. In any year, only a small part of his debts are due for repayment."

Mungo considered that. "So I would have to create a situation where all his debts were called in at once."

"That is possible," Camilla agreed. "If he defaults on one loan, all his other creditors are entitled to demand immediate repayment of theirs. One loose thread, and everything unravels. But even if the bank was willing to sell, Chester's debts are so vast you'd need a fortune to buy them."

Mungo gave her an admiring look. He could not believe how sure she had become, the shy serving girl he had known at Windemere. She had gained an understanding of business and finance that would rival many an East Coast banker.

For now, there was a more pressing question on his mind.

"How much would it take?"

Camilla stared at the crucifix over the door. "A million dollars."

Mungo sucked in a breath. He had realized three hundred thousand dollars on the *Raven*'s cargo—but costs, and the money he had spent already in New Orleans, had taken a bite out of the profits.

"I do not have that."

He thought hard, his mind reluctant to go where he bid it. Before he had known Camilla was alive, he thought he had all the time in the world for his revenge. Now everything was urgent, already too late. He could think of ways to get the money quickly. But at what cost?

He didn't speak, but Camilla seemed to read his thoughts in his face. He met her gaze, offering a reassuring smile. All he saw in her eyes was trouble.

"How did you get rich?" she asked suddenly.

"It does not matter."

"It does." A pause, twisting her hands in her lap. "I know why François went to Africa. I know he came back with you."

She stared at him, willing him to deny it. Mungo found he could not speak.

"I have seen the invoices from Havana," she said softly. "How many was it? Two hundred? Three hundred? How many women? How many children?"

"I tried . . ." Mungo trailed off. For almost the only time in his life, he could not speak. "I had no choice. I did it for you."

She moved so fast that even Mungo did not see it coming. A slap with her open hand, stronger than he would ever have guessed, that left a red welt stinging on his cheek.

"Never say that!" she cried. "If I thought that I had made you do such a thing—that I had been the cause of those people being locked in chains . . ."

Mungo's eyes blazed so hot she thought he might hit her back. Since the day she was born, she had imbibed the lesson that hurting a white man was the ultimate crime. She had not even thought she was capable of it. Now, she trembled with shock at what she had done, bracing herself for his retaliation.

Mungo balled his fist. He leaned closer, so much bigger than her. But he did not touch her.

"Are you any better? All these years that you have been

Chester's book-keeper—did you get nothing worse than ink on your hands? How many slaves are kept at Bannerfield? You may not have brought them from Africa, but you surely arranged for the tools in their hands and the food in their bellies that kept them alive in bondage."

His words cut so deep, Camilla would almost rather he had punched her.

"I did what I had to do to survive."

"I did what I had to do to rescue you."

A long silence hung over the room. There were only two feet between them, but it felt like a chasm. Not for the first time, Camilla wondered how much they had changed in the time they had been apart. Whether love or anything else could bridge the gap between them.

She had to believe it was possible.

"You did what you did. Maybe we both have done things . . ." She shook herself, then looked up. Tears glistened on her eyelashes, but her gaze was clear and firm. "You must vow to me that you will never go back to the black ships. You must promise that you will never again trade in human lives. Swear it, by your love for me."

Never before had she felt the difference between them so hard: his white skin, and her black. In that moment, she did not know what he would do. She could feel the energy in his body, every muscle tensed like a lion ready to spring. Perhaps he would walk out of the room, and she would never see him again. His yellow eyes were opaque, giving no clue.

Then, forgetting the Mother Superior beyond the door, Mungo took her hand and clasped it between his own.

"I swear it."

He stared into the depths of her eyes, and there was not a trace of guile or deceit. He meant what he said. Yet inside him, he was surprised to find he felt strangely unmoved by the oath he had taken. His cheek still hurt from the slap she had given him, but it had not stung his conscience. To apologize for what he had done would make him a hypocrite, and he would never be that. Why should he want forgiveness?

Somewhere between Pendleton's compound and the slave market of Havana, a change had happened inside him. The heat of his anger had cooled to something adamant, so hard that the mere guilt could not scratch it. If he felt anything, it was only a pang of unease at how little he could feel: a vestigial memory that once there had been deep emotion in him.

That was easily brushed away. *There is only one law on this earth—the law that gives the strong and wealthy power over the weak and poor.*

He kissed Camilla's forehead. In his mind, he had already moved on to more practical problems. Perhaps there was a way he could find the money.

"If I had a million dollars—what then? I would just go to Mr. Jackson and tell him I wished to purchase Chester's loans? Would he even sell them to me, as a private individual?"

"He would sell them to anyone if there was profit in it, but he makes a fortune off his loans to Chester. You would need to give him a reason to sell. Shake his faith in Chester."

"How would I do that?"

To Mungo's surprise, Camilla actually laughed. Risking the Mother Superior's disapproval, she reached out and put her hand on his cheek, feeling the rough-hewn lines of his face.

"Something I think you would be very good at. You would have to start a panic."

That afternoon, Mungo paid two calls in New Orleans.

The first was to the Bank of New Orleans, in an imposing building behind marble columns on Front Levee overlooking the river. Though he did not have an appointment, the clerks recognized him at once and ushered him into the private office of the bank's president, Jonathan Jackson. The office smelled of cigars and money.

"You know that I have two hundred thousand dollars deposited with you," said Mungo.

"Indeed I do," said Jackson. "We are honored to be your bankers."

"I came to you on the recommendation of my good friend François de Villiers, who conducts a great deal of business on behalf of Chester Marion."

Jackson smiled at the name. "I venture to say that through our prudent management of his finances, we have helped Mr. Marion become the greatest planter on the Mississippi."

"You advanced him the money for his projects?"

"We did."

"And you still hold these debts?"

"We do."

Mungo nodded, as if something he suspected had been proven. "You know there are rumors that your bank may be in some difficulties."

A bead of sweat broke on Jackson's brow. As a ship's captain feared even the smallest flame, so a banker lived in terror of any spark of a rumor of insolvency. If it were not quickly put out, it could become an inferno that could devour the whole institution.

"What rumors?"

"I overheard two men talking at Maspero's coffee house this

morning. They were thinking of withdrawing their funds from here and transferring them to the Union Bank."

A second bead of sweat joined the first. "Why should they do that?"

"Chester Marion has not been seen in New Orleans for months."

"That is true."

"These men said it was because he could not pay his debts. They say he has holed up at Bannerfield, surrounded by armed guards, to hide the fact that his crop has failed. One of them even said—I do not credit it myself, but he certainly said it—that Chester had taken his own life, and his overseer was hiding the fact while he sought a buyer for the estate."

Jackson thumped the desk. "That is the most infamous pack of lies. I do not know where these rumors began, but I can assure you that there is no risk. Chester Marion is a dependable customer. Rock solid."

"I am relieved to hear you say it," said Mungo. "You have seen him recently to confirm that all is well?"

"Well, no," Jackson conceded. "But I have heard nothing amiss from Bannerfield. I am sure . . ."

He broke off. Mungo was giving him a stare so piercing he felt like a schoolboy with his breeches down.

"As one businessman to another—as well as a client—permit me to give you some advice," said Mungo. "It would be well for your bank if Chester Marion showed his face in New Orleans, sooner rather than later."

Jackson drew himself up to his full height. "Chester Marion comes and goes as he pleases. But when his cotton reaches New Orleans next week, all the world will see that he has more money than he knows what to do with. I will be at the wharf myself to ensure its safe arrival."

Mungo gave a smile that, for some reason, sent a shiver

down Jackson's spine. He told himself it must be a draft. It was November, and an autumnal chill had crept into the city.

"I am glad to hear it."

Jackson showed Mungo out with a firm handshake and a sense of relief. He could not imagine where these rumors could have come from, but he felt he had done enough to quell his client's doubts.

Nonetheless, as soon as Mungo had gone he took paper and pen from his desk and wrote a brief note.

There is some disquiet that you have been absent so long from New Orleans. I believe it would be advantageous to your affairs, and reassuring to the bank, if you were able to visit the city and dispel any ill-informed rumors concerning your good health and prosperity.

He sealed the letter and gave it to his secretary to dispatch immediately by steamboat upriver. He was confident Chester would come—he owed the bank too much money to ignore Jackson's request. And that would be an end of these disagreeable rumors.

Mungo's second call was to the house on Rue Royale. He did not know if he would be welcome after their previous encounter, but Solange received him in her salon, lounging on a *chaise* and sipping a glass of chilled wine. Bars of late afternoon light shone through the slats of the shutters.

"I have an investment opportunity for you," Mungo told her.

She looked bored. "I am rich enough."

"I could make you mistress of the finest plantation on the Mississippi. Five thousand acres of land, a thousand slaves, and half a million dollars in cotton every year."

Still she showed no interest. "Is the man who owns it a bachelor?"

"He is."

"Then if I wanted it, I could achieve it through a simple act of matrimony—without whatever scheme you want to propose."

"If you married him, you would be a widow within a week."

That piqued her interest. "Is he in poor health?"

"He will be—when he has my bullet in his heart."

She laughed with delight. "This is the man you told me about? The man you came to destroy?"

"My web is closing around him. But to complete it, I need a million dollars."

"That is a lot of money." Solange beckoned him toward her. "Come and sit with me."

Mungo hesitated. Her intentions were as clear as they had been the night he entered her cabin aboard the *Blackhawk*. The fact that he had spurned her on his last visit seemed to have deterred her not at all.

But he needed a million dollars from her.

He went across to the chaise and sat on the end of it. Solange put her feet up on his lap.

"What if I do not give you the money?"

"I am not asking for a gift—only a loan. As I said, you will gain a fine estate in return."

She kicked off her slipper and nestled her stockinged foot between his legs.

"If it is such an irresistible proposition, why are you offering it to me?"

"Because I do not have a million dollars."

"And if I say no?"

"I will find another way."

"I do not doubt you will. You are the most determined man I have ever met." She leaned forward, giving him an ample view down the front of her dress. Her foot began to move slowly, rubbing against his groin. She smiled as she felt him go hard under her touch. "Perhaps if you come upstairs, we can discuss this further."

Mungo did not move. He could tell by the gleam in her eyes that she was toying with him, testing his resolve. But what did she want? Would she give him the money if he succumbed? Or would she just mock him as a hypocrite and spurn him?

"I have an appointment elsewhere."

Solange pouted. "You come to ask for a million dollars, and then tell me you must go so quickly. Even if your request was for something less *excessive*, I would think that showed a certain lack of delicacy."

"I apologize if I seem rude."

"Then come upstairs."

Mungo still did not move. "I told you last time I came here, Camilla is alive."

Solange's eyes narrowed. "You want my million dollars to buy back your sweetheart?"

"The money is to ruin Chester Marion."

"I wonder." Solange stared at him, as if trying to see behind his golden eyes. "If you had only one choice—to save the woman you love, or destroy your enemy—what would you do?"

"I do not intend to have to choose."

Solange stood. She went to the ice bucket where the wine bottle stood, and refilled her glass. The cold wine made beads of condensation bloom on the rim. She stared at her reflection in the mirror over the mantelpiece, tucking back a loose strand of hair.

"If you had not killed my brother, I would have had nothing." She said it quietly, almost to herself. "All the inheritance would have gone to Afonso when our father died. I would have been at his mercy."

Mungo had risen as well. He faced her across the room.

"I was only protecting your honor."

"*Honor?*" A scathing expression came into her voice. "Do you really believe in honor? Is that why you did everything you have done—for *honor*?"

"No," Mungo admitted. "Honor is merely a dressed-up word for pride."

"And a pretty excuse for revenge."

Why deny it? "Yes."

"Then why not come to my bed to get the money you need? Any other man would have done that and thought himself doubly lucky. Would you not sleep with me in exchange for what you want?"

"If you insisted," said Mungo. "It would not be the worst thing I have done for money."

"That is not very gallant." She said it with mock indignation, but Mungo did not think he had offended her.

She looked into her glass, swirling the wine. "Your sweetheart must be a precious woman indeed to be worth so much. Beautiful, accomplished, witty, doting. A Messalina in the bedroom."

"She is the one I want."

"Then I shall give her to you." She drained the last dregs of her wine, stepped forward and put her hands on his hips. She looked up into his eyes as if getting ready for a dance. "I will loan you the million dollars, in consideration of the debt I owe you for killing my brother. But remember it is only a loan. I will expect repayment—one way or another."

Mungo realized he had hardly drawn breath for the last ten minutes. He felt dizzy; his head swam with Solange's perfume and the wine on her breath. He looked down into her face, and all he felt was desire. He should have felt ashamed of it, but—for the second time that day—he found that he could not feel guilt.

"You do not have to give it to me," he told her. "All I need you to do is sign a piece of paper."

Ezekiel McMurran liked to say that if he knew the Mississippi any better, he'd be a catfish. His earliest memories were splashing in its creeks and bywaters. At ten, he had run away from home to crew flatboats, the rough-hewn river barges that had brought goods and settlers down the Mississippi in those early frontier days. It was one-way traffic, powered only by the current. He would help navigate the boats down to New Orleans, avoiding shallows and fending off obstacles with poles. There, the vessels would be broken up for lumber, and McMurran would trudge the two hundred miles back upriver and wait for another boat to pass.

Then one day, near New Orleans, he had seen a preposterous ship without oars or sails, spouting smoke from her funnel and churning the water behind her as she made her way upstream—upstream!—at a stately three knots. From that moment, he had known his calling in life. He had talked his way aboard: first as a ship's boy, then a rouster, a fireman, an engineer, and finally as captain of his own vessel. He had taken ships from Louisiana as far as Memphis; he had carried soldiers, opera singers and even a president.

But he had never carried a cargo as valuable as the one he did now. Half a million dollars' worth of cotton—so much, he had not even been certain the boat could carry it all. It was packed solid on the *Windemere*'s lower deck, a wall of raw cotton more than twenty feet high extending right around the perimeter of the boat. Heavily loaded, she sat so low in the water that every ripple in the river splashed over her guards and wetted the cotton that bulged out from her sides.

And as if that was not enough, he also had the cotton's owner to contend with. The day before the *Windemere* left Bannerfield, a letter had arrived from the Bank of New Orleans that threw Chester Marion into a black mood. Shortly afterward, he had announced that he would be accompanying the cotton downriver—and bringing his son with him. That had necessitated a rushed job emptying the stateroom of the cotton that had been stored within, and somehow finding somewhere else to stow it.

Now, from the pilot house above the *Windemere*'s hurricane deck, McMurran could console himself that his journey was nearly finished. On the left, the wharfs and spires of New Orleans moved past, while off the starboard side the city's river traffic made its way up the main channel. The *Windemere*, her owner and her cargo were almost at their destination.

It had not been without difficulty. The previous day, when they tied up for the night, his engineer had gone ashore to find extra wood for the boilers. It was unclear exactly what had happened next. Some said he had been drinking, others that he had got in a fight with a negro, others again that he had been accidentally knocked out by a piece of firewood. In any event, the man had been carried back to the boat insensible, with his head stove in and no prospect of him resuming his duties.

Fortunately, luck had smiled on McMurran. There had been another steamboat tied up at the landing, the *Nellie Mae*. Her captain had heard of McMurran's difficulty and offered him the loan of his own engineer. McMurran had blanched when he saw the man—a giant, probably mulatto, with an entirely hairless head. McMurran had been minded to refuse. But when he put the man in front of the boilers it had quickly become clear he possessed extraordinary skill. McMurran had gratefully accepted his help. Better, the rapid resolution meant there was no need to inform Chester of the incident. McMurran did not dare give his employer any reason to doubt him.

And now they were nearly there. Only a quarter of a mile, and he would have discharged his duty. McMurran could see the wharf ahead, and the brick warehouse behind it. The arrival of the Bannerfield steamer was always an event in New Orleans, and this year—for some reason—more people than usual had gathered to witness it.

McMurran gripped the wheel. He was almost there. He would not let anything happen to Chester Marion's cargo.

The day was cloudy, and a brisk wind whipped the wharf. Among the crowd who had gathered were some of the most eminent businessmen in the city: François de Villiers, as was to be expected; but also Jonathan Jackson, the president of the Bank of New Orleans. Some men whispered that the banker had come because there were doubts whether Chester's credit was still good. Those who did not have money in the Bank of New Orleans laughed at the gossip and laid bets; those who were the bank's customers glanced anxiously over their shoulders. There were no secrets in New Orleans. Everyone knew how much the bank's fortunes were tied to the *Windemere*'s cargo. Though if they had doubts, the two dozen guards in the uniforms of the Bannerfield Militia should have allayed them.

Amid the men in their sober suits, two women stood out. One was Chester's mistress—some said a slave, though others insisted she was a free woman of color—in a pure white dress that dazzled the dreary dock. Another was the Marquise Solange de Noailles, dressed in shimmering red silks, the most eligible lady in the city. No one knew why she had come. A slave girl stood behind her holding a parasol, though it cast no shade on a sunless day, next to a man in a black suit and a frown. Behind them, a handsome black carriage was drawn up awaiting the arrival of Chester Marion. Six black horses were harnessed in front of it, while Granville Slaughter sat up on the driver's box with a pistol in his hand.

Also present was Mr. Thomas Sinclair, though very few of the spectators noticed him. He lounged at the back against the warehouse wall, looking over the heads of those in front, smoking a cigar. Occasionally he checked his watch, and sometimes a woman would catch his eye and receive a polite tip of his hat; otherwise his gaze stayed locked on the approaching steamboat.

The captain was bringing her in quickly. She raced past the

other ships in the river, rocking the smaller craft with her wake. One of these boats, a cutter, was sailing so close that she was almost swamped by the bow wave. The *Windemere* paid no notice. Her stern-wheel beat the water, while smoke poured from her twin funnels.

In fact, a keen observer might have noticed, there was rather a lot of smoke.

McMurran did not smell it at first. He was watching the little cutter that was sailing upriver toward them. In the brisk wind, the cutter was fairly flying along, heeling hard over as she came dangerously close to the wind. Her skipper did not seem to care about the *Windemere* steaming toward him, but held a course almost as if he meant to ram her.

The cutter's crew, McMurran saw from the pilot house, were mostly black. That was not uncommon—the crews of Mississippi boats were filled with free blacks and slaves—but something about them made him look again. He lifted his binoculars and scanned the faces of the men in the cutter. The man at the bow was short and lithe, with tightly cropped hair and very dark skin, but it was the look on his face that caught McMurran's eye in particular. There was a strength to it, a sense of possession that to McMurran did not look right on a black man. It seemed not just liberated, but as if it had never occurred to him he might be inferior.

"Sir!" Belatedly, McMurran realized the first mate was tugging his arm. Not only tugging, but shouting and gesturing frantically over the side. "*Captain!*"

McMurran looked. Black smoke was billowing up from the main deck, gathering in ominous clouds around the pilot house.

"Is something wrong with the boilers?"

"It's not the boilers!" The mate was screaming at him, almost beside himself. "The cotton's on fire!"

McMurran let go of the wheel and ran outside. He almost collided with Chester barging into the pilot house.

"What is happening?" Chester shouted. The boy was with him, clutching his father's hand. "Put it out before we lose everything!"

The men had already run to the pumps. They worked the handles, while others trained the hoses on the lower deck. But as hard as they tried, no water came out.

"The stop-cocks must be closed."

The pumps were fed by pipes that took in water from the river. The taps that opened them were on the lower deck, packed deep in cotton.

Cotton that was now on fire.

Flames started to lick over the hurricane deck. The crew began to panic. Shouting, cajoling and threatening, McMurran organized them into bucket chains, hauling water up over the side and throwing it onto the cotton. But it was too little, too late. As quickly as the water put out one patch of flame, the heat of the fire dried out the cotton and set it alight again.

With sickening certainty, McMurran realized he was about to lose his ship.

"Abandon ship!" he called. "Save yourselves!"

It was a sight that no one in New Orleans would ever forget. Decades later, those who witnessed it would still talk of it in awestruck voices to their grandchildren.

With the cotton packed solid all around her main deck and her boiler deck, the flames caught hold of the *Windemere* like a bale of straw. But it had not yet reached her stern wheel; indeed, the heat only seemed to make her go faster. She streaked along the river, streaming smoke and flames behind her, cutting a swathe of destruction through the river traffic. Small boats were smashed to pieces under her bow. The larger vessels at anchor tried to get out of her way, but there was no time. She barged them aside, smashing great holes in their hulls—and everything she touched was itself set alight and joined the conflagration, until the whole river seemed to be on fire. It was an utter panic. Many in the crowd tried to flee, while the horses waiting with the carriage reared up and lashed out with their hooves.

Only one man on the wharf remained entirely calm. Mungo did not move from his position by the warehouse, but surveyed the scene with an almost serene look on his face.

Camilla found him there.

"What have you done?" she screamed. Smoke blowing off the water had turned her white dress gray. Ash had landed on her face and been smudged black by her tears. "My son is on board."

The letter had only arrived that morning from Chester confirming that he and Isaac were coming on the steamboat, but the news did not seem to surprise Mungo.

"Isaac is quite safe," he said.

A crash rang out across the water. The fire had burned through the pillars that supported the *Windemere*'s hurricane deck; now it collapsed in an eruption of sparks that threatened to set the whole town alight. A gout of flame shot into the air as the deck planks were consumed in the inferno. Camilla screamed.

But one vessel had escaped the destruction unscathed. The little cutter sailed away from the burning steamer, blown on by the hot breath of the fire behind. Sparks and burning cinders rained down around her; it was a miracle she had not caught fire. One flaming coal touched her sail; a black hole began to open in the canvas. The spectators on the wharf gasped, but the crew were alert to the danger. They hurled buckets of water onto the sail to damp it down.

In the bow stood three bedraggled figures who had obviously been pulled from the water. One was an olive-skinned giant of a man, bare-chested and bare-headed. The second was a child. The third was Chester Marion.

The cutter nudged up against the wharf. The crowd surged down the steps, so eager to help they almost sank the boat. Hands reached out; it seemed there was no way through. But the giant found a way. Hoisting the boy on his shoulders, he moved forward; the crowd had to give way or risk being pushed aside into the river. Chester followed, dripping wet, and if anyone was tempted to console him for his loss, or congratulate him on his escape, one look at him made them shrink away in terror. His bare scalp was scalded red and blistered. His eyebrows had burned away, and there was a livid burn mark down his cheek where a burning fragment of wood had hit him. His face was black with soot, while his shirt hung off him in charred ribbons. It must have caught fire before he jumped in the water. Through the rents in the fabric, you could see more blisters covering his body like the scales of some hideous reptile.

Tippoo put Isaac down on the dock. Camilla ran to the boy and lifted him in her arms, stroking his face as she carried him away. She made her way around the edge of the crowd until she found Mungo.

"We are free." Tears still streaked her face, but her eyes were bright with astonished delight. "We should go at once, before Chester sees you."

Mungo's jaw was set tight. "Not yet."

"But you have achieved what you wanted." She tugged on his arm like a child. Mungo did not move. "You have destroyed Chester, and I have my son back. If we wait, we risk everything."

Mungo barely looked at her. He was still watching the stricken steamboat, a rapturous expression on his face.

"I have not finished with Chester yet."

The flames on the *Windemere* had started to lick lower, for there was not much left to burn. They glowed a dull orange, silhouetting what remained of her charred skeleton. A curtain of steam rose from her waterline where the fire touched the river. The watchers on the shore began to breathe again.

Then her boilers exploded.

The noise hit New Orleans like a thunderclap, shivering windows and making the church bells moan in sympathy. Fragments of machinery, timbers, furniture and human bodies were shot up in a column of fire that reached a thousand feet in the air. As they reached their apex, they arced out like the jets of a fountain, raining down all over the city. One of the iron connecting rods was shot through the wall of a house like a cannonball. Mangled corpses, and parts of corpses, dropped into the square in front of the cathedral and caught in the branches of trees. A hail of burning embers fell on the city. Men going about their business, women taking a promenade and babies in their carriages suffered terrible burns. Wherever the coals landed, new fires sprang up. The city was in uproar.

Out on the water, the explosion had split the *Windemere*'s hull in two. It collapsed inward and sank in a whorl of steam, the two halves of the boat folding together like a monstrous jaw closing. Then she vanished. All that remained was flotsam, and the hiss as burning debris rained down on the water.

Like the eye of a storm, the wharf remained strangely detached from the carnage. The power of the explosion had thrown the debris far over the spectators' heads. While blood and fire consumed other parts of the city, the dock and the levee remained untouched.

All eyes turned to Chester. The crowd had formed a semicircle around him, keeping a wary distance. But one man pushed his way through. François was weeping, his hair askew and his face gray with shock. He clutched Chester's arm like a child.

"What will we do? What will we do?"

At the back of the crowd, a young clerk sidled up to the president of the Bank of New Orleans.

"I think you had best come back to the bank," he murmured.

"Why?"

"Rumors are spreading."

He pointed back down the levee, to the marble columns that fronted the bank. Even with the city on fire, people were not insensible of their savings. A crowd had already started to gather outside the doors. Their mood seemed nearly hysterical.

"What do they want?"

"People are saying that all our capital was invested in Chester Marion's enterprise, and now he is bankrupt."

Jackson went pale. "Keep your voice down."

It was too late. One of the bystanders had overheard the clerk and was hurrying toward them. To Jackson's dismay, he saw it was his client, Thomas Sinclair.

"Your bank has the bulk of its capital invested in Chester Marion," said Mungo. The emotion of the moment seemed to have got to him. He spoke in a loud voice, apparently oblivious to the effect it was having. "You told me that there was no risk attached to it—now I see that is not the case. I shall require you to return the money I deposited with you."

Jackson seemed to be struggling to breathe. "How much?"

"All two hundred thousand dollars."

The people around them had begun to listen. Some were already hurrying away down the levee toward the bank. Panic threatened.

"We do not have two hundred thousand dollars left in the vault," the clerk whispered in Jackson's ear.

Down the levee, the crowds outside the bank were now hammering on its doors.

"Well?" Mungo pressed. "Can I have my money?"

Jackson stared at Mungo, and every fiber in his body seemed to rupture with the effort of what he had to say. The words every banker dreads.

"I do not have your money," he croaked. "If you could wait a few days . . ."

"Perhaps I could be of assistance."

A new voice—that of a beautiful woman in a striking crimson

dress who had come up beside Mungo. A stern-faced man in a black coat trailed behind her.

"I am the Marquise Solange de Noailles," the woman announced herself, though Jackson knew who she was. "And this gentlemen is my attorney. I am willing to buy all Chester Marion's debts from you, for the sum of one million dollars."

Jackson looked at the woman as if she had suddenly started speaking in Chinese.

The attorney produced a sheet of paper from his case.

"I have drawn up the contract. Everything is in order."

Jackson seized it like a drowning man grabbing the rope. He read it quickly.

"Why are you doing this?"

"The Marquise does not want to see your bank collapse in a panic," said Mungo. "She knows how vital it is to the commerce and prosperity of New Orleans."

"The alternative does not bear thinking about," murmured Solange.

So many extraordinary things had happened that morning, Jackson had lost all sense of reality. If he had paused to think, he might have started to wonder at the remarkable chain of events, each more sensational than the last, that had driven him toward this conclusion. He might have asked himself how Solange came to be there at that moment, so well prepared that the paperwork was already written. He might even have wondered at the role of Thomas Sinclair in all that had transpired. But at that moment, the only thing he knew was that the city was on fire, and he had a few minutes at most to save his bank. All his fortune was invested in its stock. If it went under, he would lose everything. His wife would be impoverished, his children destitute.

He signed the contract.

The moment he had finished, the attorney took the paper from his hands and passed it to Mungo. Holding it close to his chest, protecting it from the cinders and sparks that still occasionally drifted down, Mungo shouldered through to the front of the crowd.

The guards Chester had placed around the warehouse had made a line across the door to hold back the throng. Chester stood in their midst, still staring in disbelief at the wreckage of the *Windemere* floating on the water.

Mungo stepped out in front of him, holding the paper aloft. The wind blew back his hair and a shining light filled his eyes.

"Chester Marion!" he called, in a voice that rose above the chaos in the city. "It is time to pay your debts!"

It was a moment Mungo had long anticipated. In the darkness of the *Blackhawk's* hold; in the steaming jungles of Africa; in the long days aboard the *Raven* listening to the groan of the slaves, he had dreamed of it. Since the day he returned to Windemere, face down in the mud outside the observatory, he had worked to achieve it. And now that the time had come, it did not disappoint.

Chester had imagined it too, but not like this. All the defenses he had built against this moment had proved worthless. Now he turned to see the vision from his nightmares standing in front of him.

Mungo St. John.

Their eyes met: steel gray and smoldering yellow. A snarl of surprise and fury twisted Chester's mangled face. He went so still, Mungo wondered if the shock had stopped his heart. Only his eyes moved, darting between Mungo, Isaac and Camilla. A thousand agonies seemed to shatter those steel-gray eyes as he took in the breadth of the destruction Mungo had wrought.

Then he remembered himself.

"What are you waiting for?" he shouted to his guards. "This is the man I warned you about, the man I pay you to protect me from. Shoot him!"

"Yes, shoot me," said Mungo coolly. "Shoot an unarmed man in front of two dozen witnesses. You will hang for murder—and why? To defend the honor of a bankrupt man? You will never see another penny of the wages he has promised you."

He turned in a slow circle, looking each man in the eye. One by one, they lowered their guns.

"Your power is finished," Mungo said to Chester. "This piece of paper I have in my hand is the bill for all your debts. I am calling them in."

His lips twisted in a cruel smile. "Do you remember what you told me once? Credit is as vital to a man as the air that he breathes. Cut it off, and he dies."

Chester took a deep breath. It caught in his throat, sparking a fit of coughing. Spittle and black phlegm sprayed out over the wharf.

"It does not end here," he said. His voice was hoarse and rasping. "You can burn my boat, kill my men and steal my property—but if you attempt to repossess Bannerfield, I will fight you every inch of the way. Even if you hired the fanciest attorneys in New Orleans, I will run rings around them in a courthouse. You will die an old man, still without the thing you crave."

Mungo did not dispute the truth of what Chester had said.

"There is a faster way to settle this." His eyes flashed with the challenge. "Like gentlemen."

Chester stared at him. "A duel?"

Mungo could see the fear in his enemy's eyes. Mungo was tall, lean and strong; Chester was scarred and burned from his ordeal aboard the boat. Even without that, he was shorter by eight inches and carried a hundred pounds more weight.

"I will not fight you," said Chester.

Mungo waved at the crowd. "Then every person in New Orleans will know that Chester Marion is a man without honor."

"If you believe in honor, you are a greater fool than I thought."

"A man without honor is a man without credit," Mungo reminded him.

He saw Chester's calculation changing. The jibe had struck where it counted. A Southern gentleman placed so much weight on his honor—and would be so quick to defend it—because his bank credit depended on it. And a man in the South was nothing without credit.

"I will give you another reason to fight." Solange stepped into the circle, drawing gasps from the onlookers. She plucked the piece of paper with Jackson's signature scrawled across the bottom from Mungo's hand. "This is the deed to all your debts. If you win the duel, it is yours."

Chester's mouth dropped open. "That is worth a million dollars."

Mungo, too, looked astonished. "This is not your fight."

"It is my name on the deed. I can do with it as I want." Her eyes met his in an ironic smile. "For the sake of your honor."

The paper crackled in the wind. Chester gazed at it like a chained dog eyeing a piece of meat.

"Where and when?"

"Now," said Mungo. "Here."

Chester blanched. "That is impossible."

"Why?"

"You challenged me. I have the choice of weapons."

"Indeed."

"And I choose pistols. We must wait until suitable weapons can be found."

Mungo nodded to Tippoo. The giant stepped forward with a heavy rosewood box that he seemed to have produced from nowhere. He snapped it open and presented it to Chester. Inside the velvet-lined case were a magnificent pair of percussion dueling pistols. Their barrels were forged from mottled Damascus steel, inlaid with a hunting scene of horses and hounds and huntsmen in bright gold.

"I anticipated your choice," said Mungo. "Please inspect them. You will find they are all in order."

Hesitantly, as if touching a snake, Chester took one of the pistols. He checked the hammer, the chamber and the barrel, as if to satisfy himself that Mungo had not tampered with it.

"You may choose whichever one you like," said Mungo. "It makes no difference to me."

François loaded the guns. Chester took one, Mungo the other. The crowd shuffled back to leave clear space along the front of the dock.

Mungo and Chester stood back to back. They paced out ten yards, then turned to face each other.

Mungo held his pistol steady at his side, staring down the space that separated him from Chester. The prospect of dying did not worry him. This was all he had wanted: a gun in his hand, and a straight shot at Chester.

Yet he did not underestimate his opponent. Chester's one good eye stared at Mungo with the intensity of a madman. His burned face throbbed with hatred. If it was possible to guide a bullet by sheer force of will, he would surely find a way to put it in Mungo's heart.

Silence gripped the wharf. The crowd shrank back, as if they could feel the blistering heat of the hatred between the two men. Flakes of ash from the *Windemere* drifted down like snow. François raised his handkerchief.

"One . . ." he called.

Mungo let his arm hang loose. He thought of Windemere, his mother and his father.

"Two . . ."

He curled his finger around the trigger. He thought of the slave girl aboard the *Blackhawk*; the village he had raided with the Punu; the hundreds of anonymous faces he had brought across the Atlantic to this place. He thought of Camilla.

"Thr—"

Suddenly there was a commotion in the crowd. Camilla

stumbled out, shoved forward by Granville. She staggered in front of Chester.

Mungo's arm was already swinging upward, his finger tightening on the trigger. The sudden motion only heightened the adrenaline pumping through his veins and made his muscles move even faster. The spring that held the hammer stretched; the hammer began to quiver.

But Mungo's senses had been honed by years fighting for his life. His golden eyes, fixed on his target, missed nothing. Just before the hammer sprang, he saw Camilla.

For a lesser shooter, it would have made no difference. His brain would already have given the command, leaving the machinery of his limbs no choice but to complete the irrevocable action. But Mungo, his mind and body calibrated finer than any watch, saw her in time to make a split-second choice.

He let go of the trigger.

Chester grabbed Camilla. He held her in front of him, one arm wrapped around her neck while the other held the pistol to her temple.

Mungo kept his pistol level. But though Chester's head was just visible behind Camilla's, the weapon was not so accurate that he could risk the shot.

"Let her go," said Mungo. "Let her go, or dishonor yourself forever."

"Honor?" Chester gave a cackling laugh. "You would lecture me about honor, when you would rather save a slave girl than avenge your own father. You are a coward, Mungo St. John."

"Let her go, and I will show you how much of a coward I am."

"I do not think I will." Chester edged away, dragging Camilla backward toward the carriage. "You will not defeat me so easily." His voice was loud and wild. "At Bannerfield I have five hundred armed men loyal to me. I own more land and slaves than any other man in the state. You will not pry me out of there so easily."

"Let her go," said Mungo. "Let Camilla go, and I will forget what you have done to my family."

"What you doing to Milla?" cried Isaac.

He tugged at his father's arm, but Chester's grip never loosened on Camilla, or on the gun at her temple.

"Get in the carriage," Chester told him.

When Isaac hesitated, Granville scooped the boy up and pushed him in. Chester followed, dragging Camilla in after him. Granville leaped up onto the box and whipped the horses. Before the doors were even closed, the carriage was flying down the levee and away to the city.

Mungo ran after it, but it was hopeless. He could not overtake six strong horses. He stopped, staring after the disappearing carriage.

"Where will they go?" Tippoo had come up beside him.

"Bannerfield," said Mungo. "It is all he has left."

"You want me to find horses?"

"He will not go by coach." Mungo stared at the cloud of dust and ash the coach had kicked up, second-guessing Chester's plans. "He cannot risk me getting there first. A steamboat is the fastest way."

Tippoo bared his teeth. "He has no steamboat."

"He will be able to charter one."

Mungo glanced back at the river. Inside him, feelings raged through his veins like fire: fury at Chester's escape; shock at how close he had come to killing Camilla; fear for her now in Chester's possession. Outwardly, his expression remained ice cold.

"Fire up the boilers on the *Nellie Mae*."

The steamboat *Cleopatra* tore up the Mississippi under full steam. Her boilers hissed and strained in protest, for she was not used to this frantic pace. She had been built for the passenger trade, no expense spared, and she would normally cruise the river with the deliberate, regal progress of the queen she had been named for.

There was nothing stately about her today. She had been fired up and ready to leave her moorings to pick up passengers, when Chester Marion arrived at her wharf and offered the captain ten thousand dollars to take him to Bannerfield. Even so, the master had hesitated. He had seen the fire that engulfed the *Windemere*, and Chester Marion's appearance—filthy, burned and ragged—did not inspire confidence. But the carriage had outrun the news of everything else that had happened on the wharf; so far as the master knew, the name of Chester Marion still had more credit than any man in Louisiana. So he had agreed.

Three hours later, he had begun to wonder if even ten thousand dollars was enough. First, there had been the rush to get the *Cleopatra* underway. Then, Chester had demanded he shovel on fuel until the pressure gauges on the boilers rose so high they threatened to blow. Even now, with the boat running dangerously fast up the twisting river, Chester did not seem satisfied. He paced the hurricane deck, staring back the way they had come, as if he expected the hounds of Hell to come after them.

Below his feet, Camilla sat in the lonely splendor of the grand saloon. The room was two hundred feet long and twenty feet high, like the nave of a cathedral. All around her were the trappings of luxury: gilt mirrors, crystal chandeliers, a marble-topped bar and stained glass skylights that admitted a strange, yellow-blue light. Yet to her, it felt like a tomb.

She sat on a plush sofa wide enough to accommodate a dozen people in comfort. Isaac sat on her lap.

"What's happening?" he wailed.

Whether by some deep-rooted instinct that recognized his mother, or simply because she was the only reassuring presence on the boat, he buried his face between her breasts and wept.

"You must be brave," she told him. "We are taking you home."

Amid all the chaos and carnage of the day, she felt a serenity within her soul she had never known before. She wrapped her arms around her son and hugged him tight. She had what she wanted. Nothing else mattered.

Up above, the captain descended from the pilot house and found Chester.

"We cannot keep up this speed much longer. We are burning through our wood too fast. We will have to stop and resupply."

Chester pointed aft. They had entered a straight section of the river, three miles long. Behind them, just coming out of the last turn, he saw the bow of another boat. The steam pouring from her funnels, and the speed with which she churned the water, made it clear that she was no ordinary cotton carrier or packet ship.

"If we stop, she will overtake us."

"But we do not have enough fuel to reach Bannerfield."

Chester stamped his foot on the deck. "What is this made of?"

The master swallowed. "White oak."

"And the superstructure?"

"Pine and cedar."

"Then we are standing on all the fuel we need. Break it down and feed it to the furnaces."

The master stood his ground.

"You chartered my boat so I could take you to Bannerfield. Not destroy her."

"I am willing to change the terms of our agreement. A hundred thousand dollars to buy her outright."

The master's jaw dropped in shock. A hundred thousand dollars was many times what the *Cleopatra* was worth. But it was not his decision to make.

"I ain't the owner. I couldn't agree that even if I wanted it."

"You could tell him after the fact."

It was a tempting offer. With a hundred thousand dollars, the master could pay off the owners for the loss of the ship, throw in ten thousand dollars more by way of apology, and still have enough left to retire handsomely.

But he was an obstinate man.

"It ain't right," he said.

"Very well."

Chester paused for a moment, as if preparing another offer. Then, changing his mind, he took the dueling pistol from his belt. It was still primed and loaded from the unfinished duel. Without warning, he aimed it at the captain and fired. The bullet hit him just below the sternum. The man tottered backward, clutching his chest, and fell with a scream into the brown water below.

One of the crew who had been keeping watch for hazards had seen everything. He stared at Chester in amazement.

"What'd you just do?"

"I am the master now," said Chester. Beside him, Granville had drawn his own gun and trained it on the sailor. "You will follow my orders, or follow the captain overboard. You understand?"

The crewman made a quick analysis of his options. "What do you want me to do?"

Chester waved the pistol at the deck beneath his feet. "Tear her apart."

A mile back, the *Nellie Mae* raced on. All four boilers were running hot, but Tippoo kept a wary eye on the pressure gauges to be sure they did not blow. Mungo found him on the main deck, stripped to the waist with the heat of the furnaces.

"Can you get any more speed?" he shouted over the roar of the engines. "Chester is pulling ahead!"

It should never have come to this. He had not expected Chester to leave the wharf alive. Knowing what would happen to the *Windemere*, he had moored the *Nellie Mae* well downriver of the wharf so that the fire and the explosion would not touch her. When Chester escaped, it had meant a long, hard pull in the cutter to reach the steamboat, and then more delay while they fired up her boilers and took on wood. That had given Chester enough time to board the *Cleopatra* and set out ahead of Mungo.

At least it had not been hard to identify the boat Chester had taken from New Orleans. Mungo had watched her leave the docks so fast she almost capsized a yawl sailing by. Soon afterward, he had seen Chester's unmistakable silhouette out in the open on the hurricane deck.

Tippoo shouted an order to the firemen. One came up bearing an armload of logs. He deposited them on deck and began feeding them into the furnace. As each one went in, the pitch of the engine increased.

"We cannot go too close," Tippoo pointed out. "He still has Camilla."

"I have not forgotten it," said Mungo. "We must keep pace with her and wait until she makes a landing. She cannot run forever. Then we will make our numbers tell." He had the entire crew of the *Raven* aboard the *Nellie Mae*—thirty men in total. "He cannot keep us all at bay."

"Captain!" called Henderson from the bow. "Look at this!"

Mungo ran forward. Ahead, something about the *Cleopatra* had changed. Her stern seemed to have shrunk. He examined her through his spyglass.

"They are dismantling her." He swore. "Chester will raze her to the gunwales in order to keep ahead of us."

"We'll run out of firewood before they run out of ship to burn," said Henderson.

In their haste to leave New Orleans, they had not had time to fill the wood stores completely.

Mungo reached up and snapped off a piece of molding from the column that supported the boiler deck. He tossed it to Tippoo, who threw it into the furnace.

"Do whatever you must, even if you have to destroy our own ship. We cannot let him get away."

The two boats continued upriver like two slaves in a coffle, joined at the neck by a pole that would let them neither halt, nor draw apart, nor close the gap—only carry on remorselessly. Even when night fell, the *Cleopatra* did not stop. She went on, the glow of her fire visible across the water, like a distant comet streaking upriver.

"Follow her," Mungo told Wisi, up in the pilot house. "Do not let her out of your sight."

"The river is dangerous in the dark," Wisi warned.

"As long as we keep the same line, we know we are safe. If there is anything in the way, Chester will hit it first. And then we will have him."

But luck was with Chester that night. It seemed as if the Devil himself must be steering the boat, past sandbars and shallows and floating trees, sometimes so close their branches brushed the hull. All Mungo could do was follow in her wake.

As dawn rose, they could see the full extent of the destruction the boats had suffered. Both had been stripped to their water-lines. The decks, cabins, walls and supporting timbers had all been dismantled and fed into the furnaces. All that remained were the engines and machinery on the main decks, the steering cables, and the pilot houses perched high above on stilts. Each ship looked like a body that had been flayed of its skin, leaving only the muscles and vital organs.

"He has nothing left to burn," said Henderson.

"Neither do we," said Mungo.

But as the sun rose over the river, he saw it did not matter. They were passing through cotton fields now. Little more than a mile ahead, he could see the warehouses and landing stages of Bannerfield. Chester must have found a way to signal ahead.

Through his spyglass, Mungo saw blue-jacketed militiamen mustering by the dock.

"The news from New Orleans has not reached here yet," said Mungo. "They do not know their master is bankrupt."

The *Cleopatra* nosed up to the dock. As soon as she touched, Mungo saw Chester, Camilla, Granville and Isaac leap off and hurry up the track toward the main house. The *Cleopatra* cast off and drifted slowly back downstream.

"We have lost the race," said Mungo.

He stared at the deck, his fists balled, his yellow eyes smoldering with fury, conscious of the men gathered around him. He had brought them this far on his quest for vengeance, and he had failed. They watched expectantly, waiting to find out what would happen next.

"I meant to shoot Chester dead on the wharf at New Orleans, fairly and honorably," Mungo said. "When he denied me that victory, I hoped to catch him on the river and finish it there. Now, my only recourse is to fight my way into his estate. But he has an army waiting for us."

The men listened impassively.

"This is my own fight. There is no profit or glory to be had in it. I cannot ask you to risk your lives on account of my revenge. If you wish to take the *Nellie Mae* back to New Orleans, I will not blame you."

Still the men gave no sign of what they were thinking.

"On the table in the *Raven*'s cabin, you will find a deed that divides the ownership of the ship between all of you. I signed it this morning, in case the duel did not go in my favor. All I ask is that you put me ashore before you turn back."

The men glanced at each other. None of them dared speak. One by one, they turned to Tippoo. Mungo followed their gazes, searching his friend's eyes.

"What do you say?"

The giant shook his head. "No."

"No?"

"No," said Wisi.

"No," said Virgil Henderson. "You're our captain. We'll fight with you to the end."

The others all nodded their agreement. Their brave, eager faces were black with soot from the furnaces; their hands were blistered from ripping the ship apart. But not one of them showed any hint of doubt.

Mungo nodded. A speck of soot seemed to have got in his eye, making it water. He rubbed it away impatiently.

"So be it."

"The men we are fighting," Wisi asked. "Do we take them to sell?"

Despite everything, that drew a smile from Mungo.

"If I had my way, I would ship them to Africa in chains and sell them to your father, the Nganga, as his personal slaves. But we will have to content ourselves with killing them."

Tippoo pointed to the dock. The militiamen had formed two lines—one along the wharf, the other on the riverbank above. They must have outnumbered the *Nellie Mae*'s crew at least two to one, with more, no doubt, waiting further back on the plantation. They raised their rifles as the boat approached.

"Many of them," Tippoo grunted.

"Then we will fight twice as hard." Beneath his feet, Mungo felt the boat slowing against the current. While they had been talking, no one had been feeding the fires; the boilers were going cool. "How much more fuel do we have?"

"It is gone." Tippoo pointed up to the pilot house. "That is all."

"Without it, we cannot steer the ship," added Wisi.

"It does not matter." By now, the landing stage was little more than a quarter of a mile away. "Our course is set."

They cut the hawsers that connected the wheel to the rudder, and lashed them down. Tippoo and his men chopped away the timbers that supported the pilothouse with their axes, until the whole structure collapsed. They fed it into the flames, not even bothering to cut it. The engines pumped harder; the long iron rods that ran to the wheel pounded like horses driven to the gallop. The wheel churned faster, powering the boat through the water with a final burst of speed. Waves spilled over the side.

Gunshots rang out, but they did not hit anything. Mungo and his men sheltered behind the boilers, protected by the stout iron. He could not see where they were going, but it did not matter because they could not steer anyway. Like a drunken knight, the *Nellie Mae* continued her last glorious charge, bearing down on the dock.

The shots stopped as the militia realized what Mungo meant to do. Those on the landing stage turned and fled up the bank, running straight into the line behind them. Chaos ensued, a scrum of blue jackets fighting on the steps. Some lost their footing and slipped back down; others, trapped at the back, could not get up at all.

Mungo nodded to Tippoo. At his signal, Tippoo ran forward to the little cannon on the bow. It was not much more than a signal gun, so badly rusted it was as much danger to the men behind it as in front. But—like the boat—it had one shot left in it. Tippoo had loaded it with a vicious mix of musket balls and nails pulled from the dismantled boat's timbers. He lit the fuse, then ran back to the shelter of the boilers and hurled himself to the deck.

The *Nellie Mae* rammed into the dock. At full speed, her bow smashed the pilings and splintered the landing. Some of the militia were thrown into the water; others, less lucky, were crushed between the hull and the riverbank. A second before she struck, the cannon fired a storm of jagged metal upward at the men caught at the top of the slope. The power of the blast blew the cannon apart, adding jagged iron fragments to the onslaught and cutting Chester's men to pieces.

Before they could recover, Mungo's crew rose from behind the shelter of the boilers and came at them through the smoke. Mungo led them. He vaulted over the smashed bow, splashed through the shallows and charged into the bloodied mass of men in front of him with his sword. Tippoo stood on his left, wielding a boarding ax, while Wisi stood on his right with the stabbing spear he had brought from Africa.

Chester's militia was composed of some of the roughest men in the county: brawlers, roustabouts and vagabonds. But they were more used to bar fights and street brawls than pitched battles. They had been guarding Bannerfield for months against an enemy who never came, taking Chester's money and drinking his whiskey. Now that the assault had finally come, they were utterly unprepared. The air was filled with terror: the death-throes of the *Nellie Mae* as she broke apart; the hiss of steam from her ruptured boilers; the screams of men dying and drowning.

The militia broke and ran, fleeing into the cotton fields toward the big house in the distance. Mungo went after them, pausing only to grab a pair of abandoned rifles and sling them over his shoulders. He ran so fast, he overtook some of the flee-ing militiamen. He cut them down with his sword and left them writhing in the dirt for Tippoo or Wisi to finish off.

He reached the slave quarters, row upon row of whitewashed shacks. Though it was the middle of the day, the inhabitants had disappeared, scattering like birds before an earthquake. They were not willing to defend their master, but if they took up arms they would suffer the most hideous deaths imaginable. Instead they melted away, leaving Mungo to pass through their dwellings unhindered.

Beyond the slave village, the ground rose in a grassy slope. And there, at its center, stood the house.

The scale of it took his breath away. Chester's mansion was nothing less than a castle, mounted on a hill and surrounded on all sides by broad ponds like a moat. The only access was a narrow causeway between the ponds that led to the front steps.

And it was well guarded. A bullet thudded into the earth at Mungo's feet. He threw himself to the ground, behind the shelter of the little wall that ringed the moat, as more bullets struck. The militia might have fled the landing, but they were more than ready to defend the house.

Tippoo crawled up beside him and risked a glance.

"Chester is there?"

"I guess so," said Mungo.

"You need cannons to get inside."

Mungo took another quick look. "We could swim the moat."

Tippoo shook his head. He pointed to the far edge of the pond, where something like a long tree trunk lay on the mud at the foot of the wall.

"Crocodiles."

"Alligators," Mungo corrected him.

He had seen their cousins many times in the rivers of Africa, enough to know the folly of trying to swim. He thought hard.

"Maybe there is another way."

For the men guarding the house at Bannerfield, it had been a bewildering morning. Since Chester learned that his enemy Mungo St. John had been seen in New Orleans, the militia had waited on high alert; but after Chester departed aboard the *Windemere* three days earlier, they had relaxed their guard. The crop was in, their master was gone. Surely there was nothing to fear now.

Then they had been roused by news from the river of Chester's sudden return. Before they were fully awake, they had heard shots—then a thunderous boom that had echoed across the fields. Shortly afterward, Chester—together with his overseer, his son and his slave mistress—had come running up the track, bellowing orders to prepare for battle.

They had grabbed their guns and taken up position, though on a sunny morning in the heart of Louisiana it was hard to imagine who might invade. Soon, though, they had evidence of terrible fighting. Men came back from the river—some running, others limping—all bloodied and stained with powder smoke. They gabbled out extraordinary tales: hordes of blacks swarming off the river; ships on fire; massacres in the cotton fields. For the men in the house, it was hard to credit. But the wounds were real enough.

The tide of fugitives had slowed, but now a last knot of men came running out from the slave quarters toward the main house. There were half a dozen of them, dressed in the militia's blue tunics and black forage caps. They ran over the embankment, toward the causeway between the ponds. A dozen black men waving spears and guns charged after them.

Perhaps the guards in the house did not immediately recognize the fugitives running toward them. But then, their faces were shaded by the forage caps, and they had their heads down to avoid the pursuers' bullets. In any case, Chester had enlisted so many men it was impossible to know them all. And one thing was incontrovertible. The men in uniform were white, and the men chasing them were black.

A black man, armed, rising against his white masters, was something that no man in the house could permit. Without hesitation, they opened the doors to let in their comrades.

Mungo raced over the bridge that crossed the moat, afraid he would burst out of the borrowed militia coat he wore. Every instinct in his body screamed it was madness, running headlong toward enemy guns, but he could not let that emotion show. Confidence was his only protection now. If he gave the men in the house any hint he was not who he appeared beneath the blue jacket, he would be dead.

At the far end of the bridge he paused, turned and let off a shot at his pursuers. It flew wide of Wisi's head—though close enough to be convincing. Wisi threw himself to the ground, rolling behind a stone urn so that the men in the house could not hit him.

Mungo ran on. The stairs were in front of him, leading up to the great door of the house—and it was open. He took the stairs three at a time, with Virgil Henderson and the other white men from the *Raven*'s crew pounding up behind him.

A scarred face peered out like a rat from behind the door.

"Get in!" he cried.

Mungo ran in. The cavernous entrance hall had become something between a field hospital and an arsenal. Wounded men lay bleeding against the walls, while the back of the room was stacked with cases of ammunition and casks of powder. Sandbags had been hastily piled at the foot of the stairs to make an impromptu barricade.

"Don't shut the door," said Mungo. "There's more of us coming."

The scar-faced man looked out again. The blacks had retreated behind the earthen embankments again, though occasionally they would sneak out to let off a shot.

"Who the hell are they?" he said. "Mr. Marion said we might come under attack. But I never thought it'd be niggers that did it."

"I don't suppose you did," Mungo said, and drove his knife into the man's heart.

With the chaos in the hall, no one noticed for a moment. The man slumped to the floor, oozing blood from his chest, but that did not make him any different from the other wounded in the room. It gave Mungo time to move deeper inside. Henderson and his men fanned out around him.

"Who's in charge here?" Mungo demanded.

A man with a lieutenant's epaulet turned.

"I am."

Mungo drew a pistol and aimed it at him. The lieutenant's face went wide with shock. Even then, he did not understand the danger. All he could see was a white man in uniform.

"What in God's name—?"

"God has no interest in this."

Mungo fired; the lieutenant's brains erupted from his skull and splashed over the faces of the men behind. They were still wiping it out of their eyes when Henderson's men launched into them with their swords and axes.

Chaos erupted. Unable to tell who was friend or foe, most of the militia simply fled. The wounded, who had just escaped one massacre, tried to join them. Those who could not walk dragged themselves across the floor, tripping up others and clogging the doorways. That left them easy targets for the *Raven's* crew.

The men on the upper floors did not know what had happened, but they heard the shots and shouts from downstairs. Somehow, the enemy had got in. They left their posts and ran—some to join the battle, others to flee it. That left the way clear for Wisi and his men to approach. They ran across the causeway and burst through the door, just in time to engage the militia reinforcements that had come down the stairs.

Soon the hall was cleared. The only militia left alive were those too weak to go elsewhere to die.

"Search the house!" Mungo shouted above the din. "Find Camilla! Find Chester!"

The *Raven*'s crew spread out, moving from room to room in pairs, pausing only to fire or to reload. Some of the militia tried to hide behind curtains, or under furniture; they were dragged out and killed. Some hurled themselves from windows, but then they found themselves trapped in the moat. A few tried to swim it; none reached the other side.

Mungo moved through the smoke and carnage like a demon, screaming Camilla's name. In one room, he saw a whole wall decorated with a map picked out in gold. Blood spattered the neatly painted fields; holes pocked the plaster where bullets had struck it. In another room, a grand piano had been turned on its side as a barricade.

He stopped for a moment to reload his pistols. The pause gave him the chance to listen. The sounds of battle were sporadic now—his men had mostly cleared the militia from the house. All he heard were occasional gunshots, and the agonized cries of injured men.

And—much closer by—the sound of a child wailing.

Mungo followed the sound, through a billiards room and a parlor to an open door. It led outside onto a broad marble terrace, filled with statues in classical poses. And there, among the stone figures, four living people: Camilla, Isaac, Granville and Chester.

They were filthy. Under the gaze of those flawless white statues, they seemed like creatures from beneath the earth. Soot, blood and mud stained their clothes; their hair was ragged and wild. They must have fled through the house, hoping to escape across the terrace into the east wing, but a huge cabinet had been pushed against the opposite door and blocked their way out. They had nowhere else to run.

Granville saw Mungo first. He aimed his pistol and fired, but the flint snapped on an empty pan. Mungo smiled. He raised his own gun, and shot Granville straight between the eyes.

Isaac screamed. Mungo advanced across the terrace, staring at Chester. The gray eyes, once so cruel and confident, were rimmed with red and weeping from the smoke. The blisters on his face had burst, streaming blood and pus. He had always been a monster, Mungo thought. Now the evil inside him was manifest for all the world to see.

Vengeance sang in Mungo's heart with the clarity of angel voices. He had destroyed Chester. He had bankrupted him, humiliated him, proven him to be a coward and torn apart his house. He had stripped him of everything he possessed—every single thing. All that remained now was to finish it.

Mungo stepped closer. He raised the pistol and pointed it at Chester's head.

"You took my whole life from me," he hissed. "I swore I would do the same to you, that I would make you watch while I dismantled your life brick by brick and crushed it to dust."

He was about to pull the trigger when a burst of motion distracted his attention. Isaac ran out from behind the statue where he had been cowering and threw himself into Chester.

"Don't hurt my daddy."

It was the last thing Mungo had expected him to say. He paused in surprise and lowered his gaze to look at the boy, who was pressing himself back against Chester's legs, staring defiantly at Mungo. His complexion was darker than Chester's, his hair black and stiff. But when Mungo looked into his eyes, wide and frightened, he saw the same strength of purpose as the man behind him.

Mungo went still. He looked at Camilla, his eyes brimming with a terrifying emotion.

"I thought he was your son."

"Yes," she whispered.

"You told me the father was one of Chester's overseers."

Camilla did not answer. It didn't matter. The truth was written clear and bold on Chester's face.

"If there is one ounce of human kindness in your heart, I beg you to spare him," Chester pleaded. Isaac had started to cry. Almost without thinking, Chester lifted him up and cradled him against his chest. "He is innocent."

Mungo looked between them: Chester, Isaac and Camilla. For perhaps the only time in his life, he seemed to be paralyzed by indecision.

"Why didn't you tell me?" he said softly.

"Because I was afraid you would kill him," said Camilla.

"You did not trust me?" Fire flashed in Mungo's eyes. "When were you going to tell me? When I had killed Chester and set you free? When I had adopted the boy as my own? When I had named him as my own heir? Did you think I would be deaf to the sound of Chester laughing at me beyond the grave, his ultimate revenge to have planted his cuckoo in my nest?"

"You would not understand," said Camilla. Her eyes were pregnant with tears. "You say Chester took everything away from you. But did you ever lose your freedom? Your name? The very right to call yourself a human being? Isaac is all I have ever had of my own."

"You had me," said Mungo.

"And if that means anything—if you truly love me as you say—then spare Isaac."

The gun swayed left and right, like a compass in a storm. Camilla and Chester; love or revenge. The two emotions warred in Mungo's breast so fiercely, he thought he might split apart. Chester stood at the back edge of the terrace with Isaac in his arms. The boy's body blocked Chester's torso and part of his head, leaving Mungo with little to aim at. Even if he hit, the force of the shot might push Chester backward, off the terrace and into the moat. He would carry Isaac with him.

"Let him go," said Camilla. "You have done enough."

Mungo hardly heard her. How could he spare Chester, leave his revenge incomplete? But if Isaac died, Mungo would lose Camilla forever.

I do not intend to have to choose, Mungo had told Solange. Once again, just as he had on the shores of Africa, he heard the Fates laughing at him.

What will you do?

Once again he found himself in the slave hold of the *Blackhawk*. The stench, the suffering, the sounds—the pit of human misery—and a young girl with frightened eyes. If Mungo did not kill Chester, every terrible thing he had done would be for nothing. The thirst for revenge that had driven him to the darkest places of the earth would never be quenched.

"Please," Camilla begged.

Mungo nodded. His face cleared. Deep in his soul, some great knot seemed to have unbound itself.

He aimed the pistol at Chester's head and fired.

The shot crashed around the marble terrace, echoed back by the mansion's walls like the full broadside of a man-of-war. Yet even above it all, Mungo heard a high-pitched scream that cut through the noise, then abruptly cut off.

Smoke stung his eyes, but not so much that he could not see what he had done. Across the terrace, Chester stood petrified in shock. He was not looking at Mungo. He stared at the floor, where a figure in white lay bleeding at his feet. A round hole, just above her left breast, showed where the bullet had struck as she threw herself in its path.

"Milla!" Isaac screamed. He wriggled free of his father's grip and jumped down, bawling like a baby taking his first breaths in the world. He ran to Camilla's side. He tugged her arm but she did not move. "Mammy!"

Mungo could barely take his eyes off Camilla. But behind her, he saw Chester's hand reaching into his coat—just as he had in the study at *Windemere*, the day Mungo returned from Cambridge, when he had pulled out the little pearl-handled revolver he kept there.

Chester never finished drawing it. With a roar, Mungo sprang at him over Camilla's fallen body. Chester's right hand was still inside his coat; he was not ready to defend himself. Before he could react, Mungo grabbed him by both arms. He lifted Chester's whole body into the air, took one step forward and hurled him off the edge of the terrace.

Chester fell, arms and legs flailing like a broken insect, and landed in the water below. As the ripples spread across the surface, dark shapes surged from the banks, converging where he had fallen. The water began to boil.

Mungo did not see it. He was kneeling by Camilla, cradling her in his arms, stroking her face, calling her name again and again as her blood soaked into his shirt. Tears flowed down his cheeks and fell on her face. She did not move.

A thin line of blood ran over Mungo's hand and curled around his wrist.

Camilla was free.

After the battle, Mungo sat on the front stairs alone, staring at the ponds and the empty cotton fields beyond. Wisi and his men were bringing out bodies from the house and piling them up like firewood on the drive. Smoke rose away to his right, but it was only cooking fires in the slave village. As soon as the fighting finished the slaves had returned, going back to their homes and their chores as if they had never been interrupted. For them, nothing had changed.

A song came from the village and drifted over the fields. A low, sad lament. Mungo had heard the tune at Windemere and he knew what the words said.

O Satan told me not to pray, he want my soul at Judgment Day.

Somewhere in the bottom of one of those ponds, what remained of Chester Marion would be settling into the ooze. Mungo had done what he set out to do. He remembered the promise he had made to Solange. *I will dismantle every brick of the edifice he has built his fortune on, until he is left naked in the ruins of his life.* Now that he was sitting in the desolation of Chester's life, it seemed a hollow boast.

He grasped the locket that hung around his neck. With a jerk of his arm, the chain broke; the silver heart came away in the palm of his hand. With trembling fingers, he undid the little clasp and stared at the picture inside. It was not even a very good likeness. He had drawn it himself by lamplight in the Windemere observatory. He had never been a good artist, and had struggled to make the picture small enough to fit the locket. But he had captured something of the life in Camilla's eyes, her smile and her beauty. He remembered her giggling as he drew it: he trying to make her sit still, she trying to distract him, impatient to get back into bed.

"This is important," he'd told her. "When I go to Cambridge, this is all I will have to remember you by."

He could not bear to look at it now. With a sudden spasm, he snapped the locket shut and hurled it away. The moment it left his hand he wanted to take it back, but it was too late. The locket soared through the air, flashing for a moment in the sun, then fell in the pond and sank.

He was still staring at the ripples it had made when he heard the clop of horses' hooves, and the rattle of wheels on gravel. A carriage was coming up the drive, drawn by four white horses. The coachman reined just in front of the pile of bodies, jumped down and opened the door.

Solange's head peered out. She took in the scene: the corpses; the guns and bullets littered over the ground; the pockmarks in the walls and the smell of powder in the air. She did not look terribly surprised.

She walked across the causeway, stepping delicately around the pools of blood and the spent cartridges. She stopped at the bottom of the steps and looked up at Mungo.

"Why are you here?" His voice was barely more than a croak.

"To inspect my new home. Thanks to you, I have become the new owner of this property." She put her finger in a bullet hole in the balustrade. "Though it will need some work. It is not in as good condition as you promised."

Mungo did not smile. Solange squinted at him.

"Did you kill him?"

Mungo nodded.

"Then it is done. You have achieved your heart's desire." She cocked her head. "It does not seem to have made you happy."

"Camilla is dead."

The words came out of him as a tortured howl, torn from his soul. He gazed at the ground, wanting it to swallow him up, but Solange would not let him. She stared at him, until the strength of her gaze forced him to look up. Her almond eyes held his.

"I am sorry."

She came up the steps and sat down beside him, ignoring the

dust that stained her dress. She put her arm around his shoulders and held him close.

"You cannot stay here," she said. "Not after what you have done."

"Who will care that I killed a slave?"

Mungo tried to pull away from her, but she gripped his arm tight, digging her nails into him.

"Chester Marion was the most powerful man in the state. They will care about him."

"I challenged him to a duel in front of half of New Orleans. They do not prosecute for that."

"They prosecute for waging a private war. Even in Louisiana, that is frowned on." She pointed to the pile of blue-jacketed corpses. "And you cannot pretend all these men never existed. Someone will want to know how they died."

Mungo said nothing.

"We will tell the authorities there was a slave revolt," Solange decided. "They were overwhelmed—Chester died in the fighting."

Mungo nodded.

"But you cannot be here when they arrive." She pointed to Wisi, standing guard at the top of the steps. Stripped to his waist and with his stabbing spear in his hand, he looked like a vision from a slave owner's nightmare. "It would go hard on your men."

"Yes."

"Go away for a time. Go to Texas, or California. There are fortunes to be made there."

"No."

"Only for a time," she said. "I want you to come back. Remember the bargain we made. The money I gave you was a loan, not a gift. I will expect repayment."

"You will get your money back," Mungo promised.

He had seen what debt had done to his father, and then to

Chester. He would never be beholden to any man or woman. He would pay what he owed, whatever he had to do.

"Of course, I have Bannerfield. That is worth something—though not as much as it was."

Mungo did not care. "Burn it down and add it to my account," he said savagely. "I never want to see this place again."

She stroked his arm. "You will think differently later, when your wounds are not so raw."

My wounds will never heal, he wanted to say. She seemed to read it in his face.

"All our cuts turn to scars eventually," she said. "And a scar is only skin. We do not have to show what is beneath."

She got up and beckoned to where Tippoo and Wisi had been waiting. They came forward and helped lift Mungo to his feet. Together, they descended the stairs.

At the foot of the steps Mungo remembered something. He turned back and called to Solange.

"There is a child somewhere in the house. An orphan. See to him"

"I am sure you have made many orphans today."

"This one is different. He is Camilla's son."

An unreadable look crossed Solange's face.

"Then you had better find a good home for him."

Mungo did not go to California. He and his men went to New Orleans, smuggled downriver on a coal barge. In the dead of night, they went aboard the *Raven* and slipped her cable. No one saw them go. The only cargo they loaded was a long, lead-lined box they had brought from Bannerfield. They sailed to Chesapeake Bay, up the James River, and anchored by a little island in the mouth of the creek at Windemere. The path had long since grown over, but Tippoo and Wisi cut a way so they could carry the casket up to the observatory.

They buried Camilla in the soft earth of the clearing. Mungo and Tippoo dug the grave. Mungo placed no marker, for the land was not his. Instead, he scattered roses over the freshly turned soil, and planted a dogwood tree where its blossoms would fall on the grave in spring.

Then the *Raven* headed out onto the ocean.

The world had little sympathy for a fallen hero. Edwin Fairchild had discovered to his cost how fickle the public could be. The same illustrated newspapers that had once carried pictures of him standing defiant on the *Blackhawk*'s deck, surrounded by blood-curdling cut-throats, now printed cartoons of him lying at the bottom of a hole, while a trio of monkeys sat in a tree and laughed at him. *By gad*, said the caption, *these termites are a bigger nuisance than the slavers*. To his eternal mortification, Fairchild had become a laughing stock.

But he would not be deterred. He still had his faith—in God, in his cause—and that gave him strength. For months, he haunted the corridors and anterooms of the Admiralty, begging any man he could find for a ship. He had used every family connection he could lay claim to, called in favors from Cambridge friends. He had even considered proposing marriage to a young woman whose uncle sat on the Admiralty Board.

Sense—and the lady's indifference—had quashed that particular plan. But in the end, his persistence had prevailed. Now, through the window of his room at the boarding house, he could see his reward lying at anchor in Portsmouth harbor: a handsome little sloop of sixteen guns, ready to take the fight to the slavers once more.

All he needed was a crew. His fall from grace meant there were fewer men eager to join him, even without the hardships of the West Africa station to deter them. But there were a few who believed in the cause and were willing to serve under his command. One of them was standing in front of him now. He was an odd-looking child. His hair was angelic gold, his skin pasty white, except where it erupted in the angry red pimples that covered his adolescent face.

Fairchild glanced down at the letter of recommendation the boy had brought from his father.

My son has never been to sea, but he burns with the zeal for the liberty of mankind. You will find him a willing apprentice, and in time I venture he will make a fine officer.

"You wish to serve aboard the *Wanderer*?"

The boy nodded vigorously.

"It is a hard life," Fairchild warned. He felt a twinge in his leg, and winced. It had not healed properly; for the rest of his days he would walk with a limp. "There is disease, privation, the hazards of the sea . . . To say nothing of the dangers of battle."

"All I want is to free the slaves."

The boy was so young his voice had not yet broken. The words came out with an ungainly screech. Even so, you could not miss the strength within him.

"Then I am glad to have you in my crew. Congratulations . . ." Fairchild's eyes drifted down to the letter, to remind himself of the boy's name. "Midshipman Codrington."

Despite his age, the boy's handshake was firm as a grown man's. The blue eyes fixed Fairchild with a purpose so intense that even Fairchild found it unnerving.

"Thank you, sir. I will not—"

A knock at the door interrupted him.

"Come in!" called Fairchild. "It is probably the sailing master," he told the young midshipman. "I asked him to call. He will be in charge of your instruction."

But it was not the sailing master who stepped through the door. It was two people Fairchild had never seen before in his life. One was a woman, with gray hair and a kindly face, bundled up in a traveling cloak. The other, clutching her hand and peeking out from behind her skirts, was a small boy. He had tousled black hair, a little bow mouth and olive skin. He could barely be three years old.

Wordlessly, the woman extracted a letter from inside her

cloak and gave it to Fairchild. It was written on heavy paper, embossed with a crest and the name "Bannerfield."

The boy who accompanies this letter was a slave who came into my possession. I have set him free. As an admirer of your deep commitment to the emancipation of the negro races, I have chosen you to be his guardian. I trust you will take care of him and see he receives a proper education.

There was no signature—only three initials: M. S. J.

Fairchild felt faint. His leg throbbed. He stared at the paper, reading and rereading it.

"Where did you come from?" he asked the woman in a whisper.

"From New Orleans. We arrived this afternoon aboard the *Raven*. We—"

She did not get the chance to finish. Leaving the woman, the boy and the midshipman in astonishment, Fairchild tore out of the room and down the stairs as fast as his aching leg could carry him. The landlady was cleaning the doorstep; he almost knocked her over as he barged through the front door.

He ran all the way to the harbor master's office.

"The *Raven*!" he gasped. "Where is she?"

"There."

A clerk pointed out of the window, where a sleek Baltimore clipper was beating her way out of the channel. Fairchild felt a stab of memory, more painful than the wound in his leg, at the sight of her.

"She has sailed already?"

The clerk nodded. "Arrived this morning, and put out again on the afternoon tide."

There was a terrace outside the office, where the comings and goings in the harbor could be observed more easily. Fairchild went out and leaned on the rail, staring after the departing ship.

What had Mungo done? Why on earth had he sent the boy to him? In truth, Fairchild was not at all sure how he could discharge the duty. He had no wife who would know what to do. And then there was the question of the boy's race. How could he raise a black child as his own?

But for the moment, all those considerations were forgotten in the righteous joy of being proved right. There had been good in Mungo. He had seen the error of his ways and repented. He, Fairchild, had redeemed him.

"God bless you, Mungo St. John," he whispered to the departing ship.

A squall was approaching. Fairchild turned to go back into the warmth of the office, and almost bumped into the clerk, who had emerged carrying a large ledger.

"I have the ship's manifest, if you would like to see it."

"Thank you."

Fairchild spread the ledger on the balcony rail and read the entry the clerk showed him.

"What . . . ?"

Fairchild's joy turned suddenly cold as he ran his eye down the cargo manifest. Iron ingots. Glass beads. Trade cloth. All the goods that England's factories turned out in such abundance to satisfy the market in West Africa, where they could be readily exchanged for human lives.

Fairchild stared at the receding ship, silhouetted against the horizon. Black clouds bruised the sky; the wind blew stinging spats of rain against his cheek.

"Damn you, Mungo St. John!" he shouted into the storm. "Damn you to Hell!"

THE FIRST IN THE EPIC BALLANTYNE SERIES

A FALCON FLIES

Dr Robyn Ballantyne has always worked hard for what she wants. Coming home to Africa after twenty years, she fears there are only three men who may still stand in her way.

Zouga, her brother, is the only family she's known for much of her life. Yet she and the celebrated soldier will never quite see eye to eye.

Codrington, an ambitious British naval officer, wants to give her a perfect life. But does she want to be tamed to fit his idea of perfection?

Mungo St John, the notorious American merchant, repels her with his slave trading. But Robyn cannot forget what once passed between them.

As her adventures begin, Robyn must make decisions that will shape the future for all of them.

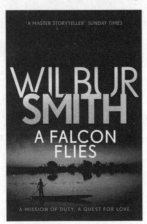

AVAILABLE NOW

BETRAYED BY BLOOD. FREED BY FATE.

GHOST FIRE

A new generation of Courtneys fight for freedom in epic story of tragedy, loss, betrayal and courage that brings the reader deep into the seething heart of the French and Indian War.

1754. Inseparable since birth and growing up in India, Theo and Connie Courtney are torn apart by the tragic death of their parents.

Theo, wracked with guilt, seeks salvation in combat and conflict, joining the British in the war against the French and Indian army. Connie, believing herself abandoned by her brother, and abused and brutalised by a series of corrupt guardians, makes her way to France, where she is welcomed into high society. Here, she once again finds herself at the mercy of

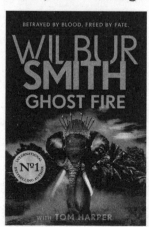

vicious men, whose appetite for war and glory lead her to the frontlines of the French battlefield in North America.

As the siblings find their destinies converging once more, they realise that the vengeance and redemption they both desperately seek could cost them their lives . . .

AVAILABLE NOW

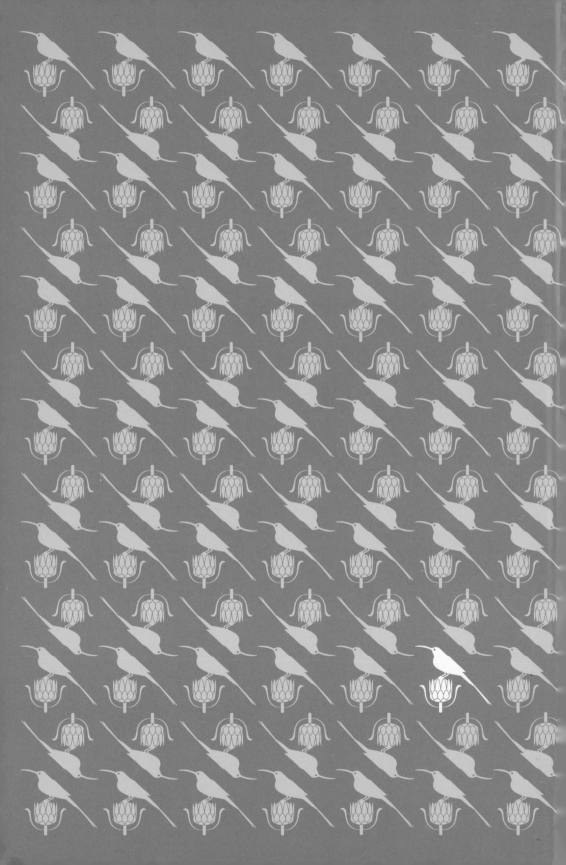